Shadow of the Pyre

R. T. Silveus

979-8-218-48605-1

to the teachers and librarians who sowed
seeds of story in my heart

Contents

PROLOGUE

Esen

BLOOD AND CHARRED FLESH. That's all the coliseum was ever used for. Esen tried to prepare himself for the looming Fire Purification, but how could anyone be prepared to watch someone burn to death? When possible, he avoided attending events in the coliseum, but no one had been able to escape today's spectacle. Not unless they wanted to be "reeducated".

Guards in sleeveless black uniforms escorted a group of human prisoners to the base of a large pyre. Even from the stands, the height difference was obvious as the Gurvel soldiers towered above their captives.

The other spectators around Esen stood completely still, only moving their lips to whisper softly to their neighbors. He opened his mind and touched the forethoughts of those around him. Not surprisingly, the Gurvel on this level of the coliseum were hiding their fearful thoughts behind blank crimson faces. Glancing across the arena, his chest tightened as he saw all of the human citizens who had been forced to watch as well. Their punishment would have been far worse than reeducation if they had refused.

A sudden silence fell over the crowd. He looked over to the left where the king's advisor, Khartsaga, had stepped forward on the viewing platform, his arms raised to gain the audience's attention. "Ladies and gentlemen, King Chono and I welcome you to this momentous occasion!"

From where he stood, Esen could see hints of gray growing on the sides of the advisor's otherwise short black hair. Much like himself, Khartsaga was still young for a Gurvel, probably only a few hundred years old.

The king and queen both leaned forward, eagerly listening to Khartsaga's every word. To them, the advisor was something akin to a prophet because of his connection to Firekin. But the real power came from the leader, who stood behind the throne with white hair that stood out in stark contrast to the black wall behind him.

Ever since that terrible Shadow War when King Chono had partnered with Firekin, the cult had grown in popularity throughout the city. Esen hadn't seen their leader attend many events in person, but these prisoners in particular had been caught scheming against the cult's presence in the city. Something that hadn't been attempted in over a century.

"Today we'll have not one, but twenty Fire Purifications," Khartsaga said. "These humans that you see before you have broken not only the king's trust but the trust of every law-abiding citizen in Galynkhot."

Movement in the pit below drew Esen's attention away from the speech. Another set of guards led a small group of human children toward the viewing platform. Esen's breath caught in his throat. Why had they brought children to the coliseum? Some of the prisoners had noticed the procession as well and began calling out for mercy.

"We have Fire Purifications because they remind us of our past," Khartsaga said. "A couple centuries ago, my father, Ukhel," Khartsaga waved behind him toward the Firekin leader, "created the Fire Stimulant, allowing Manipulators to control not only objects, but fire itself!"

Some of the children tried to run to their parents, but the guards held them back, forcing them to continue walking toward the viewing platform where Khartsaga continued on, seemingly oblivious to their cries. Esen glanced around him to see if anyone in the crowd would stop this from happening, but no one dared move.

"At that same time, King Chono wisely accepted the advice of Firekin and used the Fire Stimulant to wage war on the Speki, our greatest enemy." Khartsaga paused as cheers erupted around the coliseum. The Shadow War had killed an entire race of people. It had been genocide, not glory. Even now, King Chono's guards were still hunting down the last remnants of the Speki, all for the sake of the New Age.

Drummers began a strong and rhythmic cadence as Khartsaga continued, playing just low enough that the crowd could still hear him. The guards took the prisoners up to the top of the pyre and began binding them to wooden stakes.

"But the Fire Stimulant was not the only discovery that was made. Thanks to my father, the Eternal Flame, we learned how to control the most fearsome beast in all of Amidral—the shadowmongrel!" Khartsaga leaned forward and held his fist in the air as the crowd erupted in more thunderous cheers.

A woman beside Esen scrunched up her face in worry, but luckily everyone else was too entranced to notice how the ridges above her eyes bent in concern. Until the Shadow War, no one had ever dared to tame a shadowmongrel. There were only two in this part of Amidral and Firekin now controlled them. With that kind of weapon, few had the courage to contradict them.

Finished with their task of binding the prisoners, the guards saluted the king, each by moving a fist from his forehead to his chest. King Chono stood up and joined Khartsaga at the front of the viewing platform, signaling the guards to step away from the pyre.

"Today we celebrate this Fire Purification ritual," Khartsaga continued, "because these humans have chosen to blaspheme the New Age with their rebellious meetings. We use fire as a reminder of what Gurvel glory can attain. May the New Age rise!"

The guards each lifted a vial of Fire Stimulant to their lips and drank the dark amber fluid that had drastically changed the forces of power in Amidral. Before, Manipulators had only been able to control inanimate objects, but now, with the Stimulant's power, they could create fire. And because the vast majority of Gurvel were Manipulators, it had made them a force to be reckoned with. As a Seyr, Esen would never be able to control fire, but then again, it wasn't an ability that he coveted. Not when it was used like this.

Murmurs filled the crowd as the guards crouched into an offensive position and in unison moved their arms toward the prisoners, sending blasts of fire toward the dry wood.

Screams echoed off the coliseum walls as the prisoners began to burn. The children's cries grew louder as they were forced to watch. A little boy with hair as black as the coliseum dropped the book that he had been clutching to his chest as he fell to his knees and vomited. One of the guards grabbed the book and flipped through it before tossing it onto the pile of wood and yanking the boy to his feet. Esen's heart broke as he watched the boy staring into the raging inferno.

A heat as hot as the pyre burned in Esen's stomach, flushing his already crimson cheeks a deeper shade of maroon. No one was going to stop this. No one was going to fight against Firekin. This small group of humans had tried to. But they had failed.

He leaned over the railing, forcing himself to look at the thick black smoke and smoldering pyre. Fear and maybe a healthy sense of logic kept him from jumping into the coliseum at that moment. He wouldn't get more than three steps before the guards arrested him. Not today, anyway. It would take more tact and strategy than that.

A knot twisted in his gut, mixing with the heat of anger as he looked over at the Eternal Flame of Firekin. The cult leader was smiling. No. That was too jovial. It was more of a smirk. And why shouldn't he be filled with gleeful confidence? He was arguably the most powerful Gurvel in all of Amidral. At this point King Chono was nothing more than a figurehead, following Firekin's every whim. Who could fight against that kind of power?

The image of the boy kneeling in the sand before the smoldering pyre filled Esen's mind. It would only get worse from here. Even if he failed, he had to do something or the tension raging in his core would surely rip him apart. Passivity was no longer an option. He continued to watch the horrid display in the arena below, all the while trying not to dwell on the inevitability that he would likely end up burning on his own pyre someday.

CHAPTER 1

The Games

Long ago, when the four races still lived in peace with one another,
rumors of a new dark threat spread throughout Amidral.

Twenty Years Later
Ronan

RONAN PULLED THE PRISONER out onto the sandy arena, trying to keep a grip on the struggling man's arms. The black walls of the coliseum towered above them, covered in small holed pockmarks like all the other buildings grown from Sklera. Directing the rock-like plant to grow into a structure like this took Sklera sculptors hundreds of years. Under normal circumstances, he might have called it art, but this was where people were sent to be slaughtered. It was a bloodbath. Not art. Standing guard at The Games was never a coveted position, but human soldiers didn't have a say in the matter.

Sensing the condemned farmer's next attempt at escape, Ronan tightened his grip on the man's wrists a moment before he tried to yank his arm away. It was Ronan's sharp instincts that had earned him the rank of top soldier in the king's human militia. Not that the position meant anything. They'd never give him an official title. Even if they did, he wasn't so sure he'd take it.

Up on the higher seating levels, humans peered down into the sandy pit, looking anxiously to see if it was their loved one he was dragging in. On the lower levels, Gurvel lounged in their seats, watching him and the prisoner as if they'd come to see some kind of play. They were no better than piles of Sklera dust. Today wasn't a mandatory event, which meant every Gurvel spectator had chosen to come and watch the innocent die.

Now that they were in the sun, it was easier to see how dirty the farmer's simple work shirt and slacks had become during his time in the holding cells. Some of the dirt had likely rubbed off on Ronan's uniform but no one would be able to tell. All the king's militia wore outfits that were as black as Sklera.

Kendra used to tell him that he looked good in black because it matched his hair, but that had been years ago. Back when they had still dreamed of someday working their way to freedom.

Looking up at the viewing platform, he waited for the king's signal to start The Games. At the moment, it looked like he was talking to his advisor, Khartsaga, so Ronan stood in the center of the coliseum, forcing down the heat of anger that threatened to boil up inside him as he held onto the trembling man.

The murmuring of the crowd crescendoed into a thunderous roar as they waited in anticipation. He gritted his teeth, feeling the eyes of the stadium directed at him and the farmer who likely hadn't done anything worthy of death. And yet they came to watch. Some of them had even brought their children and pampered pets as if it was some kind of weekly family event.

A Gurvel woman in the stands across from him had her pet fox with her today. Its tail was dyed hot pink to match the brightly patterned shirt it had been dressed in. The very idea of owning another living being made his stomach churn. No human in Galynkhot would dare keep a pet. Not when they heard whispered slurs directed at them while walking the streets. *Gutter pet.* The derogatory phrase was becoming all too common.

Finally, a loud gong signaled the crowd to quiet down. Everyone's attention turned toward the viewing platform where King Chono's tall figure stepped forward to address the crowd. Ronan and the other soldiers guarding The Games saluted in unison, each by raising a fist to his forehead and moving it over his heart in homage to the king.

The sun glinted off King Chono's regal white uniform embellished with red and gold embroidery that suggested flames climbing up the sides of his tunic. The white brought out his deep crimson skin and graying hair. A fitting appearance for the king who had waged war against the Speki with fire and shadowmongrels.

With the crowd's attention, the king waved over Khartsaga. His uniform was black but had the same red and gold embellishments along the side. Ronan and the other soldiers saluted Khartsaga by raising a fist to their forehead and snapping back to attention. He kept his hand in a fist and clenched it harder than he should have. Khartsaga was responsible for increasing the weekly number of Games from one to three.

"Welcome one and all!" Khartsaga said, his voice echoing around the coliseum. "Today, I'm happy to announce that the queen will give birth to our long-awaited heir in the coming week."

Khartsaga paused as the crowd cheered. The king and queen had been trying to conceive for centuries. Gurvel didn't produce many offspring, so last year when the royal couple announced their pregnancy, the celebration lasted for weeks.

"In honor of the queen's fast-approaching due date, we will begin adding Fire Purifications after each Game, starting today. May the New Age come!" Khartsaga nodded toward the gong.

Tapping it gently around the edges, the Gurvel gong ringer readied the large instrument and slammed his mallet against the vibrating metal to signal the start of The Games. Ronan released the farmer's wrists as the Champion's side door opened across the coliseum.

The man crumpled to the ground, clutching handfuls of sand as a sob escaped his lips. Ronan kept his face straight despite the burning anger coursing through his veins and walked back to the side of the stadium to stand in parade rest beside his squad mate. Manton kept his hair cut close to his olive-toned skin, unlike Ronan who kept his black hair just long enough to run his fingers through. They exchanged quiet looks of understanding and readied themselves for the coming spectacle.

A set of drummers played a cadence to enhance the experience, but it was soon drowned out by the jeers and shouts of the crowd. Abaka, the current Gurvel champion, stepped out of the Champion's door and waved at the crowd as he entered, showcasing a long scar down the side of his arm. The thunderous roar grew louder as he grabbed a sword from the rack near the entrance and held it up above his head, his deep blue tunic open down the middle to display his crimson skin.

The farmer was still trembling in the middle of the arena floor where Ronan had left him. Abaka threw the sword down in front of the terrified man as the roar of the crowd swelled. A sword was always handed to the human defender, not that it did them any good.

Grabbing the sword with tentative fingers, the farmer slowly rose to his feet, holding the weapon out before him with a trembling hand. Even while standing, the man looked like a child compared to the lumbering Champion towering over him.

Abaka laughed and dropped into a firm stance while reaching into his pocket for a small vial of amber Fire Stimulant. Another clash of the gong signaled the start of the fight. With hands clenched into fists behind his back,

Ronan focused on the farmer whose shirt was already wet with sweat.

A burst of flame shot toward the farmer's feet. He barely managed to jump out of the way by slipping on the sand and falling flat on his back. Abaka shot another ball of fire that burst upon the sand right beside the man. With each burst of flame, heat surged through Ronan's core, but there was nothing he could do.

Ever since the Shadow War, the Manipulators in the city of Galynkhot favored the Fire Stimulant above all other Stimulants. They saw it as a symbol of purity, but Ronan was all too familiar with what it really stood for—death.

Manton nudged Ronan from the side. Wiping the scowl off his face, Ronan quickly straightened back up at attention. The heat in his core abated slightly, replaced by a cold shiver. He quickly glanced at some of the other guards, but none of them had appeared to notice his momentary slip of emotion.

The farmer flailed the sword before him, shielding himself with his other arm as a blast of fire whipped past him. The fights were never fair. Gurvel and humans were both allowed to use any means necessary to win, but that meant nothing if you didn't have Seyring or Manipulation powers. Humans couldn't possess either power, so The Games were just prolonged death sentences.

Abaka lunged toward the frightened farmer and landed beside him in a sweep of fire. His hand that held the flame brushed against the man's shirt and singed the edges. The farmer quickly rubbed the embers away and thrust the sword toward Abaka, but the champion easily dodged the attack and shot another burst of fire at him. This time it collided with the man's chest and caught his shirt on fire. The man flew back into the sand from the impact and screamed as the fire burned through his shirt, singeing his skin. Quickly tearing the garment off, the farmer scrambled back to his feet.

Not skipping a beat, Abaka jumped into the air, a sneer spread across his burgundy lips. The farmer barely had time to shield his face with his arm as Abaka shot a series of short blasts toward him mid-jump. Sand sprayed up as the Gurvel Champion landed and towered over his prey. The farmer glanced around for his sword but it had been flung close to where Ronan and Manton stood at the side of the stadium.

The crowd started chanting Abaka's name, stomping together in rhythm. The sound echoed off the coliseum in a sea of noise. Ronan gritted his teeth; this was the part he hated most.

But he was powerless. If he so much as nudged the sword closer to the man, his whole squad would suffer the consequences. So despite his hatred for The Games, Ronan kept his face blank and stood his ground. He wouldn't jeopardize his squadmates for some farmer he didn't even know.

Diving toward them, the man scrambled to grab the sword, spraying up sand at Ronan and Manton. With a wobbly hand, he held the sword out toward Abaka again.

The Champion kicked the sword out of the farmer's hand and wrestled him into a headlock. He squeezed his arm around the farmer's neck and looked up at the crowd, smiling as they cheered him on. After a moment, when the man's body became motionless, Abaka threw the corpse aside in the sand, like a child finished with a toy.

Beside him, Manton shook his head and stepped back inside to retrieve the next prisoner. In a few minutes he returned, dragging a miner covered in dirt toward the center of the coliseum where Abaka waited with a new sword.

The next fight went much the same way. Abaka drank another vial of Fire Stimulant and threw blast after blast at the prisoner until he dropped his sword. Like before, he wrestled the man into the same choke hold, but this time something would be different. Ronan's instincts told him to glance away and he was glad when he did. The audible snap of the prisoner's neck breaking sent a shiver down his spine. Throwing the new corpse aside, Abaka stood and raised his hands in the air, the scar on his arm visible as he accepted the praise of the satisfied audience.

Cheers thundered around the stadium while Ronan and Manton dragged the bodies out of the main part of the arena and dropped them in a wheelbarrow near one of the exits. Abaka caught Ronan's eye briefly as he passed them by, his eyes void of any empathy or guilt at what he had just done. To him, humans were nothing more than an entertaining pastime. Pets to be played with. Ronan had never spoken to the Gurvel, but he could practically feel the condescension radiating off of him.

"Poor wretch," Manton muttered, nodding at the corpse of the farmer in the wheelbarrow.

Ronan looked at the frozen terror displayed on the farmer's face. Firekin claimed that The Games would somehow bring about the New Age where all creatures would prosper, but after witnessing the merciless slaughter of hundreds, he knew better. Keeping quiet was the only way to survive.

Manton placed a hand on Ronan's shoulder and nodded toward the prisoner entrance where they usually stood guard.

"Why don't you head back to the barracks early? I'll stand guard during the Fire Purification," Manton said as Gurvel guards started setting up a small pyre in the center of the coliseum.

A wave of nausea churned in Ronan's stomach as he watched them set up the platform and pile on extra wood. Now that they were going to be more frequent, he wouldn't be able to avoid all of them.

Up in the viewing platform, King Chono leaned over, listening to Khartsaga. When it came to Firekin, the king hung onto every belief as if it were some kind of righteous mandate.

Manton stood at parade rest by the prisoner's entrance while Ronan slipped inside the Sklera door. Two Firekin guards with bare chests and white pants passed him as they dragged a woman with short brown hair into the coliseum. She glanced back at Ronan with eyes as dark brown as Aprika's eyes had been. His mouth went dry as they pulled her into the coliseum and shut the door behind them.

Shaking his head to clear his thoughts, Ronan turned and walked down the long hallway, passing cell after cell filled with people who were awaiting their own gruesome deaths. Most of them had been brought in for petty crimes. Even before the number of Games had increased, the king had mandated a certain number of humans be apprehended each week to keep tabs on the growing population.

There were only three punishments for humans in this city. The Games, Fire Purification, and death by shadowmongrel. Luckily the king hadn't used shadowmongrels for a couple centuries, so none of these prisoners would have to suffer an excruciating death like that. But even so, The Games were a horrible way to die.

One face looked familiar to him as he passed by. Looking closer, he realized it was the man he had arrested yesterday for insulting a wealthy Gurvel merchant. He forced himself to look each person in the eyes, feeling the weight of their fear and anguish pushing against his thoughts like a tangible pressure. This was the part he was forced to play, so he let the pain linger in his mind as punishment.

CHAPTER 2

Speki

At first, the darkness was just a rumor and nothing more.
Reports of terrifying visions and bodies found frozen in fear
spread through every town like phoenix fire.

Eira

CROUCHING IN THE DIM CAVE alcove next to her brother, Eira closed her eyes and focused her attention on the cultists up ahead. She blocked out the minds of chroma snails and bats so she could focus on the larger group of sentient beings further down the passage. They were still too far away to read even their foremost thoughts.

She touched the leather pouch at her belt, resisting the urge to take a pinch of the Prime Stimulant. They had very little left and needed to save it for their target. Like all Stimulants, this one would extend her regular mental abilities, but it had limits. If she took it too soon, the effects would wear off before they found the Gurvel they were looking for.

After centuries of searching, they had finally found the Firekin headquarters.

She opened her eyes and turned to Einar, his shaggy hair standing out against the dark stalagmite behind him. Like all Speki, he looked similar in appearance to humans except for his pure white hair and violet eyes. They had been evading capture since the Shadow War and were finally in a position to avenge their people.

"There are some structures ahead. Probably cages." Einar's comforting voice resounded in Eira's head as he looked at her with eyes that had the faintest wrinkles forming on the edges. Usually Manipulators like Einar couldn't send mental messages like Seyrs could, but the strong bond they had formed made it possible.

"That tip paid off, then," Eira thought back. *"This is where they're taking the captives. We're not close enough for me to read their forethoughts, but there's a large*

group of people ahead. Probably a mixture of cultists and captives."

Eira felt the dagger at her belt. Usually they only killed one person at a time. Today they might not have that luxury.

"Sis, we don't have to do this, you know," Einar thought to Eira, rubbing a small pink crystal stuck to the cave floor.

She met his eyes and lifted an eyebrow in response. Einar shifted his weight and looked back toward the entrance. *"I know we've been looking for this place for centuries,"* he thought, his voice ringing in her head like warm bells, *"but we don't have to go through with it. We're the only ones left, Sister. If this mission crumbles like ashbark, the world might lose the last remnants of our people's knowledge."* Images of the two of them standing in front of a mass of pupils eagerly awaiting instruction flashed in Eira's mind. She could feel his longing as if it were her own.

"Nar, we've been through this," she thought to him, tearing her gaze away from his longing eyes. *"The minute we started teaching, we would be captured and killed. Besides, who would we teach, the Gurvel hunting us or the humans that have no potential for Seyring or Manipulation?"*

"Dear Sister," Einar thought dryly, rolling his eyes at her. *"While rare, there are humans who have powers. Just because they don't live as long doesn't mean we shouldn't teach them what we know."*

"Nar, we've come so far! This is it! This is Firekin's main base," Eira thought to him, trying to shift the conversation back to their goal. *"Their leader has to be here. Besides, we're assassins. This is what we were trained to do."* She scooted closer to him and put a hand on his knee. *"We owe it to our people."* Einar gave a halfhearted smile as he met her gaze.

After centuries of chasing rumors and interrogating fringe cult members, they had finally made it. If everything went according to plan, they would find the cult leader, kill him, and get out before any alarms were raised.

Icy hatred shot through Eira as she imagined the damage she and her brother would unleash upon the cultist leader. King Chono may have ordered the genocide of her people during the Shadow War, but within decades she and Einar had uncovered the existence of a darker mastermind behind the whole attack. And when they found him, she would relish the opportunity to make him suffer the same fate her people had.

Once he was dead, she would gladly devote her full attention to making her brother's dream come true, even if it was next to impossible to find the students he so desperately wanted to teach.

Footsteps approached from the hallway. *"They're changing guards,"* Eira thought to Einar. She carefully felt out the approaching guards and crept into their minds to suggest a small illusion, one small enough that she didn't need to take the Stimulant to create it.

As the guards drew near, Eira closed her eyes to concentrate and projected an image of an empty alcove as they passed by. With such a minor illusion, the guards didn't notice her presence in their minds. She and Einar waited until the sound of footsteps passed and all was quiet except for the soft echoing plink of cave water dripping occasionally down the walls. Now was their chance.

They carefully crept down the cave tunnel, keeping to the right side where the shadows were darkest. After a few minutes the light flickering off the walls grew brighter and the sound of a crackling fire and scuffling boots echoed against the walls.

"It's a large cavern," Einar thought to her, closing his eyes as he felt for the inanimate objects around them. Without the aid of Stimulants, Einar couldn't manipulate the objects from so far away, but he could sense that they were there. They hadn't been able to replicate a Fire Stimulant like the Gurvel had created, but they still had the Prime Stimulant that lengthened the distance and duration of Manipulation and Seyring. However, Toracini mushrooms were difficult to find in the wild, so unfortunately their reserves were running low.

"The cages are on the far side," Einar thought, opening his violet eyes. *"I'm fairly certain there are some crates or boxes right near the entrance. We might be able to hide behind them before we're noticed. Assuming you don't trip on your own feet like last time."*

"I didn't trip," she thought, continuing to edge toward the cavern entrance. *"You moved a rock from under my feet."*

"Who else is going to keep you on your toes?" Einar thought, flashing her a smile.

At the edge of the cavern, she looked up and was surprised to find that the ceiling reached higher than she could see in the dim light. At the center a small fire burned where a few of the cultists had gathered, the flames flickering against their bare crimson backs. Even the females tried to show as much of their skin as possible, wearing only white pants and a wrap around their chests for modesty.

Since none of them were looking this way, she and Einar quieted their minds to avoid detection and slipped behind a couple of wooden crates. Eira closed her eyes again and felt out the minds around them. There were numerous cultists scattered about the cave and a large group of humans clustered together in one of the cages. Ignoring the captives, she continued her scan, searching for strong emotions of respect or fear targeted toward a specific person. Against the back wall, there was a small group of Gurvel and one human. Here she paused.

Strong waves of anticipation and nervousness radiated out from this area. However, upon further reflection, it seemed that these feelings were related to whatever task they were performing. There might have been some respect directed toward a certain individual, but his thoughts didn't possess the level of confidence that she expected the main cult leader to have. Disappointed, she opened her eyes and looked at her brother.

"I don't think he's here, Nar," she thought.

"Well, we've come this far. Let's at least get the humans out. Maybe one of them knows something." Einar peeked cautiously over the crates and ducked back down. *"That fellow guarding the cages looks particularly dimwitted. How do you feel about jumping into his mind?"*

Eira raised an eyebrow and peeked around the crate. A tall female cultist was adding a greenish crystal to a boiling cauldron a few paces away from their crate.

"There are too many of them. How would we get the captives out?" Eira asked.

"Jump like a moss frog, burn like a phoenix." Einar smiled confidently.

"Surprise worked in our favor last time, but there were fewer guards," Eira thought. *"Besides, I thought you wanted to survive this so you could teach."*

"I can't teach if I don't have a pupil, and one of those humans might be a Manipulator," Einar answered. *"Besides, I thought you wanted to find the cult leader. We need more information if he's not here, and those humans are our best chance."*

He was right. They might not get another chance like this, so she agreed.

Pushing down her disappointment that the cult leader wasn't there, Eira focused on the task at hand and slunk behind another set of crates. With Einar close behind her, she waited for a female cultist to pass by before stepping behind a pile of rocks and stalagmites.

They worked their way around the edge of the cavern until they were close enough to the Gurvel guarding the cage to take control of his mind. Normally an impossible feat, controlling another living being was what Speki assassins specialized in. With the help of a Stimulant to boost their powers, she and Einar could invade someone's mind and control their body. The procedure required the use of Seyring and Manipulation, so assassins were trained in pairs. Her fingertips tingled with anticipation. Moments like this made the decades of training well worth the pain and effort.

She reached into the small pouch at her waist and dropped a pinch of silvery powder into her mouth before handing the bag to Einar. The familiar bitter flavor hit her tongue as she closed her eyes and felt the surge of power flow through her veins like a warm pulse.

Einar's comforting and warm presence entered her mind like sunlight on a cool spring day. With practiced skill, they started to push their way into the unsuspecting guard's mind. The Gurvel was apparently distracted with worry over what punishment he might receive for sleeping in so late that morning, which made it all the easier to slip into his thoughts undetected. Like walking through a cold wall of water, they entered the guard's mind and compelled him to pull out his key and unlock the door.

The humans inside backed to the edges of the cage, waiting with wide eyes for the guard to enter. But they had no need to worry. With goals aligned, Eira and Einar compelled the Gurvel to lie down on the ground and pushed his mind into a deep sleep.

Finished with their task, Eira and Einar separated the connection, shivering slightly as they pulled away from each other's warmth. It was always a disconcerting feeling, but Eira comforted herself by grabbing Einar's shoulder.

They peeked around the rocks, but no one seemed to have noticed the odd transaction. Now they just had to get the captives out alive. She glanced inside her pouch. There was barely enough powder left for two doses. With a sinking feeling, she handed the pouch to Einar. It had taken them years to find enough toracini mushrooms to make that much Stimulant. Yet again, they'd have to bide their time until they could face the cult leader.

Khartsaga

WITH BATED BREATH, KHARTSAGA watched as they began their next experiment. A stout cultist stepped toward the human test subject and drank a vial of yellow liquid. The small group leaned closer to see if this was the Stimulant that would finally allow the user to control another living being.

For years, they'd been studying the mysterious green crystals that grew in this cave. The Verdant Crystal, as they'd decided to name it, was incredibly potent. On its own it caused massive headaches, but, theoretically, if combined with other ingredients it had the potential to allow someone to use both Manipulation and Seyring.

His palms grew moist as he waited. Surely this time, they had found the correct ingredients to make the Stimulant work. His father, the Eternal Flame, could only be kept waiting for so long before discipline became necessary.

The Gurvel who had used the Stimulant frowned and turned back toward the rest of the group. "Nothing. I can't even lift a pebble, let alone make this gutter pet raise his finger."

Khartsaga jotted a note down on his sheet. That was the fifth failed experiment this week. They only had a handful of hours before his father arrived for a performance check. Could they squeeze in one more test?

"Wait," the short Gurvel said, looking off toward the front portion of the cave. "There's someone here. No. Two people. They're trying to hide their thoughts, but somehow I can still hear them."

Beside him, Tarkhan, the assistant assigned to him by his father, took vigorous notes. They had Seyrs patrolling the hallways. If there really were intruders, the guards should have detected them. The only way anyone could have slipped in unnoticed was by hiding their thoughts. So how had this cultist pierced their mind barriers? Was their failed experiment actually some kind of serendipitous discovery?

"You two, go check it out," he ordered, pointing at a pair of nearby cultists.

In perfect obedience they carefully wound their way around testing tables and barrels of supplies until they reached the area near the cages. Suddenly, their postures became stiff. Something had caught their attention. Using Manipulation, each of them quietly lifted large rocks from the edge of the cave and sent them hurling behind a stack of crates.

Khartsaga took a step forward, curious to find out who the intruders were. There had been rumors about a handful of Gurvel who were resistant to the New Age, but so far no one had openly contradicted the teachings of Firekin.

"Advisor, it's two Speki!" One of the cultists cried.

Speki? A delightful surprise. His father was sure to be disappointed about the failed experiment, but perhaps gifting him with these two Speki would make up for the blunder.

CHAPTER 3

Patrol

Kings and city officials assuaged the commoners' fears by telling them the reports were nothing more than the ravings of drunken fools.

Ronan

BEFORE SUNLIGHT HAD A CHANCE to brighten the Sklera barracks, Ronan got up, ran some water through his hair, and threw on a fresh uniform. Careful not to wake his squadmates, he slipped outside and surveyed the open training area. There were always two Gurvel guards by the gates leading out of the compound, but other than a glance every now and then, they ignored him as he jogged around the perimeter.

As sunlight began to creep over the edges of the high Sklera wall, Ronan switched to sword drills. He would be out until later that afternoon patrolling the city with Manton and Kendra, so he needed to practice now. Moving fluidly from one side of the barracks to the other, he swung through his formations, sword gripped firmly with two hands. Sweat beaded on his forehead as he repeated the sweeping motions. Up. Down. Raise and slice. Thrust. Block. Turn and guard. Each movement was more muscle memory at this point than thought.

A few of the soldiers from the other squads began to exit their barracks and make their way to the dining hut, but Ronan ignored them. There were seven human squads in King Chono's army and they knew each other well enough, but in general they kept to their own teams. Even individual misbehaviors earned punishment for one's entire squad, so everyone kept their head down and focused on the task set before them. There wasn't time to get to know anyone other than the members in one's own barracks.

The guards at the gate switched over to the morning crew as some of Ronan's squadmates began to wake up. Ronan finished his last formation before stopping to wipe the sweat off his face.

"Do you even sleep?" Manton asked, shaking his head while he leaned against the barrack.

"Of course," Ronan said, walking over to him. "You would too if you weren't out late drinking at the Seaside Tavern every night."

"It's the only thing they let us do around here! Speaking of which, we're planning to get some drinks after patrol today. You should come this time," Manton said.

Ronan didn't answer at first. It had been a few weeks since he had gone with them. Staying out late drinking made it harder to get up and train.

"Come on. Just because you're leagues ahead of the rest of us doesn't mean you can't sit back and have some fun from time to time," Manton prodded.

"I'm not leagues ahead of anyone," Ronan replied, sheathing his sword. "I just put in the practice."

"Don't be humble." Manton chuckled. "I've seen you spar with some of the Gurvel soldiers when you can convince them into a fight. You always know exactly when to dodge. I'd be clobbered upside the head before we even started."

"Practice," Ronan said.

"Whatever your secret is, all I'm asking is for you to join us for just one drink and then we can go to bed early like old men. What do you say?"

"Alright. One drink," Ronan conceded.

"Good! We've missed you!" Manton straightened up as Kendra exited the barracks and joined them. She rubbed her eye with one hand and flipped her long box braids over her shoulder, not seeming to care that her shirt was wrinkled and askew. Apparently she had slept in her uniform again.

"Look who finally decided to get up," Manton said, lightly punching Kendra in the arm.

"Ashbark tea first. Talking later," Kendra muttered as she stumbled toward the dining hut.

Manton laughed and followed behind Kendra as Ronan fell into step beside him. Lethargic morning conversation greeted their ears as a handful of soldiers grabbed their ashbark or dragonbreath tea and a quick bowl of purplish slop.

Ronan managed to swallow the slimy mush with a glass of water and waited as Kendra methodically spooned the sides of her bowl.

"How can you actually like this stuff?" Manton asked her incredulously.

"The trick is to save just enough of your Ashbark tea to wash away the bitter flavor," Kendra replied, gulping the last bit of tea. "See? You gotta follow the right technique."

Manton rolled his eyes. "Sure. I'll remember that next time while I'm choking it down."

"We should get going. The sun's almost past the wall," Ronan said, glancing out the portion of Sklera that had been cut out to let sunlight in.

The three of them set down their plates in a crate by the door and left the military compound, entering streets that were already coming to life as citizens began bustling about their day. Directly across from the military compound, the Seaside Tavern was closed after staying open late into the night. The rest of the shops they walked past were just starting to open their doors and welcome in guests.

Ronan glanced at Batu's Books as they passed. He would need to stop by later and see if Batu had picked up any copies of *The Legend of Ravenel*.

"What are we patrolling today?" Kendra asked, looking up at the large and ominous castle on their left as they passed by the Sklera gates.

"Stone District," Manton said with a sigh.

"Ugh, it's so dismal there. Who got the docks?" Kendra asked.

"Barrack Three," Ronan said.

They turned right and walked past rows of merchant stalls. The ones closer to the roadway were run by Gurvel and were usually built out of sturdy wood. Ronan peered behind the wooden stalls and checked the canvas setups behind them to make sure none of the human merchants were causing any trouble. Everyone worked with their head down, refusing to meet his eyes. That was a good sign. Maybe he wouldn't have to escort anyone to the coliseum today.

"Barrack Three had dock duty last week!" Kendra complained.

"Just be glad we're not on Games duty today," Manton said.

"There are no Games today," Kendra said. "And we're always on the slot to guard them."

This street was busier than the one near the barracks. Everyone congregated here to buy their food and haggle for goods. A Gurvel and her son passed by with a small fox dyed a bright yellow trotting happily behind them. There were a few visitors from neighboring villages as well. One couple in particular caught his attention. A woman and man dressed in brightly colored clothes were chatting with one of the human merchants. It was hard to miss them when the humans around them all wore dull colors of muted browns and blues.

"Such colorful pets," a harsh whisper said.

Ronan looked past the couple and spotted a band of Gurvel teens snickering at them as they passed by. That's why humans who lived in Galynkhot wore neutral-colored clothing. Bright patterns and dyed hair only encouraged the derogatory comment. Since he had no jurisdiction over Gurvel citizens, he looked away and continued on.

Up ahead the fire fountain at the entrance to the city gates burned as brightly as ever, towering into the sky like a large eternal bonfire. They passed right by it on their way to the Stone District where most of the humans lived. It had been built a couple of centuries ago after the Shadow War to accommodate those who had sided with King Chono. They hadn't had enough time to grow Sklera dwellings, so stone had been used instead, but no efforts to grow better dwellings for future generations had ever been enacted.

"Let's make it quick. I hate walking through this part of the city," Kendra said, shivering as she looked at the rows of stone and wooden buildings that had been haphazardly built. They sat beside and on top of one another, crammed into every inch of space available to them.

"It doesn't matter how fast we go," Manton said. "We're still on duty until later this afternoon."

"I know, but the stone in there is so dead and cold," Kendra said, placing her hand longingly on the warm archway that divided the two sections of the city.

Though he hated to admit it, Ronan agreed with her. It wasn't just the lifeless stone that felt cold. Everyone had left before sunrise to work in the mines or fields. That left only the old, sick, and crippled to wander the lifeless streets.

Even without any disturbances it took them well over an hour to make their way through the crowded alleyways and curves. Supposedly, the Stone District had started out organized, but as the population had grown so had the need for housing. By now huts were stacked and piled on top of one another, just to create space for one more family.

They came up to a deadend that Ronan knew very well. He glanced down the narrow street, catching sight of the home he had grown up in before he had been forced into the king's militia. Before the Fire Purification. His tongue grew dry as memories threatened to resurface.

Manton gripped his shoulder and quickly scouted out the street so they could move on to the next section. Before leaving, Ronan spared one more glance at the door that had once been his. It probably belonged to some other poor mining family now.

Finished with their first round, they headed back toward the merchant stalls to patrol there until lunch. More of the disturbances tended to happen there, so it was a good enough reason to stay out of the Stone District for a while.

As they approached the fire fountain, a bright and vibrant magenta filled Ronan's mind.

"Hey, I think I found a chroma snail!" Kendra cried out, running toward the fountain. "They're a pain to find because of how small they are." She carefully picked up a black and gray snail and let it slide along her hand.

"Lavender! Nice. Last time I had yellow," Kendra said.

"Kendra, this is a child's game," Manton said, sighing.

"Nonsense. It's still fun to guess. What color?" Kendra asked, handing the chroma snail to Manton who rolled his eyes.

"Blue," Manton said, and then grabbed the snail. After a moment he shrugged and handed the snail back. "Eh, it was brown. See, it's a stupid game."

Kendra rolled her eyes and then held the snail out to Ronan. "What about you?"

"Green," Ronan said, looking over his shoulder as he took the snail. They needed to get back to patrolling.

He held the snail for a moment, pretending to concentrate. For some reason he had always been able to see the color *before* he touched the snail. When he was younger his sister, Aprika, had warned him not to tell anyone because standing out could be dangerous. If only she had taken her own advice.

"It was blue," Ronan said, handing the snail back. "We need to keep going." If they were caught fooling around, the whole team might have their dinner revoked.

Kendra huffed and set the snail back down on the edge of the fire fountain where it blended in with the pockmarked shadows of the Sklera. "You two are no fun. What else are we supposed to do?"

"Patrol?" Manton said, as they walked back toward the bustling stalls.

"Evening can't come fast enough," Kendra said with a loud sigh.

They spent the rest of the day walking the same route from the military barracks to the Stone District. It had been an altogether uneventful day, but that was good. Of course too many patrols without arresting anyone would result in a light punishment from their Commander, but usually it wasn't anything too harsh. Maybe an extra patrol at night or restricted access to the dining hall.

"I'll catch up with you at the tavern," Ronan said as they neared

Batu's Books.

"Alright. Just don't forget! Or I'll drag you out of the barracks myself," Manton said, waving as they walked on without him.

Ronan stepped up to the small bookstore and opened the thick wooden door. Sklera took centuries to regrow so at times it was more efficient to use wood or stone and just coat it with ropesnare milk to protect against Manipulator thieves.

Inside, a few guests wove their way through the shelves, stopping occasionally to read the title on a spine. Ronan went straight to the front desk where an elderly Gurvel with white hair sat leafing through a thick tome.

"Did you have any luck finding that book?" Ronan asked.

Batu looked up at him from behind a pair of spectacles and licked his thumb before turning the page. "No," he replied. "There weren't many in print to begin with. It's unlikely I'll find one in your lifetime, boy."

"Alright, I'll check back in another time, then," Ronan said, forcing a half smile before heading back out into the darkening streets. He didn't have a logical reason for finding another copy of that book, but a part of him couldn't let it go.

Mentally preparing himself for the evening, he made his way to the Seaside Tavern. Before he even opened the door he could hear sounds of laughter and clinking glasses. With a deep breath, he stepped inside and was greeted with the scent of fresh bread, ale, and sweat. Beside the entrance, a group of drunken Gurvel stood around a table, debating the rules of a complicated-looking card game. He carefully stepped around them and spotted Manton at a table in the back. A man covered in soot from the mines bumped into him as he stumbled back up to the bar, an empty glass clutched in his hand. Did there have to be so many patrons here every night?

Kendra lifted her mug of spiced ale and waved him over to the seat beside her.

"Let me go order a drink first," Ronan shouted over the loud din of the room.

She nodded and took a large swig of ale, wiping her mouth with the sleeve of her uniform. Inwardly cringing, Ronan ignored the urge to reprimand her and walked up to the bar at the back. He couldn't protect them from everything, but if she was caught disrespecting her uniform, their team would probably have to run laps for hours before it satisfied their Commander.

The barkeep, Seton, made his way over with a jovial smile when he spotted Ronan. He was the only human business owner with a Sklera building in the entire city. Tonight his cheeks were flushed a deeper reddish brown than the rest of his skin as he balanced eight mugs of ale in one hand.

"Hey Ronan, give me just a sec," Seton said, masterfully sliding his way past chairs and patrons until he had delivered the mugs to a table near the front.

Proud of his handiwork, Seton raised his eyebrows at Ronan when he returned and reached under the bar to grab a glass. "Not bad, eh?" Seton said. "Bet the old grouch at the Whiskered Fox can't carry that many mugs at once."

"Probably not," Ronan responded, glancing over his shoulder as a burly Gurvel slammed his empty mug on the table.

"I hope you don't mind my saying this, but it looks like you may have forgotten something," Seton said, squinting at Ronan's face while he poured a shot of Scarlet whiskey into the glass.

"What?" Ronan asked, looking down at his shirt.

"Your smile," Seton said, handing him the glass of amber liquid.

Ronan took a swig of the whiskey and raised an eyebrow.

"Haven't seen you in a few weeks, but your friends come almost every night. I've got deals for soldiers, you know," Seton reminded him.

"If they want to waste their meager earnings on drinks, then that's on them," Ronan said, finishing his glass with a gulp and then handing it back to Seton.

While Seton poured more Scarlet whiskey, Ronan looked toward the table where his friends sat. Manton laughed as he finished off a joke with a swipe of his hand through the air.

"Ronan! What are you doing skulking in the shadows?" Kendra asked, spotting him at the bar. "Get back over here and bring some more spiced ale!" She waved him over with a smile that refused to be squelched.

He gave a wave in return and got up from his stool as Seton handed him new mugs.

"And Ronan," Seton said as he started wiping down the bar, "remember to have some fun. You've got a good group over there."

Nodding his thanks, Ronan made his way back to the table, careful to step around a puddle of spilled ale. He put the mugs down and sat next to Kendra, listening as the group picked up their discussion where they had left off. Soon everyone was joking about something or other, but Ronan didn't join in their laughter. He listened and sipped the spiced ale, holding onto the moment, willing it to last a little longer.

But eventually it would end. They would return to the barracks, sleep fitfully in their rickety bunks, and wake up dreading The Games where they would be forced to watch unfortunate merchants or farmers burned to death for petty crimes. That was something that would never end.

CHAPTER 4

Firekin

And so life went on. The rumors continued to spread, but no one believed them—not unless they found themselves alone in the woods at night.

Eira

A FIERCE HEADACHE POUNDED against Eira's skull as she started to regain consciousness. She tried to raise her hand to her forehead but her wrists were tied behind her back. Still groggy, she felt the soft texture of the bonds—ropesnare.

Wincing at even the dim light, she looked around for Einar. Every movement felt sluggish against the thick fog that filled her head. They must have drugged her with an Inhibitor. With effort, she rolled over on the chilled cave floor and found Einar beside her, bound with the same kind of thick red vine that she was. Even if they hadn't been drugged, Einar would need a strong Stimulant to Manipulate ropesnare. She knew it was pointless, but she tried sending a mental message to him anyway. Her attempt was rewarded with a sharp pain through her skull.

"It's been awhile since I've seen a Speki—let alone an assassin—duo," a calm voice said from behind her.

A Gurvel man crouched down beside her, tilting his head slightly to the side as if to get a better look at her. Firelight illuminated the flame embroidery along the edge of his black uniform and cast a foreboding glow around his large stature.

"I commend your abilities to hide your mind from detection," he said, scratching the ridges above his eye. "We almost didn't notice you were here."

Eira flexed her hands, pulling against the ropesnare. If she kept this Gurvel talking, she might be able to loosen them without raising suspicion.

"I've always wanted to learn more about the Speki," he said thoughtfully, "but my father said it wasn't worth my time."

"Why not just kill us then?" Eira said through clenched teeth.

"We might, but first I'd like to study you."

A lanky Gurvel in a black uniform approached from behind him. "Khartsaga, the Verdant Stimulant is ready to test again. No need to waste your time on these two, sir."

Khartsaga nodded and stood up, towering over Eira as light from the fire flickered around his silhouette. "Thank you, Tarkhan," Khartsaga said. "Bring me one of the humans."

Eira shifted her weight and looked over at the cage where the captives were held. They were test subjects. That's why there were more of them than they had expected.

Beside her, Nar started to stir. While Khartsaga and Tarkhan walked away, Eira managed to slide closer to him.

"Are you alright?" she asked.

He slowly rolled himself around to face her, his violet eyes dim. These cultists spared no precaution. Ropesnare wasn't uncommon, but usually drugging a Manipulator or Seyr was enough to subdue them.

"Never better. What happened?" he asked, his voice cracking as he spoke.

The soft sounds of mallets smashing herbs and spoons scraping the sides of cauldrons echoed in the cavern. All around them the crimson faces of cultists were scrunched up in concentration as they worked on preparing ingredients.

"They knew we were here," Eira whispered.

But how had they known? Hiding their minds from detection took concentration. It was possible that they had slipped at some point, but they had done missions like this hundreds of times before. Something had been different this time.

Einar nodded in thought as he looked around the cavern, wincing as he turned around.

"I suppose rescuing the hostages would have alerted them anyway," Einar said. "But at least the rumors we heard were partially accurate. This is some kind of main base."

"And yet we still didn't find the leader," Eira said, watching Khartsaga drink a vial of yellowish liquid by the cage.

He had on a uniform like a leader and graying hair at his temples, but all the reports they had heard described the true mastermind behind Firekin, the Eternal Flame, as much older than Khartsaga.

They lay there for what felt like hours, not daring to speak their thoughts aloud. Whatever the cultists had tried to do with the new Stimulant had apparently failed because now all of the cultists were scrambling at their stations. One of the female cultists nearby wiped sweat from her forehead before jotting down some notes with a shaking hand.

One of the nearby tables held a pile of toracini mushrooms and a few jars of silvery powder. Eira's pulse quickened. The mushrooms alone might be enough to counteract the drugs. But how could they get close enough to grab some?

"Sir, please reconsider," Tarkhan said, interrupting her thoughts as he and Khartsaga approached them.

"This is a rare opportunity," Khartsaga countered, crouching down once more to look at her. "We have an assassin pair! Don't you think my father would be interested to learn more about them?"

She exchanged a glance with Einar as the assistant opened his mouth to object, but his voice was drowned out by a loud bang that echoed throughout the cavern, shaking the ground beneath them. A cultist stumbled into the cavern, holding his head as hints of smoke coiled around him.

Khartsaga stood up quickly. "What happened?"

Eira craned her neck to get a better look at the entrance. The Gurvel looked at Khartsaga for a moment and then collapsed to the ground.

"Don't just stand there. Find out what caused that explosion!" Khartsaga commanded, motioning for the cultists around the fire to go investigate.

Another loud bang exploded before they reached the fallen cultist. Shortly after, more smoke poured into the large room.

Einar moved closer to Eira from behind and whispered in her ear. "Do you think we have a chance of escaping while they're distracted?"

"Not unless you have a way to cut the ropesnare," Eira replied, forming fists with her hands as she tried to loosen the bonds.

"Actually I was envisioning us rolling out the exit. Or would that be too conspicuous?" Einar asked. She glared at him and continued pulling against the rope. Now might be their only chance at escape.

Silence followed the last bang. Khartsaga frowned as the cultists disappeared down the passage. When they didn't return, he slid his foot back into a defensive position.

A few small objects flew out of the smoke and clattered to the stone floor. Eira tried to move away from one that rolled toward them but couldn't escape the blue-gray gas that began seeping out of it. Unlike the smoke coming from the hallway, this was more translucent, like vapor.

Khartsaga and Tarkhan gasped and dropped to their knees, both gripping their heads as the bluish gas filled the cavern.

"Oh good. More mind fog," Einar said with a strained voice.

She could feel it as well. They had already been drugged, so the sudden shock of breathing in the inhibiting gas wasn't as intense as it had been for the cultists. Regardless she could feel her remaining energy drain away. How had the intruders even created a gaseous Inhibitor? Usually they were injected or ingested.

Figures ran into the cave out of the smoke. Faster and shorter than the Gurvel, they dashed across the cavern, heading directly for the cage in the back. Each one wore a gray short-sleeved tunic with a cowl and black pants. As a few of them passed by, Eira was able to catch a glimpse of their faces. Humans.

She squinted her eyes against the firelight, straining to think through the mind fog. The cries of the cultists reverberated around the cave as they found themselves suddenly without power. A young woman with a red tunic entered the cave with a calm and steady gait, observing the operation. Eira was pleased to see the look on Khartsaga's face as he watched the woman round the fire pit, sword held loosely down by her side. His mouth was slightly agape, eyes wide in bewilderment as the woman passed by him. She pulled back her cowl, revealing long dark hair that had been braided down the side and quickly kneeled beside Eira and Einar.

"Are you alright?" the woman asked. "We didn't know there would be Speki here."

Eira attempted to nod, but the movement felt like a wave of water crashing against her skull, so she winced instead and stifled a groan.

"It'll wear off soon," the woman said, cutting Eira free with a knife. "We'll take you with us."

Before she realized what was happening, a young man with a scar on his face gently helped her stand. Lights and sound blurred together and merged into a pounding pain across her skull. To keep from vomiting, she closed her eyes and gripped the man's shoulder for support. It took every ounce of willpower to force her feet to move as sleep threatened to overcome her.

Through the mental fog, a sense of panic rose within her. She couldn't sleep. Pain flared across her mind again as she desperately tried to fight through the effects of the Inhibitor. If she fainted, what would become of them? Where would they be taken?

With a groan, Eira cracked her eyes open and spotted Nar stumbling along beside her, hanging on to one of the humans for support. Everything started to spin. She closed her eyes and just focused on breathing. She would not lose her wits. Not again. Not after allowing the cultists to capture them. Wherever they were taken, she would find a way out.

Khartsaga

SOFT MURMURS FILLED THE CAVE as Firekin members scurried from table to table, gathering papers and packing up vials and herbs. Khartsaga forced his eyes to focus on the ledger he was holding, trying to ignore the empty pit in his stomach. Despite his efforts he had to read the inventory notes three times before he was able to retain the information.

Signing off on the list, he handed the ledger to one of the scribes and glanced across the cave where his father, Ukhel, the Eternal Flame of Firekin, stood. His back was toward Khartsaga, his golden cloak reflecting the light of the fire that still blazed in the cavern's center, and his bare crimson chest exposed like all Firekin members. He stood as tall and strong as ever, white hair kept perfectly short and groomed. A man like the Eternal Flame demanded perfection. Those who failed in their tasks were swiftly disciplined, even the Eternal Flame's own son. Especially the Eternal Flame's own son.

He took a deep breath and walked over to his father who hadn't said a word to him since arriving at the base. In fact, he hadn't even looked at him. His father had every right to be angry. Khartsaga would gladly accept the discipline he deserved for allowing their test subjects to escape, but the emptiness in his stomach deepened with every step he took. With a dry swallow, he forced himself to steady his breathing.

"Sixteen failed tests over the past few days," Tarkhan said, clutching a stack of notes to his lean chest. "We're continuing to try different combinations of toracini mushrooms and verdant quartz because those ingredients have produced the most promising results."

His father nodded, encouraging Tarkhan to continue, not so much as glancing at Khartsaga to acknowledge his presence.

"One unforeseen effect is worth mentioning," Tarkhan continued. "One of the tests allowed us to detect the two Speki that were here. It was a brief side-effect that only lasted a fraction of a second, but it pierced their minds and allowed us to find them."

His father raised a ridged brow and held a hand out to take the stack of notes, which Tarkhan gladly handed over with a satisfied smile. Khartsaga continued to wait as his father studied the notes, wrinkled eyes roaming over the pages with deep interest. Finally he handed the stack back to the smug assistant. "Have a copy of these notes and the ingredients sent to my quarters in Galynkhot."

"Yes, Eternal Flame," Tarkhan said, raising his fist to his head and lowering it to his heart before leaving.

Khartsaga gripped his hands behind his back and waited with baited breath. The emptiness in his stomach flipped on its side when his father finally turned to lock eyes with him.

"Do you realize what you've done, son?" his father asked calmly.

Khartsaga swallowed. "Yes, Father. Forgive me. I should have anticipated an attack from the humans and—"

"No." His father cut him off sharply. "You should have killed those two Speki. Humans don't have the capacity to strategize like this. They were obviously working for the Speki, and you let them get away."

He broke his father's gaze and chose to focus on a pink crystal poking out of the ground. A flash of bright green shot through his head as he spotted a small chroma snail easing its way along the side of it. They had picked this cave because of how abundant this type of crystal was. Having so many nearby made it easier to try new Inhibitor combinations.

"You're weak," his father said. "And that weakness will destroy everything we've worked so hard to build. Or have you forgotten about your mother?"

Khartsaga cringed under his father's scrutiny. A single act of kindness had killed his mother. She had been weak, and that same weakness flowed through his own veins.

Ukhel, the Eternal Flame, sighed and put a hand on Khartsaga's shoulder, sending an involuntary shiver through his spine.

"You know what I must do, right, Son?"

"Yes," Khartsaga answered, his eyes still watching the chroma snail crawling along the pink crystal.

"Look at me, Son," his father said softly.

He looked up and forced himself to hold his father's gaze.

"Face it with dignity, Son. We'll cleanse these weak tendencies out of you one way or another."

A sharp pain ripped through Khartsaga's mind like a bolt of lightning. He fell to his knees, gritting his teeth and clenching his fists to keep from crying out. It swelled in hot flashes, piercing through him in terrible waves. Tears came unwelcomed to his eyes and tremors wracked his body. Resisting would only make the pain worse and might even leave lasting damage, so he forced his mind to stay open for his father.

But worse than the pain, worse even than the splitting headache that would last for hours after the discipline had ended, was the shame and guilt of having one's thoughts and memories laid bare. Every time he was disciplined, his father had to read his mind, deeper than forethoughts, deeper than memory. He had to purify Khartsaga at the subconscious level, where the weakest thoughts hid in the shadows. It was there that the real reason he hadn't killed the Speki surfaced for his father to see. He had claimed it was for the sake of research, but really it was because he hadn't wanted to kill them. Simple. And yet shamefully weak.

As his father read his thoughts and desires, Khartsaga trembled beneath the weight of the scrutiny, letting the pain wrack his body. He was disgusted with himself for letting his weakness dictate his actions so heavily. It was his fault Firekin had to move and find another location to continue their testing. His fault that the Speki had escaped. His fault for assuming the humans were even capable of staging a rescue plan on their own.

And so Khartsaga embraced the pain, willing it to cleanse him and mold him into a better Gurvel, for the sake of his father and for the sake of Firekin.

CHAPTER 5

The Next Phase

*During this time, there was a man named Ravenel who worked
as a merchant, traveling from city to city with his wares.*

Khartsaga

NESTLED AGAINST THE WALL that guarded the perimeter of Galynkhot, the Sklera castle stood tall and proud. It was a constant reminder of the glory that could be expected in the New Age. Khartsaga's body still ached from the discipline his father had dealt him yesterday, but he felt at peace knowing that it had purified his mind. What was more comforting was knowing that in allowing himself to be disciplined, he had been forgiven and was now able to attend the meeting with the king.

The guards saluted each of them as they walked into the entryway. With a clear mind, Khartsaga gazed upon the beauty of the Shadow War mural that glistened against the side wall. Made up of countless glass fragments, it depicted the glorious moment when the shadowmongrels had been let loose on Mikiltoft, the Speki city of knowledge. While this piece was the main feature, the rest of the room was nothing to scoff at. Ornate patterns sculpted into the Sklera over millennia decorated the walls and ceilings. He glanced at the swirling designs on the stair banisters but couldn't help returning to the mural as sunlight glinted off of the colored glass, highlighting the depiction of a woman staring up in a silent scream before one of the beasts.

"Marvelous discoveries, aren't they?" his father observed, walking up to the mural and placing his hand over the shadow.

"May they bring about the New Age," Khartsaga responded.

"A few centuries ago these creatures were still considered legends, lost to the passage of time. But because of Firekin, these last two surviving shadowmongrels were redeemed."

"It was kind of you to give them to King Chono," Khartsaga said. "Without them, he might not have been able to defeat his enemies."

"Of course," his father agreed. "His conquest against the Speki was beneficial for us as well. They had knowledge we needed and refused to trade for it. Now we've redeemed that knowledge for the glory of all Gurvel. Justice at last." His father smiled fondly at the mural and then turned toward the stairs, motioning for Khartsaga to follow. "Son, today when we report to the king, we will initiate the next phase of the plan."

"The next phase?" Khartsaga asked, pausing for a moment on the black staircase. "But we haven't yet discovered the proper ingredients for the Verdant Stimulant."

"You haven't, but I had Tarkhan run a few more tests while you were recovering last night," his father replied, pulling out a small vial from his pocket.

Khartsaga accepted the vial as his mouth went dry. He would have been the one to make the discovery if he hadn't let the Speki escape. "May the New Age rise." One of the few things that gave him hope was that the New Age would arrive, with or without his blunders.

They continued up the stairs, passing servants and guards, until they reached the third floor where the king's library was. It was early afternoon so the king was likely taking his tea right about now.

At the door, they were greeted by a young attendant who ushered them in and handed them fresh cups of dragonbreath tea. King Chono sat on the window seat, reclining with a stack of books.

"My King," Ukhel said with a deep bow, his golden cape gleaming in the sunlight from the large window that spanned from floor to ceiling behind the king.

Khartsaga bowed as well and sat in a plush armchair as the king set his book down.

"What news have you?" the king asked, leaning forward.

"My physicians tell me the queen is to have a son, my King. She could give birth any day now. Congratulations," Ukhel said.

The king sat back against the window and gave a sigh of relief. "I can't thank Firekin enough for the help over the years to secure my kingdom. Now that I have an heir, the crown is safe. You and your people will be greatly rewarded."

"It is our honor, my King," Khartsaga's father said, taking a sip of his tea. "Our desire is to see that all Gurvel prosper in the New Age. But it would still be wise to set up another heir, should anything happen to the new crown prince."

"Of course," the king said, straightening. "I'll make an official announcement during the next set of Games. Khartsaga will be the next in line should anything happen to my son."

"I'm honored, my King," Khartsaga said, bowing his head in appreciation. He had known this announcement was coming and yet hearing it now made his stomach churn. King Chono trusted him, not knowing what the rest of the plan would entail. But this was the way it had to be; why should his stomach lurch?

"On another note, my King," Ukhel continued, "have you given any more thought to my suggestions?"

King Chono motioned a servant over to refill his tea. "I have and I must say, while I'd love to see The Games happen more frequently, I don't know how we'll round up enough players. The captain of my guard tells me they're struggling to round up enough criminals as it is."

"Then open The Games to the poor. They can fight to feed their families," the Eternal Flame said with a small smile.

"The poor?" The king frowned. "But they'll almost certainly die."

"It would be their choice to fight or not. If they survive we will give them the food they need. If they die, their family won't have to feed them. Either way it will benefit both the kingdom and these poor families."

It was a genius idea. The human population would increase exponentially if not for The Games.

"I suppose that would work," King Chono said thoughtfully as he sipped his tea.

"And the other suggestion, my King?" Ukhel asked.

"I intend no disrespect, Eternal Flame, but your other request still baffles me. You want me to assign a human soldier to the queen's additional guard detachment? Is that wise? We've been trying for centuries to conceive a child, let alone a male heir. I'm not sure I'm willing to allow a human soldier to guard something so crucial for not only myself but also the fate of the kingdom."

"Your concerns are respectable, my King," Khartsaga's father said. "But what better time than now to visibly show how merciful you are toward this lesser race? The humans of today might not remember what you did for their ancestors, so we need to keep your graciousness at the forefront of their thoughts."

The room grew quiet as the king took another sip of his tea, taking his time as he thought through the idea. Khartsaga held his breath. They needed this next part of the plan to happen. Adding a human soldier to the queen's guard was essential in bringing the New Age to fulfillment.

"Neither of you has ever given me bad advice," King Chono mused, looking from Ukhel to Khartsaga. When their eyes met, a part of Khartsaga's stomach plummeted, but he didn't understand why. Everything was going according to plan.

"If you think it's necessary to put a human on the queen's guard," the king continued, "then I'll agree to it. But only if I can ask the commander of the human division to send me his best."

"Of course, my King," Ukhel said with a crisp nod. "That's to be expected."

"In that case, you have my blessing," King Chono concluded, leaning back against the window. "Is there anything else to report?"

"No, my King. That is all," Ukhel said. "Khartsaga can arrange for the human soldier to transfer to the queen's guard. Then he can work with The Games Master to increase the frequency of events. As always, my King, if you need any direction in the precepts of the Fire Creed, Khartsaga can guide you. When I am away, he is an extension of my Eternal Flame."

Warmth rushed to Khartsaga's face at the high praise. He didn't deserve it, especially after his blunder from yesterday. His father was too gracious toward him.

The king set his cup down. "Of course. Thank you, Eternal Flame. Khartsaga, I look forward to watching The Games with you tomorrow. Abaka is fighting again. He's becoming a real crowd pleaser."

"I look forward to it as well, my King," Khartsaga replied, moving his fist from his forehead to his heart.

Once they were dismissed, Khartsaga and his father stepped into the hallway where Tarkhan was waiting for them. What was he doing here?

"Thank you for meeting us," Ukhel said, motioning for the assistant to join them as they walked down the hallway. "I'm needed in one of the research facilities," Ukhel said, turning his head toward Khartsaga. "While I'm gone, I've instructed Tarkhan to be your aid. We're nearing the final phase, and I can't have you making any more foolish errors. He will be here to guide you should you start to slip again."

The roof of Khartsaga's mouth grew dry. His father hadn't ordered someone to guide him in years. While forgiven, his blunder wouldn't be forgotten so easily.

"I understand. Thank you, Father. I appreciate Tarkhan's willingness to guide my thoughts." He could already feel Tarkhan at the edge of his mind, monitoring his emotions and forethoughts. Not knowing what to feel, Khartsaga smiled and tried to keep his mind blank while they walked. This was all a necessary part of bringing the New Age to completion.

He was grateful that his father had provided a way to guard him against his own foolishness. Now that they were so close to the New Age, his thoughts about King Chono and the weaker races couldn't be allowed to surface. Those were the thoughts that had gotten his mother killed. Those were the thoughts that could tarnish his father's reputation. Those were the thoughts that poisoned his mind.

CHAPTER 6

New Assignment

It used to be assumed that humans, like Forestdwellers,
couldn't become Manipulators or Seyrs.

Ronan

RONAN CHECKED THE OFFICIAL seal on the bottom of the royal summons once more. It was still there. He thought maybe it had been some kind of dream, but here he was, standing before the king's guards. According to his Commander, he was to report to Sergeant Batzorig for his new assignment in the castle that, to his knowledge, no human had ever entered before.

One of the guards snatched the paper out of his hands, studying the contents while his partner eyed Ronan skeptically. He couldn't blame them. Who in their right mind would believe that a human had been transferred to the queen's guard? Even Manton and Kendra had thought he was joking until he had left the compound that morning.

Unable to find anything wrong with the summons, the guard handed it back to him and escorted him through the Sklera gate. On the other side, a crew of Sklera sculptors chipped away new outgrowths on the wall, but they stopped their work abruptly when they saw him.

"What's with the gutter pet?" A large-nosed worker asked, loud enough for everyone to hear.

Ronan kept his eyes forward. The pressure of this assignment loomed over him like the Sklera walls around him. One mistake here could cost his squadmates more than restricted dining hall access.

Without a word, the guard pointed at a set of stairs that led up to the castle and walked away. Ronan looked up at the magnificent building, taking it in now that he was this close. Every inch of it had been decorated with intricate swirls and designs. The Sklera sculptors probably had to chip away new outgrowths every week just to keep it clean.

With a steady gait, he made his way to the base of the stairs where another soldier was waiting to intercept him. If they didn't trust him on the castle grounds, then why summon him?

The soldier raised a fist to his forehead in greeting, his sleeveless uniform exposing his crimson skin. In a rush, Ronan copied the same salute. He had never been saluted by a Gurvel soldier before.

"You must be the new guard," the soldier said with a smile. "I'm Esen. Sergeant Batzorig sent me to greet you and show you around." He stood a good head taller than Ronan and had deep-set eyes beneath the ridges on his forehead.

"I'm honored to be here." As he spoke, the color yellow flashed through his mind. Instinctively he glanced down where he spotted a chroma snail inching toward his boot.

"Adorable creatures," Esen said, bending down to pick it up. "Some find them annoying, but I think it brightens the day when a random color pops into your head."

"You'd get along with a friend of mine," Ronan ventured. "She loves these things."

Esen handed him the snail. "What color do you see?"

Ronan closed his eyes as if waiting for a color and then set the snail back on the ground. "Blue." Heat rose to his cheeks when he looked up and found Esen staring at him intently.

"Blue?"

There was no way Esen knew that he was lying. Unless he was a Seyr. Most Gurvel were Manipulators so it was unlikely, but just in case he decided to change the subject. The last thing he wanted was to stand out in a place like this. "Is Sergeant Batzorig waiting for us?"

"Of course. Let me show you around."

They climbed the steps where Esen pulled open a set of double doors almost twice as tall as he was. Even with all of his training, Ronan was fairly certain that he wouldn't have the strength to open them. No man would.

When they walked inside, he stifled a gasp. The architecture was even more elegant here than outside. It must have taken centuries for Sklera sculptors to add such intricate details to the walls and high-vaulted ceiling. The sunlight streaming in through large stained-glass windows only amplified the masterpiece as it cast delicate shadows over each pockmark.

"Beautiful, isn't it?" Esen remarked.

"I never thought I'd see the inside," Ronan said, marveling at a large mural to the side of the room that had been crafted out of colorful pieces of glass. It was only after the initial glance that he realized what it was depicting. The Shadow War.

The sound of footsteps drew his attention toward a grand staircase at the other end of the room that branched off to the right and left. Even that had been sculpted like a piece of art. An attendant escorted a little dog with fur that had been dyed a light blue. It waddled happily beside him, not caring that the pink polka-dot bandana around its neck was painfully bright.

"The queen's chambers are upstairs," Esen said, walking past the attendant and motioning for Ronan to follow. "I see you carry a sword. Is that your primary weapon?"

"It is, but I've been trained in hand-to-hand combat as well. What about you? Fire Manipulation?" He still held onto the hope that the Gurvel hadn't read his mind while he lied about the snail.

"Actually, I'm a Seyr."

Ronan glanced sideways at Esen as they made it to the first floor. "I see."

"I can tell that makes you uncomfortable. But don't worry. I won't read your mind. Unless you shout your thoughts; then I'll hear them whether I want to or not."

"Shout my thoughts?"

"If I'm close enough and you have a strong thought or emotion, I might hear it," Esen explained, leading him around to the side and up the next set of stairs. "Think of it like overhearing a conversation in another room when someone starts to yell."

How loud would a "shout" need to be before it could be heard?

"It happens with chroma snails too," Esen said casually. "The colors intrude on the mind so suddenly that I can usually see them in someone's thoughts."

Ronan almost tripped on the last stair before they reached the second floor.

"Are you alright? Looks like the Sklera sculptors need to shave off the outgrowth on that step," Esen said, stopping on the second floor landing.

"It's fine." Ronan's ability to see colors before he touched a snail didn't deserve disciplinary action, but the thought of standing out concerned him. Not just for his sake, but for Manton, Kendra, and his whole squad.

"This is where the queen's chambers are," Esen said, pointing down a hallway to their right. "We'll either be guarding her door, or walking around this balcony that looks over the foyer below. Unless the doctor clears her majesty to move around more, that's everything."

It didn't look like Esen was going to say more about the snail. Maybe he had forgotten that humans normally have to hold it first. Or maybe he just didn't care.

They walked around the balcony, checking the various entry and exit points. There were lots of windows that could be infiltrated, but it would be difficult for someone to climb that high without being seen. The third floor was set up like the others with a wraparound balcony and hallways that branched off to the sides.

"That's it," Esen said, leading him back down to the second floor.

It sounded like a simple enough job, which was good. With any luck, he would be able to keep his head down and make it through this assignment without drawing attention to himself. He was feeling surprisingly optimistic as they walked down the hallway toward the queen's chambers. At least until all four guards on duty snapped their heads up to stare at him.

"Oh good, here comes Esen with his new pet," one of the soldiers said with a laugh that wrinkled the black birthmark under his eye.

Intent on ignoring the comment, Ronan fell into parade rest across from the queen's bedroom.

"Not feeling very clever today are we, Ulagan?" Esen challenged, stepping toward the guard who had spoken.

The soldier beside Ulagan smiled, pulling his already thin lips into a tighter line. "He was just teasing."

Esen stepped back with a coy smile and stood beside Ronan. "Of course. But he could at least try to engage his brain a bit when he speaks."

Ulagan blushed a deeper shade of crimson. He took a step toward Esen as if to strike him, but the thin-lipped soldier held him back. Evidently his intelligence was a sensitive topic.

"At least I'm not stupid enough to *ask* for that weakling to be my partner," Ulagan said.

"That's interesting coming from a Gurvel who can't lift a sandbag without a Stimulant."

Ulagan growled, pulling against his friend's grip.

"Just teasing," Esen said.

Would Sergeant Batzorig blame Ronan if a fight broke out? Luckily he didn't have to wonder for long.

The thin-lipped soldier tugged on Ulagan's arm. "Walk it off. Let's do a round." Reluctantly, Ulagan followed him, hands balled into tight fists at his sides.

The two remaining guards glanced at Ronan from time to time but otherwise kept their thoughts to themselves. Occasionally they would all take turns checking the window at the end of the hallway, but otherwise no one spoke, which gave him time to think. Why would Esen intentionally ask to be Ronan's partner? Ulagan had been right in one regard. If they were forced to fight against Seyrs or Manipulators, a human soldier would only get in the way.

Ulagan had calmed down by the time he and the other soldier returned from their rounds. Instead of hurling more insults he stared resolutely at the wall, which seemed to suit everyone else well enough.

After that, the time passed quickly as the day wore on. When it was dusk, the next squad came to relieve them, accompanied by Sergeant Batzorig. He was tall, even by Gurvel standards, and had a long scar across his lip that stretched as he spoke.

Other than a short glance in Ronan's direction, the Sergeant showed no indication of even noticing his presence. "Before I dismiss you, the queen requested to meet her guards personally. You will line up in squads. One on each side of the room."

Ronan's heart leapt into his throat. Was she aware that one of her guards was human? What if she demanded he be removed? They could theoretically punish his human squadmates for something so shameful.

With great effort, Ronan forced his breathing to calm and followed the rest of the soldiers into the room. He kept his gaze down as they passed the queen's bodyguards and stood beside Esen at the end of the line. Maybe no one would notice him.

Out of the corners of his eyes he caught glimpses of colorful and ornate furniture scattered about the large room. The bed was by far the largest focal point. A handful of attendants stood near the headboard, ready to serve the queen's every need. Beside the bed stood a small table piled high with books. Despite his curiosity, he resisted the urge to look for *The Legend of Ravenel*. One of the attendants might assume he was a thief.

Once everyone had gathered, all eyes turned toward the pregnant monarch who sat up in bed with her hands folded primly over her bulging belly.

"Thank you," the queen said with a voice both stately and gentle, "for your loyalty to the kingdom. I'm honored to meet the additional detachment of soldiers who are to guard us in the final stages of my pregnancy. Each and every one of you has my gratitude." She smiled kindly and gazed down the line of soldiers.

Ronan held his breath. This was it. She would either ignore him like Sergeant Batzorig had or she would demand he be removed.

To his horror, the queen turned her gaze specifically toward him and gave a subtle nod. With haste, he straightened his posture. Since she hadn't ignored him, he had a pretty good idea of what was coming next. He only hoped the punishment wouldn't be too severe.

"Thank you, Sergeant Batzorig," the queen said. "You have some fine soldiers."

"My Queen," the Sergeant said, raising a fist to his forehead. Then he turned around and led both squads out of the room.

For a moment, Ronan stared at the queen in bewilderment. She had acknowledged him. Shaking off his perplexity, he tore his eyes away from the pregnant mother and fell into line behind Esen.

Back in the hallway, the new squad took up their positions outside the queen's chambers and prepared to stand guard the rest of the night.

"You're dismissed," Sergeant Batzorig said to Ronan's squad. "Report back here before noon tomorrow."

It was over. Ronan forced his shoulders to relax and followed Esen through the corridor and down the stairs. Somehow, he had survived even the queen's scrutiny. Maybe there was finally hope for human soldiers after all these years. Other than the near altercation with Ulagan earlier that day, nothing had gone wrong, which meant no issues for his friends either.

They passed an attendant carrying a green cat with a yellow zigzag bow on its head. Why did they always have to choose the brightest colors for their pets?

Once outside the castle gates, the rest of the soldiers sauntered off toward town square while Ronan turned down the road that led back to the barracks. Many of the shops were still open, their lights glinting off the cobblestone road. If he hurried, he might be able to stop by the bookstore before Batu closed for the night.

"Care for a drink?" Esen asked from behind him, jogging to catch up to him.

"Thanks," Ronan said, looking at him curiously, "but I think the others are headed toward the Gurvel tavern."

"You mean where the spiced ale tastes like Sklera dust? I'm headed to the Seaside Tavern. You're welcome to join me."

There was no sign of deceit on Esen's face; in fact Ronan's gut told him that the Gurvel was being genuine. Since his instincts had never been wrong before, he decided one drink wouldn't hurt. "Alright. Mind if I stop by a shop along the way?"

"Not at all," Esen said, falling into step beside him as they walked along the street.

A couple of fishermen stared at them as they walked by, torn nets slung over their shoulders so they could repair them at home. Shortly after, a man covered in soot from the mines glanced at them wearily, making the hair on the back of Ronan's neck stand on end.

They weren't doing anything wrong, but regardless he didn't like the attention they were drawing. Esen would be his partner for the foreseeable future, so he decided to go for at least one scarlet whiskey. After that he could retreat to the quiet of the barracks.

CHAPTER 7

Seton's Ale

*But fear has a way of forcing discoveries about the unknown,
as Ravenel soon found out.*

Ronan

GRATEFUL TO LEAVE THE PRYING eyes of people on the street, Ronan slipped inside Batu's Books and walked up to the front desk while Esen wandered around the shop. "Hey Batu, any luck finding the book?" Ronan asked quietly, hoping Esen wouldn't overhear them. He didn't want to explain why he was looking for a children's story.

"You've been asking for that book for almost two decades, kid. What do you think the answer is?" Batu said, closing the book he had been reading with a hard snap.

Ronan forced a smile. "Just figured I'd check."

He turned and shrugged at Esen who had been looking through a stack of small leatherbound books. Even though it had been a long time since he had seen *The Legend of Ravenel*, he still knew it by heart. It was looking like the odds of him ever finding another copy were becoming slim to none. Was it even worth searching for anymore?

"What book were you looking for?" Esen asked as they stepped outside. A small Gurvel child skipped down the street as the light from the shop windows glimmered on her fox's sparkling collar.

"Nothing important," Ronan said, hoping Esen would leave it alone. When he and the other orphans had been taken to the military barracks, they had been forced to cut all ties to their families. The king had been gracious enough to let them live even though their parents had been traitors. In return, all they had to do was serve him for the rest of their lives. But he hadn't been able to forget about *The Legend of Ravenel*. It had been a gift from his sister and one of the guards had just tossed it into the flames like a piece of trash. His stomach churned as he remembered the way the fire had melted the cover and devoured the pages. The faint scent of charred flesh accompanied the memory whenever he thought about it.

"It must be important if you've spent twenty years looking for it," Esen remarked, tilting his head to the side. For a moment, his eyes widened just a sliver as if he had realized something.

Earlier Esen had said something about being able to hear "loud" thoughts. Instinct told Ronan to calm his emotions and quiet his mind, but it was already too late. He had probably seen the memory.

A mother clutching a sleeping child in one arm passed them on the street. She smiled tiredly at both of them and entered one of the shops. Ronan forced himself to relax. It wasn't a crime to remember that day. Besides, he had no intention of rebelling like his family had.

"It's just a book my sister used to read to me when I was a child," he said. "I lost it when I was taken in by the king."

"I'm sorry," Esen said softly, his voice catching in his throat. The ridges on the Gurvel's forehead scrunched together as if he were deep in thought. Somehow, Ronan actually believed that he cared, even though no Gurvel soldier had ever shown an ounce of empathy to him or the others.

Music and rowdy laughter poured into the streets as the door to the Seaside Tavern burst open. A muscular Gurvel staggered out and sauntered toward them. Ronan anticipated the direction of the man's lumbering movement and managed to step to the side before he was knocked over. Things like that didn't phase him. What did phase him was the wall of sound and mirth that slammed into him as he opened the door. At the bar Seton looked up as they walked in and gave a wide smile, waving them over to a couple of barstools.

"Ronan! Esen! Good to see you!" Seton yelled over the din as he filled a small glass with scarlet whiskey and handed it to Ronan.

"You know each other?" Ronan asked, fighting to be heard.

"This guy?" Seton pointed his thumb at Esen while grabbing a mug from under the bar. "Of course! He's a regular."

Esen laughed and accepted the tall cup of spiced ale from the young bartender. "Where else would I get ale this good?"

"I aim to please," Seton said as he picked up an armful of mugs and wove around tightly packed chairs and tables.

Ronan took one look around the room and felt his chest tighten. Each table was full of either Gurvel or humans but never both races together. A few burly fishermen glanced over at him while they waited for a new round of cards to be dealt. Just a little longer and then he could retreat to the quiet of the barracks.

He turned back around and listened to the crowd while Esen drank his ale, the faint sound of music barely perceptible over the shouts and laughter of the more rowdy tables.

"You were pretty quick on the way in, dodging that drunkard like you did," Esen said over the din. "Your dexterity will come in handy."

Ronan downed the shot of whiskey, relaxing as the warmth ran down his throat. "Maybe, but I think Ulagan's right. If it comes to a fight, I'll only slow you down. I'm weak."

"That's not true, but regardless, don't underestimate the power of underestimation."

"What does that mean?" Ronan asked.

"If we were attacked, who would the enemy go for first, you or me?" Esen asked.

"You," Ronan said as realization dawned on him. "Which means I can attack before I'm seen as a threat."

"Exactly," Esen said before downing the rest of his ale. "There's something I wanted to talk to you about, but it's too loud here. Mind taking a quick walk?"

Discussing strategy away from potential eavesdroppers was a good idea, so Ronan left a coin beside his glass and followed Esen outside. Now that all the shops had packed up and closed for the night, the streets were quiet. They walked down the street a bit and stopped in front of a mercantile shop.

"There's something I've been wanting to tell you because I don't think anyone has ever told you," Esen said, keeping his voice low. "You're a Seyr."

Ronan raised an eyebrow, certain he had misheard, and waited for Esen to crack a smile. He couldn't be serious.

"I'm serious," Esen said.

Trying harder to control his thoughts so Esen couldn't read them, Ronan glanced over his shoulder to make sure they weren't overheard. "That's impossible."

"Surely you've noticed a few oddities about yourself. Earlier today you saw a color in your head before you picked up the snail. That's something only Seyrs and Manipulators can do."

So he had noticed. Ronan shook his head. This was foolish. All part of some elaborate joke. "Humans can't be Seyrs."

"They can be. It's incredibly rare, but it is possible. There aren't many

Seyrs among the Gurvel, so I could be the first one to notice your powers, but it wouldn't surprise me if others have known and didn't tell you."

It wasn't true. It couldn't be. He glanced back toward the military compound, his mouth suddenly feeling dry like ashbark. Surely he wasn't that different from everyone else. Manton always chided him for his skill, but that was because he worked hard, not because he had any powers. "I think you're mistaken. Surely I would know if I had the ability to read minds."

"That takes intentional practice, which I could show you if you like."

"I'm not a Seyr," Ronan said.

Without warning, Esen stepped toward him. Instincts kicked in, alerting Ronan that his patrol partner was about to throw a punch at his head. He raised his arm, blocking the attack before it could make contact, then dropped into a defensive position, ready for the next move.

Esen stepped back and smiled. "See? You anticipated my attack."

"No, I responded to your attack, and just barely in time," Ronan argued, straightening back up slowly.

"You started moving at exactly the same time I did."

He had always had quick reflexes, even as a child. And like other children, he had pretended to be Ravenel, running through the streets while brandishing sticks at stray dogs. But to have powers like Ravenel? That was just fanciful dreaming and downright dangerous.

Esen leaned forward, his voice still low in the quiet street. "I'm sure you think you've climbed your way to the top because of practice and hard work—and that's part of it, I'm sure—but that's not the whole story. You can catch glimpses of your opponent's next move. That's not instinct, Ronan. It's Seyring."

Feeling a little dizzy, Ronan took a few steps away and shook his head. "You're wrong."

"You don't have to believe me," Esen said, holding out his hands calmingly. "I just figured someone should tell you."

"I appreciate the gesture, but I need to get back to the barracks." Suddenly the quiet streets felt ominous and oppressive, as if the shadows were silently waiting to drag him into the darkness.

"Alright. I'll see you tomorrow," Esen said. He nodded his farewell and left toward the castle where the rest of the queen's guards slept.

Ronan quickly walked back to the compound, his ears ringing with every step he took on the cobblestone streets. Once inside, he sat down outside his barracks and leaned his head against the warm rock, thoughts swirling too fast for him to fall asleep.

Seyring. That was impossible. Had anyone else noticed? His stomach churned. This was dangerous. The only way to stay safe was to keep your head down and blend in with the other soldiers. Standing out got people killed, or worse. He couldn't be a Seyr. He didn't want to be one.

His breathing became quick and ragged so he closed his eyes and forced himself to breathe more slowly. Once his heartbeat returned to normal he looked around for something to distract his thoughts. It was a clear night, so he sought out the safety of the stars, searching for Ravenel's Cap and then systematically worked his way through the rest of the constellations—just like his father had taught him. But unlike his father, he wouldn't gamble with his friends' safety by making himself stand out. If he had some kind of rare ability, it was bound to draw attention to his teammates. That's why Esen was wrong. He had to be.

CHAPTER 8

Scarlet Forest

One day, Ravenel was on his way to the great Speki city, Mikiltoft, when his cart broke down, forcing him to make camp in the woods.

Eira

WITH A START, EIRA opened her eyes and sat up, grabbing frantically at her waist for the Prime Stimulant that was no longer there. Scanning the room, she surveyed her surroundings to get her bearings while reaching out with her mind to detect enemies nearby.

She was on a bed in a small wooden hut. A long table lined the wall to her right. Herbs hung from the ceiling. The faint smell of smoke filled the air. Windows covered with thick curtains lay to the front and left.

"Welcome back to the land of the living." Einar's warm voice flooded her head. She turned to the left where her brother sat at a small dining table across from a rather stout woman. *"The new hairstyle suits you,"* Einar thought as he raised a mug in the air and smiled.

Eira rolled her eyes and began running her hands through her long white hair to get the kinks out. Without drawing too much attention she casually glanced at the door that was on the opposing wall. It was wooden and easy for Nar to Manipulate if the need arose.

Now that it appeared they weren't in immediate danger, a sharp and dull ache surfaced behind her skull. Likely from the blow she had received to the head or leftover symptoms from all the Inhibitors. Probably both.

"Good to see you're awake!" the woman said, standing up from the table. She walked to an area near the door where a portion of the wall stuck out at the base with a small fire crackling inside. There was just enough room for a pot to sit over a roasting stick. The woman used a thick towel to lift the pot out and poured the steaming liquid into a wooden cup.

"Here, dear, this will help with the headache," she said, her brown ankle-length skirt swishing through the air with graceful movements as she brought the hot drink over to Eira.

She accepted the drink, studying the woman's features in case she needed to remember her face later. Wrinkles around the eyes. Hair graying at the roots. A round face with dimples in the cheeks.

"It's not poisoned, Sis, I tested it myself," Einar said before taking a large gulp from his own cup.

"You're too trusting, Nar," she replied, searching the liquid for flecks of Damiendill. She had witnessed the effects of that particular poison enough times to always check her drinks, even if they came from a trusted source. Satisfied, she wafted the smell of the drink over the mug. It wasn't sour but instead had the comforting scent of spice mixed with relief leaves. She took a tentative sip.

"Not necessarily!" Einar said, raising his eyebrows in mock offense. "I've just been awake for long enough to have a pleasant conversation with Gleda. Did you know we were rescued by Alvina, the leader of the Scarletts, who live in—wait for it—the Scarlet Forest?"

Scarlet Forest? At this, Eira stood up and walked briskly toward the closest window, yanking the curtains apart. Her heart sank. There wasn't a drop of green anywhere. Just blood-red leaves contrasted against ashen bark. Even the cabins she could see in front of this one were coated in reddish mud like the dirt path they sat on. Apparently the humans were even more foolish than she had given them credit for if they had dared to set up camp in this curse of a forest.

Nar, we need to... Eira started to message her brother when the door to the cabin opened, interrupting her concentration.

A small figure entered and closed the door behind him. She stepped back defensively, assessing the person before her. He was wearing only shorts, which made it easy to see that his skin was covered in small green scales. Tail curled around his ankles, the boy looked up at her with large eyes. He had no hair and large ears like a bat. That's when she recognized what he was: a Forestdweller. She had never seen one before. They were rare a few hundred years ago before the Shadow War, but had been especially elusive since then.

"It's alright, Wren, dear," Gleda said. "Would you like to meet our guests?"

The boy nodded sheepishly and stared up at Eira again. Turning back to the window, she looked outside, judging the distance to the treeline. They could easily make a run for it if the humans decided to keep them here. The challenge would be making it out of the forest unscathed, especially if they encountered a corpse tree or phoenix flock.

She jumped as the door flung open again, this time revealing a man with a burly expression and gray-and-black-peppered hair.

"Wren, I told you to wait," the man said before giving Gleda a quick peck on the cheek.

Wren's ears flattened against the side of his head, but he continued to stare up at Eira. Wonderful. She hated to be scrutinized. It only served to remind her of how rare her species had become.

"This is Holt, my husband," Gleda said, smiling warmly as the man took a seat beside Einar at the table.

"Nice to meet you, Holt," Einar said, lifting his fist to his heart and bowing his head as was customary for Speki greetings. "And is this your son that Gleda was telling me about?"

The Forestdweller finally tore his gaze away from Eira to look toward the table instead.

Einar leaned forward so his arms rested on his knees. "Wren, was it?"

The boy moved his hands in a series of gestures and looked up at his mother.

"He wants to know what your name is," Gleda said.

"Einar, and this is my sister, Eira. You'll have to teach me how to speak with my hands like that. I'd love to learn."

Wren smiled sheepishly again and looked up at Gleda who was about twice as tall as he was. Adult Forestdwellers were significantly shorter than humans but not quite this short. He was still a child.

"Holt found him alone and injured in the forest one day. We nursed him back to health and have been caring for him ever since," Gleda explained, pulling Wren in for a hug while Holt nodded quietly. Wren's face flushed as he wrapped his tail around his ankles and peeked at Einar from Gleda's arms.

"He's a little shy." Gleda chuckled. "He's never met a Speki before."

"Well, we're honored to meet you, Wren." Einar held his right hand to his heart and bowed his head. Eira was intrigued to see Wren pull away from Gleda's hug so he could copy him.

"Now that Wren is here, I actually have something to ask of you," Gleda said. "He has some abilities that aren't normal for humans, or Forestdwellers, for that matter." Wren nodded his head in agreement as Gleda reached into her pocket and pulled out a small stone. "Go on, show them what you can do, dear," Gleda said, tossing the stone into the air.

As it started to fall, Wren held his hand out as if to catch it, but before it touched him it stopped in mid-air, hovering in place. Eira leaned forward curiously. It was incredibly rare to find a human with powers, let alone a Forestdweller. Seeing their interest, Wren smiled and started moving the stone through the air, keeping his hands just under it as if guiding it along. Einar stood up and walked closer to Wren, watching as the boy started tossing the stone up in the air and catching it, all without letting it touch his scales.

"That's impressive, Wren!" Einar said. "Looks like you're a Manipulator. It's a rare trait to find in Forestdwellers, but obviously not impossible." Excitement shone in his violet eyes.

"Nar…" She messaged to him. *"I know what you're thinking. We can't stay here."*

He glanced at her but deliberately didn't respond.

"Would you train him?" Gleda asked. "Holt and I can't help him, but we'd love for him to learn more about what he can do."

"I'd be honored to," Einar said, smiling as he looked at Eira.

"Nar, we need to continue our mission!" Eira messaged.

"That's the beauty of it, Sis!" Einar thought back, keeping his eyes on Wren and the floating stone. *"These humans have the same goal that we do. This whole group has been trying to stop Firekin's influence from spreading. And besides, what would it hurt to pass on some of what we know?"* He looked up and met her eyes. *"Please, Sister. For me?"*

Eira sighed quietly. She hadn't seen his eyes light up like this in centuries. *"Fine. But only until we learn enough to make our next plans."*

Her brother flashed her a wide grin and started showing Wren how to increase and decrease the speed of the stone's path in the air.

A couple days while they got their bearings wouldn't be too much of a setback, but they wouldn't be able to stay here for long. Not with the speed at which Firekin was spreading.

CHAPTER 9

Partners

The air had grown unusually chilly for that time of year,
so when Ravenel laid down to sleep, he used an extra blanket for warmth.

Ronan

RONAN STOOD BESIDE THE QUEEN'S door, lost in thought. It had been a few days since his conversation with Esen outside the Seaside Tavern. They hadn't talked about Seyring since then, which was a relief, because as far as he was concerned, he planned to finish this assignment and go back to being a regular guard. Only he couldn't get the idea of being a Seyr out of his mind. Every time he passed a chroma snail, the flash of color reminded him of what he might be.

Surprisingly, Ulagan held his tongue whenever he was around but grimaced every once in a while as if disgusted with having a human on the squad. In that respect, Ronan was used to feeling different. But being a Seyr on top of that was one step too far.

"Ready for a round?" Esen asked.

They left the queen's hallway to check the second level entry points. As they walked, Ronan decided to break the tension between them with the question that had been nagging at the back of his mind.

"Why did you request to be my partner?" he asked. "Ulagan mentioned it a few days ago."

"I thought it would be a good opportunity to meet someone new," Esen said, scanning the main foyer down below. "I've tried meeting humans at the Seaside Tavern, but they don't stay to chat for very long. I don't blame them, of course."

"So you didn't know anything about me before we met?" Ronan asked.

Esen straightened and paused with his hands on the banister. "Well, not at first. But on the way to the tavern I realized who you were when a memory flashed through your mind. I was there at the coliseum. On the day your family was condemned."

Ronan's breath caught in his throat, but he forced a swallow. He had still been a child on that day. How had Esen recognized him? The book. That was also the day he'd lost *The Legend of Ravenel* to the fire. He must have seen it happen and made the connection.

Esen turned and looked down at him. "But other than that, I didn't know anything about you or your...skills before we met."

Words failed to come to him. Esen spoke with such sorrow, as if he had lost something that day as well. Somehow knowing that someone else had been there, witnessing that horrible scene, was comforting.

They continued walking around the balcony in silence, checking windows as they went. Maybe he had overreacted the other night. At the very least, Esen seemed genuine, even if he was mistaken. Since no one else had ever mentioned his possible Seyring abilities, Ronan was inclined to think that it was just an anomaly. Humans couldn't be Seyrs. Not unless you believed in fairytales like *The Legend of Ravenel*.

Finishing their patrol on the second floor, they walked downstairs to check the main entrance area. The Shadow War mural sparkled as midday sunlight reflected off the glass fragments, contrasting the dark scene that it memorialized.

"Ever since that horrible war, Firekin has rooted itself deeper and deeper into this city," Esen muttered quietly.

Ronan stood still, not daring to move in case a passing attendant overheard them. He had never heard anyone say something so blatantly against the cult.

"They're planning something," Esen said, glaring at the mural. "But we can stop it."

"Esen..." Ronan whispered, shaking his head as he stepped back toward the stairs. This was treasonous. If anyone caught them talking about something like this, his teammates could be killed.

"If we do nothing, everyone you love will be in danger."

Ronan held his ground, clenching his jaw in resolute silence. His parents may have been foolish enough to entertain wild ideas like this, but he had learned from their mistakes. He followed orders. He kept his head down.

When Esen could see that Ronan wasn't going to respond, he nodded and then relaxed. "I'm sorry. This mural always sets me on edge. Forget I said anything. Let's finish our rounds." He gave a small halfhearted smile and started checking the windows and hallways around the main floor.

Ronan followed him, but the ideas that Esen had spoken echoed in his mind, bringing up old emotions that he had long since laid to rest. For years after his parents died, he absorbed everything the militia taught him. A part of him hoped to grow strong enough to someday fight Firekin like his parents had. But that was only until one of the new recruits ran away. They killed that man's entire squad the following day.

Finished with the main floor, they made their way back upstairs. As they climbed the steps, a headache started to pound in the front of his skull, likely from the continued thoughts reverberating through his mind. It was too much to consider right now. Once this special assignment was over, maybe he would think about it in the secret of night when he was alone in his bunk. But not now.

The door to the queen's chamber burst open as a servant scampered down the hallway, followed by Sergeant Batzorig. Snapping to attention, Ronan and the other guards lifted their fists to their foreheads.

"The queen is in labor. Stay alert and hold the hallway. I want one pair on patrol constantly," the Sergeant ordered, licking the scar on his bottom lip.

Ulagan and his partner quickly set off to start the first patrol, leaving the rest of them behind to guard the door. This was good. After today, he could get back to his normal life of guarding The Games and patrolling the city. The Fire Festival was coming up soon too. Maybe he and Manton would get placed near the main gates where they could enjoy the music and sweet aromas like last year.

Occasionally when a midwife opened the door to bring in new towels or water, they could hear commotion inside but otherwise the hallway was quiet. After an hour or so, Ronan's dull headache suddenly flared into a hot and sharp pain in his skull. He rubbed his forehead, grimacing.

"Are you alright?" Esen asked.

"Just a headache," Ronan muttered, forcing himself to stand at attention. The next time they left to patrol the entryway, he would ask an attendant for some relief leaves.

"Are you sure?" Esen asked. "For a moment it felt like…"

Sergeant Batzorig opened the door to the queen's quarters. "It's a boy," he said with a smile.

A sharp stab in his skull made Ronan pause and grab his temples. He somehow managed to stay standing but his vision began to blur around the edges as if he were standing in a long tunnel. The Sergeant was still speaking, but he sounded faint and distant—his words indistinguishable.

Ronan looked up but quickly shut his eyes as the hallway started to spin. It felt like he was standing in thick water, barely able to move. In fact, the water felt like it was getting thicker. Straining against the sensation, he tried to lean against the wall, but with rising panic he realized he wasn't able to move at all. Muffled voices spoke all around him, but he couldn't make out any of the words.

Then he began to move again, only he wasn't trying to. He opened his eyes as an icy jolt of fear passed through his spine. Without willing it, his body began to step toward the queen's door that the Sergeant had left open.

Desperately trying to fight whatever was happening to him, he managed to keep himself from taking another step. For a brief moment he was even able to make his hand twitch, but the force controlling him quickly intensified until he lost control of his movements again.

Someone stepped in front of him, but Ronan couldn't lift his head to see who it was. Instead, he felt himself push past the person, muffled shouts erupting behind him. As he entered the room, the queen looked up at him with wide eyes, clutching the newborn heir to her chest as Ronan drew his sheathed sword. Straining against the power that held him, he slowed his forward momentum slightly, but not enough.

Now beside the bed, he looked directly at the queen whose mouth was slightly agape in terror. He couldn't look away from her quivering pupils as he lifted his sword and in a quick movement, stabbed the queen and newborn heir through the heart.

Releasing his grip on the sword, he stumbled backward away from the bed.

Suddenly shouts and cries of panic hit his eardrums as his vision began to return to normal. Like a jolt of lightning, pain flashed through his body, hot and sharp. He had control of himself again, but was quickly tackled to the ground. There was no chance to curl up as the guards beat him in the sides and back. Struggling to catch his breath, he was relieved when the blows subsided. Someone bound his arms behind his back and yanked him to his feet where Ronan had a good view of the bed. There lay the queen and her newborn son, pinned beneath his sword. Their blood pooled around the blade and dripped onto the floor. Bile rose in the back of his throat.

All he could do was stare in disbelief. What had just happened? He hadn't done that. He wasn't a killer. The queen had actually accepted him as one of her guards. She had trusted him. Like a sick nightmare, the memory of what he had just done played in his mind. Sergeant Batzorig stepped up to him, fury bulging from the veins in his neck.

"Sergeant, wait," Esen said, stepping up beside Ronan. "This isn't what it looks like, I felt—"

"Stand back, soldier," the Sergeant growled.

"But…" Esen stepped toward the Sergeant who grabbed his shoulder and held him at arm's length.

"Take the human to a holding cell," the Sergeant ordered.

"No. It wasn't his fault!" Esen shouted.

Ulagan eagerly grabbed Ronan by the arm and dragged him out the door. Everything hurt, but he couldn't tell if the pain was from the beating or the strange power that had overcome him. Craning his neck around, he caught sight of Esen glaring up at the Sergeant.

Oddly he didn't feel fear. He knew he would likely be sentenced to death, but at the moment he didn't care. All he could think of was the look of terror on the queen's face and the blood pooling around the newborn's chest.

CHAPTER 10

Guilt

He also noted that the moon that night wasn't shining as brightly as it should have been, even though the sky was clear.

Khartsaga

"WHERE IS THE HUMAN?" Khartsaga asked Sergeant Batzorig, who stood beside the bed where the queen and newborn prince lay covered with a blanket. Standing so close to the corpses sent a shiver down his spine, but he shook it off. This was a necessary part of the plan.

"In an isolation chamber. And the guard who tried to defend him is being questioned."

"Good. That will be all for now, Sergeant. Thank you for your cooperation. Please continue supervising."

As Khartsaga turned to leave, the Sergeant visibly relaxed, probably blaming himself for the incident. A wave of nausea passed over Khartsaga as he walked into the dim hallway. Others had reported migraines after taking the Verdant Stimulant, but he was the first to have any other symptoms. The feeling intensified whenever he lingered on what it had felt like to control that guard. To see the world through his eyes. To feel the weight of the sword as it sliced through flesh. His vision swam as another wave of nausea passed through him. Best not to think about it for the time being. Perhaps it was a lingering effect of using Seyring for the first time?

Tarkhan met him in the hallway and walked beside him, never more than a few feet away in case his mind slipped again.

Now that the interview with Sergeant Batzorig was over, he only had one more task before this phase of the plan was complete. The king had sentenced the human to death as soon as he had heard the news. All Khartsaga had to do was tell one of the guards or attendants to inform the warden.

He looked over the edge of the banister and spotted an attendant on the main floor. It was almost over. Now that the newborn prince was dead,

Khartsaga was the king's only heir. The New Age was only a few steps away. As he and Tarkhan descended, his vision swam and his heartbeat quickened. He gripped the wall for support until it passed.

"Are you alright, sir?" Tarkhan asked.

"Fine. Just some side-effects from the Stimulant."

The edge of his mind prickled as Tarkhan reached inside to test his thoughts. "You did the right thing," the assistant said after he had finished probing.

"Of course. This is the beginning of the New Age."

Tarkhan smiled, his black uniform relaxing on his shoulders.

At the bottom of the stairs, the attendant looked up from the pile of books he was straightening. Khartsaga took a step toward him, intending to pass on the king's sentence for the human, but the words wouldn't come. Instead, he felt the weight of the sword. The look on the queen's face. The horror he had felt. In a snap decision, he turned away from the attendant and headed outside.

Tarkhan probed into his mind again. "Sir? Are you not going to inform the attendant of the king's command?"

"The attendant was occupied and since we have the time I think it would be appropriate if we deliver the sentence to the warden."

He headed toward the prison entrance between the castle and the military barracks while Tarkhan scrambled to keep up.

Something about the whole ordeal ate at the back of his thoughts. The Verdant Stimulant had briefly given him the ability to use Manipulation and Seyring. It had been tested on numerous humans before today, and yet when he had taken control of the guard, something had been different. The man had almost broken his hold over him. Almost.

The prickling in his head grew more forceful as Tarkhan penetrated his mind. New thoughts formed in place of the treasonous ones that he had been about to think. *It had been his first time using the Stimulant. He just needed more practice to learn how to balance both powers.* That made sense.

He shook his head to clear his thoughts as they entered the prison and descended down to the main floor. It had taken centuries for Sklera sculptors to grow the prison into the ground, but it had been worth the effort. As a Manipulator himself, Khartsaga always marveled at the sensation of being surrounded by living rock and thus unable to sense the world around him. They were still trying to develop a Stimulant that would enable a Manipulator to control Sklera, but as of yet had been unsuccessful.

At the bottom of the stairs, the warden looked up from his desk and quickly stood up to offer a salute against his receding hairline.

"I have a sentence to issue from the king," Khartsaga said, "but first, show us where the human is being held."

Tarkhan looked at him sharply but didn't stop the warden from leading them down one of the twisting hallways. The cells here were rounded out like large eggs with barely enough room to lie down in. The warden unlocked the Sklera door and stood to the side.

Since there wasn't enough room for everyone, Khartsaga motioned for the other two to stand by the door while he stepped inside.

The human had been chained to the back of the wall with his hands above his head. They'd lowered the chains as far as they could but his feet still barely touched the floor. These cells had been designed for Gurvel, not humans. The man looked up as he entered, recognition crossing his bruised face. He tried to straighten up a little, but between the bruises and tattered uniform, his attempts did little to improve his appearance.

"I've come to inform you of the king's verdict," Khatsaga said.

The man furrowed his brow and opened his mouth to speak as blood trickled down his face. Blood. Like what he saw as he drove the sword into the queen's heart.

Before the man could say anything, Khartsaga decided to cut him off. "After hearing various testimonies, including Sergeant Batzorig's account, you've been sentenced to death by shadowmongrel."

With eyes wide and mouth open in shock, the man just stared at him. Death by shadowmongrel hadn't been used as a death sentence since the Shadow War. To humans it must have seemed more like a legend than anything. Khartsaga turned to go but stopped cold as the man called out to him.

"My name is Ronan," he said with a voice that cracked. "Please, talk to my squad mates and Commander in the barracks. I would never do something like this. I would never—"

"Your squad was sentenced to death immediately after your crime," Khartsaga said, trying to ignore that he knew the man's name now. His father had warned him about naming lesser creatures. It only made it harder to cling to the truth.

The man inhaled sharply. A pit formed in Khartsaga's stomach, almost as if he could feel the man's sorrow weighing on him. Despite the prickle he felt in his mind as Tarkhan pushed into his thoughts, he turned to look at the man.

Ronan stared back at him, eyes still wide in disbelief and swollen lips parted slightly.

The prickling in his head turned into a sharp stab. He closed his eyes and turned back toward the door. This had all been necessary. The city needed to see humans for the creatures that they were. That's why it had to be a human soldier who committed the murder. And now, without an heir, Khartsaga was free to take the throne once King Chono died, securing the New Age for Firekin. This was the way it had to be.

CHAPTER 11

Corpse Tree

Not able to sleep because of the silence, Ravenel got up to look around.

Eira

RED AND GRAY, AS FAR as the eye could see. Eira held back a shiver as she stepped around the gray and white trunk of an ashbark tree. The Scarlet forest wasn't supposed to be habitable. It was teeming with dangerous plants and animals. At any moment they could walk unknowingly into a phoenix fire or find themselves encased in a man-spinster web. She took a steadying breath and kept her wits about her as they continued searching through the underbrush.

The same plants her people used to make the Prime Stimulant might grow here like they did in the north. Ashbark trees were abundant, so gathering a few fresh leaves wouldn't be an issue, but they would likely turn the Stimulant a reddish hue instead of silver.

"What are we looking for again?" Dwennon asked, rubbing the burn scar on the side of his face.

Eira had hoped to go alone to collect the ingredients but Alvina had insisted she bring company. So here she was, in the middle of the most dangerous forest in Amidral, with a manchild and Alvina's surly Commander Holt.

"Kelby root," she said, choosing to bend down and inspect the base of a bush instead of looking at the boy as she answered. They had gone over this twice before leaving the camp.

"I remember the name," Dwennon said, crouching down beside her. "But how do you know where to look? Kelby root has pink flowers, right? That's not going to be easy to see with all this red."

Eira pursed her lips and moved over to the next bush to look under the branches.

"Pay attention, boy," Holt grumbled from a different bush a few paces ahead. "Kelby root has pale yellow flowers in this forest. Not pink. Weren't you listening?"

"Of course I was listening!" Dwennon contended.

"No, you weren't," Holt said, standing up and waving them on to the next clump of bushes. "You were staring at that new girl from the herding village, Edalene."

Embarrassment rushed through Dwennon's thoughts as he tripped over a tangle of roots and fell face first into a pile of ashbark dust.

"And pay attention to your surroundings, boy," Holt added. "One lapse in judgment could land you paralyzed beneath a corpse tree."

Stepping around the fallen youth, Eira checked her surroundings again. By using Seyring, corpse trees lured unsuspecting prey into a trap where it would paralyze and wait for the body to decompose. While this area of the forest had supposedly been checked for the carnivorous plant, caution was still necessary.

"Aren't we looking for a mushroom too?" Dwennon asked, carefully brushing off ashbark dust.

"Yes," she said. "Toracini mushrooms. But they only grow in extremely nutrient-rich soil. My people used to grow large fields of them, tending and caring for them constantly."

They continued their search in silence. It wasn't imperative that they find the ingredients today, but Eira was anxious to create more Stimulant. Without it, she and Einar would only be able to do so much against the cultists.

The sun moved its way across the sky as they scavenged the forest, not having any luck with either ingredient. Eira could sense Dwennon and even Holt growing frustrated with their lack of success. If they looked for a little longer, she would be content to go back and try a different section, but they couldn't give up entirely.

"What in Amidral's shadow is that?" Dwennon cried, stumbling back after sweeping aside a section of foliage.

Beside her, Holt's head snapped up from where he was checking behind a large moss-covered boulder. Reaching for her empty Stimulant pouch, Eira felt the area around them with her mind as she and Holt ran over to the boy.

There weren't any threatening minds that she could detect, but she stood on edge as Holt drew his sword and crept toward the foliage. With the proper training, anyone could learn to hide their thoughts.

She stepped up beside Holt as he bent down to inspect something on the ground, pushing aside red vines and brush. Dwennon scrambled up from where he had fallen and stood behind her, shifting from foot to foot.

On the ground, face frozen in a horrific screech of terror, was the broken and mangled body of a phoenix. They were large birds with a wingspan as long as Eira was tall. She had never seen one up close like this before. Despite the blood covering the corpse, it looked like it had once been mainly white and gray with red and orange feathers spotting its head and neck.

"What creature could have done this?" she asked.

"Don't know," Holt replied, looking up at the tree branches above them. "Phoenixes travel in flocks and don't have any natural predators."

"There are more," Dwennon whimpered behind them, clutching the scar on the side of his face with a trembling hand.

"No," Holt said, peering around the forest before them. "Our scouts haven't seen any phoenix flocks in this part of the forest." Dwennon moaned softly and took a few steps back away from the bird. "Dwennon, look at me," Holt said with a mixture of firmness and gentleness that seemed almost uncharacteristic of the Commander. "We're not in danger of phoenix fire. This one has been dead for a few days. We're going to be fine."

The boy nodded with wide eyes, his breathing short and quick. His hand still gripped the side of his face as if to shield his scar from further damage.

"Do you think whatever did this is still nearby?" Eira asked.

Holt inspected the wounds more closely. "No. Whatever killed it likely moved on days ago."

"It was a shadowmongrel," Dwennon said weakly.

"The only shadowmongrels in Amidral are with the king in Galynkhot," Holt said. "This was something else."

Eira caught a wave of uncertainty flare before Holt's foremost thoughts for a brief second before he hid it behind his usual brusque demeanor. This dead phoenix unsettled him.

"We'll head east and search in the next section over on the way back to camp," Holt said, sheathing his sword.

"Wait!" Dwennon cried, pointing just up ahead past the bird.

Eira looked up quickly, hair prickling on the back of her neck. But she relaxed when she saw a handful of pale yellow flowers growing between the roots of a large ashbark tree.

"Good. We'll gather the Kelby root and head back to camp for lunch," Holt said, starting to walk toward the tree. "We can come back later to look for the mushrooms."

Dwennon stayed where he was, shifting from one foot to the other, his eyes focused on the treetops.

Carefully stepping over the mangled carcass, Eira followed behind Holt, relieved to have found at least one of the ingredients. They would need the toracini mushrooms soon, but for now she was content to get back to the safety of camp. The dead phoenix was a fresh reminder of the dangers that lurked here.

Walking around the base of the tree, Eira scanned the foliage. The Scarletts had already surveyed this area thoroughly, but she felt the need to check for corpse trees herself. With proper training, a Seyr could learn to detect illusions by looking for anything that seemed too believable.

Meanwhile, Holt crouched next to the trunk and started harvesting the Kelby root like Gleda had instructed them, gently pulling the plant up from the base of the stem. One of the taller plants must have been deeply rooted because he needed to use the trunk for support to pull it out of the ground.

Nothing appeared to be out of the ordinary, so Eira bent down to harvest more Kelby root when Holt suddenly collapsed beside her. Surprise and fear jumped to the front of his mind.

"Don't touch the bark!" Dwennon screamed. He had backed farther away from the phoenix and was now waving his arms frantically from some fifty or sixty yards away.

A sharp pain pierced the back of her skull. That's when she felt it: The force pushing on her mind, willing her to believe the reality it had cast over her. She had missed it. The tree had fooled her. It had somehow created an illusion so ordinary, so mundane, that she had failed to detect it.

Shaking herself out of shock, Eira grabbed Holt under the arms and started to pull him to safety when she saw the small purple head of a toracini mushroom. She yanked it up and pocketed it before continuing to drag the surly commander out from under the tree's branches. They needed to get away from the base of that tree.

"Hurry!" Dwennon shouted, running toward them.

Small black seeds pelted the forest floor around her as she dragged the deadweight of Holt's paralyzed form. One of them hit her shoulder and burst open, oozing a hot liquid onto her tunic. She cried out as it burned through her cloak and onto her skin.

Another one hit her arm and exploded. Green liquid oozed out, burning everything it touched. Tears streamed down Eira's face at the hot, searing pain. Holt was hit as well, but she could only tell the pain he was in from the emotions filling his foremost thoughts. The poison on the bark paralyzed everything but the mind.

Dwennon ran just past her and picked up Holt's feet so they could carry him faster. With his help, they finally made it past the edge of the tree's umbra. But they couldn't stop here. From what she remembered, someone poisoned by the corpse tree only had so much time before their internal organs shut down.

Sweat ran down the sides of her face as they trudged along. She gritted her teeth as they wove around ashbark trees, trying to ignore the burning in her skin where the acid was eating away at her flesh. All she could do was keep moving, her muscles straining from carrying half of Holt's weight.

Finally, the faint scent of cinnamon from the grass at the edge of camp wafted toward her. She gladly handed Holt over to the pair of Scarletts that had seen them approach and come running. Stumbling through the grass, she fell to her knees to catch her breath as the acid continued to burn. She would recover in time, but did Gleda even have an antidote to help Holt? She should have been able to see through the illusion. If that man died, it would be her fault.

CHAPTER 12

Shadowmongrel

*What he encountered that night, alone in the woods,
was a beast like death itself.*

Ronan

COLDNESS GRIPPED RONAN'S STOMACH as he hung from the prison wall. Dead. Manton. Kendra. All of them. Because of him. He squeezed his eyes shut, but that only burned the image of the queen's terrified expression deeper into his mind.

It wasn't any different with his eyes open. Without a light source, the cell was just as dark as his eyelids. How long had it been since the king's advisor had talked to him? Hours? Days? It didn't matter. Sooner or later they would come back for him so they could feed him to the king's shadowmongrels.

An icy shiver ran down his spine. Death by shadowmongrel. He had heard stories about the Shadow War and how those creatures tormented their prey before killing them, somehow feeding off their pain and fear. No one had ever survived one, unless you counted Ravenel, but even the Gurvel didn't believe he actually existed, and their history stemmed back centuries further than the records humans kept.

He choked back the sense of overwhelming panic that rose in his throat, threatening to burst out of his chest. Terror and hollow loneliness like this hadn't gripped him since the day he had watched his family burn to death.

Close to hyperventilating, he forced himself to focus on his breathing, imagining himself running through a sword drill. But other thoughts bombarded his meditation, disrupting any semblance of peace.

If he hadn't walked in on that secret meeting all those years ago, Aprika might still be alive. Sweat slid down the side of his face as he shook his head to clear the memories, but new thoughts took their place.

His squad was killed without a trial for something they hadn't even witnessed. Leaning his head back against the warm Sklera, he stared at the black void above him, a few tears mixing with the sweat on his face. None of it made sense. None of this should be happening.

Thoughts and emotions tumbled through his mind like icy waves until finally the door to his cell swung open. Two grim-looking guards walked in. Once they released him from the wall, the soreness covering the rest of his body intensified. Every movement he made caused his disheveled uniform to brush up against the numerous welts and bruises that covered the skin underneath. His captors didn't seem to care.

Grabbing him by the arms, the guards dragged him through the hallway and up through the militia compound exit where moonlight lit the practice ground. As they led him past the barracks, Ronan squinted through the window, hoping beyond logic that Manton would be inside, laughing with Kendra and the others. But it was empty.

The reality of the situation settled on him like a cold blanket. They really had been killed. Of course they had. What else should he expect? An icy chill swept along his skin. He had slaughtered the queen and heir to the throne.

The shops were just closing up for the night as a handful of humans and Gurvel milled around. Ronan kept his gaze on the cobblestone streets as some of them spat snide comments, their hot stares boring into the back of his neck. As they passed Batu's Books, he looked up, hoping to see *The Legend of Ravenel* in the window display, just to know that it still existed. But it wasn't there.

They turned onto the main road and passed by the merchant stalls that had mostly closed up for the night. Each step drove the sense of desperation deeper into his core. Thoughts of escape flitted through his mind, but they all fell flat. Even if he could break free from the guards' grip, he couldn't physically outrun them, not when they were a good foot or so taller than he was.

As they neared the city gates, they passed by the Fire Fountain, burning brightly in the night. A blue flash of color shot through Ronan's mind. His head snapped up, instinctively looking for the chroma snail. It was too dark to see, but he knew it was there, slithering somewhere on the fountain.

One of the guards smacked him and forced him to look forward as they exited the city walls. His conversation with Esen outside the Seaside Tavern replayed in his head. It was impossible for him to be a Seyr, but as they marched around the outer wall of the city, he toyed with the idea in his head. Could all of his success have been in part because he was unknowingly a Seyr? But even if that were true, it was too late. He had never given Esen a chance to teach him anything.

Moss frogs chirped their nightly song from the shadows of the forest as they neared the cave systems behind the city. He peered through the darkness as the guards led him past the fields and patches of vegetables that the humans farmed. The cave entrance was barely distinguishable against the mountainside.

Ronan pulled against his captors as panic began to settle in his bones, but the guards only tightened their grip and pulled him toward the looming cave. Closer to the entrance, he could make out the forms of Khartsaga and a skinny Gurvel standing just behind him.

Stepping aside, the king's advisor waved his hand toward the foreboding entrance to let them pass. Dread settled in Ronan's stomach, his legs almost giving out beneath him as the guards roughly pulled him with them into the cave.

Even if he was a Seyr like Esen said, what good would that do against a shadowmongrel? How could he fight a beast made of shadow?

His heart beat faster as the cool air of the cave blew against his face. What could Seyrs even do? They could read minds and cast illusions, but would a shadowmongrel fall for that?

Firelight from torches on the walls cast eerie shadows against the bare rock as they traveled down a steep incline deeper into the mountains. Every step pounded the sense of dread deeper into his core, like a stake of ice being hammered into his stomach. It was a death march.

What had Ravenel done? Aprika had read that story to him every night. He knew it by heart. But unfortunately, there weren't any details about *how* Ravenel had defeated the shadowmongrel. He should have asked Esen to teach him something about Seyring.

Finally they approached a large Sklera door at the end of the long tunnel. This was it. A new atmosphere of coldness hung in the air, seeping into his bones. The flickering firelight on the walls grew dimmer as if covered by a thin veil. Breath caught in his throat as fear and desperation tightened his chest. He couldn't fight whatever was behind that door. If he was going to escape, he needed to do it now.

Seyrs can project illusions. But how? If he imagined the illusion, could he force the image into the minds of the guards to disorient them?

The guard on his right stepped toward the Sklera door, hand reaching into his pocket for the key. Now. He needed to try it now.

Squeezing his eyes shut, Ronan envisioned the Sklera door slowly opening of its own accord, a dark shadow floating out of the crack, like the one he had seen in the Shadow War mural. The image was so vivid in his mind that it sent a shiver down his own spine. With focus powered by sheer desperation, he pushed the image outside himself, willing the guards around him to see it too.

With a gasp, the guard still holding his left arm took a step back. Reacting quickly, Ronan yanked his arm out of the guard's grip while he was distracted and took off running up the tunnel. He didn't know a lot about Seyring, but he figured the illusion wouldn't last long, so he ignored the soreness in his muscles and sprinted.

Not long after, he heard footsteps running after him. Pain flared in his side. His ribs were likely bruised, but he didn't stop. He couldn't.

Bolting out of the cave, he saw Khartsaga and his assistant out of the corner of his eye, standing near the entrance with mouths agape. Their shock didn't last. They joined the guards and chased Ronan as he dashed toward the forest.

Thankful that they hadn't taken his boots, he tore through a wall of bushes and lept over fallen logs, hoping his smaller stature would allow him to avoid debris easier than his pursuers. At first his plan appeared to be working. The four Gurvel running after him were slowed down by the number of branches and bushes in their path, but despite the obstacles they were still gaining on him.

He looked around for anything that might help him. A few paces ahead there was a large rock that was large enough to hide behind. Maybe he could get away with the same trick twice.

Sliding behind the boulder, he shut his eyes and envisioned himself continuing to run into a thicket of trees. As soon as the footsteps were close to him, he pushed the image out from his mind like he had in the cave. A throbbing ache formed in his skull, intensifying with each breath he took.

His pursuers passed the boulder and continued running after the illusion. It wouldn't take long for them to turn back, so he scrambled up and ran in a different direction, deeper into the forest.

Slipping around trees and keeping to the shadows, he moved as quickly as he could to put distance between himself and the guards. Sweat beaded on his forehead as he concentrated on his every move. With each step, the crunch of fallen ashbark sent spikes of fear across his skin. Every ounce of strength went toward listening for signs of pursuit and keeping his progression as quiet as possible.

Just when he was beginning to hope that he had lost them, a heavy fatigue fell over him. The force of it was so strong that he tripped on a branch and slid up against a fallen log.

His entire body felt limp and exhausted. Even his early days as a soldier, training from sunup till sundown, hadn't left him this drained of energy. It took every ounce of willpower to crawl over the log and continue moving deeper into the forest. He had to get far enough away that they couldn't catch up to him.

Not able to even stand, he dragged himself along the forest floor, crawling when he could and clawing at the dirt to pull himself forward when he couldn't. A splitting headache blurred his vision and filled his head with a dense fog. But the innate drive to survive pushed him forward.

Fighting to stay awake, he continued his slow progression until sunlight started to brighten the forest around him. The dark grays of night began to shift into hues of blue and brown. Had he gotten far enough away? He hadn't heard or seen any signs of the guards. They would have caught him by now if they knew where he was. Although even if they were still hunting him, he didn't think he'd be able to keep his eyes open for much longer.

He stopped crawling and flipped himself over onto his back, groaning as the world spun around him. Before letting sleep overcome him, he looked up at the sky and gasped. The leaves on the trees were a deep shade of red.

It had been so dark, he hadn't noticed the leaves changing color. Somehow he had wandered into the Scarlet Forest. The immense wall of exhaustion weighed on him, threatening to take over and pull him into sleep. Alarm wracked his body. This forest was infamous for the dangers that lay within.

But he was fading, and fast. His vision began to blur and his eyelids drooped. With one last ounce of strength he cried out for help as loud as he could muster, but only a whisper escaped his lips before darkness overcame him.

CHAPTER 13

Cleansing

At first, Ravenel thought he must be dreaming.
His surroundings were the same, but he found himself
running from every fear he had ever imagined.

Khartsaga

KHARTSAGA SAT PERFECTLY STILL as he watched the small gray frog lift a pebble into the air with its mind. It had its eye on a fly that had landed a short distance away and slowly moved the rock over top of it. When the fly tried to leave, the frog dropped the pebble and crushed it. Then it hopped over to its successful kill and began licking up the squished remains.

These frogs were incredibly fascinating. Somehow they were able to draw on the powers of Manipulation despite having no consciousness. As a boy, Khartsaga had always tried bringing home moss frogs as pets, but his father never let him keep one. He reached over to pick up the creature and study it further when a large black boot came down on top of it, crushing it.

Evidently, he had been so enamored by the frog that he hadn't heard the approach of his father, Ukhel. They were meeting in the forest today to avoid being overheard.

The Eternal Flame of Firekin sat down on the rock that Khartsaga was kneeling in front of, the squashed remains of the frog plainly visible beside him. "I thought we discussed this, Son," his father said, shaking his head. "Your heart for these small creatures is your greatest weakness. You should be spending your time practicing, not entertaining these worthless beasts."

"Forgive me, Father, I was studying it."

"They aren't worth the time to study, Son. Small creatures like this won't even live as long as a human." He gestured to its squashed remains. "Your people need you to focus, Son. We can't afford to slack off when we're so close to welcoming in the New Age."

Khartsaga bowed his head and looked down at the grass growing around the boulder. He should have been using the extra time to become stronger, not wasting it on weak creatures that barely had time to grasp the concept of life.

"Give me your progress report," Ukhel ordered.

"The humans aren't happy about the increase in Games, but we arrested any aggressors and had them purified by fire," Khartsaga said, glancing up at Ukhel.

Ukhel leaned back on the rock and crossed his legs. "Good. Good. That will help the city transition into the New Age. And the special task I gave you?"

"Yes," he said tentatively. "The queen and prince are dead."

"Well done, Son. I wasn't sure you'd be up to the task after the incident at our research location." Ukhel tilted his head and stared at him for a moment. It was uncomfortable, but Khartsaga knew he deserved the scrutiny. He relaxed when his father broke his gaze to look around at the lush leaves thriving with all sorts of creatures chattering in the afternoon sun. "We're nearing the day when you will take the throne in Galynkhot," Ukhel said. "Don't lose sight of the end goal."

"I won't, Father. I will fulfill my role in the New Age." He had too. For the sake of his father's reputation and for the sake of Firekin.

Ukhel smiled as he picked at the frog. "You have the right intentions, but unless you remember that humans are no more than worthless animals, you'll never meet your true potential. That soldier would have killed the queen on his own, but he lacked the capacity to do so. That's why you had to intervene with the Verdant Stimulant. The city deserves to know how feral humans are."

Khartsaga nodded absentmindedly. It was necessary for the queen and newborn prince to die, but his heart didn't yet believe the truth. Last night he dreamt about a Gurvel boy playing by the edge of a steep cliff. Before he could intervene, the child tripped and fell. With dread Khartsaga peered over the ledge to find his own mother standing beside the boy's mangled corpse. The morbid scene would have been enough to disturb anyone, but what had really unsettled him was his mother. Despite the distance, he was somehow able to make out every detail of her tear-stained face, including the horror and grief in her eyes. Eyes that were looking directly at him. She was ashamed of him. Now, every time he was reminded about the queen or prince—which was often—the pain in his mother's eyes pervaded his thoughts.

"Speaking of the human guard, has he served his sentence?" Ukhel asked.

"He...escaped," Khartsaga admitted, refocusing on the conversation. He didn't know how Ronan had escaped. The man had come running out of the cave and somehow eluded them in the forest. When questioned, the guards claimed that they had seen the shadowmongrel escape its prison, and yet the door had still been securely shut. It didn't make any sense.

Ukhel's head snapped up, the ridges above his eyes furrowing. "What happened?"

"I don't know, Father," Khartsaga said, his voice cracking despite the effort to keep his tone even. "He got past the guards on the way to the shadowmongrel lair." He tensed in anticipation of what would come next. The New Age could not have mistakes or weaknesses. Especially from the Eternal Flame's own son.

Ukhel stood up, his expression as hard as the rock he had been sitting on. Preparing for the punishment, Khartsaga looked down at the ground. Ronan shouldn't have been able to get away. Obviously, this was a result of his own weakness. It shouldn't have been so difficult to control the human's body with the Verdant Stimulant either, but he had struggled. His father had entrusted this task to him and he had failed.

Regarding Khartsaga in silence, Ukhel tilted his head and stared at him. The time before the punishment was always the worst because it gave him time to wallow in his mistakes. But he deserved even that.

A sharp pain erupted across his mind and entire body as the cleansing began. Dropping to the ground, he didn't utter a single sound. The punishment served to help him, so he would face it with as much dignity as he could muster. Pain would cleanse him and remind him of the truths he had forgotten. Pain would purge him of his failings and weaknesses. Pain would prevent him from ending up like his mother. Even so, he gripped the grass and tore it from the ground as the pain pierced his thoughts and memories.

CHAPTER 14

The Seyr

But worse than his own fears was the beast itself.

Eira

EIRA STOOD WITH HER ARMS crossed, pondering the mess of notes that Alvina had laid out. Next to her, Holt scowled at the papers with both palms pressed flat against the table, patches of skin still raw from the corpse tree's acid. Luckily, after they had returned to camp yesterday, Gleda had been able to counteract the paralysis poison in time, but the burns on his skin would take longer to heal. Eira subconsciously rubbed her arm where a large spatter of acid had burned her own skin.

In silence, they pored over their combined notes about Firekin, trying to find any clues they had overlooked. Einar was supposed to be with them, but he had been disappearing more and more to train the little Forestdweller. She looked out the window at the red leaves and vines of the Scarlet Forest, antsy to get back on the road to find the Eternal Flame.

"Let's go over what we know," Alvina said, holding up a sheet of paper. "Firekin has been kidnapping humans for decades, taking them from small towns. But recently the number of disappearances has gone up. Why?" She looked at Eira and Holt, her black braid resting on her red-cowled tunic.

"To experiment on," Holt said. "They need test subjects to try out a new Stimulant."

"And they're preparing for something," Eira stated. "They're trying to speed up the process, but we don't know what Stimulant they're trying to create. They detected Nar and me even though our thoughts were hidden, but the discovery seemed to surprise them. I'm not convinced that piercing a mind barrier was their final goal."

Alvina grabbed a smaller slip of paper. "We know what some of the ingredients are. The survivors said the cultists forced them to mine for some kind of green crystal when they weren't being used as test subjects."

"A few of them mentioned that the cultists took their blood too," Holt added.

"Were they adding blood to the Stimulant?" Eira asked.

"It's hard to tell," Alvina replied, handing her the paper. "Maybe they were just being thorough in their examinations, testing the blood to make sure something like disease wasn't skewing the results."

The door to the cabin opened and Einar walked in with a large smile. "Sorry I'm late! Wren is doing a phenomenal job, Holt. You should be very proud." He slapped the burly man on the shoulder as he walked by.

Holt winced, but his eyes lit up from the praise.

Alvina smiled and took a seat in one of the chairs that they had pushed back from the table. "Wren enjoys learning from you. Thanks for taking the time."

Eira's brother leaned over the table and squinted at the mess of notes and maps. "I'm honored to do it. Discover anything new?" Holt just shook his head and went back to studying the papers. Nar looked up at Eira and raised an eyebrow. "Sister? We must have learned something."

"Not really," she said with a heavy sigh. "None of the survivors overheard what the Stimulant was supposed to do. We know a few of the ingredients, but nothing more definite."

She froze as the hair on the back of her neck stood on end. A thought passed through her mind, but it wasn't her own. It was a desperate cry for help from a Seyr.

"Sister?" Einar said with concern.

She caught her breath and looked in the direction that the message had come from. "Someone is in danger. I heard them. In my mind. They can't be too far away."

"Could be a trap," Holt said, furrowing his eyebrows into a more serious expression than before.

She considered it for a moment but pushed the concern away. "No. It didn't feel like a Gurvel mind." But if a Gurvel hadn't sent the message, then who had? Her heartbeat quickened. Could it be another Speki? Someone else who had survived the Shadow War like they had?

She exited the cabin, running toward where the message had come from. King Chono's guards had been hunting Speki survivors for centuries. If this cry for help had been from one of her people, she needed to find them and fast. A small flicker of hope burned in her heart.

Einar and Holt ran with her past the cinnamon grass. She cringed when the tall stalks brushed her skin and momentarily Inhibited her Seyring ability. It returned as soon as she was past the border, even though the scent of cinnamon lingered in the air.

"Where did the cry come from? I can get there faster!" Einar's voice filled her head as he ran beside her.

"Just up ahead."

Even without a Stimulant, Einar was strong enough to launch himself into the air by pushing off of nonliving objects with his mind. Some of the boulders in the Scarlet Forest were too large to move, so when he pushed on them, his body, smaller in mass, was propelled in the opposite direction away from the boulder.

As he pushed himself through the air ahead of them, she and Holt continued to run on foot, red leaves and moss whirling past them. Could it be true? Could there be another Speki that had managed to evade capture? No. She couldn't get her hopes up. King Chono had been very thorough in his quest to wipe out their race. But then who could it be?

She listened for other minds around them but whoever had sent the message seemed to have disappeared. Darting around an ashbark trunk, she tried again, feeling for intellectual lifeforms, but all she found were the small minds of creatures hidden in the underbrush. After a few minutes she and Holt found Einar bending down beside a fallen log. A jolt of energy warmed her core as she caught sight of the body lying on the ground next to him. She jogged the rest of the way, slightly out of breath, and looked down at the man.

It wasn't a Speki. Not unless he had dyed his hair black. She bent down and carefully lifted his eyelids. They weren't violet. Confused, she stood up, looking around them for someone else. "He's human. He couldn't have sent the message."

"Sis...I think it was him," Einar said, feeling the man's wrist for a pulse. "This is where the message came from. Who else could it have been?"

She closed her eyes and concentrated on the minds around her, blocking out the animals hiding in the shrubs and leaves. There had to be a Speki hidden nearby. Yet, after a couple of minutes she finally gave in to the truth. The only other sentient being she could sense besides Einar and Holt was the man lying on the ground.

"There's no one else," she said, looking down at the man. His face was badly bruised and from the look of his tattered uniform, the rest of him was likely just as injured.

"He's from the city," Holt observed, bending down. "This is a soldier's uniform."

Einar looked at the man with concern. "We should take him back. If he sent the message, he likely pushed himself into a Seyr coma."

"Nar, that's—"

"Don't say it's impossible," he said, catching her eye. "Wren is a Forestdweller and he's a Manipulator. It's rare, but it *is* possible. Besides, we can't just leave him here. He'll die."

"He could be dangerous," Holt said, looking skeptically at the man.

"Even if he is, he's in no condition to fight us," Einar insisted, taking his cloak off and laying it on the ground next to the man.

Holt pursed his lips but helped Einar move the man onto his cloak. As they dragged him back to camp, Eira looked down at him every now and then. Could the cry really have come from this human? He was so young. If he was a Seyr, he had likely had little to no training. So how had he sent a message from so far away? Even for an experienced Seyr, it would have taken an incredible amount of strength to send a message even with the aid of Stimulants. There had to be another explanation, but nothing came to mind.

CHAPTER 15

The New Heir

*Clicks in the shadows. Yellow eyes that bore into the soul.
And an inescapable sense of unending dread. Terrible, eternal terror.*

Khartsaga

A THUNDEROUS ROAR ERUPTED around the coliseum as Abaka, the favored Champion, finished off one of the prisoners by throwing them against the Sklera wall. Khartsaga clapped from his chair beside the king as soldiers brought in another prisoner to continue The Games. In anticipation of the next fight, the crowd chanted Abaka's name and stomped their feet as the Champion raised his hands and walked around the center of the coliseum. It was a glorious day.

Glancing to the side, he caught sight of the king's glazed expression as he half-heartedly clapped along with the crowd. They had increased The Games to daily in remembrance of the queen and heir—a suggestion that the Eternal Flame had insisted upon. King Chono had accepted the idea, but it didn't seem to ease his pain. Tonight he would go over the Fire Creed with the king before bed. That would help put his momentary suffering in the right light.

Fire purifies all impurities. Abaka shot a series of fireballs at the female prisoner who scrambled away.

May the New Age rise and Gurvel prosper so that all creatures may prosper. With a spinning attack through the air, Abaka swept the bottom of the woman's trousers with fire, causing her to shriek in fear and pain as her pants began to smolder.

Together we rise. Together we prosper. Together we ascend. Abaka feigned an attack and laughed as the woman flinched and fell on her back, sand spraying into the air.

May the children of fire rise. Abaka mocked the woman, motioning for her to stand as he handed her the sword. She stood to her feet, trembling.

The Champion lunged forward and chased her around the arena, laughing as she tried to hide behind one of the soldiers. As ordered they stepped to the side and pushed the prisoner back into the arena where Abaka swiftly pelted her with fireballs.

The fight didn't last very long after that. Abaka grabbed the woman, ripped the sword out of her hand and stabbed her with it. The crowd roared with excitement as blood stained the dead woman's tattered clothes. Standing to his feet, Khartsaga joined the crowd, clapping in excitement. What a marvelous display of strength. And this was only the beginning! Abaka was a perfect example of the kind of prosperity that the New Age would bring. As always, his father was right. Weakness would only slow down their goals. That's why he needed to become stronger. That's why King Chono could not remain king forever.

Now that the regular fights were over, the king was supposed to announce the Fire Purification, but he remained sitting with a glassy look coating his eyes.

Tarkhan cleared his throat. "Perhaps you should make the announcement, sir?"

In surprise, Khartsaga looked over his shoulder at his attendant. He had forgotten he was even there. Since meeting with his father in the forest, Tarkhan's presence hadn't seemed as noticeable as before, likely because his thoughts didn't need as much adjustment. A good sign.

Standing up, he raised his hands to quiet the crowd, like he had seen his father do on countless occasions, taking command of the coliseum with ease.

"Ladies and gentlemen, we still grieve the loss of the queen and newborn crown prince. We can never bring them back, but we can honor them through Fire Purification and by ushering in the New Age. Join me in celebrating the life that only fire can bring."

The people clapped with reverence as the soldiers scurried to prepare the pyre. He took his seat beside the king as Tarkhan nodded in satisfaction. Soon the transition to the New Age would be complete. It would be everything he had ever hoped for. Yes. It was all coming together perfectly.

A flash of pale orange filled his mind. Looking around, he found the small chroma snail slithering calmly along the armrest of his chair. It didn't have any concept of glory or honor and yet it continued to live its simple life, slowly moving wherever it pleased.

No. He shouldn't be amazed with such a weak creature. Without another thought, he raised his fist and smashed the snail, wiping off the slime it left by scraping his hand against the rough Sklera seat. Turning his attention back to the pyre, he forced a hard swallow and ignored the tightness forming in his chest. *May the New Age rise and Gurvel prosper so that all creatures may prosper.*

CHAPTER 16

The Scarletts

*Ravenel fought for his life, trapped in his own mind by
a beast born from the shadows of fear.*

Eira

WALKING BESIDE THE TALL cinnamon grass at the edge of the Scarletts' camp, Eira inspected the perimeter to find any areas that were too thin. Alvina followed beside her with a wooden board and sheet of paper to note the patches that needed more grass. The camp wasn't incredibly large, so it shouldn't have taken them this long to make it all the way around, but to her annoyance, the chatty tavern keeper from the city had decided to tag along.

"I'm telling you, Alvina, even my secret ingredient won't be able to keep patrons coming to the tavern for much longer," Seton said. "For the past few days I've only had a handful of customers. It's a sad time indeed when even spiced ale doesn't tempt the tongue. Do you know how long it took me to discover that scarlet moss compliments the earthy flavor of the ale ten times better than the moss used in other taverns?"

"That's because we thought the scarlet moss would be poisonous," Alvina said.

Eira stopped walking briefly as the fog in her mind lessened and pointed to the patch of grass that was weaker so Alvina could jot a note. They were almost back to the point where they had started, which hopefully meant she could excuse herself to go find Nar. Anything to get away from this human's incessant blabbering.

"True. But as it turns out, not everything in the Scarlet Forest is deadly," Seton said.

"We wouldn't have figured it out if you hadn't so boldly decided to try it yourself," Alvina responded with a laugh.

"Someone had to do it," he said. "How else was I supposed to compete with those big-shot Gurvel taverns?"

Stepping farther away from the cinnamon grass, Eira was able to clear her head from the fog. She had heard of other plants like this before, but they were rare. Apparently Alvina's father had discovered a patch of this grass in the Scarlet Forest and figured out how to cultivate it. The implications and possibilities were a little unnerving, but at least it meant they could keep some of the more dangerous creatures out of the main camp.

"Thank you, Eira," Alvina said. "I'll give this list to Gleda so she can work on patching up the weaker areas."

Eira nodded and looked around for signs of her brother. Scarletts milled around the wooden structures of the camp, already busy about their day. One of the scouts walked down the main path with a bundle of ropesnare in his arms, likely on his way to coat their weapons in ropesnare milk as a precaution against Manipulators. They didn't have enough to keep all the cabins coated, but at least their weapons would be safe.

"Do you think the death of the queen had anything to do with Firekin?" Alvina asked the tavern keeper.

This piqued Eira's interest, and she found herself turning back toward the conversation.

"Undoubtedly," he said grimly. "I knew the man who supposedly killed her. He wouldn't have done that willingly."

"What happened to him?" Alvina asked.

"They sentenced him to death by shadowmongrel. And they killed his entire squad too. They take extreme measures like that from time to time. It was horrible."

"Why do you think Firekin was involved?" Eira asked.

"I can feel it. King Chono declared that in the event that his own son is unable to claim the throne, Khartsaga would legally be next in line. And now the crown prince is dead. Does that sound like a coincidence to you?"

If Firekin was bold enough to kill the crown prince, then they were moving faster than she had feared. And if the cult took control of Galynkhot, they would become too powerful to stop. Where was Nar? They had stayed in this forsaken forest long enough.

As they talked, the little Forestdweller ran up to them, a wide grin across his face. He moved his hands excitedly and pointed back toward the main camp.

"He's awake already?" Alvina asked. She turned to Eira. "He said the soldier you found in the forest is awake. Einar and Gleda are with him now."

"Soldier?" Seton asked curiously.

"You can come see him if you'd like. Maybe you'll recognize him. Don't the soldiers go to the Seaside Tavern in the evenings?"

"They do," he said with some hesitation. "But if you found a soldier out here...that likely means he ran away, which wouldn't bode well for his squad..." The man trailed off as he followed behind Eira.

"If he's feeling up to it, we can ask him what happened," Alvina said over her shoulder.

They walked by more wooden structures, some of them on stilts that wrapped around trees, others on ground level that were built in two lines to form a kind of street. It was a well-organized camp, and yet the dangers that lurked just beyond the grass couldn't escape Eira's thoughts. Not with the deep red hue of all the plants. From the leaves, to the moss, to the grass, everything was a deep shade of scarlet. The ground they walked on had been tilled into soil, but otherwise the forest was ablaze with red.

The soldier recovered faster than she anticipated. For the past few days she had spent time helping the man's mind to heal. He would have recovered on his own eventually, but his level of Seyring fatigue was so severe that she and Nar thought it best if she helped guide the healing process.

Though she hated to admit it, her brother had been right. The man was a Seyr after all, despite the improbability. What had driven him this far into the forest? She wanted to pry into his memories to find answers, but his thoughts were incredibly guarded. Not wanting to harm him by forcing her way in, she had only been able to catch glimpses of dreams and emotions. Whoever this man was, he had suffered something horrible enough to push him far past his Seyring limits.

The earthy smell of herbs wafted over her as Eira stepped inside the small medical cabin. Immediately inside the entrance stood Commander Holt, his eyes locked on the stranger. Until they learned more about the man, Holt had insisted that someone watch him at all times. A precaution that Eira agreed with wholeheartedly.

Nar flashed a smile at her from beside the soldier's bed where the man was holding his arms out to the side so Gleda could change the bandages. His face, as well as the rest of his body, was still covered in bruises.

"Ronan?" Seton cried, pushing past Eira. "What are you doing here?" The tavern keeper ran to the soldier's side.

"I could ask the same of you!" The man said weakly, his eyes wide in surprise.

"Me? I come here once a month. But you're…" Seton paused and looked more intently at the man. "You're supposed to be dead. Alvina, this is the man I told you about who…was condemned to death by shadowmongrel. Ronan Ashwood."

Ronan parted his mouth slightly as if to say something but closed it again, looking down at the floor as Gleda finished wrapping the bandage.

"Wren dear, would you go fetch me some more water?" Gleda asked.

The boy glanced from her to the soldier and then slowly left the cabin, looking back over his shoulder once more before closing the door.

As silence hung in the air, Eira carefully felt the edges of Ronan's mind to see if any memories or thoughts were accessible now that he was conscious. He winced slightly, so she pulled away.

"Ronan Ashwood." Gleda whispered.

The man looked at her, as did everyone else.

"Many of us in this camp knew your parents and sister," Gleda continued. "They were some of the bravest and kindest people that I've ever known."

Alvina took a few steps toward Ronan, but he gripped the edge of the bed tighter as if ready to push it away and bolt toward the door.

"Our fathers were close friends," Alvina said, offering a gentle smile. "Together they started our rebellion against Firekin."

Ignoring Alvina's statement, Ronan swallowed hard and then turned his attention toward Eira, not loosening his grip on the bed. "Einar told me you healed my mind. What does that mean?"

"You overexerted yourself," she said, crossing her arms. "The mind is like any other muscle. It can be damaged and overworked. All I did was speed up your recovery by soothing your mind so it could heal."

Suddenly a thought from the man reverberated in her mind. His emotions were so strong that he practically shouted it. *Did she see my thoughts?*

"Some of them," she said with a sigh. "But we didn't have many options. You might have died."

His emotions quieted down as he loosened his grip. "I'm grateful for your help." The control he had over his own emotions spoke volumes about his discipline. If they had time to stay, he might have proven to be a good ally, but it was time to move on.

"We're glad to see you feeling better, but what happened?" Seton asked, taking a seat beside Ronan on the bed.

The soldier looked down at the floor. "I don't really know what happened, but I didn't kill...I would never..." He stopped and closed his eyes.

"Just start at the beginning," Nar said, putting a hand on his shoulder.

"I was summoned by the king's advisor to serve on the queen's guard," Ronan began, staring intently at the wooden planks on the floor. "Everything was going well, until the day when the queen gave birth. And then..."

Eira caught glimpses of strong memories as his emotions magnified his thoughts. A Gurvel baby's bloodied corpse. A sword thrust through the queen's chest.

He shook his head to regain his composure and continued. "And then something went wrong. I had a piercing headache and my vision started to blur. I couldn't move." Now that he had started to speak the words seemed to come easier to him. "Then it was like watching something horrible through someone else's body, only I knew it was me...but I didn't want to do it."

Eira's chest tightened. She had seen glimpses of this event in his mind, but not enough to know what had truly happened.

Ronan gripped the edge of the bed tightly again. "I ran into the queen's room, slipped past the guards and...and I killed them," he whispered, keeping his eyes on the floor. "And because of me, my entire squad is dead too."

The headache, the blurred vision, the loss of control. It all confirmed what she had feared. "Impossible," Eira whispered.

Ronan tore his gaze away from the floor and looked up at her.

"What you described," Eira said, "are symptoms typically felt when an assassin team is trying to control your body. But I doubt it was actually an assassin duo. That secret was lost during the Shadow War. Einar and I are probably the only ones left who know how to do it."

"Then somehow Firekin has found a way to control someone's body without an assassin duo," Alvina said. "Eira, you and Einar were discovered in the cave despite hiding your thoughts. Firekin must have created a Stimulant that can break through mind barriers and control people."

If that were the case, and it sounded like she was right, then they would have to stay here longer. They didn't stand a fighting chance against those monsters until they had more Prime Stimulant. Heat rushed from her stomach to her face. Firekin had already razed her homeland and killed her people. Now they had stolen one of the most sacred Speki traditions and marred it with their putrid crimson hands.

"This makes more sense!" Seton said, drawing Eira out of her head. "Ronan wouldn't hurt anyone unless he had to."

Ronan looked up gratefully at the bartender but didn't smile. His eyes were heavy and downcast.

"It also means our theory about Firekin being behind the murder could be true," Alvina said, jotting down some notes on her sheet of paper.

"But why frame a human for the murders?" Eira asked. "With a Stimulant like that they could have forced the king to drink poison or jump off the top of the castle."

"Well, that much is obvious," Seton said, looking up at the ceiling as a firebug crawled around the rafters. When no one spoke up, he looked around at them in surprise. "Oh, come on! From what I've heard, Firekin would have humans as their slaves. If they want to take over the city, they'll need the majority of the population to hate humans and treat them like animals."

"Of course," Alvina said. "Now the whole city thinks a human is responsible for the death of the queen and prince."

Eira glanced over at Ronan who was running his hand through his hair, his breathing slightly faster now. She had healed his Seyring fatigue, but it would take a lot longer for the rest of his mind to heal.

"Well, Ronan," Alvina said, looking up at him with a smile, "we owe you our thanks. You've helped us uncover some vital information. You're welcome to stay here in the camp with us if you'd like."

"Thank you, but I couldn't..." he said, trailing off.

"We would be honored to have you," Gleda put in, putting her hand gently on his shoulder as her emotions swelled with sympathy and warmth.

Hesitantly, Ronan nodded his acceptance.

There had been other memories that surfaced as Eira had helped the soldier heal, but the only thing she gathered was that he had lost something precious in a terrible fire.

"Seton is heading back to the city today, so you can use his hut while he's gone," Alvina decided.

"That's my cue," the bartender said, slapping his knee as he stood to go. "I need to head out so I can make it back before dark."

"You come here often, then?" Ronan asked, standing as well.

"Of course! Where do you think I get the secret ingredient for my ale?" Seton winked. "Ronan, glad to see you again. Try to get some rest."

"I'll show you where you can sleep tonight," Einar said, ushering Ronan toward the door.

Once they left, Eira turned to Alvina. "This is good. We know what they're planning, but we won't have much time to act. We need to move quickly."

"I agree. Let's work on a plan."

Eira suppressed the desire to roll her eyes. Another plan. Every moment they spent brainstorming and strategizing left them one more step behind Firekin. As it turned out, working in a group required excess meetings and preparations. Things were more efficient when it was just her and Nar. By now, the cult had likely accumulated enough supporters to become practically unstoppable. Of course that wouldn't prevent her from carrying out her own plans. She owed it to her people, regardless of how powerful Firekin became.

CHAPTER 17

Reluctance

*But somehow, Ravenel found a way to survive. He barely escaped
with his life that day and claimed that something
inside of him had been awakened.*

Eira

THE MORNING AIR WAS CRISP as Eira walked through the camp. Scarletts were already busy at work, cleaning weapons, preparing food, or gathering supplies to make Inhibitors. A small child ran past her, giggling uncontrollably as a boy chased after her, brandishing a moss frog like some kind of weapon. To her right, the door to one of the raised cabins opened to reveal a woman carrying a woven basket filled with clothing.

One thing she appreciated about the humans was their work ethic. Many of them started their day before the sun rose and worked late into the evening. They were nothing if not diligent.

Eira avoided the main campfire pit where most of the Scarletts were finishing up their breakfast. Right now, she needed to find Nar and tell him about an idea she had. He wasn't going to like it, so she had waited until morning to tell him, but he had already left their cabin by the time she woke up, likely out training with the Forestdweller again.

Reaching the last of the cabins, Eira entered into the small area cleared for training. Like the rest of the camp, the ground was just dirt with patches of reddish grass and small stones scattered about. A handful of Scarletts practiced formations with one another, their wooden practice swords thudding as they collided.

Off to the side, Nar stood across from Wren, his hand outstretched toward a small rock that hovered in the air between them. The boy's tongue stuck out in concentration as he focused on pushing the rock toward Nar. Eira was impressed that they were able to run that drill already. It had only been about a week since Einar had started teaching him.

Sitting on a moss-covered rock, Ronan watched the two of them with intensity, his hand resting on one of the wooden practice swords. While improving, the blue and yellow bruises on his face and arms still looked fairly fresh.

As Eira approached, Einar glanced over at her and flashed a smile. "I was wondering when you'd decide to join the land of the living." He pushed the rock toward Wren more intently. The Forestdweller narrowed his eyes and forced the rock back between them where it shook in the air from the two forces pressing against it.

Ronan slid off the rock and approached her, shoulders pushed back in determination. This was the moment she had been dreading. Before the words had even formed in his mind, she knew what he was about to ask her.

"Eira," he said, nodding a greeting. "I wanted to thank you again for helping my mind to heal."

"You're welcome," she said curtly, catching Einar's eye as he glanced over at them, still pushing the rock back toward Wren.

"I know you're busy," he continued, keeping his gaze steady, "and I have nothing to offer you in return, but would you train me to be a Seyr?"

It wasn't that she didn't think he could learn. But she didn't have time for this right now. "No," she said, ignoring the look Einar shot her. "I'm impressed at what you've been able to do so far, but I can't teach you."

"I'm a quick learner," he persisted, taking a step closer.

Slightly shorter than he was, Eira had to tilt her head up slightly to meet his gaze. "I don't doubt it. You've likely been using your powers without knowing it your whole life, always having a slight edge over your peers."

"I'll do whatever you tell me to and practice as often as I can."

"I admire your determination," she said. "But I can't teach you. Firekin is already two steps ahead of us. I can't waste my time training someone who won't even live past a century."

Wood cracks from practice swords rang throughout the training area. Ronan furrowed his brow and opened his mouth to argue, thoughts forming in his mind as his emotions began to amplify them.

"That's enough for now, Wren," Einar said, setting the rock down between them. "Why don't you take a break?" Covered in sweat, the boy eagerly plopped down beside the large rock to catch his breath while Einar walked over to her. "Sister, mind if I have a word with you?"

With a shrug she reluctantly faced him.

"If that's alright with you, Ronan," Einar said, smiling kindly.

Ronan stood there for a moment as if deciding whether or not to continue the argument, but eventually nodded curtly and walked back over to the boulder, sitting on the ground beside Wren.

"You skipped breakfast, didn't you?" Einar asked, raising an eyebrow.

"What does that have to do with anything?"

"I can tell. Do you want to know how I can tell?"

"I don't. But you're obviously going to tell me anyway."

"You're more brash on the days you skip breakfast," he said, flashing his typical jovial smile.

"Nar, please," she fumed, holding the bridge of her nose with her hand. "I'm glad you found a fun hobby, but we need to stay focused on the mission. Firekin doesn't play games, and neither should we. They've always been two steps ahead of us. We can't let anything slow us down. Especially now that we know what Stimulant they've created. I'm starting to think we need to move on. After I figure out how to create more Prime Stimulant, we should leave. We're more efficient on our own."

"Listen to yourself," he said, shaking his head. "You're so focused on the mission that you're missing out on the most advantageous opportunity we've ever encountered." He nodded toward the rock where Wren was teaching Ronan some of the hand signs in his language.

"Advantageous opportunity?" she asked.

"Do you really think the two of us can stop an entire cult on our own?"

"Yes. That's how it's always been."

Einar squinted his eyes as if lost in thought. "If I recall, you mentioned something about Firekin being two steps ahead of us? Which, if I'm not mistaken, means we're fighting a losing battle."

"Nar, wasting time on training these two isn't going to give us any advantage."

"Yes, it will!" he said with a broad smile. "Think about it. Since working with the Scarletts, we've come closer to developing an actual plan than you and I have ever come before. And on top of that, we now have Wren and Ronan who could be assets even at novice levels.

"Take Ronan, for example," he continued, excitement lighting up his eyes. "He's had absolutely no training whatsoever and yet he was able to project illusions and send out a distress message, all while running for his life. Just think of what he could do with a Stimulant!"

His excitement was almost contagious. Almost. And while she hated to admit it, he had a point. They had been trying to figure out a way to infiltrate and destroy Firekin since the day their city had been demolished. With help, maybe they would stand a chance. And like he said, even a novice Seyr and Manipulator could be useful if they learned how to use a Stimulant efficiently.

"I suppose it wouldn't hurt to train him while we make plans," she said slowly.

"That's the spirit!"

"Ronan," Eira called, turning her head to look at the man, "my brother has convinced me that it would be beneficial for both of us if I teach you."

Not hesitating, he stood up and walked back over to them. "Thank you," he said, nodding his head. "I'll be diligent in learning."

"You'll need to accompany me around the camp so I can teach you in between meetings and preparations. I don't have time to go searching for you every time I have a spare moment."

"I understand," he said, his eyes sharp with determination.

"Good. Then we start now. While we walk through the camp, I want you to try and read my thoughts. Listen and speak aloud anything you think you hear."

Not waiting for him to ask any questions, she turned and headed back toward the main part of camp where the meeting cabin was. It might be beneficial to teach him, but she wouldn't waste any more time than she had to.

◇◇

LATER THAT NIGHT, EIRA sat by the campfire and watched as the Scarletts gathered to eat the evening meal. Stringed instruments played off to the side while children danced around in a circle holding hands. Nar walked over and handed her a bowl of rufescent hoppers—an interesting dish with cheese, frogs legs, and spices. It was nothing like the food she was accustomed to, but it was growing on her.

Over the centuries, she and Einar had avoided humans because they often regarded Speki as odd and quite frankly, she didn't think it worth the time to get to know them anyway. Their lives were so short, it wasn't even worthwhile to learn their names unless she worked beside them frequently. And yet, she had to admit that they were an innovative race. Somehow they had managed to survive here, in the Scarlet Forest, without the aid of Seyring or Manipulation. They might not be a powerful or long-living race, but they did have persistence and ingenuity. She had to give them that.

"How are your talks with Alvina going?" Nar asked in between bites.

"You would know if you came to the meetings more often."

"True, but then I wouldn't have as much time to train Wren. After you and Ronan left this morning, I gave him some Kelby root. He was able to lift a small boulder from across the training clearing."

Eira chewed her frog leg, yet again impressed by the Forestdweller's progression. He would be capable of a lot more if he used a full Stimulant. They had made a small amount with the toracini mushrooms she had grabbed by the corpse tree, but they needed to save that for Firekin.

"Amazing, isn't it?" Einar asked. "I think our people had the wrong idea about Forestdweller Manipulators. They learn at a faster rate compared to Speki. And I bet humans do too."

"It's possible," she admitted, looking across the campfire where Ronan sat on a log copying Wren's hand motions. Throughout the day he had proven himself to be a quick learner, just like he promised, even though it was hard for him to focus at times. His mind still had a lot of healing to do. "Your stubbornness may have paid off this time." She looked at Einar from the corner of her eye.

"That's what makes me a good assassin," he said with a wink.

She raised an eyebrow and finished off her frog leg, very much looking forward to crawling under the covers after a long day of teaching and attending meetings. As she got up to return her plate to the cook, it dawned on her that she had never told Einar her plan.

The way her meetings with Alvina were going, she suspected that sooner or later they would infiltrate Galynkhot. When they did, she intended to find the leader of Firekin, the Eternal Flame, and kill him herself. Alvina was resistant to the idea of targeting the Eternal Flame directly because she claimed it would be more beneficial to persuade King Chono to join their cause. But if the opportunity opened up to kill the Eternal Flame, Eira was going to take it.

It would lead to an argument when she told Einar, but he needed to know. He just didn't need to know right now. She would tell him in the morning.

CHAPTER 18

The Ocean

What was once impossible suddenly became a reality for Ravenel.

Ronan

RONAN JERKED UPRIGHT IN BED, drenched in a cold sweat. His heart pounded and he could still feel the weight of the sword in his hand as he plunged it through the small crimson newborn. He gasped for breath and looked down at his hand as if the weapon would still be there, covered in blood. But his hand was empty.

He held his pounding head and worked to calm his breathing, focusing on the moonlight that poured through the cracks around the door to the small hut. Trying to fall asleep again seemed pointless, so he got up, threw on the gray hooded shirt he had been given, and stepped outside into the chilly night air.

Torches lit up the outskirts of the camp, flickering against the red backdrop of the forest. Everything was quiet except for a few chirping moss frogs and the distant hoot of an owl. He started walking toward the main fire pit which had been extinguished for the night and noticed a few Scarletts standing watch near the camp's border. He recognized one of them from earlier that day. What had Einar said her name was? Edalene. The woman from one of the small towns outside Galynkhot. He nodded as he passed by and tried not to stare too long at her purple hair blowing in the late night breeze. Now that he was away from the city, he could probably dye his hair if he wanted to, but it still didn't feel right. Not after years of hearing derogatory slurs. It was fine if others like Edalene wanted to do it, but he would never be able to dye his hair like the Gurvel dyed their pets.

He sat on one of the logs and watched the firebugs light up the red leaves in a nearby tree. His breathing calmed down slightly, but he couldn't get the images out of his mind. Clasping his hands together to keep them from shaking, he stared off into the forest.

A set of footsteps approached from behind him, drawing him out of his thoughts. Eira walked over and sat beside him without a word, staring off into the forest with him.

When she didn't initiate a conversation, he relaxed and looked up at the sky, trying to comfort himself with constellations, but instead of relief he felt an overwhelming sense of numbness. He had experienced nightmares before, but Manton had always been there to help ground him. His friend had never said a word when Ronan used to wake up in terror, memories of the burning pyre fresh in his mind. He had just been there, sometimes sitting next to him on the bed until he had calmed down. Now he was completely alone.

"Couldn't sleep?" Eira asked after a few minutes, her white hair reflecting the flickering of the torchlight.

"Not as well as I'd like to. You?"

"I haven't slept well in centuries," she said, her eyes piercing the cold embers of the firepit.

For the first time, the weight of what she and Einar must have suffered settled on Ronan like a cold chunk of metal in his core. The image of a smoldering city passed through his mind along with a deep sense of dread. With confusion he held onto the image, examining this city that he had never seen before. Then just as quickly as the image had come, it vanished.

"Don't ever do that again," Eira said, gritting her teeth together.

Blinking in surprise, he tried to comprehend what he had even done. Had he just read her mind? He hadn't meant to.

Eira sighed softly and relaxed. "If someone's guard is down, their emotions and even memories are easier to read. Especially if it's at the forefront of their thoughts. But it usually takes years of practice to learn how to do it. Have you done that before?"

"No," he said.

Raising an eyebrow, she stared at him for a moment but then turned her head back toward the firepit.

"How do you go on?" he whispered. "After losing so much?"

Eira was silent for a few minutes. He honestly didn't expect her to respond. It was the question he had been asking himself all day, and so far he hadn't found an answer.

"I wouldn't have been able to go on if Einar hadn't been there for me."

Ronan nodded in understanding, but inwardly felt his stomach plummet. He had no one. In the blink of an eye, his entire world had been ripped away, and he hadn't been able to stop it from happening. Even though he knew the night air was chilly when he first left the hut, he could hardly feel it now. Instead he just felt...nothing, as if his senses were muffled to the world.

"Seeing as neither of us is going to get any sleep, let me show you something," Eira said, standing up.

Drawn out of his thoughts, Ronan looked up at her. There was still no hint of a smile on the woman's face, but something in her violet eyes had changed. With a small shrug, Ronan stood up and followed her down the main path past the majority of the wooden huts and cabins. With most of the Scarletts fast asleep, it was quiet and peaceful unlike during the bustle of the day. Other than a few guards like Edalene, the camp was empty.

They approached the wall of tall grass that separated them from the dangers of the Scarlet Forest, the tall red trees blowing ominously in the wind.

"Wait, we're not going into the forest, are we?" he asked, halting a few feet from the border.

Eira stopped and reached into her pocket, pulling out a small vial of clear liquid. "Einar showed me a place not too far from the camp that the Scarletts visit frequently. Take this." She handed him the vial. "It will protect you against mind attacks. But don't drink it unless you have to—we only have so many on hand."

"How will I know if I need to drink it?" he asked, taking the vial and gripping the cool glass in his hand.

"If you feel oddly curious about something and filled with a desire to touch it, drink this first to make sure it's not a corpse tree."

Not wanting to go back to the hut where he would be tormented by his thoughts again, he followed Eira. As he moved through the grass, a fog filled his mind, passing as soon as he exited through the other side. The faint scent of cinnamon brushed past his nose as the fog wore off.

"Cinnamon grass," Eira said. "I don't like it either, but it has the same effect on creatures with Seyring abilities, so it's not a bad idea to have."

"The others don't feel that when they pass through it, do they?"

"No. Only Seyrs or Manipulators would be affected," she explained, leading him deeper into the forest. Neither of them spoke, which was fine with him because after the past few days, he didn't have any energy left to keep a conversation going.

Everything they passed was a deep shade of burgundy, lit only by the light of the moon. While he was still numb, the exercise and fear of what might be lurking in the darkness distracted him from his thoughts.

After a while, the sounds of chirping moss frogs and rustling leaves were replaced by crashing waves. "An ocean?" he asked. The only ocean he had ever seen was the one by the docks.

"This one is different from the one by Galynkhot," Eira said. "It's filled with salt and has an...interesting look to it."

As they climbed a shallow hill, the dirt beneath their boots turned to soft sand and the sound of the waves grew louder. When he got to the top, the sight left Ronan speechless. Everything, from the scent of salt in the air to the moonlight reflecting off of the white sand, was breathtaking. The beach stretched off to the left for a good distance until it ran up against a rocky cliff face that towered over the ocean like a stone guardian. But what immediately caught his attention was the water. Wherever the waves moved and crashed against the sand, a soft blue glow burst across the surface.

"Mesmerizing, isn't it?" Eira whispered beside him. "Nar brought me here a few nights ago. He said he wanted to remind me that there was still beauty left in this world."

All Ronan could do was nod in agreement as he stared at the firelike glow of the water. Yearning to know what it felt like, he took a couple of steps forward. A small burst of heat flashed through his chest as he remembered the dangers that lived in the Scarlet Forest. Immediately he stopped walking and pulled the vial out of his pocket.

"Wait," Eira said, grabbing his arm. "You don't need the Inhibitor. The Scarletts come here often. It's real."

"I've never seen anything like it before," he responded, putting the Inhibitor back in his pocket as he followed Eira to the water's edge.

He slid off his boots, watching as Eira bent down and ran her fingers through the moist sand, leaving a trail of glowing light wherever she moved her hand. Wanting to touch it for himself, Ronan approached the tide as it slid toward him and took a few steps in, amazed by the tendrils of soft light that followed him.

"What is it?" he asked.

"Einar thought it might be some kind of small plant or animal that reacts to movement."

After a few minutes, they walked back onto the beach and sat down at the edge of the tide, cool wind whipping through their hair. Ronan looked up at the sky and the moon and stars. Earlier he had felt empty, but now he felt a small flicker in his heart again. "When I was little and had nightmares, my dad used to take me outside and teach me the constellations," he said. "The Phoenix Feather. Azrael's Dagger. Dolgoon's Cave." He gazed at each pattern in the sky, finding a small sense of comfort in their stability, as the water continued to lap just out of reach of his feet. "But my favorite one has always been Ravenel's Cap. My dad told me if I ever got lost in the forest I could just follow the bottom point and I'd find my way back to the city."

They sat in silence for a few moments, the wind blowing in with the tide. "It's my fault they were discovered," he whispered, looking down at the sand that clung to his wet feet. He wasn't sure if Eira even cared, but now that he had started, the words seemed to tumble out of him, as if a dam had broken and released the torrent of memory inside.

"I was eight," he said, not taking his eyes off of the sand. "I was on my way to school that day when I realized I'd left my jacket at home, so I went back to grab it. It was on my bed right where I'd left it. When I opened the door to leave, I saw a group of people slip inside our neighbor's house across the street."

The memory was burned into his mind like a scar that wouldn't heal. "Our teachers told us to report anything odd to them, like secret meetings or conversations that sounded like they were about the king. They told us it was our duty to the city and that it would help the future of humankind. So I told my teacher what I'd seen when I made it to class.

"Later that day, I was brought to the coliseum with a few other students. The militia had arrested everyone at my neighbor's meeting. Including my parents and sister."

Forcing a swallow, Ronan looked up at the distant horizon across the ocean. "I watched them burn. And then, because I was suddenly an orphan, I was taken to the militia."

He had never told anyone the full story of what happened before. Not even Manton or Kendra had known that he was responsible for his parents' deaths. A deeper sense of regret settled in his stomach like a cold rock as all of their faces came to mind, haunting his thoughts. It was his fault. All of their deaths were his fault.

"That must have been horrible," Eira said softly, her usual hard and cold tone more gentle now.

They sat in silence staring up at the stars for a while, water crashing against the sand and rushing up to meet their toes. Ronan took a deep breath of the cool ocean breeze, feeling oddly calmer than he had in a long time, as if the water had accepted his confession and was now carrying it away to some far off ocean. It would probably return again. It always did.

"If I ever had a nightmare, my mother would sing to me," Eira said quietly, her gaze fixated on the moon. "I would join her until I couldn't remember the dream anymore. But that was a long time ago." Straightening her shoulders, Eira got to her feet. "We should head back before the night guards think something happened to us."

They pulled on their boots and silently headed back to camp, the sound of the ocean fading behind them. As they walked, Ronan's mind wandered back to the city and the life that he had left behind forever. What would he do now? He had been a soldier his entire life, and now he was a Seyr, living in the Scarlet Forest with the same group of rebels his parents had been a part of. What they were doing was dangerous, but he needed to learn from Eira so that no one could ever take control of his body again. The thought of what it had felt like sent a shiver down his back and made his hands grow cold. No. He would learn to use his abilities this time, if only to prevent that from ever happening again.

Back at camp, they passed through the tall cinnamon grass and walked toward the main firepit. "Thank you," Ronan said as Eira turned to leave.

"Don't tell Nar. He'd never let me hear the end of it."

They said goodnight and each headed back to their cabin. After the trek to the beach, laying down in a cot felt good. With relief, Ronan closed his eyes and fell asleep almost immediately.

CHAPTER 19

Counter Plan

Not only could he read thoughts and cast illusions into minds,
but he could also perform skills that would normally require a Stimulant.

Ronan

STANDING BEFORE A TALL bookshelf in Gleda's hut, Ronan quickly skimmed the leather covers, searching for Ravenel's name. One of the books on the top shelf was faded enough that he couldn't quite make out the words, so he reached up to grab it, wincing as the movement irritated the bruises on his back and arms. With bated breath, he opened to the front page, but it turned out to be an old flora and fauna dictionary.

He placed it back on the shelf with less vigor and walked over to Gleda and Eira who were busy poring over a pile of herbs. "You don't have *The Legend of Ravenel*, do you?" he asked.

"That's a book I haven't seen in years, dear. I'm afraid we don't have a copy," Gleda said as she grabbed more ashbark to crush in a small mortar.

"Isn't that a children's book?" Eira asked, inspecting a bushel of red berries.

"It is. I just wanted to look through it again," he said, leaning up against the wall. "Have you found a replacement for the toracini mushrooms?"

Eira sighed and set the berries down. "No. I was able to make a small amount of Prime Stimulant with the few mushrooms that I had, but it won't be nearly enough. We might be able to make a weaker version with some of these herbs, but that won't do much good against Firekin. I was trying to avoid it, but we're going to need to gather more mushrooms by that corpse tree."

"That shouldn't be too hard if we use Inhibitors."

"I didn't want to waste it on the tree," she said. "We have a limited stock of them that we'll need to use as protection against Firekin, but at this point I think it will be worth the trouble if it means more Stimulants."

The door to the hut swung open as Alvina entered with a roll of papers tucked under her arm. She smiled brightly at them despite the dark circles showing under her eyes and set the papers down on the small dining table in the corner. "Ronan. How are you feeling?"

He shrugged, still mostly numb. "What's all of the paper for?"

"Maps of Galynkhot," she said, unrolling one of them. "Would you mind taking a look at them? Seton helped us with landmarks, but you might have more knowledge about defenses."

He walked over to the table to take a look while Eira helped Gleda hang up some of the herbs to dry from the rafters.

"Seton said these were the two areas he was least familiar with." Alvina pointed to the castle and militia grounds at the back of the city.

"I can fill in some missing areas," he said, glancing over the map. "Civilians aren't allowed in the barracks, and as far as I know, I was the first human to enter the castle grounds in centuries." He pointed to one of the blank areas on the map. "There's a door here between the castle grounds and barracks. It's used to transport prisoners sometimes. I've heard there's a door within the castle that leads to the prisons as well, but I haven't seen it."

Alvina grabbed a quill pen and scratched a few marks onto the map. As she did, Ronan felt a tug on his mind, like a small poke to the head. Looking up, Eira's violet eyes met his gaze. She nodded with satisfaction and went back to hanging berries from the rafters as if nothing had happened. So he would be tested throughout the day then. Good. He needed to be ready. Picking up even the practice sword the other day had made his stomach churn, so he was hoping to hone his mental powers as a weapon instead.

"So we have a more accurate map now," Eira said. "But what do we do about the cult?"

"Somehow we need to convince the king to outlaw Firekin," Alvina replied.

Eira walked over to the table. "We don't have time to convince the king. Firekin was confident enough to have the queen and heir murdered. We need to act fast."

"I agree," Alvina said. "But we can't attack them head on. We're vastly outnumbered and don't have the resources to fight Manipulators *and* the king's shadowmongrels."

"Einar and I could pick them off one by one," Eira said. "But not without more intel."

"Could you and your brother take over an entire city by yourselves?" Gleda asked, wiping out her mortar with a damp cloth.

"No," Eira admitted with a sigh.

What they were doing was impossible. Eira was right, the king would never listen to them. And attacking the city was just as dangerous as trying to assassinate key leaders. They needed to learn more about Firekin's plans first.

"What if you capture one of the leaders?" Ronan asked, an idea coming to mind. "You could remove some of the influence controlling the king and try to interrogate them for more information."

"Who would you suggest?" Alvina asked, leaning forward across the table.

"I'm not really suggesting anything," he said, looking from Alvina to Eira. "You're better off staying here, hidden from Firekin, but if you're deadset on continuing this suicide mission, you should target Khartsaga, the king's advisor. King Chono trusts him and would never listen to a reasonable argument as long as he's close by."

"That might work," Alvina said slowly. "If we separate the king from the influence of Firekin, he might be persuaded to listen."

"That, and you might be able to use Khartsaga as a bargaining chip," Ronan added. "You could offer to return him to the king once he's listened to you."

Eira folded her arms in front of her and walked over to the window. "Firekin will replace Khartsaga. They can't afford to lose their foothold in the city."

"Not if we move fast enough," Alvina said, jotting down some thoughts on a scrap piece of parchment. "We could capture Khartsaga and speak to the king on the same night. They wouldn't have time to replace him."

Capturing the king's advisor wouldn't be an easy task. Not only was he a Manipulator himself, but he was never alone. Ronan pursed his lips as he thought through the gravity of what they were planning.

"We have to try it," Eira said, staring at the wall of ashbark trees. "Firekin is moving too fast to sit here in endless meetings."

Assuming the cult wasn't already too powerful. Maybe there was still a chance, but trying something like this would put them all at risk. Did it matter if Firekin took over the city? Why couldn't they just hide, here in the forest, safe from the cult's violence? Eira shot him a glare from across the table, shaking him out of his thoughts.

"Let's find Holt and Einar and come up with a plan," Alvina said. "If we're going to do this, I want to make sure we've thought through everything."

"Ronan, stay here," Eira ordered, moving toward the door. "I'll find Holt and Einar. See if you can feel our minds before you hear us approach." Before he could respond, Eira was out the door, leaving him in the cabin with Alvina and Gleda.

"She doesn't waste much time, does she?" Alvina gave a tired half smile.

"No, she does not," Ronan said. Closing his eyes, he tried to clear his mind so he could focus, but the new plan they had come up with continued to cling to his thoughts. They were safe here. Why would they risk the wrath of Firekin? He took a deep breath and tried to feel the minds around him. Once he had found Alvina and Gleda, he tried to extend his reach outside the cabin.

For a few years after his family was killed, he had dreamed of fighting back like Eira, but that had been beaten out of him eventually. Instead it had made more sense to improve his skills silently, perfecting his swordsmanship in case he needed to use it someday. But even that plan had backfired. Despite all his efforts to blend in, he had still gotten his squad killed.

A scream shot through the camp. Ronan leapt up and flung open the door as two Scarletts in gray tunics dragged a body behind them through the main path. The corpse was almost unrecognizable. Deep gash marks traveled down the length of the torso, innards spilling out across the stomach. But the face was what really sent a shiver down his spine. It was frozen in a silent scream of terror.

What could have caused something like that? Silence fell around the camp except for a few muffled voices as all activity stopped. He couldn't make out the whispers, but one word kept surfacing. *Shadowmongrel.* A shiver passed through his spine, churning his stomach. But it couldn't have been a shadowmongrel. The only two in existence were up at the castle in Galynkhot. Had Firekin found the camp and sent a shadowmongrel?

The Scarletts dragged the body over to a small patch of land near the training ground where a temporary cemetery had been set up.

"That's the second one this week," Holt muttered from nearby.

Ronan turned. The man was standing beside the cabin, grimly watching the procession pass by. Beside him, Wren hugged the side of his leg, eyes wide as he watched the Scarletts dig a grave.

"Second what?" Ronan asked.

"Death. We have precautions set up, but that doesn't protect us from everything. Something's out there. A corpse tree won't leave a man cut up like that. And phoenixes burn their prey."

Maybe it wasn't a shadowmongrel then. Not if they had had deaths like this before. If the king had sent a beast after them, it would have continued to kill. But even so, something that could leave a man in such pain and terror like that wasn't a creature he wanted to run into. More determined, Ronan went back inside Gleda's hut and sat down at the table to concentrate on feeling the minds of others nearby. They might be safe from Firekin for now, but this was still the Scarlet Forest. He wouldn't be safe until he learned how to use his powers.

CHAPTER 20

Preparation

But there wasn't time to explore these new powers.

Eira

EIRA STOOD BELOW A LARGE ashbark tree just outside the camp in the early morning light. Beside her, Ronan looked up at the highest branches, observing a few of the Scarletts as they carefully worked on unwrapping a section of ropesnare. The vines typically grew from the ground and wrapped themselves around the trunk until they were long enough to hang from the upper branches. This tree had mature vines that would be perfect for holding Khartsaga. Their plan was to capture him during the city's Fire Festival and keep him under heavy drugs while she and Alvina spoke to the king. The ropesnare was just an extra precaution.

"Ready?" A woman with thick curly hair called from the top branches. She had managed to unwrap the vine and needed to drop it.

"Go ahead!" Two men called from below, prepared to catch the bundle. The men quickly coiled the vine into a more manageable loop and helped the woman climb out of the tree. Eira turned to Ronan beside her. "Have you seen ropesnare before?"

"Not really. The city prisons are made out of Sklera, so they don't need it, but they do coat their chains in ropesnare milk if they need to arrest a Manipulator."

She nodded in affirmation and inspected the ropesnare coil, testing the thickness of the cords. Satisfied, they all made their way back to camp, keeping a careful watch on their surroundings. Rumors of a shadowmongrel lurking in the forest had spread like phoenix fire, putting everyone on edge even though they knew it was impossible. Eira subconsciously felt the Inhibitor in her pocket. She would take it if necessary, but would rather avoid it if possible.

At the edge of the camp, they passed through the cinnamon grass. Even though it was temporary, the heavy fog that settled in her mind still made her skin crawl. She shrugged the sensation off once they were on the other side. "We need to find my brother so we can test our plan."

Nar was likely with Wren in the training clearing again, so they walked past the main campfire where a handful of children were jumping over the logs like moss frogs. The Scarletts went to a nearby tree to start prepping the ropesnare while Eira and Ronan continued toward the training area.

Sure enough, when they made it to the clearing, Nar was observing Wren juggling three large rocks in the air. The boy had his tongue stuck out in concentration and was covered in sweat from the exertion, but he was successfully keeping the rocks rotating. Though she tried to hide it, she was truly impressed.

"Nar! We need you to test the ropesnare!" Eria called from the edge of the clearing.

Einar looked up and beckoned them to come over. She sighed and approached, antsy to test out their plan.

"See the progress he's made?" Einar asked, smiling at Wren who grinned back and dropped the rocks to the ground.

"Yes. Quite unexpected," she said. "Now, brother, if you would be so kind, we need you to test the ropesnare."

"I hoped you'd forgotten." He gave a long sigh. "But first, how's your training coming along, Ronan?"

"It's going well," Ronan answered, glancing at Eira.

"You haven't told him how fast he's progressing, have you?" Einar's voice filled her head as he raised an eyebrow toward her.

"Yes, it's going well," she said. "Now, please, Nar. We're trying to capture the king's advisor. We don't have time for games."

Einar sighed again, this time with more gusto, and started walking toward the main tree where Holt waited beside the coil of ropesnare. "Come on, I know you're dying to watch me sit beside a tree while heavily sedated. Gleda said the Inhibitor she's been working on should last three or four hours. Honestly, I hope she's wrong."

Eira held back a smile and followed Einar back through the camp. Wren picked up the rocks they had been using and scampered behind her and Ronan to catch up.

"That was impressive," Ronan said, motioning with his hands as he spoke. "It looked like it took a lot of concentration."

Wren grinned and nodded tiredly, his tail swishing proudly behind him as they walked.

"It takes a lot of strength and stamina to do that," Einar said, turning around to face them while continuing to walk backward toward the tree. "Seyring requires the same kind of strength. It's like muscles. The stronger you are and the more stamina you have, the more you can do."

"And Stimulants increase that," Ronan ventured.

"Stimulants enhance the abilities you already have, but it comes with a price. The stronger the Stimulant, the stronger the fatigue you'll feel afterward. When you take something to enhance your powers, you're pushing your brain past its normal capacity."

"If you push yourself too far, you'll get a migraine, or worse," Eira added. "Like when you fell unconscious in the forest. Your mind had been pushed too far."

As they approached the base of the tree, Holt started uncoiling the ropesnare. Alvina walked around the trunk, inspecting the area for debris that could be used to escape.

Wren gestured with his hands to Einar who bent down to be on eye level with him.

"Good question, Wren."

"What did he say?" Ronan asked, kneeling beside them. Eira listened to the conversation but watched Holt to make sure he was making the proper knots.

"He asked why Manipulators can't control ropesnare once it's been uprooted," Einar said. "It's no longer living, so you'd think a Manipulator would be able to control it. It has to do with the milk inside the vine. That's why ropesnare milk is used to coat other items like chains or swords to stop Manipulators from controlling them."

Eira looked at her brother, crouched down beside Wren. Ropesnare milk was quite useful, but the effects wore off with time. Usually, anything coated with ropesnare milk required fresh application every so often. It worked, but you had to be diligent about the upkeep.

"We're ready if you are," Alvina said from the tree.

"Let's get this over with." Einar heaved another sigh as he straightened up and walked to the trunk.

"Keep sighing like that and the whole camp will hear you," Eira said.

"Let them hear me," he retorted, sitting back against the trunk. "Then they'll know of my sacrifice."

Holt tied Einar to the tree, careful to inspect the knots as he went. Once he was finished, Nar struggled against the binds. "Yep, that'll do," he grunted.

"We can't thank you enough for this, Einar," Alvina said, pulling out a syringe.

He smiled and sighed again, pointedly looking at Eira as he did so. "Alright, give it to me."

A knot formed in the pit of Eira's stomach as she watched the dazed look overcome her brother's violet eyes when Alvina injected him. She didn't like it, but they needed to know how well the Inhibitor worked.

"How do you feel?" Alvina asked.

"Like I've been drugged," he replied, wincing as he spoke.

"Try to escape," Eira said.

"Believe it or not, dear sister, but I'm trying to." Einar squirmed beneath the ropesnare, but it didn't give way. He leaned his head against the tree. "I commend Holt's rope-tying skills. And Gleda's Inhibitor."

"So far so good," Alvina observed.

Eira nodded and took a seat on the red grass to keep her brother company. Beside her, Ronan and Wren sat down as well. The boy looked at Einar with wide eyes, the tip of his tail flicking against the ground.

"Don't worry, I'm fine, just a little tired." Einar smiled.

"Now, we wait. While you practice," Eira said, looking at Ronan.

He turned toward her, listening intently. So far, he seemed to understand everything she had taught him and managed to make progress, despite how busy they had been.

"You need to learn how to hide your mind from other Seyrs. This is the most important thing you will learn. It takes concentration and control." She felt the edge of Ronan's mind, easily able to hear thoughts as they passed through his head. "Close your eyes."

Taking a deep breath, he closed his eyes and waited.

"Now imagine yourself somewhere that gives you peace. It needs to be a place with meaning specific to you. Somewhere that you can picture with absolute clarity."

As he concentrated, she caught glimpses of locations flashing through his mind. One kept coming to the front of his thoughts and eventually he held the image there. It was the ocean near the camp.

"Good," she said. "This image will serve as your starting point. It represents your mind. Whenever we practice you must imagine this location clearly and center your thoughts around it. Do you understand?"

Ronan nodded, keeping his eyes closed.

"Now hold that image in your head until I tell you to stop."

From the tree, Nar raised an eyebrow and smiled tiredly. They both hated this exercise as children. Manipulators could learn this technique as well, but Seyrs usually picked it up faster. Eira rolled her eyes and smiled back at him.

To her surprise, Wren was copying Ronan, sitting with his eyes closed and face screwed up in concentration. It wouldn't be bad for him to learn this as well.

A different image crossed Ronan's mind and the ocean vanished. She elbowed him, drawing him out of his thoughts. He looked at her and opened his mouth, ready to object.

"Start again, you grew distracted," she said, cutting him off.

Frowning, he closed his eyes again and willed the image of the ocean to come back. His mind and soul were still healing, making it difficult for him to focus at times. To his credit, he hadn't given up yet. She wouldn't push him too hard, of course. That would only harm him.

They sat in silence as the camp cook started the fire, preparing for the next meal. After a few minutes, Ronan was distracted by another passing thought so she pushed him over. Scrambling back up, he opened his eyes and glared at her.

"Again," she said.

They went through this process for the next few hours. Sweat dripped down the sides of Ronan's face as the concentration drained his strength. She was impressed by his determination. Even after hours of being shoved over, he hadn't complained once.

Finally, Nar's Inhibitor began to wear off. Holt loosened the ropesnare and helped him up so he could stretch. Wren scrambled up and gestured something to Nar.

"Still a little foggy, but I can think again," he answered, rubbing his head.

"That's enough for now," Eira said, tapping Ronan's boot with her foot.

He opened his eyes and wiped his brow with his sleeve. They would need to practice a lot more before he would be able to hide his mind completely. Picturing that ocean was only the beginning. But all in all, she had to admit, she was pleasantly surprised. Never before would she have imagined coaching a human through this vigorous exercise.

LATER THAT NIGHT, THE WHOLE camp gathered for the evening meal as was their custom. Children ran around chasing after firebugs as soon as they cleared their plates, giggling gleefully as the insects evaded their grasp. Eira sat next to Einar around the fire finishing off the last bite of stew. When most of the adults had finished, the bowls were packed away and the musicians took out their drums and flutes, preparing to play. Nar lifted his head, his eyes lighting up as they began to tune their instruments.

Eira braced herself for the usual barrage of strong beats and rhythmic tempo. With any luck, she might be able to slip away after the first song. But she was surprised. Tonight the musicians played a different tune.

The fast beat and minor scale was warm and familiar. She glanced curiously at her brother who smiled and stood up with an outstretched hand, inviting her to join him.

"How do they know this song?" she asked. The last time she had heard it played was during the Celebration of Scholarship in Mikiltoft, but that was centuries ago, before the Gurvel had attacked.

Nar smiled mischievously, the firelight glinting in his violet eyes. "I taught it to Edalene and Ferren. Shall we show them how to dance?"

Everyone watched them with baited breath. They had never heard Speki music before. Of course they would be curious. Suddenly, the stew didn't seem to sit well in her stomach.

Einar pulled her to her feet and brought her closer to the fire. "Don't worry about them, just let your feet do the talking."

The musicians circled back to the beginning of the beat as she and Einar stood across from each other. Something tugged at her heart in anticipation as the rhythm filled her soul. This was the song that her mother used to sing to her every night. As a child, Eira loved singing with her mother. She hadn't found it within herself to lift up her voice since witnessing the desolation of the Shadow War. Every time she tried, the horrible image of her parents' terror-stricken faces filled her mind. She shook the memory away and looked around the campfire at the Scarletts. Even Holt, sitting beside Wren on a log, had a sense of curiosity playing at the forefront of his mind.

Einar lifted his arms and clapped in rhythm with the drums as the music swelled. She matched his movements as they swung around each other and swapped places. Despite how many centuries had passed since she had last danced, her feet and hands had no trouble remembering how to move. It was as if the song was a part of her that had been asleep. Her energy and confidence grew with each step.

Across from each other again, she and Einar followed the pattern they had learned as children. Memories flooded her brain from long ago. The music grew faster and faster, building in complexity as they danced in the firelight. The mixture of warmth from the flame and chill air from the wind was energizing as they continued to swirl and clap in unison. With a final spin they landed back where they had started and the music came to a stop.

The Scarletts stood and cheered as warmth flushed her face. Surprisingly, that felt...good. Einar smiled at her and then turned to thank the musicians.

To dance again to her people's music was invigorating. Memories of Speki festivals and traditions swirled around her mind in fresh waves. Then suddenly, everything turned sour.

These shadows of the past fueled a growing hunger inside her. This music. This culture. It should still exist, but all that was left was a ruined city filled with bones and ash. She and Nar had walked the streets in shock, trying to make sense of the puddles of blood and tattered corpses frozen in fear. They had managed to find their parents' mangled bodies and buried them. Otherwise they left the city as they had found it. Utterly demolished. She didn't just want to resist or fight against Firekin. She wanted them to *pay* for what they had done. To feel the same agony that she was cursed with.

Eira followed her brother back to their log and sat beside him, her thoughts distant. Their plan to capture Khartsaga might work, but convincing the king to forsake Firekin was a fanciful daydream. She wanted more. She still hadn't told Einar about her plan, but watching him now, laughing with one of the musicians who had come over to talk, she couldn't bring it up just yet. It would ruin the night that he had worked so hard to set up. She would try talking to him in the morning.

CHAPTER 21
Fire Festival

As the rumors of attacks in the night increased, Ravenel became more aware
of the danger that lurked at the edge of civilization.

Khartsaga

TONIGHT WAS A SPECIAL occasion, so Khartsaga wore a black uniform lined in gold with a large embroidered flame on the chest, similar to the robe that the king wore. All eyes were on the coliseum pit where Abaka stood laughing over a cowering human.

Once The Games finished, the king would give his speech to initiate the start of the Fire Festival, but Khartsaga didn't feel like celebrating. What was wrong with him? They were almost ready to start the next phase of the plan. The New Age was finally upon them, and yet his stomach felt like it was filled with lead.

Tarkhan placed a hand on his shoulder, reminding him to focus on the fight. The crowd cheered as the human grabbed his sword and shakily stumbled to his feet. Tonight, King Chono was engrossed in Abaka's technique, leaning forward on his throne in anticipation. But was it really a glorious fight? This human wasn't even a prisoner. He was a farmer, fighting to earn his family extra food portions.

Abaka shot a burst of fire that hit the man squarely in the chest. These fights were always one-sided. Didn't that make it more of a slaughter than a competition? The farmer fell to the ground and screamed as the flames burned through his clothes.

Without pause, the next and final human was dragged into the center of the arena where she was left shivering before the towering Champion. Abaka raised his arms above his head, the scar along his arm glimmering with sweat, as he drank in the enthusiasm of the audience.

As usual, there were human soldiers posted around the prisoner's entrance.

Normally Khartsaga didn't pay any attention to them. They were merely there to keep the fighters from escaping. Tonight, however, he was reminded of Ronan, the man that had escaped from right under his nose.

Ever since the queen died, he had been caught in a cycle of restless sleep, reliving the same horrific dream every night. The child. The cliff. And his own mother's tortured eyes looking up at him. No matter how many times he convinced himself that it wasn't his hand that had slayed the prince, the ache in his stomach remained. The only thing that brought him comfort was knowing that Ronan had somehow managed to escape. But why should that give him comfort? He had been nothing more than a tool to bring about the New Age. What did it matter if he lived or died?

But the man wouldn't have suffered merely death. He would have been tormented by that shadowmongrel. Tortured by fear, when the assassination hadn't even been his fault. But if Ronan was innocent, then what did that make Khartsaga?

A sharp pain stabbed the front of his skull.

"Anything I can bring you, sir?" Tarkhan asked, grabbing his shoulder.

Khartsaga gripped the edge of his chair. His mind had slipped from the truth again. "No, thank you."

Tarkhan nodded and took his place at the back of the viewing platform.

In the arena, Abaka knocked the woman to the ground. Focusing again on the fight, Khartsaga forced himself to admire the Champion's form as he drank a fresh Fire Stimulant and expertly ended the prisoner's life with a burst of flame to the head.

As the crowd cheered, the king stood and walked toward the edge of the platform for his speech. Still grieving the loss of his wife and son, the king was doing an admirable job showing his strength before the people.

"Tonight we commemorate the discovery of the Fire Stimulant and our partnership with Firekin! With their help, we conquered our enemies 200 years ago and ensured a brighter future for Galynkhot. The queen's death has been hard on us all." His voice cracked as he paused for a moment. "But in her honor, we will celebrate the glory we have attained in anticipation of the New Age to come. So tonight, enjoy all the festivities!"

The king lifted his hand, signaling a band on the arena floor to start playing. The song was a traditional Fire Festival cadence with strong drum beats and dissonant vocals. The audience flung confetti into the air, making it rain orange and gold as the king sat down and turned toward Khartsaga.

It had only been a week since the incident but already there were strands of gray flecking the king's hair line. And yet he still carried himself in a regal and earnest manner. "I can't thank you and Firekin enough. Your presence has been a great comfort to me this week."

"Of course, my King. It's been an honor to serve with you," Khartsaga replied, bowing his head in respect while inwardly cringing. The king trusted him. Was there truly no way to bring the New Age without removing King Chono?

"Feel free to enjoy the festivities," the king said. "You deserve it. I'll be here to represent the Fire Purifications if you want to walk around. The people would enjoy seeing you."

"Thank you, my King," he said, standing as he motioned for Tarkhan to follow. Usually he would jump at the chance to watch Fire Purifications, but suddenly the idea wasn't as appealing.

A sharp stab in his skull pulled his thoughts back toward the truth. Fire Purifications were a glorious tradition. A symbol of Gurvel superiority.

He and Tarkhan left the coliseum where they were met with more music and dancing in the streets. Colorful gold and orange streamers decorated every shop, and torches of fire burned brightly at every corner. Beside the fire fountain a group of Gurvel Manipulators performed for a gathering crowd. Beside them a crate full of Fire Stimulants lay ready for their use. He didn't envy them the headache they would feel in the morning from using so many Stimulants.

Civilians bowed their heads in respect as he passed. He didn't deserve any of it. His father was the one who deserved their honor. He directed Tarkhan around a few stalls, nodding as guards saluted him with fists to their foreheads.

The nostalgic scent of spicy fire cakes and scarlet whiskey pervaded the air, but he still had no desire to celebrate. What was wrong with him? He should be filled with joy, and yet the only sensation he could coax out of himself was a cold ache in his core.

Something caught his attention in a side alley. Behind a stack of crates, a small human child peered at him, eyes wide in fright. When he made eye contact with her, she yelped and scampered away, her limbs thin and covered in dirt. Where were her parents? Had they fought in The Games tonight?

Suddenly, he felt closed in and desperately wanted to get away from the crowd. He started walking up the street toward the castle, Tarkhan following quickly behind him.

"Sir, where are we going?"

"We're just taking a walk, Tarkhan." They passed by a few more stalls with dwindling crowds, most of them run by human merchants. There was no laughter here and the sound of music grew more faint. And why should they celebrate when their families and neighbors were forced to fight in The Games for food?

Tarkhan caught up to him, the ridges on his face bent in concern. "I must insist that we stay with the main crowds. We don't have your guards with us and—"

"Your concern is appreciated, but I want to take a walk," Khartsaga interrupted, heat rising to his face.

The assistant reached out and grabbed his arm as they passed the last festival stall, "Sir, I must insist—"

"Just give me five minutes," Khartsaga snapped, pulling his arm away. The outburst was unbecoming, but his chest was tight and it was getting harder to breathe. Something was wrong. He just needed some room to catch his breath, and then he would return to the festivities.

Tarkhan followed without another word as they continued up the path toward the castle. All the shops on this street were closed for the festival, so no one else was walking this way. There were still streamers and torches, but for the most part it was quiet except for the distant sound of drums. Finally he could hear himself think. A small prickle stabbed the front of his skull, but he ignored it this time. His father would surely hear about it, but he needed to gather his thoughts. However, the cleansing would be especially painful for refusing to let Tarkhan into his head. Wavering in his determination, Khartsaga stopped and started to ask for forgiveness when a small object like a rock fell to the ground beside him.

"Look out!" Tarkhan cried, trying to pull him away.

It was too late. Gas leaked from the device, enveloping them in seconds, just like when the rebels infiltrated their research base. He held his breath and looked up in time to see four shadowed figures fall from nearby buildings. They would dare attack the king's advisor?

Dropping into a crouch, he readied himself for a fight. There were loose cobblestones around him that he could shoot even without the aid of a Stimulant, but he didn't think it would come to that. These were humans. He should be able to fight them in hand-to-hand combat without any trouble.

A man with graying hair rushed at him with a dagger, but when Khartsaga tried to grab the weapon with Manipulation, he wasn't able to sense it. So they came prepared. Most of their equipment would be coated in ropesnare milk as well then. Time to change tactics. He stepped to the side and grabbed the man's arm, swinging him into the side of the building.

Beside him, Tarkhan was tackled to the ground. He struggled with the assailant, knocking off her hood. It was the woman with the long braid from the cave. Why was she here in the city? There weren't any test subjects here. What did these humans want?

Khartsaga took a step back, intending to leave the cloud of gas as he reached for the Base Stimulant in his pocket. But he stopped himself. He wasn't that desperate. Not to fight humans. They may have caught him by surprise, but there was no way they would actually be able to kill him.

One of the figures lunged toward him, dagger flashing in the torchlight. He stepped to the side, flinging a handful of loose pebbles in the assailant's direction, but to his surprise, the attacker vanished into the fog, as if evaporating into smoke. How was that possible?

He took another step toward the edge of the gas, but was stopped by an odd sensation. His mind became muddled and his movements slowed down until he was frozen in place. It was as if he had lost control of his body. As if... no. That would be impossible. Who would be controlling him? No one but his father and a handful of Firekin members had access to the Verdant Stimulant.

Against his will he fell to the ground and took in a large breath of gas. Fatigue filled his mind and bones. He gained control of his body again, but it was too late. The effects of the Inhibitor left him with a splitting headache that pounded against his skull.

The four figures approached him from all sides. He was just aware enough to notice Tarkhan breathing weakly on the ground nearby. Barely able to think straight, he tried to struggle as they shoved a bag over his head and bound his arms behind his back, but he didn't have enough strength left for it to do any good.

"We'll meet you two back at the camp," a gruff voice said beside him.

"And please, try not to get yourselves killed," another voice said.

One of them pulled Khartsaga up and shoved him forward. He was too disoriented to figure out which direction they were taking him. This shouldn't be possible. They were human. Weak and insignificant. This must be his fault. Somehow his own weaknesses were the reason these creatures had been able to defeat him. Any attempt to think left his head throbbing and his stomach churning, so he shuffled along where his captors led. He would find a way to escape, and when he did, he would bring back any information he could gather about these rebels. That might be the only way to redeem himself.

CHAPTER 22

Audience with the King

*If left unchecked, the beasts would destroy every human, Speki,
and Gurvel town from the Ashcapped Mountains in the north
to the Turbulent Sea in the south.*

Eira

EIRA PULLED HER HOOD down to keep her white hair covered as she and
Alvina scrutinized the looming wall. Once the festivities had died down, the
king had finally returned to the castle. Now all she and Alvina had to do was talk
to him while he was alone and convince him to see reason.

It would never work. Even before Firekin's influence, King Chono had
been her people's adversary. He was infamous for the ruthless slaughter of a
shipwrecked Speki crew that had landed near Galynkhot. He had claimed that
it had been a misunderstanding, but the order of Knowledge Keepers knew
better. King Chono couldn't be trusted. However, at the end of the night, it
wouldn't matter if Alvina's plan failed because Eira had a better one.

Alvina slipped on a pair of gloves with thin metal plates attached to the
fingertips. Like their outfits, they were dark and mimicked the texture of Sklera.
She handed a pair to Eira and started climbing the wall with boots that had
razor blades on the tips. By design, her cloak flared out behind her, blending
into the wall like an outcrop of Sklera.

Following suit, Eira dug her gloves into the wall and pulled herself up.
It had taken some convincing, but she had reluctantly accepted a cloak like
Alvina's. Besides the camouflage benefits, it had been coated in a fire retardant
which might be useful if they were discovered. Otherwise she never would
have parted with her own cloak that had gotten her through countless missions
before.

At the top of the wall a guard passed by. She and Alvina froze, keeping
their faces close to the warm rock until his footsteps grew faint. With caution,
Eira felt for any other minds nearby. Other than Alvina and a few chroma snails,

they appeared to be alone, so she signaled that the coast was clear and slid onto the walkway.

There wasn't any cover here, so they quickly crossed and descended down the other side where they hid behind some shrubs. Ronan had suggested they scale the wall near the king's garden in case they needed to hide. Not bad advice considering the ground they still needed to cover. Alvina tapped her on the shoulder and pointed to the side of the castle where a side door was left with only one guard.

"Let's go," Eira messaged with her mind.

Alvina jumped, but nodded in understanding. They made their way through the garden as far as they could and hid beside the trunk of a wide and gnarled tree. Alvina took out a small dart shooter and aimed at the guard. They must not expect intruders to make it this far or else they would have heavier security. Then again, why should they expect this kind of assault? They were prepared for Seyrs and Manipulators, not humans.

With a soft whisper the projectile hit the guard's leg. Before he could pull it out, the Gurvel collapsed, slumping against the wall. They quietly dragged his body behind a large bush, removed the dart, and slipped inside the castle.

A dim, narrow hallway opened up before them. Probably the servant's entrance. Eira closed the door behind them and followed Alvina, keeping to the shadows. Soon they reached the main entrance where a crackling fire illuminated a large glass mural. The flickering light made the monster in the scene appear to lunge toward them. She clenched her jaw and tore her eyes away from the image so she could concentrate on nearby minds.

Someone was coming down the stairs. She pulled Alvina back into the hallway as a guard came into view. They held their breath until he was gone. Heart hammering inside her, Eira led Alvina toward the stairs, still listening for nearby thoughts. This was the closest she had ever come to actually finding the Eternal Flame. He was sure to be here in the castle. Especially if Firekin was narrowing in on the throne. But if they were caught...

She held back a shudder and rounded the corner to climb the next flight of stairs. Best not to think about that.

At the second floor landing, they peered over the last step and looked for guards, but it was empty. This was where Ronan had guarded the queen's chambers. Apparently it was some kind of Gurvel custom for the husband to sleep apart from the wife when she was pregnant. Theoretically the king's chambers would be on the same hallway; otherwise they would have to search the castle.

She couldn't sense anyone within the rooms because of the Sklera, but that meant they wouldn't be able to sense her either. Not unless they took an extremely powerful Stimulant.

They crept onto the empty floor without any trouble, but something didn't feel quite right. It had been too easy to sneak in. They had seen a few guards who probably didn't expect human intruders, but even so, she had expected more security. The Fire Festival was supposedly the biggest celebration of the year, so it was possible most of the guards were out celebrating, but the lack of resistance still left her on edge.

A large stained glass window sat at the end of the hallway next to the king's chambers. Careful not to make any noise, they snuck along the passage until they came to a Sklera door with flecks of crystal in it. Embellishments made for a king.

Exchanging a glance, the two women got to work. Alvina gently tested the handle but it was locked like they had expected. Dropping to one knee, the woman took out a kit of lockpicking tools and quietly fiddled with it.

Eira took a sleeping dart out of her pouch and loaded it into the shooter. Her aim wasn't as good as Holt's, but she had practiced enough to fulfill their mission. The king would have at least one guard with him. Maybe even two. She would shoot one with the dart and Alvina would shoot the other. Hopefully that would give them enough time to talk to the king alone.

There was still no sign of the Eternal Flame. Once their attempt to persuade the king failed, she would leave Alvina and go searching for the cult leader. He had to be somewhere in the city. When Nar heard about it he would be furious, but he would forgive her eventually.

Alvina put her tools back and stood up while Eira gripped the dart and calmed her breathing. No time to strategize about finding the Eternal Flame now. She would figure it out after they spoke to the king.

Swinging the door open, they stepped inside and shot the guards on the left and right before either of them could react. Satisfied, she looked toward the bed, expecting to see the king's terrified expression. The king was there, sitting upright with his night clothes on. But he wasn't alone. Five bare-chested cultists grinned at the two women as if they had been expecting them.

It was a trap. They were outnumbered. Even with the small amount of Prime Stimulant she brought, she couldn't fight five Manipulators at once. Not without Nar.

The cultists ran toward them. With her mind, Eira lashed out with a wide force as she and Alvina backed into the hallway. While not buying them a lot of time, her attack made the cultists stumble as they each raised a vial of green liquid to their lips; the new Stimulant that had allowed them to control Ronan.

As quickly as she could, Eira yanked an Inhibitor out of her pocket and downed it. She wouldn't be able to use her mind to attack but it would stop them from reading her thoughts. If this new Stimulant truly gave them Manipulation and Seyring, the sanctity of her mind might be her only advantage. She cringed at how dead the world felt without her powers.

A surge of guards rushed toward them from down the hallway. There was no way out. She pulled her dagger out of its sheath, prepared to put up a fight. Maybe she would get to meet the Eternal Flame after all, just not under the circumstances she had hoped for.

"You're in danger, my King!" Alvina yelled. "Firekin is planning to kill you!"

What did it matter? The mission had failed. Even if the king believed her, which was unlikely, the cultists would never let them escape.

Alvina grabbed her arm, pulling her toward the stained glass. Before Eira could stop her, the woman grabbed onto a sconce and swung herself into the window, kicking the pane with her razored shoe. The sound of shattering glass followed them as they fell out of the window and into the night.

An involuntary gasp of air escaped Eira's lips as they plummeted toward the ground. With effort, she and Alvina dug their razored boots into the wall to slow their descent and grabbed onto a window ledge. One of the more zealous cultists dove out of the stained glass window and used Manipulation to slow his fall.

"Jump!" Eira cried. Without the ability to use her powers, their only chance was to run. A few more cultists leapt out of the window, white pants almost glowing against the black wall.

She and Alvina dropped the rest of the way to the ground and ran toward the easternmost wall. They had some cover as they ran through the garden, but the plants quickly went up in flames as fireballs shot past them.

Grateful now for the fire-retardant cloak, Eira shoved the climbing gloves on and threw herself at the wall. She could feel the impact of each fireblast but none of them burned her. At the top, they were met with a line of guards, each holding an empty vial.

They were so close! Gritting her teeth, she lunged forward and slashed at the nearest guards with her climbing gloves. The blades tore their flesh, causing them to pull away from her. In the opening, she and Alvina bolted through their line and swung over to the other side of the wall. Fiery stones pelted them on the way down. Once they were close enough to the ground the two women pushed off of the wall and ran toward the treeline.

The shouts of the guards grew distant once they entered the forest, but they didn't slow down their pace. Eira jumped over a fallen log and exchanged a glance with Alvina. They were fortunate to even be alive. Somehow, the cultists in the king's room had been expecting them. She had been outmaneuvered once again.

CHAPTER 23
Alone

So Ravenel met with the Speki order of Knowledge Keepers,
but they turned him away, refusing to accept his claims.

Khartsaga

THE MUSIC FROM THE FIRE Festival had long ago been replaced by the sounds of rustling leaves and scurrying animals. His captors stopped and shoved Khartsaga down on the ground. How long had they been walking? He could see light through the bag on his head, but the mind fog made it difficult to gauge the passing of time.

He tried to get back up and run when they untied his hands, but there were too many of them to fight, even with his larger stature. They held him against a tree while someone wrapped a cord around his torso and fastened it to the trunk.

"Bind his hands again too."

Weakened by the Inhibitor, his attempts to struggle were only met with tighter grips and muttered curses. When they had finished their knots, the bag was finally yanked off his head.

He grimaced as his eyes adjusted to the morning light. Pulling against the binding did no good. It was ropesnare too. Even under normal circumstances, he would need a strong Stimulant to Manipulate his way out of this.

The humans surrounded him in a half-circle watching him with careful eyes. This was ridiculous. He had been a fool to leave the festival. And for what? Time alone to get his thoughts in order? That was what Tarkhan was assigned to do.

"Give him another dose, just to be safe," said a gruff-looking man, glaring down at him.

"I'd give him another two if it wouldn't be a waste of Inhibitor," responded a man with hair as white as the light. He was one of the Speki from the cave. At least that explained how they were able to capture him. No mere human could do that.

"What do you want from me?" Khartsaga asked.

Neither of the men responded. Instead a woman with a strand of purple hair approached him with a needle.

"Wait," he started to say, but the human injected him with the Inhibitor anyway. Some of the mind fog came back, but it wasn't quite as bad as it had been before. He was able to think without his head threatening to crack open, but the dull throbbing persisted.

Two of the humans sat down in front of the tree while the rest of them left to sit by a nearby campfire.

"Why am I here?" he asked.

But again, the humans only glared at him in response. From what he could gather, he appeared to be in some kind of camp. It was decently populated. A number of the humans were at the campfire, but many of them walked along a path of wooden structures. That's when he noticed the coloration of the plants. Most of the camp was made up of dirt, but there were patches of grass here and there. Red grass. He looked up. The leaves above him were also a deep shade of red.

The breath caught in his chest and a chill swept across his skin. The Scarlet Forest. Were the humans really foolish enough to try living in a death trap like this? He nervously craned his neck around to see if the rest of the forest was as red as the legends claimed. The leaves shimmered against the gray sky like drops of blood on a piece of steel.

He tested the strength of the ropesnare again, but the knots were incredibly tight. If the leaves were as vivid as the stories claimed, then that meant everything else he had heard about the Scarlet Forest was likely true as well. Man-spinsters. Corpse trees. The legends claimed that wild shadowmongrels used to live here too, but luckily he wouldn't have to worry about them.

He managed to catch the names of some of his captors as the morning wore on. Not that it mattered. Learning the names of humans was pointless because of how short their lives were, but it gave him something to do. Every so often children would run around the firepit, giggling and chasing after one another. More than once they stopped their game to look at him, their eyes wide in a mixture of curiosity and fear. He probably looked half-deranged after the hike last night. Not to mention the heavy drugs in his system.

Around noon, the humans gathered around the fire for lunch. Khartsaga's own stomach growled as the hearty aroma wafted over to him, but he didn't expect to be given anything from these creatures. They were driven purely by instinct, not by love or passion like Gurvel. Would he starve to death here? Tarkhan was the only one who had seen the attack, but he could be dead by now, for all Khartsaga knew.

He leaned his head back against the tree. Without Tarkhan he was alone. Now it was his responsibility to keep his thoughts from slipping. *May the New Age rise and Gurvel prosper so that all creatures may prosper.* He repeated the familiar chant in his head, accepting the throbbing headache that accompanied it as his punishment.

"Be careful, Wren," Holt said, breaking Khartsaga's concentration.

A small Forestdweller stepped up to him with a sheepish grin and a bowl of stew.

Khartsaga accepted the food and studied the creature with curiosity. He looked young, even for a species that didn't live long to begin with. "I don't think I've ever encountered a Forestdweller before."

Wren, or at least that's what Holt had called him, smiled and then ran over to the firepit. Why was a Forestdweller living here? With humans?

Holt and the Speki named Einar switched places with the guards and eyed him as he drank the soup. Maybe they would answer his questions.

"Why am I here? What do you want with me?"

Like before, neither of the men answered him. Khartsaga returned to his soup. At least he wouldn't starve. If they weren't intending to kill him, then what did they want? Information? Surely they knew he would never give that to them.

After he finished, he set the bowl down and dozed for a bit, the exhaustion from the long trek finally overcoming him. Dark figures accompanied his usual fitful dream by the cliff. They surrounded his mother whose face was stained with blood-red tears.

He awoke with a start as someone injected him with a fresh Inhibitor. It was approaching evening now and the guards were changing again. At this rate he was losing hope in the possibility that he could escape between doses.

One of the new guards caught his attention. "Ronan," he whispered. The man who had escaped into the forest. The man he had controlled with the Verdant Stimulant.

Ronan looked at him but didn't respond. The female Speki from the cave sat down beside him in silence, just like all the others. But he had to try.

"What do you want with me?" he asked.

The woman's gaze made his stomach churn. He didn't need to be a Seyr to feel the hatred seething out of her.

"Please, I just want to know why you've captured me. Why me specifically?" he asked, trying to remain calm. The humans were turning out to be rather strategic creatures.

"You're here because of Firekin," the Speki spat. "So sit tight and do what you're told."

Einar and Holt hadn't answered his question either, but at least their eyes didn't seethe with hatred like this woman's. Not getting anywhere with answers, Khartsaga went back to dozing against the tree. Sooner or later he would find an opening to escape. It was only a matter of time. Besides, if they were trying to stop the New Age from happening, kidnapping him wouldn't prolong anything. Even now his father was preparing the final phase of their plan.

His stomach churned as he thought about the next phase. King Chono needed to be replaced with someone from Firekin. His father was adamant about that part. This was how the New Age must come. *May the New Age rise and Gurvel prosper so that all creatures may prosper.*

While meditating, he managed to pick up enough of Ronan's conversation with the Speki, Eira, to realize the topic. She was teaching him about Seyring.

How ridiculous. Humans couldn't have powers of Manipulation or Seyring. It was a fact that every Firekin member was taught. However, it had been difficult to control Ronan with the Verdant Stimulant. Then the man had somehow escaped the guards too. Even Tarkhan had seemed baffled when they had lost him in the forest. Frowning, Khartsaga listened more closely.

No. Shaking his head, he quickly refocused his thoughts on the truth. It was impossible. Humans were animals. They couldn't possess such powers. Closing his eyes, Khartsaga meditated on the Fire Creed again. *May the New Age rise and Gurvel prosper so that all creatures may prosper. Together we rise. Together we prosper. Together we ascend.*

He repeated the phrases in his mind, over and over, concentrating on each separate part, until the sound of footsteps nearing the tree drew him out of his meditation.

A woman with a thick braid crouched in front of him. "I'm Alvina, leader of the Scarletts. Welcome to our camp." It was the woman that he had seen in the cave on the day the Speki had escaped. Ronan and Eira stood just behind her, watching him intently. Maybe now he would finally get some answers.

"What do you want with me?" Khartsaga asked, meeting her gaze evenly.

"What does Firekin want with the throne?" she asked, her voice crisp and clear. So they planned to interrogate him after all. Shifting his position slightly, he sat up straighter but didn't answer.

"Alright, we'll start easier," she said. "Are you the leader of Firekin?"

Now this was a question he could answer. It was time for these ignorant creatures to learn who to thank for their coming prosperity. "No. My father, Ukhel, is the Eternal Flame. He was the one first enlightened with the vision of the New Age."

"So why are you next in line to take the throne?" she asked.

"King Chono trusts me," he replied, pushing down the knot in his stomach. "Speaking of which, he'll be very unhappy when he finds me missing."

"We're counting on it," she said, straightening. "As soon as he grants us an audience with him, we plan to reveal who really killed his son. Then we would be more than happy to hand you over to him."

His breath catching in his throat, Khartsaga's chest tightened as he weighed the possibility. Could they prove it? If the king knew what had really happened, he would send them all to the shadowmongrel pits. They had gained a decent amount of new Firekin members, but the king still had a number of guards loyal only to him.

Looking satisfied, Alvina walked away, leaving him alone again with Ronan and Eira, both of whom returned to their seats on the grass to continue practicing. Khartsaga clenched his hand into a fist and tried to calm his thoughts, but memories of the dead queen continued to flash through his mind. It was necessary. It was *necessary*. It *was* necessary. Tarkhan had reminded him of this again and again, but somehow, without the lanky Gurvel nearby, the truth wasn't nearly as convincing.

During the next change in guards, the rebels actually let him walk around a bit, taking him into the forest to relieve himself and stretch. He looked for an opportunity to escape, but the two Speki stayed close beside him, glaring at every move he made. Eventually someone would let their guard down, and when they did, he would run and hope that he could make it through the Scarlet Forest without encountering too many dangers. With any luck he might make it back to the city in time for the next phase.

And so the pattern continued. Every so often, the guards would change and he would be given a new Inhibitor dose. On occasion, the guards would let him get up and stretch, but otherwise he was bound to the tree, stuck watching the humans go about their lives while the New Age was nearing in Galynkhot.

As days passed, the emptiness he felt without Tarkhan or his father monitoring his thoughts plagued him. Without their guidance, his weakness was in danger of overcoming him. So he repeated the Fire Creed to himself, over and over, desperately clinging to truths that didn't seem quite as relevant out here in the Scarlet Forest, surrounded by creatures that seemed to be thriving well enough on their own, without the prosperity of the Gurvel.

CHAPTER 24
Assassins

Ronan

PEERING AROUND THE CRUMBLING trunk of an ashbark tree, Ronan scanned the forest, looking for the presence that he had felt with his mind. It had been so close, but the only living things he could see were red vines and mossy rocks. Now he felt nothing, as if the mind had vanished. Did he imagine it? He wiped the sweat off of his forehead and eased himself around the tree, scanning the boulders and bushes for signs of movement.

Somewhere between a large scraggly bush and a patch of weeds, Ronan found his mind drifting off toward the glowing ocean. That water looked so much like fire, but not like the kind that killed. This felt different. Calmer. Maybe even more like healing. He caught himself and shook his head to clear his thoughts. They had been at this exercise for almost an hour. It was becoming difficult to focus, so he found himself constantly dragging his attention back to the task at hand. Something he had been doing more frequently even when they weren't practicing.

Someone tapped him on the shoulder. Spinning around, he dropped instinctively into a defensive crouch, but no one was there. Again, he reached out with his mind and caught the flicker of a thought from someone nearby, but his senses told him he was alone. Somewhere up above him, Eira and Einar watched, obscured from his view by the thick canopy. Their thoughts were completely hidden, but his task wasn't to find them.

Curious, Ronan started scanning the branches of the treetops, searching for Wren's green scales. Surely he would stand out among all the vivid reds of the forest? He had to give it to the kid. Even with his trained eyes and ears, he wasn't able to pick up any movement or sound from Wren. It was truly an exercise of the mind.

A brief thought caught his attention. It hadn't been his own, but he still couldn't see anyone. This time he was sure it had come from the bush directly in front of him. Where was that kid? He began to wonder if he was just picking up the presence of a squirrel or frog when the air before him began to shimmer and shift, transforming into the form of a person. Wren stood before him, a wide grin stretched across his face as the scales on his skin turned back to their normal shade of green.

"You can change the color of your scales?" Ronan asked, relaxing his stance.

"All Forestdwellers can," Wren signed.

After a week or so, he was finally starting to pick up enough of Wren's language to understand basic sentences. "That was impressive."

Eira landed beside them, jumping down from the higher branches of the ashbark tree. "You shouldn't have doubted your mind."

Landing beside her, Einar chuckled. "It was only the first try, sister. It's amazing that he picked up Wren's presence at all!" He turned toward Ronan and grinned. "Still want to learn how to use your powers, or has my sister's attitude scared you off yet?"

He stifled a small smile as Eira raised an eyebrow toward her brother. Despite her initial reluctance, she had actually taught him quite a bit this past week. He was looking forward to continuing the training today, even if she was a little cold toward him at times.

"We'll try the exercise again before we go back," Eira said. "Right now we need to focus on scavenging for toracini mushrooms."

"We're sure this is the only way to find them?" Ronan asked. He had been dreading this task all week.

"They only grow in extremely nutrient-rich soil," she answered.

Still not keen on the idea, he followed Eira's lead, carefully walking around ashbark trunks and rock clusters as they scanned the foliage for signs of the corpse tree. He was only willing to take the risk because confronting Firekin without a Stimulant would be suicidal. Although if he could have his way, they wouldn't confront Firekin at all. He didn't have to help them. In fact he could leave anytime he wanted to, but he felt obligated to stay. Eira had saved his life. The least he could do was help them plan the cult's downfall so long as he didn't have to go back to the city.

He stepped over a gnarled root, wondering if there were any books in Batu's shop about the dangers in the Scarlet Forest. That thought led him to wonder if Batu had found any copies of *The Legend of Ravenel* yet. Not that he would ever see it.

He wasn't sure how long it had been, but he tripped over a stone and realized his mind had drifted far from looking for the corpse tree. Shaking his head, he refocused on the forest. Daydreaming now could be deadly.

"Has the king responded to our meeting request yet?" he asked, trying desperately to keep his mind from wandering.

"No," Eira said with a sigh. "He's either ignoring all of our messages or someone is intercepting them. I'd bet a bag of Prime Stimulant that he's just buying time in hopes that Khartsaga will escape."

"At least we've learned about the inevitability of the New Age," Einar said. "That's been helpful."

Eira rolled her eyes, continuing to scan the treeline. "Like I've said, if we want answers we're going to need to do more than just guard and feed him."

"But alas, Alvina isn't too keen on the suggestions of an assassin," Einar said.

"What exactly do Speki assassins do?" Ronan asked.

They were both silent for a moment, or at least they appeared to be. From the way Eira glanced at her brother he got the impression that they were speaking in their heads.

"We're called assassins, but that's not entirely accurate. We work in pairs, only killing when necessary," Einar explained. "One Seyr. One Manipulator. The two train together from childhood, forming what's called an Assassin Bond. When they're ready, the Speki counsel sends them out on missions."

"It's a coveted position," Eira said. "We protect the knowledge of our people."

"And we gather new knowledge," Einar added. "As you can imagine, we have various methods of obtaining information. Like the kind that our Gurvel friend back at camp is reluctant to give up."

Wren walked in front of them so he could be seen. *"Would you hurt him?"*

Einar stopped walking and thought for a moment. "Not unless we had to."

"That's the tricky part about Assassin Bonds," Eira said over her shoulder. "Both parties must be in complete agreement. Even if torture would be more likely to yield the kind of information we need."

"Even if Alvina would allow it, we don't know that pain would loosen his tongue," Einar said.

"It would eventually," Eira muttered, shoving aside a branch.

The hatred in her voice cut like ice, but she had a point. Since the king wasn't listening to their warnings, they might have to force the information out of Khartsaga. At the moment they didn't even know how many cultists there were.

"There," Eira said, pointing to an average-looking tree with a large canopy of leaves in the distance. "Be quick. We need to uproot the mushrooms and get outside the range of the umbra before it drops seeds."

"Get your Inhibitors ready," Einar said. "Wren, your job is to stay back as a lookout and guide us out of the tree's illusion."

"I want to help," Wren signed.

"You are helping," Einar answered while signing with his hands. *"We need someone to keep an eye on us, in case something goes wrong."*

Wren pursed his lips but nodded in understanding.

This was it. Ronan took out the vial of Inhibitor and drank it, expecting something bitter. Instead he was surprised to find that it didn't taste like anything. A thick fog clouded his mind as he ran alongside Eira and Einar, similar to the effects of the cinnamon grass but stronger. Thinking became more difficult, so he tried to focus on the task at hand. Don't touch the trunk. Uproot the mushrooms. Get away from the leaves.

Once they were close enough to see the black thorns on the trunk, he felt an odd prickling sensation at the edge of his mind. He shook off the feeling and knelt beside the soft purple mushrooms, hoping the Inhibitor was strong enough to block the deadly plant.

It was oddly quiet this close to the tree. There were no chirping moss frogs or scuttling squirrels. Even the sound of wind seemed to vanish. He worked faster, stashing mushrooms into Eira's satchel as the hair on the back of his neck stood up. Were they being watched? No. Of course not. It was the tree.

They worked quickly but still had to be careful or else they would knock the spores loose. Without them, the mushrooms would be worthless. Sweat trickled down the side of his face as he glanced up at the ominous dark green leaves. He would have thought a splash of green would bring comfort to him after days spent in the Scarlet Forest, but it didn't. Not when he knew there were acidic seeds waiting in the branches above them.

"That's enough. Get back," Eira ordered, standing up with the bulging satchel.

They ran back to where Wren was waiting, tail curled around his ankles. Once they were outside the range of the tree's exploding seeds, Ronan let his shoulders relax. He could still feel the prickling sensation in his head, but it had lessened.

"Good! We managed to survive the deadly corpse tree," Einar said. "Now we just have to wait a couple of hours for this aching fog to fade."

"It will be worth it," Eira said, lifting up the sack. "This should make a decent amount of Prime Stimulant."

"Now maybe we'll have enough for our pupils to practice with."

"Don't count on it," Eira said, slinging the bag over her shoulder. "We're going to need every ounce of this when we confront Firekin."

"Of course," Einar agreed, but he turned away from her and winked at Ronan and Wren.

What would it feel like to use a Stimulant? Ronan wondered. Maybe it would allow him to read minds.

After running through a few exercises that could be done with Inhibitor fog, they walked back toward the camp. Even after they were far away from the corpse tree, he couldn't shake the feeling that they were being watched. It was too far away for the tree to reach their minds, so it must be something else. He had never used an Inhibitor before. Maybe it was just a side effect. He made a note to ask Eira about it later and focused on keeping up with the others.

CHAPTER 25

The Beach

*Finally, Ravenel appealed to the courts of men to help him find a way
to defeat the shadow beasts before it was too late.*

Khartsaga

FIRE PURIFIES ALL IMPURITIES. He could use a purifying fire right
about now. It had been about a week since the humans had brought him here.
With each passing day, it became more difficult to hold onto the truth.

May the New Age rise and Gurvel prosper so that all creatures may prosper.
And yet the humans appeared to be prospering well enough on their own. In
fact, he had discovered that the Speki weren't in command like he thought.
Alvina was their leader. A mere human.

Together we rise. Together we prosper. Together we ascend. But what if he was
alone? How could he prosper? How could he ascend? Without Tarkhan, his
thoughts slipped more frequently. Last night he found himself almost admiring
the humans. They had a culture of their own, complete with music, traditions,
and beliefs. Was his father mistaken?

Khartsaga squeezed his eyes shut and started over. *Fire purifies all
impurities. Fire purifies all impurities.*

"That was good," Einar said. "I heard you."

"Did you respond mentally?" Ronan asked.

Khartsaga opened his eyes and looked over at the two men who were
guarding him this morning. That was another thing. Humans couldn't be Seyrs
or Manipulators. Or so he had been told.

"I did, but you didn't hear me," Einar replied. "The message was clear,
though. You're progressing at an impressive rate."

"Not fast enough," Ronan said, looking off into the forest.

Every day Ronan listened intently to one of the Speki and practiced until
sweat rolled down his face. He did this despite the fact that he couldn't possibly
have any powers. Then again, it had been difficult to control him with the

Verdant Stimulant. Could his father be wrong about that too?

Einar held his hand out and bounced a small rock in the air, never letting it touch his palm. "Even something as simple as this took me a decade to perfect. But you've only been practicing for a couple of weeks and look how far you've come!"

"That's impossible," Khartsaga interjected. "You shouldn't have any powers at all. And if you do, they should be much weaker. You're just a by-product of Gurvel creation."

"That's assuming a lot, Gurvel," Einar said coldly. "Perhaps your theories are incorrect."

"They're not theories. That's a fact from the Great Beginning," he argued, shifting his position as best as he could while tied to the tree.

"Ignorant scum," Einar muttered under his breath.

Khartsaga chose not to respond. It was the truth whether they believed it or not, but today he struggled to believe that truth himself. Arguing with them might only confuse his thoughts further.

Wren joined them, somehow communicating to the others with his hands. When Khartsaga was much younger, his mother had taught him a little about Forestdwellers. Supposedly, none of them spoke audibly, choosing instead not to disturb the natural sounds of the forest. But what really intrigued him was that this child was the only one who didn't seem to hate or fear him.

Ronan and Einar stood up, monitoring him while Wren administered a new dosage of the Inhibitor. They didn't need to worry. He wasn't going to hurt the boy in an escape attempt. Of course his father wouldn't approve of that. Escape should be his number one priority, at any cost. But it didn't matter. He had nothing to cut the ropesnare with anyway. A fresh cloud of mind fog washed over him, accompanied by the ever-present ache in his skull.

"Alright, let's get this next bit over with," Einar said, bending down to untie him. "He desperately needs a bath."

After a week he probably looked worse than he smelled. They pulled him up by the arms, leaving his hands tied. At least he would be able to stretch his legs.

Nearby, Wren watched them with his tail wrapped around his ankles. Where were the others of his kind? From what Khartsaga could gather, Holt was like a father to him. But why would humans take care of a different species?

Wren saw Khartsaga looking at him and smiled. Despite everything, he couldn't stop himself from smiling back. His father would be furious.

Leaving the boy behind, Einar and Ronan led Khartsaga to the edge of the camp. Escape would be difficult without his powers. He might have had a chance with just two guards, but Holt and Edalene joined them on the other side of the cinnamon grass.

"Remember the plan. We get in, wash him, and leave," Holt said, leading them past red shrubs and trees covered in burgundy moss. "We want to get back with ample time before his dose starts to fade."

In response, Einar and Ronan walked closer to Khartsaga, both carefully watching his movements while Edalene guarded the rear. The humans were more thorough in their vigilance than he had anticipated. He couldn't find any holes in their defenses. But it was only a matter of time. Sooner or later someone would make a mistake.

They wove their way through the forest, stepping on ashbark flakes that dusted the ground like snow. What if they didn't make a mistake? Waiting for the Inhibitor to wear off was out of the question because they had likely brought more with them. Running wouldn't work either. Not with the Speki Manipulator nearby. They had thought through everything.

One of the trees along the path had a large spider dangling from the upper branches. The body was as large as a man's hand and looked like it was covered in ashbark. So man-spinsters really did exist. Luckily it was to the right of the path so he wasn't going to run into it. He figured Ronan would see it and duck under it like Holt had, but the man continued walking, seemingly lost in thought. Khartsaga opened his mouth to warn him of the danger, but Einar was faster.

"Ronan! Watch your step."

With a start, Ronan stopped in his tracks and looked up, finally seeing the spider.

"Gotta watch out for those," Einar said. "Man-spinsters won't kill you, but their bite will paralyze you for days."

They carefully passed the spider and continued along the path. Had he really been about to help Ronan? If Ronan had been bitten by the man-spinster, Khartsaga could have escaped during the confusion. What was wrong with him?

With renewed determination, he refocused his thoughts on the Fire Creed. *Fire purifies all impurities. May the New Age rise and Gurvel prosper so that all creatures may prosper. Together we rise. Together we prosper. Together we ascend.* This time he didn't question the statements. He just repeated them, forcing the words into his mind like a hammer on an anvil.

By the time they reached the beach, he had gone over the creed dozens of times and yet the truth still felt far from him. He needed to be cleansed. And to be cleansed, he needed to escape.

He went through his options again as Einar and Ronan led him over the crest of a small hill. But at the top, his desire to escape momentarily vanished, replaced with breathless awe. Before them a field of white sand disappeared into the water where the waves crashed against the beach in a spray of foam. A flock of birds flew overhead, landing next to a large cliff face to the left where they basked in the gleaming sun. His mother would have loved this. Khartsaga wanted to stand there for the rest of the day, breathing in the salty air and listening to the cries of the birds mixed with the rushing water.

But he wasn't free to do so.

Holt led them onto the beach and brought them to the edge of the water. "Let's make this quick. Gurvel, take off your boots and rinse off. Edalene, you're with me in the water. Ronan, Einar, stay on the beach and keep watch."

Khartsaga sat down on the sand and pried his boots off, struggling to get the right grip with his hands still bound. Normally he would have been concerned about getting his uniform wet, but the pristine outfit he had worn for the Fire Festival was now disheveled and covered in dirt. A little salt water might actually be an improvement.

All four of his captors watched him intently as he stood back up and entered the ocean. The sand was mostly smooth and slipped easily between his toes, but there were a few shells and rocks scattered about that felt sharp against his skin. If he could grab one without them noticing...another one stabbed his foot. He curled his toes around it and continued wading further out.

Once he was about waist deep, Holt grabbed his arm. "That's far enough. Rinse off."

The cold water chilled his face as he ducked beneath the surface, but he didn't care. It felt so good to finally wash off all the sweat and grime. Keeping his foot on the shell, he came back up for air and started to rub away the dirt that had accumulated on his clothing. His mind was still filled with fog, but if he was fast enough he could cut the ropesnare and swim away. Even if Einar had a strong Stimulant with him, he wouldn't be able to Manipulate the sand or water. No Manipulator could.

He took a deep breath and ducked back under the water. In a swift movement he held the shell firmly between his toes and slipped the tip of it between the ropesnare and his wrists. He pulled his arms back, cringing as the shell cut his skin along with the rope. But the pain was minor compared to the exhilaration of finally being free. With a push, he propelled himself toward the open ocean.

Edalene stepped in front of him, so Khartsaga reached out and pulled her below the surface. She thrashed around in his arms, struggling to get back above the water. Seizing the opportunity, he let her go and swam away while she splashed back up for air. His own lungs burned but he forced himself to stay under for another few seconds. Once he was farther out, he swam up and caught his breath.

"There!" Ronan yelled from behind him. "Can't you control the water?"

"It's too fluid!" Einar yelled from farther back. "So is the sand. I can't..." His voice was drowned out as Khartsaga dove back down.

He should have been able to outswim all of them because of his stature, but being tied to a tree for so long had left him weaker than he anticipated. Spinning around, he peered through the dark blue void. Someone was treading water a few paces behind him. If he could disorient whoever this was like he had done with Edalene, he might be able to get away.

He propelled himself toward the person and grabbed their ankle. It was Ronan. The man let out a stream of bubbles as he was pulled under. But he didn't thrash like Edalene. Instead he kicked with his other leg and broke free.

Gritting his teeth, he swam after Ronan, grabbing his ankle again. This time the man kicked more forcefully and landed a blow to the side of Khartsaga's face.

Mixed with the Inhibitor, the blow to his head clouded his vision so he swam to the surface and gulped in air until he could see again. The current had carried him farther down the beach. He could barely hear the sound of the Scarletts shouting from the shoreline. A few arms' lengths away, Ronan treaded water, a dagger held defensively in his hand.

This wasn't good. He needed to get past Ronan, but the tide was pulling them both toward the cliff face. With renewed determination he dove back under the waves and grabbed Ronan around the waist, dragging him deeper below the water this time. He hadn't intended to kill him before, but now that he was this close to freedom he didn't have much choice. *May the children of fire rise.*

CHAPTER 26

Enemies

But even his own people turned him away,
claiming his tale was a fluke of nature and his powers a danger to society.

Ronan

YEARS OF TRAINING KICKED in as Ronan was dragged deeper into the depths of the ocean. He tried to open his eyes but the sting of the salt was too intense. Instead of panicking, he stabbed his dagger at the arms that held him. Khartsaga tensed but didn't release him.

The weight of the water pressed against his ears, sending an icy jolt of fear through his heart. His lungs burned as he fought the urge to breathe in something, anything.

In an act of desperation, he swiped the dagger out in front of him while also envisioning the weapon piercing Khartsaga's mind. Under normal circumstances he never would have tried Seyring against someone affected by an Inhibitor. It wouldn't work. Not even a shadowmongrel could break an Inhibitor barrier. But with death clinging to him like the cold abyss around him, he reacted by instinct, not logic.

The dagger made contact with something and Khartsaga's grip weakened enough to let him pull free. He pushed himself away from the Gurvel and swam back up, head pounding.

When he finally reached the surface, his ears were met with the screeching cry of seagulls flying overhead. He gasped for air while looking around to reorient himself. The beach was nowhere in sight.

"Einar!" He choked, still struggling to breathe. They probably wouldn't be able to hear him anyway. The tide had carried him to the other side of the cliff where a cave sat nestled inside the rocks.

Khartsaga came back to the surface a few arms' lengths away, gasping for breath. Blood trickled down his face from where the dagger had cut just below his eye.

Even while treading water, the tide pulled them both closer to the rocks. Ronan started swimming toward the mouth of the cave, propelled by the force of the ocean. He didn't like the idea of being trapped in there with Khartsaga, but at least he would be on solid ground where he could fight.

A large wave pushed him from behind and slammed him into the cave. He scrambled up, ignoring the throbbing in his head, and looked around for Khartsaga. The Gurvel stood across from him, gripping the wall for support. Good. He stood a better chance against an injured opponent.

The roar of another wave grew louder as it rushed toward the small opening. Neither of them would be able to fight against the power of these waves. He looked around for something to hold onto and spotted a passage that led farther into the cave.

Darting toward it, he barely missed the wave as it crashed against the rocks behind him. Khartsaga dove after him, slamming onto the rocky ground as the water receded. With a head start, Ronan ran down the passage until he came to an open room.

It was about 15 paces wide and lit by sunlight that was streaming through a hole in the ceiling. Heart pounding, he looked around for a way to get up there, but other than a few crystals glinting in the sunlight, the cave was empty. There was another passage that likely led deeper into the cave, but he wouldn't be able to see in there, and fighting a Gurvel in the dark sounded as bad as fighting one in the ocean.

He backed up against one of the walls and pulled out his dagger as Khartsaga stumbled into the room. Fighting him here was his best bet.

Khartsaga glanced from the hole in the ceiling to the passage they had entered by. Both of them knew the waves were too strong to swim against. If they were going to get out, it would have to be up through that opening. Unfortunately, it looked like the Gurvel might be tall enough to reach the edge if he jumped.

Gritting his teeth, Ronan dug his heel into the ground. If Khartsaga escaped and managed to get back to the city, he would lead the army to the Scarletts' camp and destroy them all with shadowmongrels and fire. None of them would survive and it would be his fault. He took a few steps forward to block the escape route.

Instead of attacking him, Khartsaga looked right past him, eyes widening in fear and surprise. Ronan's breath caught in his throat as the air around them froze. The sunlight that had lit the cave moments before dimmed as if smothered by cloth.

A shiver ran down his spine when the sound of crashing waves and whistling wind suddenly fell silent. He and Khartsaga looked at each other in utter shock. It was impossible. Like a cold rock in his stomach, a deep sense of dread washed over him. The rumors were true. Somehow, a wild shadowmongrel had survived out here in the Scarlet Forest and they had just stumbled into its lair.

He jumped as a sharp click tore through the silence and echoed off of the rocks. A series of smaller and lower pitched clicks followed the first one. Then the creature fell silent, leaving behind an eerie quiet that felt almost tangible.

Not daring to move, Ronan looked at the passage from his peripheral vision. Somehow it seemed even darker than before. Fighting Khartsaga now paled in comparison to the danger that lurked just out of reach. He looked back at the Gurvel. All he had to do was escape through the hole and leave Ronan to be tormented by the shadowmongrel.

Khartsaga bent down to inspect one of the pink crystals growing out of the cave floor. Was he toying with him? Why didn't he just run?

Ronan crouched into a more defensive position. Cold sweat dripped down the side of his face. Survival at this point was unlikely, but discipline kicked in like muscle memory and kept him from giving up before the fight even started.

The darkness in the passage hadn't moved, but he could feel something watching them like he could feel the cold rock under his bare feet.

Khartsaga pulled up one of the crystals and inspected it. There should have been more sound accompanied by that action, but the silence around them absorbed most of it. Ronan watched him warily and glanced up at the hole in the ceiling. He could try making a lunge for it, but even with a good running start there was no way he could reach it.

Khartsaga approached him slowly with the crystal. In response, Ronan brandished the dagger, keeping an eye on both enemies. He fought back the urge to shiver as the darkness crept around him. It was searching for him.

"Here," Khartsaga whispered, tossing him the crystal. "Put it in your mouth."

"What?" Ronan whispered back, clutching the odd crystal. Why hadn't Khartsaga escaped yet?

"Put it in your mouth. It's an Inhibitor."

The chill of the room had grown colder to the point where he could see wisps of his own breath. The creature's clicks continued to pierce through the quiet every now and then.

"Now, Ronan!"

He eyed Khartsaga, fear churning his gut and gripping his heart. It was a trick of some kind. It had to be. Before he could decide what to do, Khartsaga lunged at him, knocking him to the ground. Ronan slashed his arm with the dagger, but Khartsaga easily knocked the weapon out of his hand. Then the Gurvel shoved the crystal into Ronan's mouth and held it there. The overwhelming flavor of salt lingered on his tongue, despite his efforts to spit it out.

He tried to push the Gurvel off of him, struggling to breathe beneath his weight, but almost immediately a wave of lightheadedness and fatigue washed over him. Khartsaga released some of the pressure. It was enough that he could breathe again, but not enough to push him away.

He glared at Khartsaga, but the Gurvel wasn't paying any attention to him. He was focused on the darkness.

That's when Ronan saw it too. A cold chill swept through his veins. Something was looking at them. Two small yellow eyes. But they weren't moving. Could it see them? Ronan stopped struggling and tried to quiet his breathing. He didn't know if the crystal was hiding his mind or not, but at that moment he just didn't want the creature to hear him.

Cautiously, Khartsaga got off of him. The yellow eyes still didn't move, but the chill of the air and dim lighting was all he needed to know that the creature was alive and well. Despite the foul taste of salt, he didn't spit out the crystal.

Khartsaga started moving toward the hole. As he did, the number of clicks emanating from the beast increased.

Ronan scrambled up and blocked him. Now that he was under the hole, there was definitely no way that he could reach it. Khartsaga pulled him to the side and then jumped up, grabbing the edge of the opening before Ronan could stop him.

The shadowmongrel released a series of clicks as its eyes moved toward the hole. Ronan glanced at the dagger that he had dropped. It was a few paces away, but he didn't dare move. Khartsaga won. An icy chill swept through his veins. He wouldn't be able to escape the death sentence this time.

A soft tapping came from above. Khartsaga reached through the hole and motioned for Ronan to grab his hand. Now what game was he playing at? Surely he wasn't actually trying to help him escape? He glanced back at the creature and felt his heart skip a beat. The deepest shadows had moved slightly outside of the passage now.

Desperate, he stepped back and took a running leap toward Khartsaga's outstretched arm. He expected the Gurvel to pull back at the last second, but he grabbed Ronan's forearm and pulled him up. High pitched clicks echoed off the cave walls below as the creature scuffled around, searching for them.

Outside, the light was still dim as if filtered through cloth, but the chill was gone. It looked like they were somewhere in the Scarlet Forest. Ronan sat on a patch of red grass, the salty crystal still in his mouth. He was alive. And Khartsaga had saved him.

He wiped the sweat off of his forehead as he worked to catch his breath. Why was he alive?

By the looks of it, Khartsaga was just as surprised and confused. He knelt on the ground and scrunched his eyes closed. The ridges on his forehead were bent and he shook slightly as he gripped fistfuls of grass.

After a few moments, the sunlight returned to normal and started to shine through the tree canopy. Ronan took the crystal out of his mouth and wiped it on his sleeve. "You saved my life."

Khartsaga frowned.

"Why didn't you leave me to die?"

"I don't know," Khartsaga admitted, rubbing his forehead with the palm of his hand. "I could have escaped. I should have."

"Ronan!" Someone in the distance shouted.

He stood up and cupped his hands around his mouth. "Over here!"

Khartsaga didn't make any attempt to run or fight. Instead he just stared at the ground, continuing to clutch fistfulls of grass.

Holt and Edalene ran toward them with weapons drawn while Einar took out a bag of Stimulant.

"It's okay," Ronan said, holding his hands out to calm them down.

"What happened?" Holt asked, pointing his sword toward the kneeling Gurvel while Edalene cautiously approached Khartsaga and bound his wrists with ropesnare.

"We were washed into a cave and..." He looked at the crystal in his hand. "Khartsaga saved my life."

"What?" Einar asked.

"There was a shadowmongrel and he gave me this. It's an Inhibitor." He handed the crystal to Einar.

Everyone tensed at the mention of a shadowmongrel.

"I think its lair is down there," Ronan said, nodding toward the hole in the ground. "I'll explain back at camp."

He walked over to Khartsaga and gently pulled him up by the arms. The Gurvel stood up but wouldn't meet his eyes.

"Let's go," Ronan said, motioning for Holt to lead the way back.

"Wait," Einar said, pulling an Inhibitor out of his pocket. "I don't want to take any more chances."

Khartsaga winced as the extra fog entered his mind but didn't fight it. In fact he almost looked relieved. Why the sudden change of heart? Moments before he had tried to drown Ronan and now he was willingly letting them take him back to camp.

They made their way back to the main beach where his boots were still sitting in the sand. Now that a shadowmongrel had been confirmed in this area, Ronan doubted they would ever come back. He took one last look at the waves before following the group into the shaded forest.

Khartsaga refused to make eye contact with any of them as they walked. What had happened down in that cave? It was almost like he was two different people. One minute the Gurvel had tried drowning him and the next he had rescued him. A shiver passed along his spine when he remembered those glowing eyes searching for its prey. Regardless of the reason, Khartsaga had saved him from a fate worse than death.

CHAPTER 27

Independence

And so, with nowhere else to turn, Ravenel traveled across the mountains in search of the reclusive Forestdwellers, until one day he found them.

Khartsaga

WHEN THEY RETURNED, EDALENE, the rebel with purple hair, injected Khartsaga with a fresh dose of Inhibitor. He let it happen, almost relishing the new fog that enveloped his mind. It made it harder to think. Harder to dwell on the choice he had just made.

They shoved him against the tree and bound him to it with a new coil of ropesnare. He had likely just blown his only opportunity to escape. And for what? A human? His father would be furious when he found out. If he ever found out.

The headache lessened after a few minutes, but the fog was always present. Scrunching his eyes shut, he tried to settle the uneasy churning in his stomach, but it wouldn't go away. He was so weak! Somehow Ronan had been able to fight him off in the water. If he didn't know any better, he would say the man had attacked him with his mind, not just the dagger. But that was impossible. Then there was the crystal. His father would be especially displeased about that part. Now the humans had the potential to develop an even stronger Inhibitor. Why hadn't he left Ronan to die?

Because he didn't want him to die.

The sound of someone approaching drew him out of his thoughts. Wren, the little Forestdweller, tentatively approached him with a bowl of stew. He smiled at the boy and thankfully accepted the meal. Wren moved his hands in some kind of pattern, smiled, and then ran off.

A short distance away, Holt glared at him. The Speki, Ronan, and Alvina were with him discussing something quietly, but they were just close enough that he could overhear.

"How is that possible?" Eira asked.

"It doesn't matter," Holt said. "Now that we know it's there, we need to prevent it from escaping."

"Would cinnamon grass stop it?" Ronan asked.

"It's not strong enough," Einar said.

Khartsaga's father knew how to control shadowmongrels, but it was a technique that he had only shared with the king and Tarkhan. A knot formed in his stomach. When it was time, his father would share that knowledge with him too. Or so he had been told for the past few centuries.

"Any word from the king?" Ronan asked.

"No. He still hasn't responded to our request for an audience," Alvina answered.

"So we try again," Einar said, hand on his chin. "We just need to take a different approach. Maybe we can try to talk to him when he's at The Games or something."

"There might not be a next time," Eira pointed out. "They're already set up to replace the king with one of their own."

"We don't know that, Sis," Einar said. "The king is a faithful believer in Firekin. Surely they wouldn't kill him. Keep him as a puppet? Sure. But I don't think they'd kill him."

The king. Firekin would be entering the next phase with or without him. The knot in Khartsaga's stomach tightened. He hated to think about the next phase, but it was for the New Age. *May the New Age rise and Gurvel prosper so that all creatures may prosper.* He had repeated that phrase thousands of times before, and yet tonight the words felt empty.

"Ronan," he called out.

The discussion came to an abrupt silence as everyone turned to stare at him. Ronan walked over and crouched in front of him.

"The king is in danger," Khartsaga whispered. "Eira's right. They're going to kill him. I was supposed to be his successor."

"What?" Ronan furrowed his brows. "Why are you telling me this now?"

"Because I never wanted him to die. I was told it was necessary, but..." He trailed off. What he was saying was outright treasonous. If his father ever found out about the things he had done today, his punishment would last more than a few hours. He had failed them.

With a perplexed look, Ronan walked back over to the group to relay the information. Khartsaga leaned his head back against the tree. What had he just done?

Eira

SO IT WAS TRUE. EIRA cursed under her breath. A part of her had wanted to believe Nar's theory that Firekin wouldn't kill one of its own, but it sounded they were planning a coup after all.

"He could be lying," Holt said, glaring at Khartsaga.

"No," Ronan insisted. "He's telling the truth. An hour ago he saved my life."

"That's not enough proof," Holt said. "What if it's a trap?"

"He seems torn. Like a part of him didn't want to tell me," Ronan said. "He couldn't have known that shadowmongrel would be there. Why would he save me?"

To earn trust, Eira thought. This was exactly the kind of ploy that Firekin would try. Then again, they had already assumed that the king was in some kind of danger. That's partially why they had captured Khartsaga in the first place. So it wasn't really new information. It just confirmed what they had feared.

"I don't know if he's telling the truth, but I do know this," Alvina said. "Khartsaga has been the king's advisor for centuries. I'm sure that fit Firekin's needs at first, but now they want more. With the recent death of the king's son, Khartsaga is legally the new heir. They don't want or need a puppet king. They want the whole throne."

Eira nodded in agreement, watching as Ronan's eyes glazed over at the mention of the newborn's death.

"So what do we do?" Einar asked. "Barge into the castle and kidnap the king next?"

"That's exactly what we're going to do," Alvina replied.

"I know at times my wit can be confusing, but surely you realize I was joking," Einar said.

Alvina held his gaze without cracking any hint of a smile.

Eira shook her head in disbelief. "You can't be serious. How would we even get close to the king with Firekin hovering over him like a mother phoenix?"

"We do what we always do," Alvina said. "We plan. Scaling the walls isn't hard with the right equipment, and if we bring enough Inhibitor darts we can get past the guards."

That had been enough to get them into the castle before, but infiltrating would be even more difficult this time. Ukhel's defenses would be stronger by now.

"Assuming we can survive long enough to find the king, how would we convince his majesty to come with us?" Einar asked.

Alvina paused, looking off into the forest. "We can't."

"The whole city will be after us," Holt grumbled.

"That's why we don't bring him back here," Alvina explained. "We'll take him into the mountains and convince him to join us."

"He's not going to trust us if we capture him," Einar argued.

This discussion was going nowhere. Of course the king wouldn't trust them. They had already broken into his castle once and captured his advisor. What they really needed to do was figure out a way to kill Ukhel.

"We could bring Khartsaga," Ronan suggested.

Everyone glanced from Ronan to the Gurvel who was staring at the leaves above him. Bring Khartsaga? What was Ronan getting at? She felt the edges of his mind and was surprised to find regret. He didn't want them to attempt this mission. It was too risky.

"I'm serious," he said. "The king trusts Khartsaga. If he comes, we might not need to capture the king."

"It might work," Einar said slowly. "But we can't trust Khartsaga."

"We can keep giving him Inhibitor injections," Ronan replied. "I don't like this plan either, but without Eira I'd be dead, so I'm choosing to help you. For there to be any chance of survival, we need to bring Khartsaga."

He set his jaw and looked them each in the eye. For someone who wouldn't live to see a century pass, he had so much determination. When he looked at her, Eira felt the heat rise to her cheeks.

"It might work," she admitted, quickly regaining control of her thoughts before anyone noticed. Einar raised one of his eyebrows ever so slightly. Nothing ever got past him.

"It's settled. Let's start making preparations," Alvina ordered. "We leave first thing in the morning."

CHAPTER 28

Shifting Loyalties

*The Forestdwellers taught him about the art of listening. With nature
as his guide, Ravenel learned how to use his mind
in ways previously unknown to the world.*

Khartsaga

KHARTSAGA OPENED HIS EYES with a start. Mere moments ago he was plummeting to his death. Something woke him from his nightmare. The sound of his heart thudded heavily against his eardrums. This time, when peering over the edge of the cliff he had seen Ronan standing beside his tormented mother. Then the ledge had crumbled beneath him.

Before him lay the unconscious forms of Edalene and Holt, the two humans who had been guarding him that night. Except for the soft sound of moss frogs chirping in the trees, everything was quiet. The ropesnare loosened around his arms. He craned his neck around and saw a familiar tall form with crimson skin.

Khartsaga's heart plummeted. "Tarkhan?" he whispered.

"Your father is disappointed that you didn't find a way to escape on your own," the assistant said while hastily untying Khartsaga's hands. "He sent me to collect you."

"How did you find me?"

Tarkhan stood and ushered for Khartsaga to follow. "When the Eternal Flame called upon my services, I followed your tracks into the forest. Your father will be pleased with my success."

Khartsaga hesitated. The thought of going back didn't settle well in his stomach.

"What's wrong?" Tarkhan asked. "Are you injured?"

Khartsaga looked back at the camp. Torchlight flickered against the wooden buildings that the humans had constructed. What was wrong with him? He should be relieved that Tarkhan was here. Freedom was mere steps away and yet something felt wrong about returning. He had been alone without his father's guidance for an entire week. At first he had been terrified, but now he found himself reluctant to give up his independence. "I don't want to go back," he said.

Tarkhan's expression darkened. "Your father will not be pleased with how far you've slipped from the truth."

A cold flash passed through Khartsaga's core. His father would be livid to learn that he had recited the Fire Creed fewer times each day since his capture.

Cries of alarm broke the silent night. They had been spotted. Tarkhan grabbed Khartsaga's arm and pulled him toward the cinnamon grass, but before they reached the edge, Tarkhan suddenly turned around and started heading toward the camp's center.

"What are you doing?" Khartsaga cried.

Tarkhan stopped hard in his tracks and began scanning the shadows. "I was blinded by an illusion."

Khartsaga couldn't see Eira but she had to be close. Creating an illusion took a lot of concentration, so Seyrs didn't move around nearly as much as Manipulators did. That's why Seyrs never fought in The Games; unless you were the one being attacked there was nothing to watch.

Tarkhan quickly pulled out a vial of Verdant Stimulant and downed it. With a sly smile, he held out his hand toward a stack of firewood propped up against a building and shot the pieces through the darkness where they collided with a veiled figure. Eira. One of the many benefits of the new Stimulant included the ability to pierce through the mind barriers of hidden Seyrs.

Using the distraction to his advantage, Khartsaga ran toward the line of grass surrounding the camp. This was it. His chance to escape and redeem himself. Of course his punishment for being captured would be severe, but afterward the New Age would make all things right.

Except all things wouldn't be right. King Chono would be dead and the Scarletts would be hunted and killed.

Reaching out with his arm to brush the grass aside, Khartsaga briefly caught sight of the red forest beyond before someone tackled him to the ground. Heavy footsteps pounded around his head as he was swiftly surrounded and held down.

Off to the left, Tarkhan was in the thick of combat. Scarletts, dressed in hastily clad clothes, shot darts in his direction. Under normal circumstances Tarkhan wouldn't have had any trouble fighting them, but he hadn't accounted for the two Speki who attacked him with a combination of illusions and projectiles.

The battle took a turn for the worse as the Speki forced Tarkhan closer to the Scarletts. Khartsaga tried shaking off his captors so he could help, but two more Scarletts joined the others in holding him down.

Tarkhan backed toward the edge of camp as it became apparent to all that he was losing. Khartsaga struggled more aggressively. If he didn't return with Tarkhan tonight, he might miss the dawn of the New Age. He could already feel his father's disappointment settling over him like a wet blanket.

However, if he didn't return, perhaps it would delay King Chono's death. His father would eventually move on without him, but maybe it would be enough time for King Chono to escape before it was too late.

No. Such thoughts were heresy. The New Age must come. No matter the cost.

"I'll return with help!" Tarkhan yelled before running into the Scarlet forest.

A few of the Scarletts chased after him, but they wouldn't catch him. The Verdant Stimulant didn't last long, but Tarkhan still had a few more minutes of enhanced powers.

That was it, then. He had failed again. Khartsaga tried to console himself with the hope that King Chono might be able to escape, but the odds were too slim. His father would have taken precautions against that.

Alvina and the Speki strode toward Khartsaga while the Scarletts restraining him pulled him onto his feet. Ronan ran over from a nearby building, his hair still ruffled from sleep. Of all the Scarletts, he was the only one who didn't seem angry or frightened of him.

"What do we do with him now?" Einar asked with a sigh.

"If we kill him, it will be easier on our resources," Eira responded dryly.

Afraid to hear the consensus, Khartsaga looked to Alvina. Of course they would want to kill him. Why would they keep him as a prisoner any longer?

"We're not going to kill him," Alvina said firmly.

Khartsaga relaxed slightly but kept an eye on Eira. His predicament was precarious. He had already told them that Firekin was planning to replace the king. Now he was useless to them.

A man with a burn scar on his face approached Khartsaga with a fresh dose of Inhibitor. He braced for the injection, but Alvina stepped forward and put a hand on the man's shoulder.

"Wait," she said, stepping closer to Khartsaga. "You don't want King Chono to die. Why else would you tell us Firekin's plans?"

Khartsaga remained silent.

The Scarletts that had run after Tarkhan walked back into the camp empty handed. Eira cursed under her breath. "He'll lead them back here."

"We need to make our move. Tonight," Alvina said.

Einar folded his arms and shook his head. "We're not ready."

"We don't have a choice," Alvina replied, turning back to Khartsaga. "You could have killed Ronan earlier today, but you didn't. Then you told us Firekin's plans to kill the king. I'm willing to bet that if you had the chance to save King Chono, you would do it. Wouldn't you?"

The woman was serious, and unlike the glares he could feel from Eira and Einar, there was no hatred in her eyes.

"The king doesn't trust us, but he might trust you," she continued. "Will you help us?"

Again, Khartsaga remained silent. If he helped them, it would mean forsaking everything he had ever lived for. The king must die in order for the New Age to come. He didn't like it, but that's the way it needed to be. His father, the Eternal Flame, had decreed it.

And yet, his father had also taught him that humans were just another species of animal. Now he wasn't so sure about that fact. Could his father be mistaken? And if he were wrong about that, was it possible that he was mistaken about the New Age too?

"I'll take your silence as a 'yes,'" Alvina said. "Eira, can you read his mind to make sure?"

"Not until the Inhibitor wears off and only if he's willing," she replied, shooting him a look of disgust.

"Will you let Eira read your mind?" Alvina asked him.

Khartsaga pursed his lips. It was against everything he had ever been taught, not to mention the searing pain of having one's mind read. But then the thought of his mother standing at the bottom of the cliff, tears streaming down her face, pervaded his thoughts. Maybe helping the humans didn't go against *everything* he had ever been taught. His mother would have been heartbroken to hear about what he had done to the newborn prince. If she knew what was about to happen to the king, surely she would want him to intervene. With hesitation, he nodded to Alvina.

"Let the Inhibitor wear off," Alvina ordered. "Until then, tie him to the tree. We'll prepare as much as we can in the meantime."

Once he was secured to the tree and left alone with his thoughts, Khartsaga looked up at the red leaves and the stars that burned in the darkness above. Was everything he had ever been taught a lie? Someone walked over to him but he didn't tear his gaze away from the sky. The shimmering lights were so stable and calm.

"My father used to teach me about the constellations when I was a child," Ronan said. "On clear nights like this, it's reassuring to see them up there, shining just like they always used to."

They stood there watching the sky and listening to the soft chirping of moss frogs as firebugs drifted lazily past them with a faint red glow. His father had never shown him anything like this.

"What changed your mind?" Ronan asked. "Why help us now?"

Khartsaga grimaced and tore his eyes away from the stars to look at him. "I was taught as a child that humans were more like chroma snails than Gurvel. My father assured me that you and the others were just a drain on society's resources. He told me that all the other races—human, Speki, Forestdweller— were inferior to us.

"It has always been my destiny to eventually take my father's place as the Eternal Flame. That's why I became the king's advisor. So that I could help the king make decisions that would bring the Gurvel closer to the New Age. But a couple of centuries ago, I started to waver."

He paused, remembering the first time his father had told him about the plan to kill the Speki. He had been less experienced then and unable to articulate his thoughts.

"My father told me we needed to destroy the Speki because they were draining our Stimulant resources. Later, I found out that they were also hiding valuable information that was needed for the New Age. However, even after learning *why* their demise had been necessary, I could never shake the guilt."

"It sounds like your dad is pretty manipulative," Ronan said.

"What do you mean? He does what is necessary."

"He never lets you think for yourself," Ronan countered. "Have you ever done anything you wanted to do? Or have you always been forced to do his will? Forced to hurt innocent people?"

Khartsaga was taken aback. The New Age had always been more important than individual desires. Each Firekin member was supposed to forsake their own wants. Once, as a child, he had begged his father for a pet, like a moss frog or a cat, but that had been a long time ago. He couldn't recall any other desires—until today when he had decided to save the king.

"I don't know what I want," Khartsaga said softly. He looked away from Ronan. Attendants like Tarkhan had always snapped him out of this line of thinking. The minute he showed signs of uncertainty they had always guided him back to the truth.

"What about The Games? Was that your father's idea too?" Ronan asked with an edge to his voice.

"Yes," Khartsaga said. "In the New Age, The Games are a reminder of our superiority, so we increased the frequency."

"It's a bloodbath."

Ronan was right, but somehow after a cleansing from his father, The Games had almost seemed enjoyable. "Bloodbath or not, it's a part of the New Age," Khartsaga insisted. "Just like the death of the queen and heir."

Ronan visibly tensed. "Wait," he whispered. "It was you. Wasn't it? You used me."

A shiver passed through Khartsaga. Besides his father and Tarkhan, no one else knew that he had forced Ronan to kill the queen and prince.

Cold fury drained Ronan's face of color. He raised a fist as if he intended to strike Khartsaga, but then he stopped and let his arm fall back to his side. Without uttering a word he turned away and dropped to his knees.

Khartsaga considered breaking the silence to apologize, but he couldn't find the words. None of the explanations or sentiments floating across his thoughts sounded right. Finally, the mind fog dissipated, but even without the Inhibitor he was left speechless.

A warm breeze blew through the camp and rustled the leaves in the branches as Eira and Alvina walked toward them. At their approach, Ronan sluggishly rose to his feet. While calmer than before, Eira still glared at Khartsaga with a seething hatred that was practically tangible. Fear gripped Khartsaga's heart. What would they do when they discovered that he was behind the queen's death?

"Are you ready, Khartsaga?" Alvina asked.

"Yes." It would hurt, of course. It always did.

Eira stepped right up next to him. "Pay attention, Ronan. This is an advanced technique."

Ronan watched stoically, but refused to meet Khartsaga's eyes.

The front of Khartsaga's head prickled as the mind reading began.

Astonishingly, he wasn't overcome with sharp, debilitating pain like he was used to. In fact as Eira pushed further into his mind, he felt no pain at all. Her presence felt cool, like the rain on a warm summer's day. Keeping his mind open for her was easier than he had anticipated.

"He's conflicted, that's for sure," Eira said finally, opening her eyes as she pulled out of his mind. "But I'm not detecting any deception. He intends to help save the king."

"That will have to do," Alvina decided, starting to untie Khartsaga. "We need to leave. Stay close to Eira or Einar at all times. Tonight, if we want to save the king, we'll need to work together. Understand?"

Khartsaga rubbed his wrists and nodded in affirmation. He wanted to test out his powers but decided against it when he noticed Eira eyeing him skeptically.

Next to the firepit, Wren made wild gestures at Holt, his tail whipping back and forth vigorously. Holt responded with similar gestures until Wren turned around and walked away, hands clenched into fists at his side.

Holt watched the boy leave and then walked over to the tree.

"Everything okay?" Alvina asked.

"Wren wanted to come with us. Said he was ready after all the training."

Einar chuckled as he joined them. "You have one brave kid, Holt."

Holt grunted in response. "Are we ready?"

After checking their gear, Alvina led them through the wall of cinnamon grass and into the shadows of the Scarlet Forest. They had a decent chance of convincing the king to come with them—as long as they didn't run into Khartsaga's father. The saliva on his tongue ran dry. After his recent decisions, he would rather return to the shadowmongrel's lair than face his father's wrath.

CHAPTER 29

Save the King

*As Ravenel improved his skills, the Forestdwellers
taught him how to make vim tea.*

Eira

THE REDS IN THE FOREST appeared a darker shade of purple in the pale moonlight. The small party ran through the trees, only stopping occasionally to catch their breath. They had to get to the castle by morning or risk the Gurvel returning in full force. Alvina had already ordered the rest of the rebels to move the camp to their second location as a failsafe. That would buy them some time, but once the Gurvel knew the rebels were somewhere in the Scarlet forest, they would hunt them down until they were completely destroyed.

Off in the distance an animal, likely a squirrel, rustled the leaves as it moved from tree to tree. Odd time for a squirrel to be searching for nuts, but then again this was the Scarlet Forest. Everything was different here.

Soon her mind wandered, distracted by the fight with that Gurvel, Tarkhan. He was obviously a Manipulator, and yet that green Stimulant he ingested had given him the ability to use Seyring techniques, just like the cultists guarding the king. Gritting her teeth, Eira jumped over a fallen tree and followed Alvina around a large boulder. How many of those Stimulants did Firekin have?

Eventually the shrubs and leaves around them changed from red to green as they neared Galynkhot. She ducked under a low-hanging branch and checked the vials in her bag. They had been able to make more Prime Stimulant with the toracini mushrooms, but it was only enough for one or two uses. Khartsaga had also warned them that the shadowmongrels might be guarding the castle as an extra precaution. If needed, she could take an Inhibitor, but it would greatly reduce her effectiveness.

At the front, Alvina signaled for them to stop. The forest was quiet except for a few crickets and a distant phoenix cry. Whatever had been moving around in the trees earlier had grown silent as well. Beside her, Khartsaga leaned up against an ashbark tree to catch his breath. He was drenched in sweat from the exertion. They had slowed their pace more than she had wanted to, but not just for Khartsaga. Despite his attempts to hide it, the pace was difficult for Ronan to keep as well. He was getting stronger, but was continuing to heal both physically and mentally.

Alvina turned around and faced them all. "We're near the edge of the forest. This is going to be dangerous, but we have some advantages they won't be expecting." She smiled and looked each one of them in the eye. "We have the element of surprise. Even if that Gurvel from before has alerted them, they won't expect us to make our move in the same night. Plus, now we have two Manipulators and two Seyrs."

Eira raised an eyebrow but kept her mouth shut. They still couldn't trust Khartsaga. So far he had been honest, but there was a deep sense of confusion and internal tension swirling around in his subconscious. Telling the truth in one moment didn't guarantee that someone wouldn't change their mind later. She kept an eye on him, but he was harmless at the moment, bending over beside the group to catch his breath. Besides the untrustworthy Gurvel, Alvina had also counted Ronan in her estimates. He was progressing quickly, but he was by no means an asset yet.

It didn't matter though. Eira had her own plans. Once they made it into the castle, she was going to find Ukhel, the mastermind of all of this, and kill him. The rest of the party could get the king to safety, but she was going to do what she came for. Helping the Scarletts had always been a detour.

Einar elbowed her as his warm voice filled her mind. *"Don't look now, but I think a squirrel built a nest in your hair while we were running."*

She frowned and quickly ran her fingers through the strands to get the frizz out while inwardly pushing down the knot in her stomach. She had never gotten around to telling him about her plan.

"Let's go," Alvina said with a sly smile. This time they walked slowly and quietly through the forest, its colors becoming more vivid around them as the sun rose in the distance. Before long they reached the edge of the treeline that bordered the crop fields.

"They're empty," Ronan noted with furrowed brows.

"That's good, no one will see us," Eira said, taking a step out of the forest.

Ronan caught her arm and pulled her back. "No, that's not normal. The farmers are usually out working before sunrise."

"Maybe they're at The Games. Aren't they required to attend?" Alvina asked.

Concern flashed to the front of Ronan's forethoughts. "The Games aren't usually this early."

While her pupil had been improving, sudden emotions were still difficult for him to block. Regardless of how he felt, they didn't have much choice. They needed to move now or they would lose the element of surprise, and at the moment it was one of their few actual assets.

"We'll have to chance it," Alvina said resolutely.

Ronan looked up and met Eira's eyes briefly before looking away and releasing her arm.

The group ran across the open field, checking for guards in the dim light of dawn. When she made it to the city wall, she crouched down and waited for the others to gather. No alarms were raised, so Holt quietly handed out climbing gloves. They hadn't brought the boots this time, but the gloves would suffice. She monitored Khartsaga's emotions again. At the moment he seemed stable. His gloves were too small, but he squeezed them on just enough to be able to use them.

Alvina held a finger to her lips and pointed upward. A guard walked by on patrol but luckily didn't look down. Once he had passed by, they scaled the wall and climbed down the other side into the king's garden. They hid among a cluster of large bushes and waited a few moments to make sure they hadn't been seen.

"It's been awhile since we've had such a high-profile mission." Einar's voice echoed in Eira's head. She smiled and peeked around one of the bushes.

"Just don't trip on your boots like that one time," she thought back, playing the memory in her mind.

Einar rolled his eyes. *"I'm never going to live that one down, am I?"*

"Not likely."

"The side door has three guards this time," Alvina whispered. "Holt, Eira, and I will use the sleep darts at the same time. Then we'll continue to the back of the castle where Eira and I escaped through the window. We might need to break it again if they've fixed it."

Something scraped against the Sklera wall behind them. Whipping her head around, Eira saw and felt nothing. Probably just a branch. She shook her head to clear her senses and followed Alvina from bush to bush, carefully making her way toward the side castle door.

In unison, she, Alvina, and Holt shot darts at the guards. Once they were knocked out, they made their way toward the back window. New stained glass sat in the hole they had created, surrounded by wooden supports that connected it to the Sklera. All they had to do was remove some of the beams to get in.

Without hesitation they climbed the wall together and waited while she felt for any life presences nearby. Not sensing anyone beyond their party, she quietly removed enough of the supports to create a space between the glass and Sklera. With ease she slid herself through.

While everyone else climbed into the hallway, she moved up against the king's door. She thought about taking the Prime Stimulant so she could sense who was on the other side, but she needed to save it for Ukhel.

"Is there a draft in here?" Einar whispered.

Now that he mentioned it, she noticed how chilled the air around them had become. Everyone froze as realization dawned on them. Eira gripped the Inhibitor at her side but didn't take it just yet. She needed her powers to kill Ukhel.

She held her breath and listened for any signs of movement, but the silence around them was deafeningly loud. On the other end of the hallway, a slight shift in the shadows drew her attention. She peered into the darkness. Or was it the shadows themselves that had moved? She shivered unconsciously as the creature began to pry at her mind.

"It's not a wild shadowmongrel. We need to find whoever is controlling it," Khartsaga whispered.

He was right. The shadow stayed where it was, watching them as if waiting for a command. There was no one else in the hallway that she could see, unless the controller was behind the shadows.

"Well done, Son," a voice said, off in the distance, crashing through the silence. "That was quick reasoning. Why can't you think like that more often?"

Khartsaga tensed beside her, a flash of fear passing over him before he hid it. The voice had to be coming from Ukhel. This was the Gurvel who had ruined her life. Tortured her people. Destroyed her home. Despite the cold air, heat flooded her veins as ire rose up within her.

"Forget him," Alvina whispered. "We're here for the king."

She threw open the king's door with a quiet thud muffled by the shadowmongrel's silence. They filed quickly into the room as the shadows began to slide silently toward them, dampening the light streaming in from the new window. Still in the hall, Eira couldn't make out any forms, but she did see two small yellow pinpricks staring at her from the center of the shadow. Dread settled in her stomach as she made eye contact with it. With effort, she tore her gaze away and entered the king's room. Holt shut the door behind her and leaned against it to brace it.

Khartsaga took in a sharp breath beside her, drawing her attention to the large bed across from them. Sitting on the plush covers, Tarkhan smiled at them, drumming his fingers next to the dagger sticking out of the king's chest. They were too late.

"You missed the start of the New Age, Khartsaga," Tarkhan said, continuing to tap his fingers. "Your father was so disappointed you weren't here to see it."

A wave of fear passed through Khartsaga again as he looked from the corpse to Tarkhan. Eira was about to push a little further into his thoughts to make sure he wasn't about to change sides out of shock, but the door behind them began to open.

"Abandon the plan," Alvina said sharply, running toward a large set of wooden double doors on the other side of the room that opened onto a balcony.

Eira stayed where she was, watching as everyone but Khartsaga followed Alvina. He was still in shock and hadn't moved either. Moonlight streamed into the room as Alvina flung open the doors.

This was her chance. Ukhel stepped into the room as Eira turned to face him. Out of the corner of her eye, she saw Einar pause and look back. Sensing her plan, he shook his head.

"Sorry, brother. It's too good an opportunity to pass up."

Eira poured a small amount of Prime Stimulant into her mouth, focusing on her breathing as the familiar bitter taste hit her tongue. Power surged through her body, enhancing her ability to sense the people around her. More ready than she had ever been before, she pulled out her dagger and crouched low to look for a point of weakness.

Ukhel tilted his head to look at her. His hair was as white as her own, with flecks of gray mixed in, and he stood so straight and calm that for a moment Eira second-guessed her decision to stay and fight. But the memory of what this Gurvel had done to her people quickly replaced her doubt. Gritting her teeth, she stood her ground and met his gaze.

"A Speki," Ukhel observed, smiling at her from the doorway. "I haven't seen one of your kind in centuries."

Einar ran over and tried to grab her sleeve but she stepped out of the way and lunged at Ukhel, aiming her dagger at his chest. To confuse him,

160

she simultaneously projected an illusion of herself jumping toward his head. Ukhel's eyes followed her illusion, but at the last second he raised his hand up and caught her wrist, the blade inches from his chest. She broke free of his grip and projected another illusion of herself slashing the dagger at him so she could get away. Instead of dodging the fake image, Ukhel stepped through her illusion and grabbed her arm again. So the Eternal Flame was a Seyr.

Eira tried to pull free but this time his grip was too strong. He twisted her arm and forced her to drop the dagger. She grunted as it clattered to the floor. Reflexively, she tried to pry his mind open, but his defenses were too strong. There was no way in.

Another dagger shot toward Ukhel, but before it could reach him, it froze in the air, hovering inches away from his eye.

"Two Speki. This is a special occasion indeed," Ukhel said.

Einar shot his arms out to the side and brought them together quickly, Manipulating a set of chairs and a bedside table to fly toward Ukhel from either side of the room. Again, the objects froze inches from Ukhel's face before they crashed to the ground. Eira stared up at the Gurvel, still trying to pull her arm free. He hadn't even blinked when he countered Einar's attack.

Seeing their fight, Ronan and the others turned from the balcony and rushed back into the room. Holt shot a few darts, but none of them made contact with the Ukhel's skin. He was always a step ahead of them, reading their minds a moment before they attacked. That meant he had to be a Seyr, but then how had he stopped Nar's attacks?

She looked around and spotted an empty vial with a few green flecks stuck to the side. It was the same Stimulant that Tarkhan had used earlier that night. Ukhel looked down at her with a wide toothy grin.

A smoke grenade flew through the air toward Ukhel, but it paused in midair and then flew into the hallway as a group of cultists rushed into the room. They were surrounded. Why had the others followed her? This was supposed to be her mission. She had known how dangerous it was, but even so she hadn't expected Ukhel to be so strong.

Ukhel handed her off to one of the guards who immediately injected her with an Inhibitor. Her mind fogged over instantly as she watched the guards grab hold of the others.

"There's one more," Ukhel said, walking over to the corner of the room. He reached his hand out toward the wall and grabbed at the air. The shadows shimmered slightly, revealing Wren's small form, camouflaged against the Sklera.

Holt made a guttural sound in his throat as Ukhel passed the boy to one of the guards. Wren must have followed behind them, hiding his thoughts the way Einar had taught him to. Thinking back, she had heard him jumping through the trees, but his mind had been hidden the whole time. Even with the Prime Stimulant she hadn't been able to sense his presence. Whatever Stimulant Ukhel had taken was incredibly dangerous if it had allowed him to find Wren. Seemingly unperturbed, Ukhel stood watching all of them with his hands clasped before him, as if observing some kind of interesting performance.

CHAPTER 30

Reunion

*They told him that vim tea was as old as the mountains
and gave new knowledge to those who drank its leaves.*

Ronan

RONAN'S HEART POUNDED IN HIS chest as the guard's grip tightened around his arms. Khartsaga's father paced slowly in front of them with his golden cape glinting in the torchlight. Despite the fight they had just had, there wasn't a white hair out of place on his head.

"That's better," the Eternal Flame said. "Now that we've calmed down, allow me to introduce myself. I am Ukhel, the Eternal Flame of Firekin."

He stopped in front of Ronan and looked at him intently for a moment before walking over to Khartsaga. "What an interesting day. One moment you're setting up a coronation event and the next you're welcoming back your long-lost son."

Ronan glanced at the others. Eira and Einar were both pale and their violet eyes were glazed over. Alvina glared at Ukhel with a firm jaw, but Holt kept his attention on Wren who looked like he was trying very hard to keep his bottom lip from quivering. They needed to get out of here.

"Welcome home, Son," the Eternal Flame said, dismissing the guards that were holding Khartsaga with a wave of his hand. Ronan was relieved to see that Khartsaga didn't return his father's greeting. At the moment, he might be their best chance of survival.

Ukhel frowned and stepped closer to Khartsaga until he was inches from his face. "Tarkhan returned to us earlier this night with some unsettling news. He said you had the opportunity to return with him but refused to leave. Is this true?"

"Yes," Khartsaga answered, looking down at the floor.

"I see. And now you're working with these animals? Why, Son?"

"Because you lied to me," Khartsaga said, clenching his hand into a fist.

The guards around Ronan shifted uncomfortably as Ukhel's expression turned blank for a moment. Even if Khartsaga decided to side with the Scarletts, his father had too much control. The situation was crumbling like ashbark. Ronan tugged against the guard's grip again.

"Son, I've never lied to you," Ukhel said, his voice slow and even. "Why would you claim such a thing?"

Khartsaga looked up and locked eyes with his father. "You taught me that humans were stupid creatures with no aptitude for innovation or strategy. And yet they managed to kidnap me. And they developed a method for not only surviving in the Scarlet Forest but thriving there. They're not incapable. In fact, even this Forestdweller has shown himself to be highly capable when you claimed their race was the weakest of all."

The room went completely silent as even the guards held their breath. Ronan kept his eyes on Khartsaga. Their lives depended on whether he could convince his father to let them live or not.

Finally, Ukhel grinned and placed his hand on Khartsaga's shoulder. "Son, you've been under heavy Inhibitors for days. Your thoughts are muddled and confused. Listen to yourself. I've taught you better than this. Everything you just claimed can be explained.

"Like a pack of wolves, the humans have learned how to group together and capture their target. Like a flock of phoenix, they've discovered how to live in the Scarlet Forest. Like a nursing mother cat, they've decided to care for a creature not their own flesh and blood. These are all traits that we can find in nature. That doesn't mean they possess sentience or that their lives are worth as much as a Gurvel's life."

Ronan's heart sank as he watched Khartsaga frown in concentration. He was considering it. After everything he had seen. Even after saving Ronan's life, Khartsaga was still wavering internally. Suddenly his mind was filled with the image of Wren and Eira's ashen bodies beside the cold embers of a pyre. No. There had to be a way to stop this.

"That's twisting the truth," Ronan said, gritting his teeth. The Gurvel guarding him tightened his grip. Ukhel smiled in response, not taking his eyes off of his son.

Khartsaga turned to look at Ronan and held his gaze for a moment. Then he turned back to his father and took a step back. "You've never let me choose the things I want to do."

Ukhel's smile vanished.

"My whole life, you've told me what you want me to become. But you've never let me choose what I want to do."

A vein in the side of Ukhel's neck bulged slightly, but otherwise he was expressionless. He was going to kill them all. And Ronan would have to watch. Again.

"You have given up so much for our cause, Son, suffering alone for centuries without your brothers and sisters to surround you." Ukhel looked around at the guards. "I think it's time we let Khartsaga choose something that he wants to do. He's right! The New Age is upon us! It is time for rewards and celebration! And what is it that you want, Son?"

The ridges above Khartsaga's eyes bent in concentration. Ronan gritted his teeth. This guy's father had complete control over him.

"I don't know," Khartsaga said.

Ukhel nodded and rubbed his chin. "Well now, let's see. Ever since you were a child you begged me for a pet. I think it's high time I let you have one." He waved his hand toward Ronan and the others. "Choose one."

A cold shiver passed through Ronan. He didn't like where this was headed. Beside him, Alvina and Holt froze as well.

"What?" Khartsaga asked.

"Choose one of these humans to be your pet," Ukhel repeated. "This is the New Age now, and I think a pet would help remind you of your superiority to these animals."

For a moment, Khartsaga's mouth opened partially in surprise as if he were going to respond, but he quickly shut it after looking at the guards who were nodding in agreement.

"The ones you don't choose will be sent to The Games or the mines with the rest of the humans in the city," Ukhel continued. "Except for those two." He pointed at Eira and Einar. "We can learn a lot from the Speki. Take them to a holding cell."

The guards holding Eira and Einar raised their fists up to their foreheads and lowered them to their hearts before leaving the room. A salute for the king.

"Now, Son," Ukhel said, "make your choice, and just for fun, I'll choose one as well."

"When I said I wanted a pet, I meant a cat or a moss frog," Khartsaga said, staring off to the side.

"Oh, nonsense. Those creatures are pathetic. The new king deserves a better pet than that." Ukhel put both hands on Khartsaga's shoulders and turned him around so he was facing the humans.

Heat rose to Ronan's face as he watched Khartsaga look slowly from Wren down to him. There was a balcony in the room, but even if they could all manage to break free from the guards, there was no way they could fight them all.

"Pick one, or I'll pick one for you," Ukhel said.

Hesitantly, Khartsaga stepped toward Wren. The boy stared up at him with wide eyes, his tail curling around his ankles. He was so small compared to the Gurvel, barely up to his waist.

"Then, I'd like to take this one," Khartsaga said.

To the side, Holt's muscles tightened against the guard's grip but he kept silent. Wren wouldn't suffer whatever the rest of them would, but the situation was still horrible.

Ukhel just shook his head and smiled. "You've always gravitated toward the weakest animal in the room. But I always keep my word. You may take the small Forestdweller. Now it's my turn."

He stepped up to Holt and looked him up and down before shaking his head and moving on to Alvina. Stroking his chin, he looked her over briefly but again shook his head. The hair on the back of Ronan's neck stood on end as the Eternal Flame stepped in front of him. As Ukhel looked him up and down, a familiar prickling sensation touched his mind. Ronan's heartbeat quickened. Ukhel knew he was a Seyr.

"I like this one," Ukhel said. "Guards, take the other two down to the mines."

As the guards pulled them out the door, Alvina locked eyes with him for one last moment. He wondered which fate was worse. Forced labor in the mines or whatever becoming a "pet" entailed. A cold chill settled in his stomach— given the choice, he would have gone to the mines.

"Aren't you mad at me, Father?" Khartsaga asked.

"Mad at you, Son?" Ukhel responded, walking over to the bed where the dead king lay. "No, this isn't your fault. It's mine. I never should have left you alone for so long. Even the best of us can forget the truth if left alone."

He picked up a vial filled with black liquid on a nightstand and walked back over to Khartsaga. Not wanting to draw more attention to himself or Wren, Ronan was content to watch and observe for now. He had to find a way for them to escape.

"You need to be purified after your time away," Ukhel stated.

"I...understand," Khartsaga replied, shifting his gaze to the black Sklera floor.

The scrawny assistant, Tarkhan, stepped up beside Ukhel. "It's good to have you back, Khartsaga."

"We will have a double celebration tonight," Ukhel said, rolling the vial between his fingers as he spoke. "Now that my son is back, we can celebrate his return and crown him king in the same evening. The New Age is finally upon us."

"May the New Age rise," Khartsaga and all the guards said in unison. Ronan shivered and tensed his muscles against the guard still holding him. Were they all distracted enough for him to use an illusion? As the thought entered his head, Ukhel glanced at him from the side. Ronan's breath caught in his throat.

"Tarkhan, go find one of the pet groomers," Ukhel ordered. "We'll need to prepare these two for the celebration tonight."

Dread settled in his stomach as he watched Tarkhan salute Ukhel and walk out the door.

"While we wait, let's start your purification," Ukhel said, drinking the vial of black liquid.

Sweat beaded on Khartsaga's forehead as the room fell silent. The guards holding Ronan and Wren shifted their weight and each took small steps back. Khartsaga suddenly dropped to the ground, fists balled up in pain and eyes shut tight. Ronan winced as he watched Khartsaga stifle a grunt of pain, shaking as he knelt on the ground.

The cold knot that had formed in his stomach turned sour and churned within him. If this is what Ukhel was willing to do to his own son, what hope did he and Wren have? The Eternal Flame of Firekin smiled as he towered over Khartsaga and watched him suffer. Ronan turned his face away from the torture until Khartsaga's stifled groans stopped and turned into ragged breaths. Even the guards relaxed slightly when it was over, but not enough for Ronan to pull his arms free.

"We'll need a few more sessions to fully cleanse you, but this is a good start," Ukhel said, pocketing the empty vial. "Once you're fully under the truth of the Fire Creed again, I may even tell you what new Stimulant Tarkhan and I have been developing."

Still kneeling on the floor, Khartsaga looked up at Ukhel and nodded wordlessly, still trying to catch his breath. It looked like Khartsaga had no control of the situation. Ronan and Wren couldn't rely on him for help.

"You called for me, Eternal Flame?" said a squeaky voice from the doorway.

Ukhel nodded at a Gurvel who was carrying a large crate in his arms. It looked like it had been a rather difficult feat because next to the other Gurvel, he looked closer in height to a human.

"Thank you, Khurel, let's see what you have," Ukhel said, watching as the Gurvel set the crate down on the floor.

Heat rose to Ronan's face as he caught a glimpse of what was in the crate. Lying on top of some brightly patterned cloth lay two metal leashes and some bottles of what Ronan could only guess was hair dye.

CHAPTER 31

Darkness

A secret kept in mind. Feather. Ash. Crystal. Power combined.

Eira

THE DOOR CLOSED WITH a soft thud, leaving her and Einar in complete darkness. There were no torches in this cell, but from the feel of the floor and walls, the whole room was made of Sklera. She moved her hand along the length of the walls, trying to get a rough estimate of the size. There would barely be enough room for them both to lie down.

The significance of the guards keeping the two of them together was not lost on her. Ukhel wanted them to realize how gravely small their chance of escape was, even when they had the ability to plan together.

"That went well," Einar said from the other side of the cell.

"Please, not now, Nar. I'm not in the mood to laugh."

"Oh, I know, it was intended to be sarcastic." His voice had more chill than it normally did.

She couldn't see him in the dark, and the drugs made it impossible to feel his emotions or thoughts, but she knew her brother. The subtle edge in his voice would have gone unnoticed by someone less acquainted with him, but he was definitely upset. With good reason. "I'm angry too. These cultists are always one step ahead. It's like they—"

"No, Eira," he said curtly. "I'm not mad at them, I'm mad at you."

His reaction caught her off guard. He hadn't called her by her first name in centuries.

"You left the group to do what?" Einar asked. "Complete some glorified vengeance mission? Alone? When were you going to let me in on your plans?" He paused as if waiting for an answer, but she could only stand there in shock.

"Did you even stop to think about how much the group cares about you?" he asked. "Did you realize that *you* jeopardized the mission because *you* decided to act alone? They all ran after us, Eira. Not because they were trying to escape, but because they care about us. Not like you would understand. You've only cared about yourself since that stupid war."

"What?" Heat rose in her veins. "You mean the war that destroyed our city and our people? The war that left women and children mutilated in the streets? The war that destroyed our lives and took away every last thing we ever cared about? That war, Einar? Forgive me for wanting to stop the force that's now threatening to destroy another race of people."

"Wake up, Eira. You're not doing it to protect the humans. You don't even care about them. This has been a vengeance plan from the beginning, and you know it."

"I care about the humans! You think I want them to be enslaved?"

"You care about the humans? Really. Alright, name five of them. We were in their camp for weeks. Give me five names."

She took a step forward in the dark. "What does that prove?"

"Go on, if you really care about the humans, how many did you talk to?"

"Nar, you're being ridiculous."

"Five. Names," Einar said, stepping toward her.

"Fine!" Eira spat. This was pointless. Of course she knew five of the humans. "Alvina. Ronan. Holt." She paused, trying to recall other names. She remembered Holt's wife who healed them when they first arrived, but her name escaped her. There was the woman with purple strands of hair, but Eira had never really talked with her. Then there was the man with the scar on his face who had been with them during the corpse tree attack. But what was his name? That annoying bartender had been memorable, but his name wasn't coming to mind either. Now that she thought about it, she had spent most of her time with Alvina and Holt. If Ronan hadn't come along, she probably wouldn't have interacted with anyone else either.

"You never cared about them," Einar said quietly. She heard him take a few steps back and slide down the wall to the floor.

He was right. Somewhere in the past few centuries she had let her hatred of Firekin take control of every aspect of her life. But was that so horrible? So what if she hadn't learned five names? It was Nar's dream to get to know them, not hers. He was the one who wanted to teach students like Wren and Ronan.

Now he'll never get the chance, she thought, *because of me.* She slowly felt her way toward the far wall and slid down beside her brother. They sat in silence, leaning against the warm rock. Her head throbbed from raising her voice.

"Why do you care so much about them?" she asked into the dark.

"Because they're all that's left. Our people are gone, Sis. I'm angry at Firekin too. But sometimes I wonder if we're fighting the wrong battle. Maybe instead of trying to kill our way to victory, we could make more progress by teaching the humans about our people and discoveries. That way, when we die, someone will be left to remember."

Someone left to remember. They had hunted the Eternal Flame for centuries and when they finally had a chance to kill him, she had failed. Now what would become of her people? She and Einar would likely rot in this cell, if they were lucky, and all their knowledge would die with them. There would be no one left to gather their memories as was customary when a Speki died. That's when her people would truly be gone. The thought hadn't occurred to her before. She'd failed all of them.

"I'm sorry, Nar," she whispered. "This is all my fault. I wasn't strong enough."

Einar shifted position and set his hand on her shoulder. "You don't have to do this alone, Sis. We're a team, remember?"

She nodded, even though she knew Einar couldn't see her, and leaned up against him. They sat like that in the darkness until the reality of their situation started to sneak in. It was bad. They had been in some intense situations before, but this was worse. Even if they could escape this cell, the city would be filled with Firekin members.

"Got any bright ideas, Brother?" she asked, desperately hoping that he would have some kind of witty idea, even if it was a bad one.

"Not this time, I'm afraid."

Her small glimmer of hope dimmed until it was as dark as the cell. If even Einar couldn't see humor in a situation, their odds were slim to none.

They sat in the dark for hours until the door scraped open. Eira blinked profusely as light poured in from the hallway. A pair of hands yanked her up and pushed her roughly out of the cell. She tried to calm herself by gathering as much intel as she could.

She squinted up at the guard, ignoring the pounding in her skull. Like most of the other cultists, he wore only white pants. On a normal day she would be able to fight a grunt like this, but without her powers she didn't stand a chance.

Another cultist pulled Einar out of the cell and followed behind her. She hid her nervousness behind a scowl and continued studying their surroundings. Now that her eyes had adjusted, the torchlight flickering against the Sklera seemed dim. She counted the doors as they walked, trying to remember the layout. Four doors on the left, then a turn. Five more doors on the right. The cultist pulled Eira through the fifth door and lit the torches after consuming a Fire Stimulant. They must have abundant resources to use Stimulants so lavishly.

The room had four long tables with restraints lined along the back wall and shelves filled with a wide assortment of bottles, ingredients, and instruments. Her stomach clenched as she envisioned what kinds of tests the Gurvel intended to run on them. Assassin training had prepared them for torture, but that had been a long time ago. She still had scars from that lesson and didn't look forward to repeating the experience.

Two new cultists joined the guards and restrained Eira and Einar to separate tables. She tried to fight them off, but the drugs left even her muscles weak and lethargic. It was useless. Content with their handiwork, the cultists walked over to the shelves and began looking through the stockpile of ingredients.

Einar looked over at her and gave a half smile. If only she could hear his reassuring voice in her head. She tried sliding her hand out of the restraints, but they were almost tight enough to cut off her circulation. There had to be a way to escape. She racked her brain for ideas, but nothing came to mind except a splitting headache.

Soon the cultists began clinking around jars and mixing liquids over by the shelves. One of them came over to Eira and stuck her with a needle. She cringed as he extracted her blood and took the vial over to a table with more vials of dark liquid. Then he returned to extract some of Einar's blood.

"What's the blood for?" Einar asked.

None of the cultists even acknowledged that he had spoken. When she looked at her brother, ice flooded her veins. His violet eyes were usually so strong and cheerful, but now all she could see was fear.

CHAPTER 32
Celebration

These are the only words Ravenel ever revealed when questioned about the power he learned from the Forestdwellers.

Ronan

UKHEL LED RONAN AND WREN down the main hall which was lit with torches and decorated with golden streamers. Every room was full of Gurvel guests dressed in elaborate silky clothing, all of them designed to accentuate their crimson skin and tall physiques. Some of them chatted in the hallway and glanced at Ronan and Wren who were both dressed to play the part of Ukhel's pets. He refused to look any of them in the eye, but it was difficult to hide when you were forced to wear striped pants. They were dark blue, like the dye they had used on the ends of his hair.

Beside him, Wren shivered, but tried to keep his head up, his lips pursed in a brave show of courage. Neither of them had been given a shirt to go with the patterned pants, but the heat of anger kept the chill off of Ronan as they walked toward the flickering lights shimmering on the carpet outside the grand hall.

The drums grew louder as they walked. He clenched his jaw, feeling the paint on his face crack from the movement. This wasn't entirely new. He just needed to keep his head down like when he was a soldier. But this was worse. So much worse. Wren didn't deserve this. He needed to find a way to get him out of here.

Ukhel stopped just before the ballroom and bent down to look Ronan in the eye. "Listen closely, human, because I will only give you this warning once. You've been manipulating my son with your words and I won't have that. If I hear one more word come out of your mouth, today or any day, I will not hesitate to cut out your tongue. And I would relish the opportunity, so don't tempt me. You might think you have powers, but they will never amount to anything, so don't get any ideas, or I will punish you and your little Forestdweller friend. Do you understand?"

Ronan met his gaze, glaring into his yellow eyes. The Eternal Flame of Firekin didn't play games. For Wren's sake, he gave one curt nod. Satisfied, Ukhel smiled and jerked on their collars to lead them to the entrance of the grand ballroom.

At the archway, Wren stopped and stared in shock at the sheer number of people. It was packed with Gurvel dancing and moving around. The musicians were on the far side of the room playing on a raised platform; otherwise they likely wouldn't have had room. Ukhel pulled on the chains around their necks when he noticed that they had paused.

Ronan stumbled forward and helped Wren keep going. The poor kid shook and grabbed his ears as the shouts and fast music reverberated around them. Everyone was staring. Ronan could feel their eyes burning against his back, but he was powerless to stop them. All he could do was follow Ukhel. The crowd parted to let them through, pointing and laughing in delight as they passed by.

Anger burned in his stomach like a smoldering fire. This was beyond humiliating. His scalp still itched from the blue hair dye. The bright colors and busy patterns of the pants he was wearing were obviously meant to mimic the clothing that the rich put on their pets. The very thought of the word sent a jolt of nausea through his stomach.

Ukhel led them to the front of the room where the throne had been placed on another platform with a set of stairs leading up to it. With another tug at their collars, he led them up the stairs and stopped before the throne where Khartsaga was already seated. He wore the black uniform with gold and white embroidery that he used to wear with King Chono, only now he had a gold sash around his waist.

"Welcome, Father. You didn't miss much. The music just started. Ronan. Wren." Khartsaga gave them each a nod and a small smile.

Ronan met his gaze briefly and then looked out at the sea of dancing Gurvel. Many of them wore white pants and no shirt to show off their crimson skin. These weren't Galynkhot's regular citizens. They were all cultists. With the warm glow of the torches and chandeliers, the crowd looked almost like a fire flickering against the wind.

Ukhel yanked the leashes to get their attention and pointed to the top step. "Sit."

Not wanting to see Wren hurt, Ronan swallowed his anger and obeyed.

Ukhel sat down beside Khartsaga and attached the end of the leashes to his throne. "The day has finally come, Son! You should be proud of your accomplishments. Now all Gurvel will be able to attain their true calling."

"May the New Age rise and Gurvel prosper," Khartsaga said as if from habit.

Wren's eyes were wide and glazed over as he looked around the room at the dancing Gurvel. To his credit, he sat tall and didn't close his eyes to the scenes around him, but he did press his bat-like ears flat against the side of his head. Ronan scooted closer and pulled him close. They couldn't fight Ukhel, but maybe there was another way to escape. If he could distract Ukhel for long enough, Wren might be able to free himself and climb his way to freedom.

"Wren," he signed, *"tonight, you leave. Use window. Climb castle."* He wasn't fluent yet, but he had learned a few words here and there.

Wren pulled his hands away from his ears and winced from the music and general volume of voices. *"Not without you."*

"I can't climb. You can." Ronan tried his best to smile reassuringly. *"I'm okay."*

"Khartsaga knows I have powers," Wren signed.

He was right. Why hadn't he brought that up to his father yet? He had seen Wren practicing with Einar. Ronan turned his head to look at Khartsaga. The Gurvel was watching them curiously. Uhkel, on the other hand, was focused on the spice puffs that a waiter had brought over.

"Not important. Tonight, you escape. Okay?" Ronan signed, trying to hide the motions from Khartsaga.

Wren pursed his lips, hiding some of the purple paint on his mouth, and nodded. He raised his hands back to his ears and flattened them against the side of his head.

"Wren, come here," Khartsaga said, waving the boy over to the throne. Ukhel eyed his son skeptically.

Ronan tensed and watched with apprehension as Wren got up, but Khartsaga only took off the gold sash and wrapped it around Wren's head so that it covered his ears.

Ukhel raised one of the ridges above his eyes as he took a bite out of the spice puff. "What are you doing, Son?"

"He doesn't have hair. It just occurred to me that I could put a colorful sash or scarf on his head instead. And it goes with the rest of the outfit, doesn't it?" Khartsaga smiled at Wren and waved him back over to the stairs with Ronan.

Ukhel just shook his head and stood up. "Time for the speech." He took out a vial of amber liquid and downed its contents. With both hands he shot a large fire blast that burst in the air and drew the attention of the crowd. Everyone quieted down.

Ronan pulled Wren close again and looked at the sash. It was wrapped tight enough that it kept Wren's ears pinned against his head. The fabric likely helped muffle the sound too. He glanced back at Khartsaga who met his gaze for a fraction of a second and then stood up beside his father to address the crowd.

Ukhel raised a fist into the air as the crowd cheered. "Welcome, brothers and sisters, to the New Age!" He waited for them to quiet down again to continue. "For centuries we have waited for this very moment. It is time for our people to be glorified and raised up to their proper status! Tonight we crown our new king and tomorrow we will celebrate with The Games and a special Fire Festival!"

Ukhel grabbed Khartsaga's hand and raised it up in the air to which the crowd burst into more thunderous applause.

Wren winced at the sudden rise in volume but didn't raise his hands to his ears this time. It appeared the scarf was helping somewhat.

"Please, continue the celebration!" Ukhel waved at the band to start the music back up.

Most of the crowd went back to dancing or drinking refreshments, but not everyone. Rimming the sides of the room were King Chono's soldiers wearing expressions as dark as their uniforms. Ronan looked at their faces, wondering if he knew any of them. With a start he realized one of the guards was looking directly at him. Esen stood by one of the pillars to the right of the dance floor. He caught Ronan's eye and then weaved his way through the crowd toward the throne.

"Permission to approach the throne, Eternal Flame," Esen asked, saluting with a fist to his forehead. He adamantly snapped back to attention instead of moving his fist over his heart as was customary for the king.

"Granted," Ukhel said.

Esen walked up the stairs and stopped beside Ronan. "Congratulations on ushering in the New Age."

"May the New Age rise and Gurvel prosper," Khartsaga said with a nod. "What can we do for you, brother?"

"I have no needs, but I do have some questions. A couple of weeks ago I was assigned to the team that guarded the queen during childbirth. It was a rather odd night, don't you think? There were at least ten highly trained Manipulators and one Seyr—myself—on the squad that night. And yet one human somehow managed to get past all of them to kill the queen and newborn heir. Odder still is the fact that he sits here now. Last I heard, this man was sentenced to death by shadowmongrel despite never having a proper trial."

King Chono's flame on the front of Esen's uniform seemed to glimmer in the torchlight. Esen himself looked relaxed and calm, but his hand was still clenched into a fist by his side. Reaching out with his mind, Ronan couldn't feel anything from him. His thoughts and emotions were completely guarded.

"I think I heard about you," Ukhel said. "You're the Gurvel Seyr that tried to oppose the king's decision to have the human killed for such a horrific and treasonous act. I find it more strange that you would try to oppose a case with so many witnesses. Regardless, this is not the same human." Ukhel sat back in his throne with idle interest displayed across his face.

Esen looked down at Ronan and then back up at Ukhel with a raised eye ridge. "This is the man. I served on the same team as him."

"Humans all look alike, Soldier. Surely you're confused. Pet, come here." Ukhel tugged on the leash.

Ronan clenched his jaw and walked over to the throne.

"Pet, this Gurvel says he served on the same team as you once. What's his name?"

Ronan glared at Ukhel, but remained silent. He wasn't about to lose his tongue over this. He filled his mind with memories of their time serving together in case Esen tried to read his thoughts. Addressing the Eternal Flame so bluntly had to be dangerous and yet Esen had done so anyway. It gave him a small sliver of hope.

"See, if he had served with you like you say, he would surely have learned your name." Ukhel's voice was hard, insinuating a hidden edge to his jovial demeanor. "Go back to the party and enjoy yourself, soldier. The New Age has come! You need not worry about the lesser beings. They'll fall into their proper places."

Esen turned to Khartsaga. "As our new king, do you agree?"

Khartsaga sat up straighter. "Of course. That's the purpose of the New Age."

"Consider this. Perhaps true worth isn't in the length of a life or in the power of an individual. Perhaps it's inherent in them from conception." Esen held Khartsaga's gaze for a moment longer, then turned to leave. "Say what you will, Ukhel, but I was there. Ronan didn't kill the queen. Someone was controlling him, and your lack of concern speaks volumes." He nodded at Ronan and then weaved his way back into the throng of dancers.

"Why did you lie to him, Father?" Khartsaga asked. "And why does Ronan not speak?"

"Sometimes we must lie for the good of our people, Son. The New Age comes above all else. But remember what I taught you. You mustn't name the lesser creatures. It only serves to confuse you."

"But why doesn't he speak?"

"Go on, pet, what happened to your talkative tongue?" Ukhel emphasized the last word and smiled with amusement.

Ronan furrowed his brows and continued to watch Esen weave his way through the crowd. With a laugh, Ukhel pushed him toward the step so he could join Wren again.

"He's just accepted his role in the New Age, like you must do, Son. He is nothing more than an animal looking to fulfill his basic needs. If given food, water, and shelter, he will be fine."

Ronan gritted his teeth and sat down beside Wren. His stomach churned with hatred as he watched the rest of the Gurvel swinging and dancing around each other. They were either ignorant of Ukhel's real nature or just as vile and guilty. Either way he hated every one of them.

"I want to speak more with our bold soldier friend," Ukhel said, calling over one of the nearby cultists. "Go find that soldier that was here a moment before and bring him to my quarters. I want to have a word with him in private."

Ronan looked out at the crowd and saw Esen slip through an open doorway. It was a shame. That Gurvel was probably the only friend he could have depended on and surely Ukhel would arrest him. He hoped beyond reason that Esen was able to evade capture, if only so that there was one Gurvel in the world that he didn't have to hate.

CHAPTER 33
Underestimation

When Ravenel returned home, he returned to destruction.
The whole town lay strewn about the streets, frozen in fright.

Ronan

RONAN SAT ON TOP of a blanket next to Wren, the ends of the leashes chained to hooks set in the Sklera wall behind them. Compared to the volume of the party, the quiet of the bedroom sounded muffled in comparison. Wren took off the gold sash, holding onto it tightly as if he needed it to live.

In the middle of the room, Ukhel sat at the small dining table watching Khartsaga recite the Fire Creed. Parts of the creed had been spoken at The Games before, so Ronan was familiar with it. Khartsaga stood a few feet from the table with legs spread apart and arms behind his back. His posture was straight as an arrow and his gaze fixed straight ahead. They had been at it for at least an hour now and had gone through the same repetitive lines over and over again.

"One last time and then we can retire for the night," Ukhel said.

"Fire purifies all impurities. Together we rise. Together we prosper. Together we ascend. May the New Age rise and Gurvel prosper so that all creatures may prosper. May the children of fire rise," Khartsaga recited.

Ukhel stood and clapped with a smile that sickened Ronan. The worst part of it was that Khartsaga was too entranced by him to realize how wrong and illogical it all was. He almost felt sorry for him. Almost. Ignorance didn't excuse how he had led King Chono to commit genocide. It didn't excuse him for all of the deaths at The Games, and it certainly didn't excuse him for taking control of Ronan's body to murder. He rubbed his face again trying to remove the paint remnants. There were still a few spots under his eyes where the paint cracked against his skin.

"Remind me tomorrow to order a search for that soldier," Ukhel said, changing into a sleeping gown. "The guards say he slipped out of the party and hasn't been seen since."

"Of course, Father. I'm sure he'll turn up."

While Khartsaga and Ukhel got dressed for bed, Ronan prepared for what would come next. He needed to get both Gurvel out of the room long enough for Wren to escape and climb out the balcony.

"Are you ready?" Ronan signed.

Wren took a deep breath beside him and nodded.

"Find Esen. He'll help you."

Wren clutched the golden sash tighter as he prepared to run.

"Goodnight, pets," Ukhel said from across the room. "Sleep tight." He winked at Ronan with a raised finger to his lips and snuffed out the torches with a wave of his hand.

Ronan blinked until his eyes adjusted. Pale moonlight slipped into the room from under the balcony door and allowed him to see the silhouettes of Ukhel and Khartsaga heading to their beds. He began counting, waiting for them to drift off to sleep. If he timed it just right, he could project an illusion into both of their minds and draw them out into the hallway without them knowing it was him. With any luck, they would be so close to sleep they wouldn't notice the illusion.

After a handful of minutes, he squeezed Wren's hand and projected a guard crying for help. Ukhel sat bolt upright in bed and dashed out into the hallway. Close behind him, Khartsaga grabbed a vial from his bed stand and ran toward the doorway.

Waving his hand in a circle to help his concentration, Wren used his powers to unlock the collar around his neck and ran toward the balcony doors. Barely able to reach the handle, he stood on the balls of his feet and managed to crack the door open with a soft thud. Khartsaga ran back into the room and furrowed the ridges above his eyes when he saw Wren.

"Khartsaga, let him go, please," Ronan whispered, standing to his feet. There was nothing more he could do.

To his relief, Khartsaga actually stopped. Ronan spoke as loud as he dared. Ukhel would be back any second now. "He's just a kid. Please. Let him go."

Khartsaga's eyes darted back to Wren, but he didn't move. Seizing the opportunity, Wren looked back at Ronan one last time and darted through the opening out onto the balcony. Relief flooded his body as the boy's small form disappeared from view. An instant sense of fatigue settled in as well. Without Wren, he didn't have much reason to expend extra energy on keeping his strength. He leaned back against the wall and slid to the floor.

Khartsaga continued to stare at the balcony door as if frozen. Despite rejoining his father, a part of him must still disagree with the Fire Creed.

A growl erupted from the hallway as Ukhel stormed back into the room. With a wave, he relit the torches and stormed over to Ronan and the empty collar beside him.

"What happened?" he demanded.

Now he wanted him to talk. He kept his mouth closed and stared up at the enraged Gurvel. Still in a stupor, Khartsaga sank into one of the dining chairs and held his head in his hands.

Ukhel spun around. "Son, what happened?"

"I...I don't know."

Ronan held his breath as Ukhel finally saw the open balcony door and ran outside. Wren was able to blend in with the roof, of course, but he was still wearing those putridly colorful pants. *Please be hidden*, he thought desperately.

Thankfully, Ukhel slammed his fist onto the railing. Wren had done it. He had escaped. If he could find Esen, he would be safe, or at least as safe as he could be considering the circumstances.

Ukhel slammed the balcony door shut when he entered the room and immediately came for Ronan. Without warning, he yanked him up by the neck and slammed him against the Sklera. Ronan gasped for breath and tried to pry Ukhel's hand away, but the Gruvel's grip was incredibly tight. His feet dangled off the floor and scraped against the wall as he tried to find a foothold.

"You're behind this, aren't you?" Ukhel shouted with his face so close, Ronan could make out the individual gray hairs on his head.

"It's not his fault, Father. It's mine," Khartsaga said.

Ukhel looked at his son, his hand still pinning Ronan to the wall.

"The Forestdweller got out of his collar and made a run for the balcony. I wasn't fast enough to stop him. He must be a Manipulator," Khartsaga explained.

"Don't be stupid, Son. Forestdwellers can't be real Manipulators. It's much more likely that he slipped out of the collar. I was planning to have a smaller one made in the morning."

Black dots started to blur the edges of Ronan's vision. Finally Ukhel released him and he fell to the floor choking on the air. He still felt the pressure against his neck from where the collar had been pressed against his windpipe.

"I guess that makes sense," Khartsaga said as his father walked over to the table.

Ukhel sighed and put his hand on Khartsaga's shoulder. "He wouldn't have been a very long-lived pet anyway. He probably would have died from fright before too long. But what's done is done. Did the human say anything while I was gone?"

A burst of icy fear gripped Ronan's heart. He had taken a big risk in asking Khartsaga to let Wren escape. Now he would have to face the consequences.

"No. In fact he hasn't said anything since the party. What did you threaten to do to him if he spoke?" Khartsaga asked.

Why did he lie? Ronan quickly erected a mind barrier so Ukhel wouldn't overhear his thoughts. Maybe he wouldn't lose his tongue after all.

Ukhel smiled and squeezed Khartsaga's shoulder before getting back into bed. "I only encouraged him to embrace his rightful place in the New Age. Come. We have a big day ahead of us tomorrow."

Khartsaga stood up and glanced at Ronan briefly before extinguishing the torches and returning to bed.

Ronan sat in the dark, trying to get his breathing under control. It hurt to swallow, but at least he was still able to. He eased himself down on the blanket and stared up into the darkness. There was definitely some tension between Khartsaga and Ukhel. Maybe he could use that to his advantage. Then again, he couldn't rely on Khartsaga. He was too heavily influenced by his father.

Was it even possible for him to escape? He would have to pick the lock on the collar somehow. Not to mention he would need to hide his thoughts. Surely Ukhel knew he had powers, even if he denied that possibility to Khartsaga. Various escape plans whirled through his head, but each one ended in an impossible hurdle. Eventually he fell into a fitful sleep, dreaming of Ukhel towering over him with a devious smile and a pair of hot tongs.

The next morning, the weight of his situation settled on him anew. Someone got up and opened the balcony doors to let in the sunlight. Ronan kept his eyes closed, trying to muster the strength to get up, but without Wren, he found himself lacking the desire to try. What did it matter? There was no key to the collar and without Manipulation, he would never be able to unlock it himself.

Something soft landed beside him. "Here, pet. Eat up."

He cracked open his eyes and looked up at the Sklera ceiling, grimacing at the soreness that had swelled along his neck. At least they were going to feed him. Maybe he would be able to think of something if he kept his strength up.

Stomach growling, he sat up and took the chunk of bread that had been thrown at him. Ukhel stood by the table in the center of the room, watching him intently as he took a bite. It still hurt to swallow, but the bread was warm and surprisingly good despite a slight bitter aftertaste. He leaned up against the wall and ate the rest of it. Fresh bread coming from Ukhel seemed a little out of character, but he would take what he could get.

Khartsaga joined his father at the table and started eating his own breakfast while they chatted about the day. Content to be ignored for the moment, Ronan looked out at the sky, hoping Wren had found a safe place to sleep last night.

Then his head began to throb. He instinctively rubbed his temples with his hands as his thinking started to become muddled. It was like he was slipping into some kind of trance. With a start, he realized what had happened. The bread had been injected with an Inhibitor, and an incredibly strong one based on how fast his mind was clouding over. His heartbeat quickened, but not fast enough to shake away the fatigue.

He looked up at Ukhel and saw the Gurvel smiling at him, satisfied with his reaction. So potent was the Inhibitor that he started to lose his grip on reality while Khartsaga and Ukhel recited the Fire Creed. All he could do was sit against the wall, barely able to keep his eyes open. Any hope of planning an escape vanished behind the mind fog.

Barely aware of his surroundings, the rest of the day passed by in a haze. He was vaguely aware of someone painting his face again and somewhat remembered walking through the city to the coliseum, but for the most part he felt disjointed, going and doing whatever he was told.

CHAPTER 34

Mental Fog

In anguish, Ravenel began a grand search.

Ronan

DAYS LATER, RONAN SLUMPED up against the Sklera and forced himself to take a few bites of the drugged food. He was starting to lose track of how many days it had been since they had been captured. Luckily the Inhibitors he had been given since the first day weren't nearly as strong, but his mind was still in a constant fog. This evening, Khartsaga was out looking for Esen with a squad of Firekin guards, leaving him alone in the bedroom with Ukhel.

They went through the same ritual each night. While Khartsaga was out of the room, Ukhel watched him eat the drugged food and then tormented him. Tonight looked like it would be no different.

As Ronan reached the end of his drug-filled meal, Ukhel lurked nearby, twirling a dagger in the air just above his finger tips. Knowing what was to come, Ronan steeled himself as he swallowed the last bite. On queue, Ukhel approached him with a terrible smile and slashed the dagger at Ronan's head. Instinctively, Ronan deflected the attack, but Ukhel changed tactics and punched him in the abdomen.

Curling up as tendrils of pain and nausea shot out from the injury, Ronan could only watch as Ukhel sliced his arm with the dagger and licked the blade clean. Then he pressed against Ronan's open wound and gathered the pooling blood into an empty vial.

Ukhel was insane. He had to be.

"There, that wasn't so bad, was it?" Ukhel said, walking over to the table with the vial. "You'll get used to it eventually. The sooner you learn to stop fighting, the easier it will be for you."

The door to the bedroom opened and Khartsaga came in, acknowledging Ronan with a nod as he sat down at the dining table. Ukhel didn't treat him nearly as harshly when Khartsaga was present, but that was little consolation when he was still their prisoner. Only it was worse than that. Prisoners were people. He was Ukhel's pet.

"Any word on that soldier from the party?" Ukhel asked.

"Not yet. Apparently Esen climbed his way up in the military rather quickly the past two decades. He's always been an exemplary soldier, so he knows all of our tactics."

Ronan breathed a small sigh of relief. He was exhausted, but knowing that Wren and Esen were free eased some worry. With any luck, the kid was somewhere safe. But if Esen was alluding capture so well, would Wren even be able to find him? No. Wren was safe. He had to believe that.

As Ukhel and Khartsaga went through the Fire Creed, he tried to think of a way to escape again, but without the ability to create illusions his options were limited. At least his thoughts were safe with the Inhibitor so he could make plans in secret. Unfortunately, he was out of ideas. In fact, he was beginning to think it was impossible. He couldn't get the collar off without help. There wasn't even a key to steal because Ukhel had designed it to unlock through Manipulation.

Fatigue settled on him as he fought to think through the mind fog. He wasn't getting out of here. Even if he could manage to get out of the metal collar, he would never be able to get out of the castle alive. He couldn't climb like Wren and if he ran, Ukhel would hunt him down, torture him for pleasure, and take his tongue for good measure. The weight of exhaustion mixed with the Inhibitor closed in on him, making it difficult to breathe. He gave in to the lethargic fog filling his mind and laid down to stare up at the black ceiling. When the torches were finally extinguished, he slipped into a fitful sleep.

At some point in the night, he woke with a start, drenched in cold sweat and shaking. The throbbing in his head was back in full force. He gripped his arms and focused on his breathing to calm himself down, but he could still hear their screams. The acrid smell of burning flesh clung to his nostrils and the heat of the flame lingered on his skin. Since he had been captured even his dreams tortured him.

"Are you okay?" Khartsaga asked, his silhouetted figure approaching cautiously in the dark.

Breathing heavily, Ronan didn't answer. Instead he lay back down on the blanket and turned to face the wall. Even if he wasn't concerned about losing his tongue, he didn't feel like soothing Khartsaga's wounded conscience. If the

Gurvel were really concerned about him, he would convince his father to let him go.

After a few seconds, Khartsaga went back to bed. The rest of the night, Ronan dozed on and off, but he didn't dare let himself dream again. He knew the lack of sleep was weakening him, but he couldn't face their deaths again. Not tonight.

When daylight finally appeared beneath the balcony doors, Ukhel got up and lit the torches. Ronan couldn't muster the strength to sit up today. When Ukhel threw him the bread, he refused to eat it. Hunger was better than this constant headache.

Ukhel walked up to him and bent down to pick up the bread. "Eat your food, pet, or I'll have to inject you with an Inhibitor."

He forced himself up, using the Sklera as support and begrudgingly took the bread. Ukhel smiled as he ate. Resisting wouldn't get him anywhere. Satisfied, Ukhel joined Khartsaga at the dining table and commanded him to recite the Fire Creed.

Ronan closed his eyes as the throbbing in his head intensified. It was never-ending. With such a strong headache, the Fire Creed that Khartsaga recited sliced through his mind like a sharp stake. He tried his best to block it out while he waited for Ukhel to drag him to the next event like some kind of pampered fox or cat.

When they finished, Ukhel grabbed a jar of paint and applied it to Ronan's face. Hatred boiled in his blood, but he didn't fight it. His stomach was still sore from last night.

"Now you're catching on," Ukhel said, yanking on the chain to lead him out into the hallway with Khartsaga.

His anger petered out. What was the point of fighting at all? If he resisted Ukhel, he was beaten. If he tried to wipe off the paint, he was beaten. If he refused to eat, he would be beaten. And regardless, he would be forced to do whatever Ukhel ordered him to do anyway. It wasn't worth the strength to fight. Maybe it wasn't worth the strength to try to escape either.

They were joined by a squad of Gurvel wearing only military pants and boots. More and more of the guards were boldly adopting the bare-chested look in homage to Firekin. Personally, Ronan would do almost anything to get his hands on a jacket or shirt of some kind.

Ukhel led them through the castle, nodding to various cultists and staff members that they passed by. Once they exited the castle gates, Ukhel acknowledged the guards. "Report."

A Gurvel with a slight overbite held out a roll of parchment. "Eternal Flame, there's been a disturbance in the city."

Ukhel took the paper and read it as they walked. After a moment, his face darkened and he crumbled up the message.

"What's wrong, Father?" Khartsaga asked.

"Just that soldier again. We'll find him and remind him of the truth."

Esen continued to evade capture. With any luck, Wren had found him and was relatively safe by now.

Gurvel stared at Ronan as he passed by, most of them laughing or pointing, but a few did nothing more than look at him with expressionless faces. He kept his gaze straight ahead and resisted the urge to rub off the paint as it cracked against his skin. As humiliating as it was to be paraded through the streets like a pet, he dreaded their arrival at the coliseum even more.

They walked up the stairs to the viewing platform where they could watch the bloodbath without obstructions. If only his Inhibitor dose were stronger. That way he wouldn't have to witness the meaningless deaths and horrific Fire Purifications.

He cringed as a burst of flame caught a woman on fire in the sandy pit below. He shut his eyes to block out the scene as her screams echoed through the coliseum, but his mind was soon filled with the memory of his parents burning at the pyre. He tried to cover his ears to dampen their terrible cries, but Ukhel struck him in the back of the head. There was no way to hide from it.

After a handful of people had died, Ronan's emotions and mind became numb. He lost track of time as the violent scenes repeated themselves before him like a hypnotic rhythm. The champion drank a Fire Stimulant. Then the human ran. The champion chased the human until he grew bored and then he slaughtered him or her.

Finally Ukhel yanked on his chain, drawing him out of his thoughts. The sun had moved significantly. Had he fallen asleep? Yesterday The Games had lasted all day, but today it felt like he had only seen a few fights. Or had it been more than that? They all melded together. It didn't matter. Ukhel pulled on the chain again and dragged him back to the castle.

Once they were back in the bedroom, Ukhel ordered Khartsaga to recite the Fire Creed like he did every night. Ronan tried to block out their words but each repetition felt like a hammer nailing the lies deeper into his skull. He knew what they said was wrong, but some of it was starting to make sense. Maybe if he gave up like Ukhel wanted him to, he could finally get some rest.

Eventually, like every night, Ukhel sent Khartsaga on an errand with Tarkhan. Another part of the day he had come to hate.

Ukhel loomed over him and was silent for a few minutes as if waiting for something. "I'll admit that I'm impressed. I haven't heard you speak in days. I didn't think humans had the ability to be so self-controlled." He bent down so that he was at Ronan's eye level. "But I was really looking forward to cutting out your tongue."

Ronan held his gaze and tried to hide the fear that shot through his heart. There was nothing he could do.

Ukhel reached out his hand and ran his fingers through Ronan's hair. "But not right now. I have to visit the prisons tonight, so I don't think I'll have time. Your Speki friends are turning out to be great test subjects. Would you like me to pay them a visit for you?"

The image of what this monster could be doing to Eira was enough to replace some of Ronan's fear with anger. He knocked Ukhel's hand away and punched him in the jaw, knowing full well what the consequences would be.

As expected, Ukhel slammed him against the wall and kneed him in the stomach. Then he proceeded to batter his body with a series of blows. Pain erupted across his body as he struggled to breathe. His vision began to blur when finally Ukhel dropped him and stepped away.

"Now I'll have to go wash this blood off before I visit your friends. Like I said before, stop fighting and this will be easier for you."

After wiping his hands off on a towel, Ukhel shot him a smile and left the room, closing the door firmly shut behind him.

Ronan sat up gingerly, grunting as his movements irritated the bruises and cuts along his back and arms. He pulled at the chain around his neck with the waning hope that the beating had loosened something, but it was as secure as ever. There was no escape.

He sat there and let his mind go blank until eventually Ukhel and Khartsaga came back to have dinner and go to bed. They recited the dreaded Fire Creed yet again as Ronan was forced to listen. He had heard it so many times he could recite it by heart.

May the New Age rise and Gurvel prosper so that all creatures may prosper.

Maybe this was all there really was. Maybe it was what he truly deserved after causing so many deaths. All the people in The Games. His parents. Aprika. Manton. Kendra. He closed his eyes. There was nothing left to do, so he gave up.

CHAPTER 35

Thoughts in the Night

*Listening to faint rumors and myths, Ravenel tracked down
a handful of humans like him.*

Esen

A CHILL WIND SWEPT through the deserted alleyway where Esen crouched beside a pile of discarded tarps and wooden stalls. The day after the coronation feast, it had only taken the cultists and city guards a few hours to escort the human population down to the mines. Now the city felt empty in the areas where human merchants had once set up their shops.

In the pale moonlight, Esen hid behind the rubble with the weight of the city on his shoulders. There was still a chance to retake everything. If he could convince enough people to join together, they might be strong enough to contend with Ukhel's brainwashed forces.

Esen quietly eased his way over to the next pile of rubble, trying to stick to the shadows. As he moved, he concentrated his mind on his surroundings, feeling for any life presences that might be following him.

It had taken a lot of strategizing and planning to set up the meeting he was headed to. If he could convince the Purev family to join their cause, it would change everything. Their vast network of connections in the city was rooted in millennia of family history and loyalty. If they joined, most of the other large Gurvel families would follow their lead. And that in turn might be enough to overturn Ukhel's rule.

To his left, the coliseum loomed over the city like a towering storm, casting a dark shadow on all the shorter buildings beside it. Perfect for sneaking in the night.

Despite the late hour, the streets had a decent number of Gurvel wandering about. No children or families like there would have been a week ago. This crowd looked like it had crawled out of the lowest crevices in the city. Drunkards staggered from taverns to secluded alleys. Figures in dark cloaks sauntered slowly down the main streets and black-clad city guards made their constant rounds.

Pulling his cowl over his head, Esen stood up and walked with a wobbly stride down the main street, forcing himself not to go too fast. If any guards did come around the corner he was hoping they would look the other way and let him stumble down a side alley.

As he crossed the street to the dark alleyway on the other side, he caught the brief flash of a thought from close behind him. He held back the urge to spin around and see whose mind he had detected, instead continuing his charade across the street and into the alleyway.

The mind he felt had only been there for a second before flickering away, which meant the person tailing him was intentionally hiding their mind. He could drink the vial of Base Stimulant that he had brought with him, but that would alert his pursuer too quickly. Had they seen him leave the safe house? If they had, he would need to make sure they didn't carry that information back to Ukhel.

He made it across the street and stumbled against the Sklera wall of one of the buildings, using his periphery to see who was behind him. No one was there. Not wanting to relax too soon, Esen shuffled further into the alley, listening for any sounds of pursuit.

This alley, unlike the other one, was empty except for a few bits of paper and trash that had been blown in from the main street. Esen continued his slow, wobbly strides and turned down a side road leading toward the coliseum. His meeting was in the opposite direction, and only a few streets away, so he would need to take care of his pursuer quickly and double back.

He passed by an old homeless Gurvel sleeping under a ratty blanket and continued down the small street. It didn't sound like anyone was behind him, but he couldn't shake the feeling that he was being watched.

Finally, he spotted another alley between two large Sklera storefronts with numerous crates and barrels along the sides. He took a few steps into the alley and then whipped around.

Other than the sleeping homeless man, the street and alley were completely empty and yet he felt another blink of a life presence right before him.

"I know you're there. Show yourself," he said, reaching for the vial in his pocket.

Nothing moved. He looked up at the tops of the buildings but they were as silent and black as the night sky. Perhaps he was mistaken? It was possible he had just detected someone on the main street. But he had taken care to stay away from everyone, and he had definitely felt the life presence from close behind him.

When he looked back at the entrance of the alley he almost jumped. The air started to shimmer and the form of a small creature began to phase into view. Esen stepped back and squinted his eyes until the person materialized fully, peering around the edge of the building. Realization hit him as he recognized that face.

The Forestdweller boy from the castle wrapped his tail around his ankles and nervously rubbed his hands together in front of his heart. Esen relaxed and took his hand out of his pocket. The boy seemed incredibly small and frail compared to Esen's towering height.

Not moving too quickly, he crouched down with one knee to the ground to get closer to his eye level. The boy's small frame shivered in the dim moonlight, his eyes wide in fright.

"It's alright. I won't hurt you," he said gently. "What's your name?"

The boy shuffled his feet and started to move his hands around in a series of movements.

"I'm sorry," he said. "I don't know your language, but if you concentrate on what you want to say, I'll be able to hear it in your mind."

The boy took a deep breath and then screwed his face up in concentration. Esen listened and heard his thoughts as they crossed the front of his mind.

"Wren."

"Are you injured, Wren?" he asked.

The boy shook his head and shifted from foot to foot, tail curling more tightly around his ankles. Despite his nervousness, Wren looked him straight in the eye, his lips pursed in determination.

"Is Ronan with you?" Esen asked.

Tears welled up in Wren's eyes as he shook his head. Painful memories crashed to the front of his mind. Esen saw fleeting images of a balcony and Ronan sitting against a Sklera wall.

"It will be okay," he said, his heart breaking at the wave of despair that the images were tinged with. He reached out his hand toward Wren. "I'm trying to help him and the others, and I can help you too. Please, let me take you somewhere safe."

Wren stared at him for a moment as if deciding what to do. Then he ran toward him, threw his small arms around him, and clung to his shirt.

Esen wrapped his arms around him as sobs wracked the boy's body. A flash of anger hit him deep within his core. Ukhel was a monster.

The meeting with the Purevs would have to wait. He picked Wren up with ease and started walking back toward the hideout. Trying to make himself look less conspicuous, he pulled his cloak over the boy and held him against his chest. Wren was small enough and the night dark enough that someone would have to look closely to see that he was carrying someone. If he stuck to the shadows and side roads, they might be able to avoid detection, but he would need to be extra careful regardless.

In case they were being followed, he decided to take a different path to get to the main road. They walked along the coliseum and crossed the main street where some of the more expensive vendors set up stalls. Wren continued to shiver against his chest but his cries were silent and his mind had quieted again too. Esen was impressed. It had taken him years to master quieting his thoughts.

He waited for a pair of city guards to pass before darting across the street and slinking along the side of a bakery. After doubling back a few times to check for pursuers, Esen finally made it to the familiar back entrance of the safe house. It was really just an old tea shop that had been around for millennia. The owner, Sarnai, was one of the first to join with Esen and had helped him carve out a bunker beneath the store.

He knocked seven times in the agreed upon pattern. After a moment, the door opened and Sarnai ushered him inside. She clutched a large green blanket with a wrinkled hand and glanced from Esen's face to the bump protruding from his cloak.

"You're back early," she whispered, latching the door behind him. "Is everything alright?"

He pulled aside his cloak, revealing Wren who was still clinging to his shirt.

"Ah," Sarnai said. "And who is this?"

"This is Wren," he replied, kicking aside a carpet on the Sklera floor to uncover the secret door. "We'll have to reschedule with the Purevs."

"Of course," she said, helping him open the door. "I'll bring down a hot pot of tea and some extra blankets."

He climbed down into the hole with Wren and looked back up at Sarnai's dark burgundy face. "Thank you."

Wrinkles formed at the edges of her eyes as she smiled. "No, thank you, dear. This city is in dire need of change." She closed the secret door, leaving Esen in dim torchlight.

He walked along the short passage they had carved out and took Wren to the only room in the safe house. There was just enough space for a large table, a bed, and some shelves.

Exhaustion settled on him now that they were safely off the main streets. Secretly conspiring against the strongest force in Amidral had turned out to be quite the endeavor. He sat down with Wren who had yet to pull his face away from his chest and gently rubbed the boy's back until he looked up with a tearstained face.

"You're safe now," he said, wiping away some of the tears.

It wasn't entirely true. He knew the danger they were in, but at least for the moment they were as safe as they could be.

CHAPTER 36

Bloodlust

*With their help, he formed the Veiled Paladins and taught them
everything he had learned about Seyring and Manipulation.*

Khartsaga

THE CROWD STOMPED THEIR feet and cried out in excitement as the
Gurvel champion, Abaka, shot a burst of flame toward an elderly woman in
disheveled clothing. Khartsaga sat beside his father in the viewing platform of
the coliseum—the same one he used to sit at with King Chono. Now he was
supposedly king, but he didn't feel like it.

With a quick succession of fire bursts, the champion finished the job and
bowed before the audience. His father stood up and clapped emphatically but
Khartsaga remained seated. The champion had killed an unarmed elder. Where
was the glory in that?

Unable to look at the charred remains of the corpse, he turned his
attention to Ronan who was staring at the arena below with a glazed expression.
Dark circles rimmed his eyes accented by the bright purple paint on his cheeks.
His dyed hair was a mess and dark stubble covered his face. He looked horrible.

A cool wind blew through the stadium sending a wave of goosebumps
across Ronan's bruised and cut torso. A knot formed in Khartsaga's stomach.
He wanted to question his father about the beatings, but the Eternal Flame had
a right to punish his pet for disobedience. Didn't he?

As the gong signaled the start of the next fight, Ukhel sat down in his
throne and let out a sigh of content. "This is what we've been missing."

One of the guards threw a man with a crooked leg into the arena. Was
this truly the highest potential that humans would ever reach? The Fire Creed
promised that the New Age would bring prosperity to all creatures, and yet
what Khartsaga saw didn't sit well with him.

He looked away as the man struggled to his feet and tried to limp away
from the blood-crazed champion towering over him. It wasn't a fair fight. Even

if the man were perfectly healthy, it wouldn't be a fair fight.

Ukhel leaned forward to get a better view, which gave Khartsaga a chance to see Ronan again from the corner of his eye. The edge of the man's mouth twitched, but otherwise he remained expressionless. Something was wrong. His father was adding Inhibitors to Ronan's food. He had asked why, but had been forced to recite the Fire Creed in response. The more he recited that creed, the more questions he had. Humans weren't supposed to possess any real powers, so why drug him? Nothing made sense.

Down below, Abaka shot a few fire blasts near the crippled man's feet, forcing him to jump and twist out of the way. After a third blast, the man stumbled and slipped in the sand.

How was this prosperous for anyone? The man was clearly outmatched and the Gurvel champion wasn't showcasing his real strength against such an opponent. He glanced out at the crowded stands. Crimson Gurvel faces leaned over the edge of the railing crying out with gleeful shouts. They were excited by the bloodshed.

The cleansings weren't working anymore. Everyone else had accepted their placement, but he couldn't find it within himself to enjoy anything. Every bloodied corpse that fell to the ground reminded him of the terrible dreams he kept having.

The champion grabbed the man by the ankle and threw him into the air with a triumphant laugh. Ukhel stood up and clapped, which incited the crowd to stomp even louder.

This was the New Age. This was what he had longed for his entire life, and yet he hated it. The thought crossed his mind before he could stop it. Luckily his father was preoccupied with The Games and didn't hear it. He regained control of himself and turned his attention back to the arena where Abaka was drinking a fresh dose of Fire Stimulant. The champion raised the empty vial above his head and stepped toward the cowering man. Then in one swift movement, he burned him alive.

The man's mouth opened in a scream of pain, but the thrum of the crowd was too loud to hear it. Nausea washed over Khartsaga. He couldn't bear to watch this anymore, but he couldn't leave yet. Not when his father was still watching intently.

Abaka walked around the stadium with his fists raised in the air while the crowd continued to shout and stomp their praise. Meanwhile, the guards started clearing away the mutilated corpses littering the arena floor. There had been twenty individual fights today.

Ukhel sat back and closed his eyes as if savoring the flavor of a good meal. The bloodshed didn't seem to bother him at all. In fact, he looked like he relished it.

Suddenly, the world seemed to tilt underneath him. He couldn't wait any longer. He stood abruptly, drawing Ukhel's attention.

"Something wrong, Son?"

"You promised to take me to see the Speki in the dungeons. Can we go now?" Anything to get away from the violent rage of the crowd.

"I'm glad to see you finally taking an interest!" Ukhel said, standing up. He yanked on Ronan's chain to get him moving.

Ronan hadn't been the same since Wren escaped almost a week ago. Maybe it was just the Inhibitor, but the light had faded from his eyes as well. Khartsaga had tried to get him to talk, but the man hadn't uttered a single word. If he could find some time to be alone with him, maybe Ronan would say something, but an opportunity hadn't presented itself yet.

They left the coliseum and made their way through town square. Gurvel civilians saluted them as they passed by, raising a fist to their foreheads and moving it over their hearts. Even the children seemed enamored with them as they walked by. One young boy pulled at his mother's hand and pointed excitedly at Ronan as if wanting to pet him like a fox or cat. It shouldn't have unsettled him, but Khartsaga was glad when they were finally past the busy market area.

Once back in the castle, Ukhel started walking toward the entrance to the dungeons, but Khartsaga stopped him. Ronan was still with them. He didn't know what condition the Speki were in, but he didn't want Ronan to have to see them like that.

"Wait, Father, perhaps we should leave the human in our bedchamber?"

Ukhel stopped and raised one of the ridges above his eye while Ronan continued to stare lethargically off into the distance as if unaware of his surroundings.

"Why?"

"You've seen him. He's been sluggish lately. I'm afraid he'll slow us down," Khartsaga said, trying his best to push down the rising panic inside him. Like all Firekin members, he had learned how to hide his thoughts, but his father was often able to read his mind anyway.

"Perhaps," Ukhel said.

"I'll wait here if you don't mind. I've been wanting to study the murals of the Shadow War again."

Ukhel looked him slowly up and down. Afraid of giving away his intentions, Khartsaga turned his back on his father and started walking toward the mural.

Thankfully his father didn't push him any further. "I'm glad you're starting to feel like yourself again, Son," he said, leading Ronan up the stairs, "but try to look more alive during The Games tomorrow. The crowd might think you're... uninterested."

A shiver ran down his spine. His father was a Seyr, but even so, he shouldn't be able to read hidden thoughts, not without a Stimulant. But on days like today, he got the impression that his father knew what he was thinking, even when he hid his emotions.

CHAPTER 37

Something New

*His small group practiced their skills by hunting down criminals in the night,
all the while preparing for their real enemies: the shadow beasts.*

Eira

A PAIR OF CULTISTS ROUGHLY forced Eira onto the examination
table, strapping her down to the Sklera surface. It wasn't just the weight of the
Inhibitor fog that kept her from fighting them. The impossibility of their escape
had exhausted her desire to try. She would give anything to hear one of Nar's
witty quips right now, but he couldn't offer her any comfort. Sweat moistened
his forehead and his skin still looked pale and clammy from whatever Inhibitor
they had tried on him earlier that day.

Steeling herself against the next experiment, she stared up at the black
ceiling. They had tried thinking of a way to escape, but so far nothing had been
worthy of trying. Clenching her fists, she closed her eyes and ran through their
options again.

They could either fight their way out or sneak out. They might have
enough strength to fight off one guard if the cultists ever forgot to give them
an Inhibitor dose, but that was unlikely. Even if it happened, there were usually
multiple guards. So far their best idea was to fake one of their deaths. Maybe the
guard would rush in and leave the door open, but she doubted it would work.
Firekin didn't care enough about them. They would probably just leave them
both in the cell to die.

The door to the room burst open, causing the cultists to drop the vials they
had been sorting through. She opened her eyes and craned her neck to see who
it was. A flash of heat flushed her face. Ukhel.

He entered the room with a wide stride, his golden cloak shimmering as
the torchlight hit it. What was he doing back? He had observed them earlier
that day with that spineless son of his.

"Eternal Flame!" the cultists shouted, scrambling to raise their fists to their heads and hearts.

"May Gurvel prosper and the New Age rise," Ukhel said, nodding at each one. "You are all dismissed from your duties for the rest of the day."

The cultists glanced at one another in confusion.

"But, sir," one of the older cultists said tentatively, "what about the Inhibitor tests?"

"Thank you for your dedication and faithfulness, but you are dismissed," Ukhel repeated. "The Inhibitor tests can wait."

The cultist saluted Ukhel. "Of course, Eternal Flame."

Then one by one they left, leaving Ukhel alone in the room with Eira and Einar. What did he want with them now? They had already been subjected to countless tests.

Ukhel took a book out from under his cloak and set it down on the table, giving her a sly smile as he did. She gritted her teeth and watched him closely. What was he planning that required such secrecy? She glanced at Nar to see if she could read his expression, but his eyes were closed tightly in pain.

After opening the book to an earmarked page, Ukhel started gathering ingredients from the supply shelves. She wasn't at a good angle to see exactly what he was doing, but it sounded like he was grinding something up. More of those green crystals?

Except for the sound of Einar's soft groans and the clinking of glass vials, the room was silent. She forced herself to stay lucid, which was difficult with the Inhibitor blocking her mind, but necessary. Especially with Nar feeling so poorly, she wanted to be prepared to defend them both. Not that she could do much.

Ukhel continued to work methodically and scratched a note in the book every now and then. He was definitely creating something new, but why keep it hidden from the other cultists? After a while, Ukhel reached into his pocket and took out a handful of vials. She squinted her eyes to try to see them better, but they were too far away. Why did she even care? She set her head back against the table. It wouldn't be long now before she figured out what he was making. Whatever it was, he was bound to test it on them.

"I'm so grateful that you and your brother came back to me," Ukhel said, breaking the silence. He walked over to the two experimentation tables and stood in between them. "After my son let you escape from our cave that you wandered into, I thought I'd never have a chance like this again."

She stared resolutely at the ceiling, nostrils flaring slightly at the sound of his voice. Images of what he had done to their city flooded her thoughts. The shadowmongrels he had tamed had ravaged even the children of Mikiltoft. As she and Einar had searched the decimated city, they had found a small severed hand still gripping the bloody wing of a stuffed phoenix. Not having the strength to search for the rest of the body, they had left the child's hand in the streets, surrounded by the horrific remains of countless other Speki.

"Is the Inhibitor fog bothering you?" Ukhel asked, stepping up beside her table and towering over her. The torchlight flickered off of his crimson skin, casting eerie shadows above his eye ridges.

"Your reign will crumble like ashbark," she spat.

"Maybe it would have, but I stumbled across a weapon that will change the course of history." Ukhel smiled as he lifted a vial filled with a thick black liquid into the air. "This is the fifth variation I've tried, but now I've finally found the missing ingredient. Let's try it out, shall we?"

Eira tensed her arm, waiting for the injection. By now she had become accustomed to the cultist's experiments. She and Einar would be stabbed with an Inhibitor and then monitored for hours. Sometimes the cultists would test their reflexes. Other times they would test their pain tolerance. Regardless, it was always dreadful. But Ukhel didn't stab her with anything.

Instead he lifted the vial to his own lips and drank it. Nothing happened for a moment, but then a flashing pain split her forehead as she felt Ukhel's mind invade her own, slicing through the Inhibitor fog like butter. Memories flooded from the back of her mind into her forethoughts, piercing through her head like fire.

The charred remains of their sandstone home cut through her thoughts, intensified with vivid colors and emotions that normally faded from memory over time. She could even smell the burnt corpses and metallic blood in the air like she had on the day they had returned home. Bile rose at the back of her throat as the image morphed into the shredded face of Master Hertha, lying limp on the streets. Screaming in desperation, she tried to close her mind and fill the cracks, but the attack had come too quickly. The searing pain intensified, threatening to rip open her mind until suddenly it stopped.

Trembling, she gasped for breath and kept her eyes closed. It shouldn't be possible. Inhibitors blocked both the victim's own powers and protected them from attack. No one could pierce an Inhibitor fog, and yet Ukhel had invaded her mind, attacking her innermost thoughts with no struggle or hesitation. What had he created?

"That worked better than I expected it to," Ukhel said with a chuckle, footsteps moving back over to the work table. "But it could still use some work."

Cracking one eye open, she managed to strain her neck up enough to see Ukhel empty another vial into the mixing bowl. Still struggling for breath, she caught Einar's eye. If Ukhel could attack them through an Inhibitor, there wasn't much hope for them to escape.

Eira set her head back against the table and closed her eyes, struggling to think through the splitting headache that now pounded against her skull, but nothing came to mind. There was no way they would be able to fight something like that. Dread settled in her stomach like a cold corpse, spreading throughout the rest of her body as the last shred of hope drained out of her.

CHAPTER 38

Decisions

*Eventually, rumors of the Veiled Paladins reached the ears
of the Speki Knowledge Keepers and Gurvel Master Manipulators.*

Khartsaga

TARKHAN PLACED A JUICY chicken covered in a thick sauce in front of Khartsaga and Ukhel. "It is a pleasure to cook for both the Eternal Flame and my King."

"Thank you, Tarkhan," Ukhel said. "I'll see you later tonight to discuss our special project."

The lanky assistant dipped his head and left Khartsaga alone with his father in the bedchamber. It was late afternoon and the curtains had been drawn back to let in the yellow glow of the sun. Ronan sat on the floor beside Ukhel's chair, staring blankly at the wall with glazed eyes.

Khartsaga took a bite out of the chicken. It was juicy and tender, but it didn't settle well in his stomach. Since returning from the prison, Ukhel had been oddly quiet.

His father took a sip from his dragonbreath tea and then looked up at him. "What is the most important part of our beliefs?"

"May the New Age rise and Gurvel prosper."

"Indeed. Then if you believe that to be true, tell me, Son, why don't you act like it?"

His heart skipped a beat. He thought back to that moment at the coliseum when he had realized how much he hated the New Age. How did his father know? He set the chicken down and took a swig of water while he pushed his emotions down. "What do you mean?"

"Did you think I wouldn't notice?" Ukhel asked.

Khartsaga tried his best to keep his expression curious and his forethoughts blank. He would be forced to endure excruciating reeducation if his father discovered how resistant he was to the Fire Creed. "Notice what, Father? The

New Age has come and Gurvel are prospering. Just like we'd hoped." The words came easily enough, but his stomach twisted in a knot of regret as he spoke. He no longer believed in the New Age.

"You can't hide your true feelings from me, Son."

His chest tightened. Ukhel knew. Of course he knew. Even without a Stimulant, his father was bound to pick up on his emotions eventually.

"The past few days you haven't been interested in The Games at all. And you've become less passionate in your delivery of the Fire Creed."

"I've clapped at The Games," he protested, desperately trying to think of a way out of the painful reeducation that was coming.

"But without zeal!" Ukhel said, shaking his head. "And this morning, you were rather eager to leave before the crowd's passion had died down."

He didn't respond. What could he say? His breath caught in his throat. The anticipation was almost too much. His father knew. He knew that Khartsaga was beginning to hate the New Age.

Ukhel sighed and stood up from the table. "I think I know what the problem is, but I don't know how to get this lesson through your head. I've tried punishing you and encouraging you with the Fire Creed, and you still haven't changed the way you think about these creatures." He motioned to Ronan sitting on the floor. Some of the paint on his face had rubbed off, but most of it was still there. A week ago he would have rubbed the paint off the first chance he got. Now he didn't seem to care. In fact, from his vacant expression, Khartsaga wondered if he even cared at all anymore.

Ukhel pulled out an amber Fire Stimulant and twirled it in his fingers. So the punishment would involve physical pain today. He braced himself. It would be over soon enough if he just let it happen.

Ukhel drank the liquid and turned toward Ronan. "Maybe watching your beloved pet suffer will finally ingrain the truth of the New Age in your head."

Before Khartsaga could comprehend what was happening, his father kicked the man over and shot a burst of fire at his head. He stared in shock and stood up from the table as Ronan barely managed to cover his face, taking the blast with his exposed forearms.

"Stop!" Khartsaga cried, but Ukhel just shook his head.

"I don't know how else to teach you, Son. Watch. I'll show you how weak and insignificant humans really are. Maybe this lesson will finally get through that thick skull of yours."

With one hand, Ukhel grabbed the chain leash, yanking Ronan up by the collar, and punched him across the face. Ronan's feet dangled above the ground, one hand gripping the collar to keep from choking while the other shielded his face. This was wrong. It didn't matter if the New Age was the true way or not. Khartsaga couldn't stand another minute of this.

Ukhel went to strike Ronan again, but Khartsaga stepped forward and grabbed his father's wrist. "No! No more. If you're going to punish someone, punish me."

Ukhel's attention snapped to Khartsaga, a frown creasing his otherwise flawless crimson skin as he tried to pull his wrist free. His eyes were wild and filled with manic rage.

That's when Khartsaga saw it. The fear in his gut morphed into a slow burning fury as he realized for the first time what his father really was. A monster. An animal driven solely by his twisted nature.

"Let him go," Khartsaga ordered.

"Son, don't be ridiculous. This is my..."

Khartsaga yanked Ukhel's arm and forced it behind his back, twisting it until he cried out. "Let Ronan go. Now."

With a smirk, Ukhel released his grip and let Ronan fall to the floor, where he lay choking and coughing. Khartsaga dropped beside him and unlocked the collar, barely needing to wave his fingers as he did so. He cringed when he saw how bruised the skin was underneath. This had gone on too long.

"This is wrong, Father," he said, standing to face the man he feared. "All of this is wrong. The New Age has brought pain and suffering to everyone but the Gurvel. I won't sit by and let you hurt these people anymore. I won't be your puppet."

Ukhel narrowed his eyes, regarding Khartsaga as if looking at him for the first time. Gritting his teeth, Khartsaga crouched back down beside Ronan whose expression had become blank again. At least he was still breathing. Khartsaga gently pulled the man to his feet and stooped over slightly so he could support him.

"I'm leaving and I'm taking Ronan," he said, turning toward the door.

"Don't be so arrogant, Son. This isn't about you." Ukhel clapped three times and both the balcony door and main door burst open. Firekin members stood waiting, Verdant Stimulant vials ready in their hands.

Khartsaga froze. There were too many of them. Even with a Stimulant, he couldn't fight all of them. Had he really expected his father to just let him walk away?

"I told you, Son, I could tell that you'd fallen from the truth. But not to worry. We'll get you back on the right path soon enough."

Beside him, Ronan continued to stare blankly ahead as if in some kind of daze. They both needed to get out of here. Reaching into his pocket, Khartsaga grabbed an Inhibitor vial and drank it before the cultists could take control of his mind. There was no way this would work but he had to try. He owed at least that much to Ronan.

The guards rushed forward, but Khartsaga side-stepped their fireballs and smiled in adrenaline-fueled excitement when he saw the looks of confusion cross over their faces. They had expected him to drink the Verdant Stimulant, not weaken himself with an Inhibitor. Now they couldn't read or attack his mind. He grabbed Ronan's arm before they could overcome their confusion and ran through the main door toward the staircase.

Fire blasts exploded behind them as the cultists downed amber vials of Fire Stimulant. Ronan kept pace with him but still had the look of someone sleepwalking through every movement. Ahead, more guards rushed up the staircase, blocking the way down.

"Don't make this harder than it needs to be, Son!" Ukhel shouted from behind.

Khartsaga ignored him and pulled Ronan up the stairs instead of down. At the next level he rushed them through the hallway and into the library, closing the Sklera door behind him. He turned to face the windows. The curtains were long, but not nearly long enough to drop them to the ground.

He felt exposed without his powers. With the Verdant Stimulant he might have been able to lower them down while riding a table, but with the Inhibitor clouding his head he wasn't any more useful than a human. He glanced at Ronan who hadn't moved. What would the Scarletts do?

An idea popped into his head as pounding footsteps sounded in the hallway. Khartsaga dragged Ronan closer to the window and yanked the curtains down, pulling the whole rod with it. He caught the rod and jammed it into the sitting nook at an angle until it stuck. It wouldn't hold for long, but he didn't need it to.

The door burst open behind them as guards rushed inside. Khartsaga flung Ronan over his shoulder, grabbed the end of the curtain and ran toward the window as fast as he could. The glass shattered around them as they shot out into the open air, fire blasts pelting them from behind. The curtain rod caught them and directed their momentum back toward the wall of the castle where the window was on the floor below.

Khartsaga stuck a foot out and grunted as shards of glass pierced his leg. They broke through the window and tumbled onto the floor. Dark burgundy blood dripped from his ankle, but he ignored it. Ronan had a couple cuts, but nothing major.

"I'm going to get you out of here," he said, searching the man's eyes, but he gave no response. Would he ever recover? There was no time to think about that now.

He pulled Ronan along and rushed out into the hallway. The door to their bedchamber was wide open, but he didn't stop to look inside. All of the guards were likely scrambling to catch up to them on the floor above. He led them toward the stairs again, this time running down to the main floor.

Near the bottom landing, a sense of dread settled in the atmosphere as the light around them dimmed. He gritted his teeth. Shadowmongrels. His father was relentless. Both of them were drugged so their thoughts would be safe, at least, but the beasts had a nasty set of claws that he didn't want to run into. Ronan continued to follow where he was pulled and had been managing to keep up, so Khartsaga sprinted across the open room and past the dim fireplace.

"Why are you running, Son? You can't escape the New Age!" His father's voice echoed down the stairwell.

As he ran, he glimpsed a pair of yellow eyes peering at them from a side hallway. Could they make it to the door in time?

The muffled sound of footsteps made him look back toward the stairs. Ukhel stood on the bottom step with his hands splayed out before him as the mass of guards that had chased them earlier finally caught up.

"Come back, Son! You're making this difficult," Ukhel said as his face turned a deeper shade of crimson.

Khartsaga spun around and pulled Ronan toward the main entrance. With both hands, he forced the large Sklera door open just wide enough for them to squeeze through. He yanked Ronan through the crack before the guards could catch up to them.

Finally he blinked in the late afternoon sunlight, his heart racing as he noticed the horde of Gurvel guards at the gates. That was their only way out. He glanced back as the doors to the castle opened up. They were trapped. The Sklera walls surrounded them on all sides and they didn't have the climbing gear that the Scarletts had used before.

The guards at the main gates took defensive positions and drank vials of

Fire Stimulant. Khartsaga racked his brain for ideas, but nothing came to mind. They couldn't run. They couldn't fight. His father was going to catch them. What would happen to Ronan now?

Beside him, Ronan stared blankly toward a portion of wall to the right of the castle. His expression wasn't completely vacant, almost as if he might be thinking. That's when Khartsaga saw it. A door.

He grabbed Ronan's wrist and pulled him toward it. He had never used this exit before, but he knew it was connected to the military barracks. Not the way he would have chosen to go originally, but it would have to do. Reaching the Sklera wall, Khartsaga tried the door handle, but it was locked. The shouts of guards running toward them grew louder.

Khartsaga took a few steps away and rushed the door, trying to shoulder it open. Surprisingly it gave way. Unlike the large doors of the castle, this one was thinner than the others and opened under his weight. He stumbled through and turned back to grab Ronan. The palace guards were gaining on them. A few fire blasts exploded against the Sklera.

With Ronan in tow, Khartsaga dashed through the military barracks, not daring to look around to see if they were picking up any more pursuers. There were only a few soldiers guarding the entrance, so he ran in that direction at full speed, hoping they would be able to slip by. The guards turned in confusion, surprised to find a commotion coming from inside the compound. Khartsaga flew past them and turned right, running along the street.

Up ahead he could see the archway leading out to the docks. This was the only thing he could think of to get them out of his father's reach. Khartsaga kept running, breathing hard and fast as they pushed past civilians lingering in the streets. A few Gurvel fishermen stared at him curiously as he passed them. They were probably surprised to see their king running away with a human while the entire guard chased after them. Who wouldn't be?

He paused briefly to survey their options amidst the sailors bustling about with fish-filled nets and barrels. Large trading vessels lined the docks, but they required a crew to sail. He pulled Ronan along, desperately looking for something smaller and more manageable. A fisherman with a bucket overflowing with Crustfins passed by them, leaving behind his small craft. With haste, Khartsaga pulled Ronan toward the boat, hoping it would be easy to sail. He unhooked the mooring line, and half picked up and half jumped with Ronan into the boat.

The owner saw them start to sail away and rushed toward them with an angry scowl. Khartsaga waved at him with a sheepish grin and grabbed a paddle to speed up their pace. Once they were away from the dock, he climbed up to untie the sail. He had watched the fishermen do this before and hoped it would work. He just needed to get out of range of the Manipulators. The boat itself was coated with ropesnare milk, but the sail wasn't. Manipulators needed to be able to control it if the wind was unfavorable.

When the wind finally caught the sail, he looked back at the dock and watched as the entire castle guard lined up along the shore. They were out of range. He finally let out a breath of relief. His father would probably hunt them down, but they had made it out alive.

Ronan was sitting in the same place he had left him, staring back at the city as it faded into the distance. His face was swelling and bruising from where Khartsaga's father had struck him, and his skin was covered in goosebumps. Coupled with the dyed hair and stubble on his face, he looked horrible. Almost as if he had been fighting in The Games.

"What have I done?" Khartsaga whispered.

CHAPTER 39

Camouflage

With the number of attacks on the rise,
the Speki and Gurvel were finally inclined to listen to Ravenel.

Esen

DROPPING INTO THE HOLE, Esen looked up at Sarnai and waved his thanks before she closed the door. With a quiet sigh, he made his way through the short tunnel where Wren would be waiting for him. Maybe he had been too firm earlier. It was natural for the kid to want to save his friends. Logically, by saving the city, they would save Ronan and the others, but that was difficult for a kid to understand. Especially after what he had experienced.

He felt his pocket to make sure the cinnamon sweets were still there. Sarnai had managed to buy a few while he was gone as a gift for Wren. Leaving the boy in the middle of an argument had been hard, but he couldn't miss the opportunity to set up a meeting with the Purevs. The future of Galynkhot was riding on that family and their connections.

After days of trying to reschedule, he had finally managed to corner the family's contact. Tomorrow afternoon, he would meet with the Purevs at their home. It was good news, but he still had a lot to plan for. That would come later. Right now, he had someone to comfort.

"Wren?" he called as he stepped into the small safe room. The boy was in bed, nestled beneath a pile of blankets.

Esen took off his cloak and draped it on a chair. "I'm sorry I shouted earlier. Your heart is in the right place, and you had some very good ideas."

The lump on the bed didn't stir. Esen sighed and sat down next to it. Wren had a right to be angry. Everything about this situation was unfair.

"We can't march into the castle and free Ronan because he's too close to Ukhel, but maybe we can help your Speki friends. Breaking into the prison beneath the castle won't be easy, but you made some good points. Of course, we'll need to work out a plan first. I know you want to go, but it's too dangerous.

Even with your camouflage. What would Ronan think if after everything you wound up right where you started?"

Wren didn't move. In fact, it didn't look like he was even breathing. Esen placed his hand on the lump and froze. Heart racing, he yanked the blanket back, revealing a stack of pillows. Wren was gone.

Eira

THE SOUND OF CLINKING glass and murmuring cultists filled the small examination chamber, but Eira didn't bother to look. Instead she stared up at the black ceiling, her head filled with the constant fog of the Inhibitors that the cultists seemed to have an endless supply of. With all of the humans working as slaves, they probably had enough ingredients to make hundreds of Inhibitors and Stimulants.

"Don't give up, Sis," Einar whispered from the table beside her. "We'll get out of here."

Eira didn't respond. It was foolish to continue hoping for an outcome that was impossible. Even if they could break the bonds of the examination table, there were too many cultists to fight through, and once they were back in the Sklera cell, they would be too drugged to even think about escaping. They were out of options.

Closing her eyes, she held back the tears that threatened to slide down her face. It was her fault they were even here to begin with. If she had just jumped out the window with the others, they could have regrouped and formed a new plan in the Scarlet Forest. Killing Ukhel had been too tempting. Now they were being used as his test subjects, helping him grow stronger still. At least he hadn't come back to test that black Stimulant on them again. A shiver passed through her at the thought of it. Whatever it was, it was incredibly powerful.

The door to the examination room thudded against the Sklera wall as a young Gurvel ran inside. "Emergency," he said, struggling to catch his breath. "Up at the castle. All hands needed."

The sudden intrusion piqued Eira's interest slightly, but not enough for her to bother lifting her heavy head. Footsteps scuffled along the flooring as the cultists left to handle whatever emergency was happening in the castle. A few days ago she would have relished the delay in experimentation, but now she wished the cultists would come back so they could get it over with and throw her back in the dark cell where the fog would overcome her mind.

"What's that?" Einar asked.

She turned her head lethargically to look at her brother who was squinting at something.

"What?" she asked, fatigue making it difficult to care.

Einar began to shake his head in uncertainty, but then stopped. His eyes widened. Fighting against the restraints, Eira craned her head up to see what he was looking at.

"Wren!" Einar whispered.

At the edge of the table, the Forestdweller smiled at them, his scales turning back to their normal shade of green. Even after blinking a few times to clear her eyes, Eira watched in disbelief as he unfastened the straps holding Einar to the table.

"Wren, I can't believe you're here!" Einar whispered as he carefully eased himself into a sitting position. "I mean you are here, right? I'm not just seeing things?"

The boy quickly rushed over to Eira and unfastened her restraints as well. Still not fully understanding, she sat up and rubbed her head. "No, I see him too, Nar."

Wren glanced at the door, his tail twitching as he waved for them to follow him.

A smile spread across Einar's face as he got down from the table and followed Wren. "You don't think we're hallucinating from the Inhibitors they've been giving us, do you?"

"It's possible," she said, still not able to grasp what was happening. There had been no way out. They had lost. Ukhel had won. And yet here was Wren, a Forestdweller and a child, appearing out of thin air to lead them to freedom. Her head ached as thoughts and emotions fluttered through her mind.

"Come on, Sister, we need to move," Einar said, stopping beside the door to grab two cloaks that the cultists had left behind. He still looked pallid, but the possibility of escape seemed to have perked him up.

She stepped onto the floor, not daring to believe that they might actually regain their freedom. To help center her thoughts, she did a quick sweep of the room. Various instruments and ingredients were strewn about the tables, including an identical set of vials—likely their next Inhibitor dose.

Something else caught her eye. A section of shelving that wasn't completely flush with the rest of the wood. It was so subtle that even her trained eyes had almost missed it. She stepped over and felt along the edge until she found a section that could be lifted up. The book that Ukhel had been looking at the other day lay inside a small indentation. She grabbed it and then joined Einar and Wren in the hallway. With any luck they might be able to figure out what ingredients he had been using.

"The guards are still gone," Einar whispered as he handed Eira one of the cloaks. "Let's move quickly."

Eira pulled the cloak on as they went, hiding her white hair under the deep cowl. They weren't nearly as tall as the Gurvel cultists, but the cloaks would hide their Speki features. With growing urgency she stumbled down the hallway after Wren who kept looking anxiously over his shoulder. He led them down various passageways, all the while swishing his tail behind him. His large ears were tense and alert, twitching at every sound that echoed in the distance. Where had he even come from? Didn't Ukhel capture him?

Each corner they turned sent a jolt of fear through her veins. At any moment she imagined Ukhel's twisted smile would be waiting for them with a vial of black liquid pressed to his lips.

Somehow they managed to make it all the way to a set of stairs without seeing a single guard. The emergency situation must have been fairly important to warrant such attention. She climbed the stairs behind Einar and forced herself to focus. It didn't matter how Wren had escaped and it didn't matter what kind of emergency the cultists had run off to deal with. Right now, they just needed to make it out of the dungeons.

On the top step, Wren held out a hand to stop them while he pressed his ear against the Sklera door. She glanced at Einar who gave her a small smile that didn't quite light up his violet eyes like it usually did. Despite coming this far, neither of them was convinced that it was actually over.

Wren camouflaged his scales to match the wall and slowly cracked the door open to peer outside. Sunlight streamed over their weary faces after days of sitting in near darkness. It felt so warm and hopeful that for a moment her breath caught in her throat.

Satisfied that the coast was clear, Wren urgently waved for them to follow him. Heart beating violently in her chest, Eira forced her legs to move up the remaining stairs and out into the open. They were surrounded by Sklera walls and plain structures lining a sandy training ground of some kind. Expecting to see guards, she glanced quickly around, but the compound was empty.

Eira followed Wren's form which shimmered in the sunlight, moving too quickly to truly blend in with his surroundings. His shorts couldn't be camouflaged, but since he was so small it was difficult to tell what she was looking at. Passing through the archway that separated this area from the city street, she kept her head down and listened to the distant cries coming from the docks. There were a handful of Gurvel out on the streets, but everyone else had gathered near the pier to watch whatever was happening.

They moved into an alleyway and hid in the shadows. No one on the main street followed them. They were free. They had actually made it out alive.

"There you are," a voice whispered harshly from behind them.

She spun around, tensing her legs as she prepared to run. A Gurvel with deep-set eyes pulled his hood down as he looked from Wren to her and Einar. Pushing past her, Wren ran up to the Gurvel and started moving his hands in a series of signs.

To Eira's surprise the Gurvel bent down to talk to him, still glancing up at her and Einar occasionally.

"I know. I know. We'll talk about it later," the Gurvel said with a tired smile. "For now, let's just worry about getting back to the safe house."

Standing up, the Gurvel started to approach them. This didn't feel right. She took a step back and grabbed Einar's sleeve to pull him with her. After tasting the hope of freedom again, she wasn't about to stroll into another trap.

"Listen," the Gurvel said, slowing his pace and holding his palms out toward them. "I know you don't trust me, and I don't blame you, but we need to get you somewhere safe before that disturbance at the docks ends."

She agreed with him on that point. As soon as the disturbance ended, Ukhel would discover that they had escaped and launch a city-wide search. Making it out of Galynkhot alive would be incredibly difficult, but she would take her chances before trusting a Gurvel.

"My name is Esen," he continued, glancing over his shoulder at the empty alleyway. "I'm a friend of Wren and Ronan. Please, come with me. We need to go. Now."

Nar put a hand on her shoulder and nodded encouragingly. They were running out of time and neither of them was well enough to fight. This Gurvel claimed to know Ronan by name and Wren seemed comfortable with him. She wasn't completely convinced, but regardless she relaxed slightly and let Esen lead them further into the city.

She took careful notes as they snuck through the narrow alleyways, intending to fight her way out if needed. Sunlight warmed her skin as she ducked behind a stack of crates. Now that they were outside, the sense of hopelessness that had gripped her earlier had morphed into a ravenous desire to live. They weren't going to get captured again. She would die before that happened.

CHAPTER 40

Freedom

*The Veiled Paladins worked with the Speki and Gurvel
to plan the destruction of the shadow beasts,
attacking them where they were most vulnerable: the mind.*

Ronan

THE SOUND OF BIRDS chirping and leaves rustling slowly drew Ronan out of his sleep. Blinking slowly, he looked up through the canopy of tree branches above him, not quite comprehending what he was seeing. A light breeze blew through the forest, moving the leaves above him in the warm afternoon sun.

Snapping twigs and footsteps signaled someone approaching, but the scene above him was so peaceful that it didn't startle him. He didn't even feel the need to sit up and see who it was just yet. The footsteps stopped, setting something heavy down on the ground. After a few moments, he heard wood crackling in a campfire as the smell of smoke wafted over to his nose.

"We're having soup again today," a voice said from near the fire. "I think you'll like it, but if not, soup is still easier to get you to swallow, so...we're gonna try it. Whatever it takes."

The voice sounded familiar, but he couldn't place it at first. A strong sense of confusion settled on him, threatening to overtake the comforting blanket of tranquility that he was feeling.

"I'm not entirely sure where we are," the voice continued, "but we should probably move camp again today. If you're up to it. Just in case they come looking for us."

The sound of water bubbling over the fire was soon met with tempting aromas as Ronan continued to stare up at the tree canopy, the smoke drifting up among the branches. He furrowed his eyebrows as lucidity started to come back to him. This wasn't right. Where was he? Why was he in a forest?

A series of cold images crashed through his head, tarnishing every last shred of serenity. The shock of the memories made him groan as he quickly raised his hands up to grab his head. He could almost feel the cold metal of the collar around his neck. Could almost hear the condescending voice of Ukhel taunting him. This wasn't real. It couldn't be. Soon he would wake up and still be chained to that Sklera wall with those ridiculous patterned pants. Ukhel would be standing over him with a stale piece of Inhibitor-laced food and a dagger to make him bleed. That was the only reality that awaited him.

His breathing was ragged, but after the initial shock of the memories had faded he realized he could still hear the birds chattering in the trees. He wanted to open his eyes and see the lush greenery again, but surely as soon as he did the dream would end.

"Ronan?" The voice that had spoken earlier was quiet, but he recognized it now.

Slowly, he cracked open his eyes. Khartsaga's crimson face peered anxiously down at him, the canopy of trees blowing gently above him.

"Khartsaga?" he croaked. The dream didn't end. He was still in the forest.

Khartsaga smiled in relief and quickly turned around to fill up a bowl with the broth he had made. Sitting up cautiously, Ronan looked around at the small clearing they were in. He slid back the blanket that covered him and was surprised to see that he was wearing Khartsaga's black jacket and a pair of roughly sewn burlap pants. His skin was covered in scars and bruises but somehow having regular clothes made them seem less painful. How had he gotten here? The last thing he remembered was sitting alone in the bedroom, chained to the wall.

Khartsaga handed him the bowl of broth and sat down across from him on a fallen log that had been pulled near the fire. Confused, Ronan studied him for a moment, but he didn't seem aggressive. The aroma wafting up from the soup smelled so savory he decided to chance a sip.

The soup was warm and thick as it slid down his throat. Realizing how hungry he was, he couldn't take just one sip. He took a gulp and another and quickly finished the small bowl as Khartsaga watched him from beside the fire.

His hunger satisfied, Ronan tried to ask one of the many questions coming to mind, but coughed as the words came out of his mouth. His throat hurt. He rubbed his neck and cringed as his fingers brushed against raw skin and bruises.

"It's okay," Khartsaga said. "I'm sure you have a lot of questions. Do you remember leaving the castle?"

He shook his head no. Was he...free, then? Had he escaped somehow? Khartsaga filled up another bowl with broth and handed it to him.

"It doesn't surprise me. You've been unresponsive for almost two days. I wasn't..."

"Two days?" Ronan managed to choke out. Had he been out of the castle for that long? He went to run his hand through his hair, but it was much shorter than he last remembered.

"I'm sorry," Khartsaga said, looking down at his boots, "I didn't know how to get the dye out, so I cut most of it off. I thought it might make you feel better."

Taking another sip of soup, Ronan looked at him in bewilderment, still not quite comprehending what had happened. The collar was gone. His clothes had been changed. His hair had been cut. He was out of the castle. But was he really free?

"So, what am I to you now?" he asked.

Khartsaga opened his mouth but closed it again and looked down at the crackling fire.

"Your pet?" Ronan said coldly.

"No. You never were," Khartsaga assured him, still looking at the fire. "That was wrong. Everything we did...everything I did, was wrong. I'm sorry."

Ronan set the bowl down and shakily stood up. More aware of his surroundings now, he suddenly felt a strong urge to run. To get away. To test if he were truly free or if this was still some kind of sick joke. Khartsaga looked up at him but didn't move to stop him.

"Then you would let me walk away?" he asked, searching the Gurvel's eyes.

"Of course," Khartsaga said. "You're free to do whatever you'd like."

Ronan took a few steps away, expecting Khartsaga to jump up and stop him.

"However, I advise you to stay," Khartsaga continued. "You're injured and I can help."

True or not, Ronan just wanted to get moving and prove to himself that it was really over. His heartbeat quickened. At any moment Ukhel could appear from behind a tree and lock him up again. It could all be some elaborate trap to cripple his will to live or trick him into speaking so Ukhel could rip out his tongue. Hoping to hide some of the rising panic, he walked away from the campsite.

"Wait," Khartsaga said, grabbing something from beside the wood pile.

Leery, Ronan turned around and watched him carefully. The mind fog was gone, but he still didn't feel quite like himself. If push came to shove, he might not be able to cast an illusion to escape this time.

"It's not a sword like you're used to," Khartsaga said, handing him a small fishing knife, "but please take it. There shouldn't be shadowmongrels around here, but you might need to defend yourself regardless."

Ronan weighed the knife in his hand. It wouldn't do well in a real fight, but it was better than nothing. Having some kind of weapon in hand dampened his anxiety. He looked up at the Gurvel, not really knowing how to respond.

After a moment of silence, Khartsaga returned to the log and clasped his hands together. It seemed like the tension that had once controlled him was gone. Maybe he had finally decided who he was.

It was unlikely that Ronan had escaped on his own. However, he wouldn't have needed to escape in the first place if Khartsaga hadn't forced him to kill the queen. That's what started this whole mess. For some reason, he wasn't really angry like he should have been. Just tired.

"I need to clear my head," he said before turning away.

Holding onto the knife, he wandered into the forest, moving slowly so that he didn't irritate the bruises along his torso. After walking for a few minutes, he closed his eyes and breathed in the fresh earthy smells that surrounded him. The chirp of birds and moss frogs mixed with the sound of rustling leaves in the wind. It was beautiful. He hadn't left the city often as a soldier, so his time in the Scarlet Forest had been a nice change of scenery. Maybe he could start a new life out here in the woods.

Careful not to go too far from the camp, he opened his eyes and continued toward the faint sound of rushing water. Not too far ahead he found a small brook babbling through the trees. He bent down and threw some water on his face. It was cold and refreshing. The water's movement was slow enough that when he looked down he could see his reflection, shifting slightly with the ripples.

Khartsaga hadn't done a half-bad job with the haircut. He moved his hand up to feel the short hair again and sat back against a rock with his feet resting in the brook. Other than the cool water flowing through his toes, he felt numb. Dare he trust that he was really free? It didn't feel real. Other than his time in the Scarlet Forest, he had never really been free.

He picked up a smooth stone and rubbed it between his fingers.

Even as a soldier, he had been forced to guard The Games or arrest humans for petty crimes. Deserting would have resulted in his squadmates' deaths. The consequences of refusing an order were so grave that it didn't really count as an actual choice. He had been a prisoner even then.

And now? What did freedom mean? Free to do what?

He flung the rock at the water's edge and watched it skip along the surface, cringing as the jacket rubbed against his forearms. It felt like he had been burnt.

He hadn't thought about his teammates in a while. Too much had happened in too short a time. They were dead because of him, and he hadn't even had time to grieve their deaths.

No. They were dead because Khartsaga had controlled him to kill the queen and heir.

He picked up another stone and frowned. Heat rose to his face as he remembered the reasons he had to hate Khartsaga, and yet, he wouldn't be here, beside this brook, without him. Pinching the bridge of his nose, he rubbed the stone between his thumb and forefinger.

Regardless of how he had come to be here, everything and everyone he had come to love was either dead or trapped in that city. Seton. Eira. Einar. Alvina. Wren. His stomach clenched. Had Wren managed to find Esen? There was nothing he could do. He felt helpless.

The memory of Aprika standing tall and proud on that pyre shot through his mind. He had been helpless then too.

He threw the rock harder, this time watching it plink straight down into the brook.

Since that day in the coliseum he had been determined to keep his head down and do what he was told. That was supposed to protect him. That was supposed to protect his friends. But it hadn't. His squadmates had been killed anyway. He had been sentenced to death anyway.

A light breeze blew through the trees. He pulled Khartsaga's jacket tighter around himself. It was way too large for him, but he was grateful for it regardless.

The stream carried with it a handful of leaves, lazily floating along the surface. What had happened to Wren? Esen had been on the run. Even if Wren had found him, was he really safe? The thought of Ukhel finding him, alone in the streets, made his muscles tense up. It hurt, but he didn't care.

A yearning began to form in his heart as he watched the water trickle by. He needed to go back and find Wren. Was that why his parents had done it? Had they plotted against Firekin, risking their lives, to prevent this from happening? Maybe they hadn't been as foolish as he had been led to believe.

He sat by the brook until the sun started to go down, contemplating whether he really intended to go back or not. One thing was certain. He knew his father would have gone back. Months ago that thought alone would have changed his mind—his father had gotten himself killed—but today, that thought comforted him.

As the light faded behind the trees, he got up from the rock and walked back to the campsite. He had to know what happened to Wren, whatever the cost. Despite the terror that threatened to claw its way into his heart, he couldn't walk away knowing that that boy might still be in danger.

When he returned, Khartsaga looked up from tending the fire and smiled in relief. Ronan nodded his head in greeting and sat down in front of the fire, leaning back on his hands to look up at the sky as the stars became visible.

"I'm going back to the city," he said, finding Ravenel's cap in the sky.

"What?" Khartsaga asked.

"I need to find Wren."

Khartsaga was silent as he continued to tend the fire. He probably thought it was foolish to go back after the trouble it had taken to escape. "How can I help?" he asked.

Surprised, Ronan met Khartsaga's eyes across the flickering fire and focused on the edge of his mind. Unlike before when they had tried to break into the castle, Khartsaga's emotions were firm and determined.

"Did Esen get arrested?" Ronan asked.

"Esen? No. Last I heard, we still couldn't find him."

"Good," he said, straightening up. "I told Wren to look for him."

Khartsaga leaned forward to tend to the fire, pushing around some of the embers to keep them alive. "How will you find Wren?"

Ronan slid his fingers through his shorter hair. "I'm not sure. If he's with Esen I could leave a message of some kind in the city and wait for them to find me."

"What if he's not with Esen?"

A spike of fear shot through Ronan. There were fates worse than winding up as Ukhel's "pet". If Wren had been discovered by one of the low-lifes in the city...

"Then I'll just have to search for him," Ronan said. "Maybe I could work on reading minds and see if anyone has found him." With his powers there might be a chance, but it wasn't really a plan. Galynkhot was large, and for all he knew, Wren had fled into the mountains. He took a deep breath. It was either go back and look for the kid or live the rest of his life wondering what happened to him.

"Before that we'll need to get into the city," Khartsaga said.

"Right. How far away are we?"

"I'm not sure actually. We sailed through the night and then set up camp here a little ways into the forest."

"Sailed? So there's a boat?" Ronan asked.

Khartsaga nodded. "We still have it, but they would see us coming long before we reach the docks."

"How did we manage to escape by boat?"

"It was quite the feat," Khartsaga said with a hint of a smile on his lips.

Ronan racked his brain trying to remember anything about leaving the castle, but nothing came to mind. With effort, he ignored the unsettling feeling of memory loss and continued. "So we take the boat part of the way back and stop before the docks, but how do we get inside the city without raising any alarms? Could we climb the wall like we did before?"

"Possibly," Khartsaga said. "Scaling the wall shouldn't be too difficult if we find the right place. A large portion of Firekin was assigned to watch over our mining operation which resulted in fewer guards everywhere else. The only problem is, once we're in the city we're bound to be discovered."

"I've patrolled the streets countless times," Ronan said. "There are plenty of places to hide."

"Hide from view, yes," Khartsaga agreed as he placed another log on the fire. "It's our minds that trouble me. We wouldn't be able to keep our concentration up long enough to obscure our thoughts from Firekin. Even an average citizen could overhear us and alert the guards out of fear."

"Any suggestions?" Ronan asked. His chest felt tight. Finding Wren wasn't possible, was it? By going back, he would only be delivering himself to Ukhel.

They sat listening to the crackling fire, thinking through the possibilities as moss frogs began their nightly cadence and firebugs flickered in nearby shrubs.

"If we could somehow penetrate the fear that Firekin has placed over the population," Khartsaga said, "we could assemble a search party. I'm sure there would be some willing to help look for Wren. It's going to take more than two of us to find him."

"We'd have to get rid of Firekin for that to happen," Ronan said dismally.

That was it then. Were there really no other options? Did it even make sense to go back?

"Yes," Khartsaga said, looking at Ronan. "That's exactly what we need to do."

"You're not serious."

"I am. To accomplish it, we need to remove my father from power."

"You think we can find Wren if we kill Ukhel?"

Khartsaga cringed at his words and became silent. Surely he realized Ukhel had to die. Maybe Ronan had gone too far. He was about to change the subject when Khartsaga spoke again.

"My father will be looking for me. Even as we escaped the castle, he tried to convince me to stay. If we get close enough to the city, we'll likely encounter guards who would take me directly to him."

"How would that help? We'd be killed," Ronan said.

"No. He wouldn't kill me. He'd just punish me and try to reeducate me. Besides, you wouldn't be with me. You could follow us and hide your mind with Seyring."

Ronan considered it for a moment. "What kind of punishment?"

Khartsaga clasped his hands together. "For my latest disobedience? I'd probably be locked in a room and forced to listen to the Fire Creed constantly while my treachery is burnt out with fire. Not enough to kill, but enough to make a point."

Ronan felt Khartsaga's forethoughts with his mind. He was serious. Ukhel really would be so brutal to his own son. And yet Khartsaga was still determined to help.

"I don't think I can hide my mind for more than an hour, though," Ronan said.

Khartsaga stood up and paced beside the log. "That's all we need. We can time it so that they'll take me to Ukhel during The Games. That way you don't have to sneak into the castle."

"Then what?" Ronan asked. "I jump out and stab him?"

"No, Firekin would immortalize him as a martyr. We need to get Ukhel to relinquish his command."

"How?"

Khartsaga stopped pacing and turned toward him. "If Ukhel pronounces me the Eternal Flame, Firekin will have to obey me. Then I can order them to stop everything."

"But how do we make that happen? We would need an assassin pair to gain control of his mind. Even if you and I try it, Ukhel will likely give you an Inhibitor the first chance he gets."

"You don't need me. You can control Ukhel on your own. We just need to get a vial of Verdant Stimulant. That would allow you to use Manipulation and Seyring at the same time. It would only last for a few minutes so you'd have to be quick, but it might work." Khartsaga paused and looked away. "That's how I controlled you before."

Pain as cold as ice shot through Ronan before he could force the memory of that night out of his mind. It took effort, but he willed himself to keep talking. Anything to keep those horrible images away. "Assuming I can get close enough, how do we get our hands on a Stimulant? Do all the guards carry them?"

"No. Not all of them. But the ones closest to Ukhel will have a vial. Do you think you could steal one?" Khartsaga asked, looking at him tentatively.

"I'm not sure."

"That's the only way I can see this working. You take the Stimulant, control Ukhel to give up his throne, and then..." Khartsaga stopped, jaw clenching as if he couldn't bring himself to finish his sentence. They were planning the end of everything he had ever known. Let alone the death of his own father.

"I think it's the most dangerous plan I've ever heard of," Ronan said, standing up. "But I don't have a better one and we need to find Wren before someone else does. So let's try it. We can figure out exactly what we want Ukhel to say on the boat ride back."

Khartsaga nodded and quietly began packing up the few things they had in the camp. With a small push against his thoughts, Ronan could tell that this plan caused him grief. He couldn't believe he was actually working with Khartsaga, but the Gurvel had changed. It was a dangerous plan, but there was the smallest flicker of hope that it could work. And if it did, they would save not only Wren, but all of the humans trapped in The Games and the mines.

CHAPTER 41

The Purevs

They created an army made up of not only Speki and Gurvel,
but also Ravenel's human team of Seyrs and Manipulators.

Esen

SUNLIGHT GLINTED OFF OF the pockmarked Sklera door of the Purev's
house. Pulling the cowl closer to his face, Esen knocked and waited with baited
breath. Tomor and Odval Purev had suggested he come by during the day this
time. They often had guests over, so they thought it would draw less suspicion.
Besides, it was more dangerous to meet at night now that the number of patrols
had increased.

A spindly Gurvel servant opened the door and led him inside to a large
ornate sitting room, covered with dark green and blue patterned carpets and
drapes. Esen sat down in one of the plush armchairs and gratefully accepted a
hot cup of dragonbreath tea from the servant.

"So this is the Gurvel that has the city on such high alert," a refined voice
called from the hallway. Tomor Purev entered the sitting room, leaning on a
thin wooden cane to support his bad leg. His wife, Odval, followed him and
smiled at Esen in a way that drew attention to her bony cheeks and sharp nose.

Esen stood up to shake Tomor's hand. "Thank you for meeting with me.
Your support is greatly appreciated." He shook Odval's hand as well and then sat
back down in the armchair.

"Don't thank us yet," Tomor said, taking a seat on the gray sofa next to
Esen. "We haven't yet decided if we will support your little group or not."

Outwardly Tomor appeared to be confident, but Esen detected faint
nervousness playing at the edge of his mind.

"Of course." Esen nodded as he took a sip of the hot tea.

"So tell us," Odval said, eyes darting back to the hallway, "why should we
help you?"

Resisting the urge to take another sip of tea to wet his lips, Esen straightened.

224

"I know even meeting with me is a risk, so I'll keep this brief. Firekin has taken the throne and removed all of the humans from the city. That's a sizable portion of the population. We both know that the economy will plummet as a result. And who do you think Khartsaga and Ukhel will turn to when businesses and trade start to suffer?"

Tomor nodded slowly and tapped his fingers lightly on the cane. "We expect them to come to us and the other established families. But how would supporting your rebellion benefit us? Right now, should we be called upon to bail the city out of financial turmoil, all we lose is money."

"You have connections with many of the Generals in the king's militia," Esen said, leaning forward. "With your help, we can convince them to join us, overthrow Firekin, and return the human population to the city. That will slow down the economic spiral long enough for us to reestablish a governing system and stabilize the city's infrastructure."

Odval sat back and crossed her ankles, glancing at her husband while pulling at a loose thread at the end of her shirt. He had expected them to be nervous, but something about the way her eyes kept darting around set Esen on edge.

"And financial support for all of this?" Tomor asked.

"I'm not asking for your financial support," Esen said, taking another sip of his tea. "What we need is the support of the military. With that, we'll return the city to a more stable system so you can continue living the way you prefer."

Tomor ran his fingers through his short graying hair and glanced at his wife. "Well, it certainly gives us something to think about. Would you mind if we took a day or two to discuss it?"

They were scared and unwilling to commit. If he let them think for too long, they would never join him, and without them there wouldn't be much of a rebellion to fight Ukhel. "Time isn't a luxury we can afford, but I understand the weight of the situation. I'll come back tonight. If you decide to join us, light a torch and put it in this window. If not, keep the room in darkness."

"Alright. I think we can manage that," Tomor agreed. "But there's no need to leave so soon. That might draw suspicion after all."

Odval didn't make any moves to stand either and continued picking at the loose thread. Something didn't feel quite right. They had every reason to be nervous. Honestly, he was surprised they had actually agreed to meet with him. Even so, there was a rising tension in the room that was almost palpable.

He set his tea down and stood, putting out his arm to shake Tomor's hand.

Even if it drew suspicion, he felt a sudden urgency to leave the confines of this room. "Unfortunately I can't stay. Perhaps I could use a back door or window to throw off any observers."

"Oh no, that won't be necessary," Tomor said, rising to his feet. "I'll just have my servant check the street before you head out."

While Tomor called for the servant, Esen looked around the room one last time. A book on one of the side tables caught his attention. *The Legend of Ravenel* glimmered in golden letters against a soft leather cover. He picked it up. "Tomor. A friend of mine was looking for this. Mind if I borrow it in the future? Assuming we solidify this partnership, of course."

Tomor clasped his hands together on top of his cane and smiled. "Of course. In fact, you're welcome to read it now if you'd like to. I can have more tea made."

Esen set the book down and walked into the hallway where the spindly servant was waiting by the door. "That's alright. Like I said, I can't stay."

"Are you sure?" Tomor asked. "It's a short book. If you prefer, I can have the servants bring up some ale."

They were stalling. Something was wrong. He needed to leave. Now. The servant reached out to turn the handle with shaky hands as he approached the door. It was too late.

The servant barely had time to scramble out of the way when the door burst open. Esen's legs tensed as he instinctively tried to run but there wasn't enough time to move. Three burly soldiers lunged at him and tackled him to the ground.

He fought against the two that held him by pushing into their minds, but the third guard injected him with a thin needle before he could do anything. Instantly a cloudy haze filled his mind and made his skull throb with a dull ache. He groaned and continued to struggle on the ground as the guards bound his hands and hauled him back to his feet. Once he was standing, he noticed that the third guard was unfortunately familiar to him.

Ulagan gave him a coy smile. "If you engaged your brain every once in a while, maybe you would have sensed us coming."

Ignoring his former teammate, Esen chose to look at his hosts. Tomor and Odval stood in the middle of the sitting room, eyes staring blankly at the patterns on the rug. Neither of them said anything or even looked in his direction. It had been a trap from the beginning. He was a fool for thinking that Ukhel hadn't already bribed or coerced the well-established families into blind loyalty.

226

Exhaustion settled in his bones as reality hit. It was over. He stopped struggling and let the guards drag him out of the house. He had known the risks from the day he started this whole endeavor. It had always been a matter of time, and today, his luck had finally run out.

AFTER FORCING ESEN TO WALK through crowded streets, the guards led him into the coliseum where they pushed him into a Sklera hallway filled with metal holding cells. Each cell was packed with humans waiting for their turn to be slaughtered in The Games.

Ulagan stepped in front of him while the other two guards tightened their grip on his arms. Their squabble during the queen's pregnancy was apparently far from being over. He braced himself for what was coming.

With a crazed gleam in his eyes, Ulagan landed a solid punch in Esen's gut and followed with a swift blow to his head. Before Esen could catch his breath, a series of punches landed on his ribcage and abdomen. The hallway swam before him as he struggled to stay standing. Not willing to let him fall, the guards grabbed him under the armpits and held him in place.

Ulagan grabbed his jaw and forced his head up. "Look at you. You're pathetic. Where's your arrogant personality now?"

"Probably the same place you left your wit," Esen said between ragged breaths. "Oh wait, you never had any to begin with."

This time, Ulagan grabbed his shoulders and kneed him in the stomach. With an involuntary heave, Esen vomited across the pockmarked floor. Despite the pain, he was satisfied to note that a good portion of it landed on Ulagan's boots.

"Joke all you want," Ulagan said. "Soon enough you'll be burning at the stake with the worthless pets you love so much. Throw him in a cell."

"There's no room," one of the guards objected.

"Then we'll make room," Ulagan said, motioning for them to drag Esen down the hallway. "What about that cell, in the corner? There's plenty of room." He pointed to a cell with one single prisoner in it.

"She's in isolation for encouraging the others to revolt."

"It doesn't matter. Throw him in with her. Tomorrow they'll both be purified by fire."

The guards unlocked the cell, injected Esen with a fresh dose of Inhibitor and shoved him inside. Disoriented from the wave of fog that flooded his mind, he fell to the floor and barely had time to defend himself before Ulagan slammed his foot into his side.

With a loud click, the metal door locked behind him. At least the torment was over for now. He waited until he heard the sound of their footsteps fade down the hallway before trying to lift his head.

Grimacing, he pushed himself up and sat with his back against the bars. Across from him a woman with a dark braid over her shoulder raised an eyebrow.

"They never bring Gurvel here. What'd you do?" she asked.

He gingerly felt his ribs to see if anything was broken. Pain flashed through his chest as he prodded his right side. Definitely injured. "Oh, nothing really. Just attempted to assemble a resistance to fight the strongest cult in Amidral. What about you?"

"This is the coliseum. They bring humans here just for being human."

"True. But they don't give just any human their own cell." He nodded toward the larger holding cells spanning the rest of the hallway. "What made you stand out enough to earn your own prison?"

She gave him a tired smile. "I led an escape from the mines. They had us digging for some kind of green crystal that was giving us all migraines. After a few days we figured out that the Gurvel needed us to mine it because it was too potent for them. So we overwhelmed their senses with some of the ore and ran. We almost managed it, but they cut us off at the entrance."

Considering the level of importance Firekin placed on their Stimulant resources, it was impressive that they had even made it to the entrance.

"Sounds like we're on the same side," he observed. "Shame to have to meet like this. A few years ago I would have suggested we talk some more at the Seaside Tavern. Maybe order a couple mugs of Seton's spiced ale."

"I'd have taken you up on that," she said with a sigh. "I used to believe Gurvel and humans could learn to live in harmony. That dream is dead now." She looked over at one of the holding cells. "That dream killed my family and put my friends in slavery."

They were a lot alike. He had shared a similar dream once. When he had seen those people burning in the coliseum a couple decades ago, he had really believed that if he acted, others would join him. Now it was over. There was no resistance. Wren and the Speki were stuck in a city that wanted to kill them, Ronan was trapped with that tyrannical monster, and the entire human population was now subjected to slavery or mindless slaughter. He had failed.

He had failed all of them.

"I'm sorry," he whispered.

They sat in silence for a few moments until the woman slid herself over beside him. "Maybe it's not a dead dream. You tried to fight them after all."

"I failed."

"But you tried," she insisted. "That means that even after we die, there will be others who will try. One day, Firekin will fall. It's just a matter of time."

"Maybe," he said, searching her eyes. A small spark of hope glimmered in her dark pupils.

"I'm Alvina, by the way."

"Esen."

"For what it's worth, Esen," she said with a faint smile, "if we survive this, I'll take you up on that ale."

"Well, now I'll be disappointed if we never get to have that drink. Any ideas about how to escape?"

"Any chance you can use your powers?"

"No. Even if I wasn't drugged, I'm a Seyr, not a Manipulator."

"Well, that's unfortunate," she said. "I've tried picking the lock, but there's nothing thin or sharp enough."

"If we're lucky, we might be able to get our hands on one of the guard's daggers." He craned his neck to see if Ulagan and the others were still in view. There didn't appear to be any guards on duty at the moment.

"Why would they need a dagger if they have Manipulation?"

"It's a backup. Most Gurvel soldiers carry one on them."

"How do we get one?" Alvina asked, sitting up straighter.

"That's what we need to figure out," he said, but the Inhibitor in his system made it difficult to think.

For years he had been able to keep an optimistic outlook even knowing that one day he might end up here. It had always seemed worth it because he assumed if he were caught, there would be enough of a resistance built up to finish his work, but in the last few weeks he had barely made any progress. The military and major Gurvel families had sided with Ukhel. Only a few shopkeepers had agreed to join him, and they had made it clear that they wanted to remain anonymous. Without him, the little resistance that had grown would crumble.

With a sinking feeling in his gut, he rested his face against the bars. Even if they could steal a dagger, their odds of escape were low if not impossible.

CHAPTER 42
The Secret

*In preparation, Ravenel worked late into the night
creating a new Stimulant for the army. But he worked in secret,
revealing to no one what the Stimulant contained.*

Eira

THEY WAITED FOR SARNAI to return, hoping that the old Gurvel hadn't
gone missing in the middle of the night like Esen had. Eira hated to admit it,
but they needed these Gurvel because without them they would be stuck in the
middle of a hostile city with no access to food. The thought of it made the walls
of the small room feel like they were caving in on her.

"Keep pacing like that, Sister, and you might wear a hole deep enough
for us to escape through." Despite his confident jokes, Einar's white hair was
disheveled from all the times he had run his fingers through it. Neither of them
slept well. Wren looked just as weary sitting beside him at the table with his ears
drooping slightly as he read the book she had taken from the examination room.

"You realize if she doesn't come back, we're trapped here," Eira said.

"We're not trapped," Einar responded, rolling his eyes. "It would just be
difficult to leave, but it's still possible."

She shook her head and continued pacing around the room. Energy raged
through her, forcing her to keep moving. At any moment, she expected a horde
of Firekin guards to burst through the trapdoor and capture them. Sarnai had
been helpful so far, but she could easily be coerced into revealing their location.

"Listen, why don't we try and figure out how to counter the Stimulant
Ukhel made?" Einar asked, scooting his chair closer to Wren. "At least that will
be productive. Unless of course you want to continue wearing away your trench."

She walked up to the table. "Nar, we've pored over these pages for two days
now and we still have no idea how he even made the Stimulant, let alone how
to counter it."

"Patience, Sister. Let's go over what we know. Ukhel sent the other cultists away so he could use this Stimulant in secret. Then he made notes in this book, *The Legend of Ravenel*, about the ingredients that he used. Therefore, he's keeping this Stimulant to himself and he thinks this book is the key to creating it."

"Regardless of how he created it, we still don't know how to counteract it. He broke through the Inhibitors, Nar. How do we even begin to fight that?"

Perking up at their conversation, Wren leaned forward and pointed to a section of the book where Ukhel had underlined a passage.

A secret kept in mind. Feather. Ash. Crystal. Power combined. Next to the text Ukhel had scribbled down various notes to indicate which ingredients he had experimented with. Three shredded phoenix feathers, a handful of powdered ashbark, and a pinch of verdant crystal fragments. The only part of the phrase that he hadn't commented on was the first part: a secret kept in mind.

Eira sighed and continued to pace around the room. "We know what three of the four ingredients are, but that means nothing if we can't figure out the first one." Of course she had seen him make it, but the mind fog had been so strong that it continued to cloud even her memory.

They all jumped as the trapdoor thudded open from down the short hallway.

"Don't be alarmed. It's me," Sarnai called as she shuffled into the safe room.

Eira breathed out a sigh of relief. At least they wouldn't starve.

"Any news about Esen?" Einar asked, standing up to join Eira. From the table, Wren pursed his lips in anticipation.

"Yes..." Sarnai answered, shoulders drooping slightly. "It's like we assumed. They caught him while he was meeting with the Purevs." She paused briefly, her voice cracking as she continued. "He's to be purified by fire at The Games tomorrow morning."

An uneasy coldness gripped Eira's stomach. What would become of them now? She hadn't been able to completely trust the Gurvel yet, but at least Esen had kept them safe.

Wren stared at Sarnai with wide eyes and gripped the edge of the table until his knuckles turned white. The news probably meant more to him than simply losing his own safety.

"I will do everything I can to find a way for you to leave the city," Sarnai said, looking at each of them in turn. "For now you'll need to stay here until the excitement dies down."

"Thank you, Sarnai. We appreciate your help," Einar said. "I'm sorry about Esen."

"Me too," she responded, her wrinkled face sagging more than usual. "Try to get some rest if you can. I'll bring down some food in the morning before I head to the coliseum."

They were silent as Sarnai climbed out of the hole and closed the trap door. At least they weren't stranded without food, but this certainly complicated their situation.

Wren tapped the table to get their attention. *"There shouldn't be a secret ingredient,"* he signed.

Since they had been stuck in one room for two days, Eira had started to learn the boy's language, filling in the gaps with the thoughts flashing through his mind.

"What do you mean?" Einar asked.

Wren slid the book toward them. *"This sounds familiar. Phoenix feathers, ashbark, and green crystals. I think those are the ingredients for vim tea. I was too young to drink it, but I watched the older Forestdwellers make it. There was no fourth ingredient."*

"You mean like the tea mentioned in the story?" Einar asked.

Eira stepped forward and looked at the book again. If that tea actually existed and there was no fourth ingredient, then what had Ukhel done to turn it into such a powerful Stimulant?

"Well, in that case," Einar said, rifling through the book, "perhaps we're looking at this the wrong way."

"We've been scouring it day and night," she protested. "How else could we look at it?"

Einar smiled and landed on a page with an illustration of Ravenel standing beside a cart of merchandise. "It's a story, right? So instead of trying to crack a code, we should try looking at the story itself."

"Nar, it's a children's story."

"Precisely." He flashed her a smile. "Wren, would you mind telling us what this story is about?"

The boy's bat-like ears perked up as he leaned forward to respond. *"It's about a man who became a Seyr and created an army to kill the shadowmongrels before they could destroy the world."*

Einar nodded his head and flipped to another page in the book. "That sums it up fairly well, but before he created that army it says that he met with the Forestdwellers. Listen to this:

"'As Ravenel improved his skills, the Forestdwellers taught him how to make vim tea. They told him that vim tea was as old as the mountains and gave new knowledge to those who drank its leaves. A secret kept in mind. Feather. Ash. Crystal. Power combined. These are the only words Ravenel ever revealed when questioned about the power he learned from the Forestdwellers.'"

"We've read this part a million times, Nar."

"Stay with me, Sister!" Einar said, leaving the table to pace the room. "Trust the process. In this passage we learn that Ravenel was so determined to improve his powers that he explored them on his own because no one else would teach him. Sounds familiar doesn't it, Sister?"

Eira rolled her eyes. "If you're referring to my reluctance to teach Ronan, I fail to see how it's relevant."

"Ronan and Ravenel are a lot alike," Wren signed. *"Maybe he could help us figure out the other ingredient."*

"Possibly," Einar said. "If only we knew where he was. I'm still shocked that the disturbance down at the docks was Ronan and Khartsaga running from the palace guard."

Something about the similarities between Ronan and Ravenel weighed on Eira. It felt like an important piece of the puzzle was just out of reach.

"Wait. Wren," Eira said. "How would Ronan help us?"

"Vim tea is strong," Wren signed. *"Maybe if he drank it like Ravenel, he could figure it out."*

Yes. The tea was part of the solution. Ravenel was with the Forestdwellers, drinking that tea and practicing his Seyring powers at the same time. Almost like when Speki trained with Inhibitors and...

"It's a Stimulant," she whispered.

"Not on its own," Einar said. "If it were, Ukhel wouldn't have been searching for a fourth ingredient."

"It is a Stimulant. A Stimulant for human Seyrs." Eira grabbed the book from Einar and read the passage again. "A secret kept in mind. Ravenel's mind. The fourth ingredient has something to do with Ravenel...or in this case, Ronan."

"If you're right," Einar agreed. "Ukhel shouldn't be able to make more of the Stimulant without Ronan."

A wave of energy rushed Eira's heart. There was a chance. It could take Ukhel decades, maybe even centuries, to find another human Seyr. Until then he could be beaten. They could still avenge their people.

Wren jumped up from his seat. *"Then we can save Esen."*

"I'm afraid it's too late for that," Einar said.

"But you're assassins. Can't you do something?"

"That's not how it works, Wren," Einar said sadly.

The boy wasn't far off. She and Nar had performed extractions before. Occasionally it had been necessary in order to procure key intelligence. This situation was different, but perhaps if they could create enough chaos...

"We could make it work," Eira ventured.

"Sister..." Einar's warm voice filled her head.

"He's right, Nar," she spoke aloud to keep Wren in the conversation. If Nar was outnumbered, she might be able to persuade him. "We are Speki assassins. This would be just like our mission in Bellzul."

"Oh really? Just like Bellzul?" Einar asked. "We still don't know how much of the Stimulant Ukhel has already made. And, in case you've forgotten, the entire city is looking for us."

"He's a monster, Nar. If we don't kill him, who will?"

Einar gave a long sigh and sat down with his head in his hands. After a moment he looked up at her with a tired smile. "In Bellzul, I seem to recall having more Stimulants. Unless my calculations are off, we currently have a grand total of zero."

"We won't need them," she said, joining Nar at the table. "I'll get close enough to create a simple illusion that the guards will have to respond to. Then you make the kill."

"You make it sound so simple," Einar said, "and yet lately things haven't been working in our favor. Besides, how would killing Ukhel save Esen?"

"If Ukhel's body is thrown into the arena it would cause a massive distraction. That's when we extract Esen."

"Oh yes, we'll just waltz into the center of the arena and carry him out," Nar retorted sarcastically. "No one would notice that."

Wren climbed on top of the table and sat down in front of them with his tail flicking back and forth behind him. *"I can do it. I'll be invisible."*

"It's much too dangerous, Wren," Einar countered.

"We were his age when we went on our first mission," Eira pointed out. Or at least they had been the equivalent of Wren's age. For Speki, childhood lasted about a century.

"Besides," she continued, "Wren has already successfully performed an extraction."

"Dear Sister," Einar said with a chuckle, "if I wasn't born with this hair color, I'd blame you for making it turn white. Fine. We can try. But at the first sign of trouble we all need to run. Deal?"

"Thank you, Brother."

Einar smiled and then turned his full attention to Wren. *"Deal?"*

Wren nodded emphatically.

"Then it's set," Einar decided. "We'll leave tonight and find a vantage point to scout out the area. If all goes well, maybe we can leave the city and look for Ronan. I'm sure he'll love how much danger we're walking into."

Ronan. If only she had had more time with him. Despite her reluctance to train him at first, she had actually looked forward to watching his progress. If they survived, perhaps they could still train together. She wouldn't mind seeing that look of determination in his eyes again. Especially after all of this.

Ronan

RONAN CROUCHED IN THE SHADOW of the outer city wall listening intently for sounds of alarm. As anticipated, there had been cultists at the front gates ready to greet Khartsaga. Now all he had to do was scale the wall, steal the Verdant Stimulant, and take control of Ukhel's mind while he was distracted by Khartsaga. His heart felt like it was about to grow wings and fly off like a phoenix. This was insane. It wasn't too late to turn around. Khartsaga would be stranded, but he didn't really owe him anything.

Only that wasn't entirely true. Khartsaga had saved him from the shadowmongrel and without him, he wouldn't even be here right now. He would be with Ukhel, chained up like some brainless pet.

With a deep breath, he pulled out the stone daggers that Khartsaga had made for him. Now that the human population had been forced into slavery, there was a good chance that the guards wouldn't be worried about someone scaling the wall. Or so he convinced himself as he looked up at the menacing obstacle of living rock.

Before he could change his mind, he slammed the first dagger into the wall and began climbing. Using his bare feet to grip the small indents in the Sklera, he was able to take some of the weight off of his arms. Regardless, the process was strenuous, especially in his malnourished state.

About halfway up, a guard passed by on the wall walk above and paused to look across the open field. Ronan clung to the wall and tried not to make any noise, but his muscles were shaking from the exertion. Finally, the guard continued on his patrol without raising any alarms.

Sweat dripped freely down his face. Every time Ronan jabbed the dagger into the Sklera his hands burned and threatened to slip. His arms were going to give out if he didn't hurry, but he couldn't physically go any faster. With determination, he focused only on the next step until he made it to the top and was able to swing onto the wall walk.

Before anyone could see him, he ducked behind a crate and struggled to regain control of his breath. He had known the climb would be difficult, but that had been near impossible. He rubbed the palms of his hands which were red and swollen. Could he even make the climb down the other side like this?

He had to try. Otherwise someone would find him. There were a few guards farther along the wall walk, but they were focused on a card game, so he crept over to the edge facing the city and looked down.

The streets were empty. Convincing himself that everyone else was at The Games, he swung one leg over the side of the wall and stuck the dagger into the Sklera to descend.

Sweat continued to roll down the sides of his face. Worse than before, the raw skin on his palms burned as if scorched by flame every time he drove the dagger into the wall. He wasn't going to make it. With gritted teeth he kept going, forcing himself to hold onto the homemade climbing tools, but near the bottom his grip slipped. With a loud crash he fell onto a pile of barrels in the cobblestone streets below.

Not checking to see if he was injured, he scrambled up and dove behind a nearby cart before any of the guards saw him. His back hurt, but luckily nothing felt broken. There was some scuffling at the top of the wall, but eventually the guards moved on. Hopefully they assumed the commotion was caused by a stray fox or some other small creature.

He closed his eyes and recentered his mind, imagining the ocean and erecting the mind barrier again. Now that he was in the city, he needed to be more careful. The closer he was to Ukhel, the easier it would be for the Gurvel to detect him if his concentration slipped. The next step of the plan involved stealing a Verdant Stimulant from Ukhel's personal guards, but he didn't move from behind the cart. This was reckless. He should let his hands rest and then leave the same way he had come in.

And then what? He didn't know where the Scarletts' new base was. Even if he did, could he live with himself knowing that Eira, Einar, and Alvina were still trapped here? Could he sleep at night knowing Wren might have been captured by Ukhel again?

Before he could change his mind, he ran across the street and hid beside an empty booth. It didn't look like anyone had seen him, so he snuck in and out among the stalls, careful to stay out of sight.

He had patrolled the stairwell to the king's platform before, so with the image of the ocean still held clearly in his mind, he ran up the steps and slid into the first alcove. If he kept sneaking up the stairwell and waited near the entrance to the viewing platform, he might be able to grab a Stimulant from one of the guard's pockets, but if they caught him...

Wiping the sweat off of his face he tried not to think about what Ukhel would do to him, but his imagination refused to be tamed. If he were captured, he would likely burn on his own pyre, just like his parents. Since the day they died, he had always blamed them for being foolish, but now he finally understood. This was what they were trying to prevent. If they hadn't been caught, maybe Ukhel never would have gained control of Galynkhot. Now it was his turn.

He took a deep breath and moved on to the next alcove, listening for approaching guards as he went. From there he continued toward the viewing platform where the large swell of the crowd thundered in his ears. He could almost feel the cold metal around his neck again. He shouldn't be here. This was suicide.

Eira. Wren. Kendra. Manton. Aprika. Their faces flashed through his mind.

He had to try. He owed it to them.

Holding his breath, he eased himself onto the last step. All of the guards were standing behind Ukhel's throne with Khartsaga. A chill swept across his skin. Just a few days ago he had been chained to that throne, forced to watch human after human brutally murdered. He pushed the memory away. If he lost concentration now, the mind barrier would drop and he would likely find himself in the same situation again—or worse.

Luckily everyone was focused on something in the coliseum pit, including

Khartsaga, so he crept toward a guard on the end who had a bulge in his pocket. Once he was close enough, he carefully reached his hand in and pulled out a vial.

Ukhel stood up suddenly and lifted his arms up to address the crowd. "Gurvel one and all!"

Ronan practically jumped out of his skin but somehow resisted the urge to drop the vial. Thankfully, no one had noticed him yet so he forced himself to quietly exhale. Now that Ukhel had the crowd's attention, this could be the perfect moment to take control of his mind.

"Today, we'll start The Games with a Fire Purification!" Ukhel announced. "A few days ago we caught not one, but two rebellious creatures. You'll notice that one of them is a Gurvel, but his acts of treason have proven him to be nothing more than an animal at heart."

While Ukhel talked, Ronan uncapped the vial and ran through what he and Khartsaga had rehearsed. He would force Ukhel to transfer command of Firekin to Khartsaga and then explain that there was one more piece to finalize the New Age: his own death. Then Ronan would force Ukhel to stab himself with his own dagger. Khartsaga had been resistant about the plan at first, but had eventually admitted that they didn't have any other option.

"As a mercy to both of these creatures," Ukhel continued, "we will help them reach their true potential through purification. Then we have a special entertainment planned to remind us all of the glory that Gurvel rightfully deserve."

The crowd cheered so violently that the thunderous sound shook even the floor that Ronan was crouching on. He stood and raised the green flecked liquid to his mouth. Before the glass vial touched his lips, he glanced over the railing and froze. The arena was empty except for a large covered box on the far wall and a single pyre in the center. Bound to a stake on top of the pyre, Esen and Alvina stared up at Ukhel as a group of cultists on the arena floor uncapped their amber Fire Stimulants. His heart sank and in that moment, his mind barrier wavered. It was down for only a fraction of a second, but it was enough. Ukhel turned to look over his shoulder and locked eyes with him, a devious smile playing at the edge of his lips.

CHAPTER 43
Discovered

Finally, with Ravenel's Stimulant, the army marched into the Scarlet Forest where the shadow beasts made their home.

Khartsaga

DREAD FILLED KHARTSAGA'S STOMACH as Ukhel turned his head to the side and smiled at something off to the right. He followed his father's gaze and saw Ronan holding the Verdant Stimulant up to his lips. Something must have made his concentration falter. The vial shot out of his hand and flew toward Ukhel who caught it.

Ukhel looked from Ronan to Khartsaga. "What a beautiful day. First my son returns, and now my faithful pet has come home as well."

Ronan glanced at Khartsaga and then bolted toward the stairs. He didn't even make it three steps before the nearest guard caught him and dragged him over to Ukhel.

"Let him go, Father. I'm who you really want," Khartsaga said, taking a step forward. One of the other guards grabbed his shoulder and firmly held him in place.

"I'm glad to have you back, Son, but disappointed to see that you've become even weaker. If you continue down this path you'll wind up dead, just like your mother."

"She wasn't weak for offering to feed those men!" Khartsaga cried.

"She foolishly chose to invite them into the house!" Ukhel yelled. "Had she treated them like the vile animals that they were, she never would have died."

"Humans aren't animals," Khartsaga said. That much he was sure of. No level of discipline from his father was going to change his mind.

Ukhel's nostrils flared, but he took in a long breath and continued in a calmer tone. "I won't let you become as foolish as she was. Guards, take him to one of the holding cells while I welcome my pet."

A burning panic rose in Khartsaga's chest as the guard pulled him toward the stairs. He dreaded the punishment that would be unleashed upon him later, but the thought of seeing the life drain from Ronan's eyes again was somehow even more terrifying. Since they hadn't given him an Inhibitor yet, he elbowed the guard and yanked a vial out of his pocket.

Immediately, the guards started slinging anything they could at him while they scrambled to drink Stimulants. Khartsaga downed the amber vial he had stolen and dodged past a flying banner. Not the Stimulant he had hoped for, but he would make do. They would capture him again, but he could manage.

He rushed toward the guard holding Ronan and shot a series of fireballs at the Gurvel's face. Ronan broke free and darted toward the stairs. Khartsaga kept throwing fire at the other guards, trying desperately to give Ronan an opening, but there were too many of them blocking the exit.

While he fought, Khartsaga caught a glimpse of Ukhel watching with a bemused expression on his face. An intense heat washed through him. This was his father. The Eternal Flame of Firekin. The Gurvel who had forced him to endure torturous punishments. No more. Ukhel wasn't going to enslave anyone else today. Not while Khartsaga was still breathing.

Drawing upon his anger, he increased the size and speed of his fireballs, showering the guards in a reign of fire. Some of them shuffled aside to avoid the projectiles, but not enough for Ronan to get through.

Unexpectedly, Ronan gave up on the stairwell and leapt over the railing into the coliseum instead. Khartsaga stopped his volley of fireballs and anxiously looked down at the arena. Was the situation so dire that he had chosen death? He looked for Ronan's broken body, but the man was unharmed. Rolling to decrease the impact, Ronan sprung back to his feet and sprinted toward the pyre at the center.

Shouts of surprise echoed around the audience. What was he doing? There was nowhere to run! Khartsaga attempted to jump into the arena with him but was quickly apprehended by the remaining guards.

Eira

CROUCHING BESIDE EINAR AND WREN, Eira carefully scanned the viewing platform, watching Ukhel's every move. They had managed to find a lookout spot above the highest level of audience seating. From here they had mapped out their escape route and counted Ukhel's guards. It was time to move into position.

"Two extractions is going to be significantly more difficult," Einar whispered, staring at the pyre below where Esen and Alvina were waiting for the Fire Purification to start.

"Wren, do you remember the plan?" Eira asked.

But the boy only responded by pointing toward the viewing platform before quickly covering his ears again. A figure jumped over the railing and rolled onto the sandy floor. Her eyes weren't as good as Wren's, but she could make out enough of the man's features to recognize him. Her heart leapt as Ronan got back up and ran toward the pyre.

"What is he doing here!?" Einar cried.

Bare-chested guards swarmed into the arena and quickly surrounded Ronan. There was nowhere for him to go except toward the center. What was he doing? She leaned over the edge to get a better look. Ronan continued sprinting toward the center and climbed onto the pyre. He had never intended to run toward the exits. In disbelief she watched as he frantically started to untie Alvina and Esen. He was going to fail. Even if he freed them there were too many guards. Eira shook her head. "They're outnumbered."

Before he finished untying the rope, one of the guards kicked him off the pyre while another one tackled him to the ground. Eira gripped the edge of the Sklera as a cold wave of fear passed through her. Even with Stimulants they would never get down there in time. She was going to watch him die, just like she had watched her city burn.

Without warning, Ronan stopped struggling and lay still. She held her breath until suddenly, the guard released him to attack something else on the ground. Only there wasn't anything else on the ground. Ronan had created an illusion! If only she had had more time to work with him. The roar of the audience crescendoed into a solid wall of noise as Ronan sprung up and ran toward the pyre again.

"He's trying so hard to free them, but he's not going to make it," Einar said. "Can't we do something? Anything?"

Two guards leapt onto the pyre, grabbed Ronan by the shoulders, and threw him back onto the sand. She didn't want to watch, but she couldn't pull her eyes away as Ronan kicked and struggled against them.

"They're going to kill him," she whispered.

He was able to break free of the guards' hold with another illusion, but sooner or later they would realize what he was doing and adapt.

"Can you send a message to him from here?" Einar asked.

With a Stimulant it would have been easy, but they didn't have that. The only person she could message from this distance was Einar, and that was only because they had spent decades practicing. She took a deep breath and worked to center her mind. "I can try."

<hr>

Ronan

WITH A HARD PUSH AGAINST the guard's mind, Ronan yanked his arm free and ran toward the pyre. It was pointless to try and free Alvina and Esen, but he couldn't watch them burn. Not again. He would rather be subject to Ukhel's wrath than hear those horrific screams again.

Someone grabbed him from behind and started to drag him away. He tried to project an illusion, but this time the guard's grip tightened instead of loosening.

"Always full of surprises, aren't you, gutter pet."

He looked up at his captor. A familiar black birthmark sat just below his eye. Ulagan.

The roar of the crowd pounded fiercely in his ears in rhythm with his heart. Alvina and Esen were going to die. He had failed them. Again. Just like he had failed his sister and his squadmates. He craned his neck around to look at Alvina. She was standing tall against the wooden stake with her head held high and gaze set in front of her. Aprika had done the same thing.

Once they were at the base of the king's viewing platform, Ulagan gripped his arm harder and pulled him to a stop. Above them, Ukhel leaned over the railing and gave him a sickening smile. What kinds of horrors awaited him now? He could take the beatings. It was the collar around his neck that he dreaded the most. Khartsaga looked over the railing as well, restrained by two cultists, with eyes that were glazed over from an Inhibitor. He wouldn't be much help at the moment either.

Ukhel raised his hand up and waited for the crowd to quiet down while Ulagan shoved Ronan down onto his knees. It took a few moments, but when the crowd finally grew silent, Ronan looked up and waited for whatever humiliation the Eternal Flame had in mind.

"My fellow Gurvel, today I promised you a special treat as a reminder of the discoveries that we've been blessed with. We'll still have the Purity by Fire, but I think you also deserve to witness the origin of our power!" Ukhel held out his hand toward something on the other side of the arena.

A cold chill swept through Ronan as he looked over his shoulder and watched a few cultists run over to the large covered box at the other end of the coliseum. He had forgotten it was there and yet somehow already knew what was lurking inside. Working together, they lifted up the front part of the black cloth covering the box, revealing a mass of pure shadow. The only thing he could make out were two small yellow dots glowing in the darkness.

"One of the greatest discoveries of this age! Lest we forget it was the Gurvel who learned how to tame and control the mighty shadowmongrel—the most horrifying of all beasts!" Ukhel's voice dripped with ecstasy as the crowd broke out in murmurs.

Ronan stared into the cage, unable to tear his gaze away from those piercing yellow eyes. Fate had caught up to him after all. This was a death worse than Ukhel's torment. As a "pet", he could at least quietly rebel if he wanted to, but against a shadowmongrel...

Ukhel looked down at Ronan with a wide, toothy grin and motioned for Ulagan to take him toward the cage. "While I hate to lose my pet so soon after his return, I think you all deserve to see an example of the shadowmongrel's power. Besides, pets can be replaced, no matter how useful they are."

CHAPTER 44

Terrors of the Mind

A battle of the mind ensued, but as they fought,
it was clear to all that they were greatly outmatched.

Ronan

SWEAT POURED DOWN RONAN'S face as he desperately tried to project an illusion, but Ulagan only chuckled and pushed him forward. The soft murmurs from the crowd began to swell like waves crashing against the sand. When was the last time anyone had even witnessed a shadowmongrel attack?

As they drew closer to the cage, the beast remained hidden in the dark shadows, but he knew it was there. He could feel the icy chill emanating from its presence.

One of the guards unlocked the door while Ulagan shoved him inside. He tumbled to the floor and scrambled up as the door clicked shut behind him. Without thinking he grabbed the bars and tried to open it, but of course it was locked. Ulagan waved tauntingly at him from the other side. This was it.

He turned around with his back to the bars and faced the darkness. All he could see were two pinpricks for eyes glowing faintly in the shadows. He choked in a breath of air that felt thick and ancient. This creature had existed long before Firekin had been created. All it cared about was filling its hunger. How could he fight something so old and feral? He couldn't.

Slowly the sounds from the coliseum began to fade, muffled by the shadowmongrel. Even his own breathing grew distant until all he could hear were the slow, crisp clicking sounds coming from the beast in the shadows.

A wave of nausea passed through him. He winced and closed his eyes, trying to bring up the mind barrier, but it was too late.

The cage was gone, replaced by a forest lit by pale moonlight. There were no chirping moss frogs in the brush. No wind to rustle the leaves. No distant phoenix cries in the sky. Everything was silent and still. He glanced around wildly but everywhere he turned he was met with an inescapable wall of branches and vines. Something was watching him. He couldn't see it, but the hair on the back of his neck stood on end. It was there.

He took a few steps toward a sturdy tree and backed up against the trunk, ears ringing from the sound of silence. Then a familiar scent filled his nostrils: smoke and charred flesh. His stomach clenched and ice rushed through his veins.

"Ronan!" A faint voice called his name. Where was it coming from?

He closed his eyes and gripped the bridge of his nose. The smell wasn't real. None of this was real. It was a mind game.

When he opened his eyes it was no longer dark. Fire from somewhere flickered off the trees as thick smoke filled the air. He coughed and involuntarily went to bring his hand up to his mouth but he couldn't move it. His hands were tied to the tree. The fire was coming closer. He was going to burn alive.

"Ronan! The stars!" The voice was so distant he could hardly hear it. Who was calling for him? Were they burning too?

This wasn't real. The fire wasn't real. Regardless, he was consumed with the desire to escape as the heat from the flames grew hotter. There had to be a branch or something that he could grab with his foot. He looked around for something and froze when he saw a figure tied to the tree next to him. It was his sister. Her hair was braided down the side like it had been during the Fire Purification.

He tried to call her name but his voice was choked behind a cotton gag of some sort. Suddenly he found it hard to breathe. He coughed and tried to get Aprika's attention but the smoke quickly enveloped her.

His toes burned. The fire had reached his tree, destroying all of the grass and brush in its path. It singed his clothing and scorched his skin. He groaned under the pain and tried desperately to break free as the flames rose up around him. With a final tug he pulled his hands away and fell onto the forest floor.

As soon as he touched the ground everything went dark. The crackling sound of the fire stopped and everything was silent once again. He reached up, pulled the cotton gag out of his mouth, and spat on the ground. Then he gingerly touched his toes and winced. If it was all in his head, why did it hurt so bad?

He stayed still and tried to steady his ragged breathing. Could he hide from the shadowmongrel? It was probably nearby, watching him from the deep darkness. The silence was so loud he was sure his heartbeat would give him away.

His blood ran cold again when a screech pierced through the forest. Then there was stifling silence. His heart raced within his ribcage. Someone screamed again. This time he could make out a cry for help. Was someone else in the forest too? He jumped to his feet and spun around looking for the source of the cry, but he couldn't see anything.

"Where are you!" He cried into the abyss, but his words were as quiet as a whisper in the distance, swallowed by the silence. The darkness felt like it was creeping in around him, brushing against his burns and making them sting.

The cry came again, only this time directly behind him. He spun around in a defensive stance but even so was not ready for what he saw. On the forest floor was a pool of dark blood. His eyes followed the blood to the body of a Gurvel woman lying dead beside a small bundle. He took a step backward and felt his stomach lurch when a cold wet hand touched his shoulder. It was the dead queen. A maggot crawled along her decayed fingers and fell onto his singed skin. He shivered as she spun him around to face her. The skin on her face was drawn tight around her bones and her eyes were empty shells oozing with blood and mold. Before he could stop her, she pulled him toward herself and bit into his shoulder.

He stumbled backward and slipped on the pool of blood, landing on his back. The queen was gone and the forest was again enveloped in silence. His breathing was labored as he frantically scanned the trees. The cold air sent a shiver down his spine. Scorching pain flared across his skin as his muscles spasmed beneath the burns. The blood and sweat coating him only intensified the sting. He tore off a piece of his pants, wincing as his fingers brushed against his skin and wrapped it around the bite wound. Everything seemed calm, but he felt like there was something bigger he was supposed to be hiding from.

"Ronan! Look at the stars!" The distant voice was closer. Who was calling him?

He shook his head. It didn't matter. The shadowmongrel. He was fighting a shadowmongrel. Nothing else in his head was real. He started to get to his feet but something grabbed his ankle. It was too dark to see clearly, but it looked like some kind of rope. He leaned down to pull it loose and realized too late that it was a vine. Another one shot out from the darkness, grabbed his wrist and pulled him down on his back.

In desperation, he tried to rip it away, but another vine grabbed his free hand and pulled it to the ground. Pain flared across his limbs as his burned skin was stretched. Even his other foot was trapped now. He struggled, but the bindings pulled tighter. His heart pulsated with his eyes as they darted around looking for something, anything that could help him, but nothing aside from trees and shadows surrounded him. His struggling froze as a form emerged from the darkness.

It was the size of a child with arms that dragged on the ground. Its fingers were long and claw-like and curled upward as they brushed over grass and twigs. He couldn't make out much more than its shape because its skin blended in with the shadows it was concealed by. Everything except for its eyes: two small yellow dots that stared at him without blinking. He clenched his jaw and thrashed about on the ground, but the vines only tightened around his limbs.

He had no strength left to scream. Every blood vessel in his body must have been filled with liquid ice, yet sweat poured down his face. The creature watched him struggle but made no further movements. As it stared at him, another presence pressed on his mind. He could feel it trying to get in, but he fought against it. His mind was the only thing he had left.

The shadowmongrel began to trudge toward him. His stomach lurched as he choked on a scream. It leaned over him and cocked its head as it examined him. He kept pulling against the vines but couldn't get free. All he could do was watch as the thing climbed on top of his chest and lifted up one of its long claws. Then it slowly pushed the claw into his shoulder where the queen had bitten him earlier.

He screamed so violently it hurt his throat and yet the sound that escaped his lips was nothing more than a whisper. This pleased the creature because it stood up on his chest and started to drag the claw along his sternum. The pain was unbearable. Every fiber inside him erupted in heat as the claws ripped his skin. But he couldn't move. Not because of the vines; they were no longer binding him to the ground. Now he was paralyzed and unable to even tear his eyes off of the menacing beast.

The presence pushing on his mind broke through. "Ronan! Fight it! Look at the stars!"

It was a woman's voice that was familiar to him. He wanted to focus on it, but the pain was too much. He couldn't fight it. Besides, he couldn't move his eyes even if he wanted to. This creature was going to kill him. No one had ever survived a shadowmongrel attack without Stimulants, except Ravenel, and he had almost nothing in common with him. Ravenel was a hero and a legend. Ronan was an exiled soldier...and a Seyr. A human Seyr.

With nothing else to go on, Ronan used the only thing he had left: his mind.

The shadowmongrel stopped cutting through his sternum and again cocked its head to the side while it examined him. Ronan's breathing was shallow and quick, but he stopped fighting the paralysis and closed his eyes to focus. Then he reached out with his mind and found the creature's wild and instinctual thoughts. He pushed and was surprised when the creature screeched into the night. All of sudden he regained control of his body and was able to knock the beast off of his chest.

It rolled onto the forest floor and regarded him cautiously, shaken by the sudden attack. Before it could make a move, Ronan sat up and pushed on the creature's mental barrier again. The shadowmongrel screeched and took a step toward him, claws outstretched.

His sternum hurt just as much as the rest of his wounds, but he was driven by a desire to listen to that other voice. Now that he could move, he looked up through the tree canopy, expecting to see the stars, but they were wrong. There weren't any constellations. The sky was filled with meaningless pinpricks of light. If they were in his mind, why weren't the stars familiar to him? Unless they weren't completely in his mind.

He looked back at the creature and tried forcing his own illusion into its mind. The forest melted around them, replaced by the beach with the glowing water that looked like fire, and the smattering of lights in the sky were replaced by real constellations. To his surprise Eira appeared on the beach as well. The shadowmongrel recoiled as the glowing water lapped at the misty shadow where its feet should be.

Ronan walked up next to Eira and looked down at himself. The scorch marks and other wounds still covered his body, but they weren't nearly as painful as they had been moments before. He had survived, but it wasn't over yet. He slid his foot back into a defensive position, and prepared to lunge at the creature.

"Use your mind, Ronan," Eira said.

What more could he do with his mind? He had already created an illusion to bring them here. What he really wanted was a weapon. He concentrated on the weight of his sword and to his surprise, felt it materialize in his hand. The shadowmongrel hadn't moved from its position between them and the glowing waves. For some reason it didn't seem to like the ocean.

With a smile, he lunged forward and slashed the beast's arm, but the sword fell right through it. The shadowmongrel swiped at him with its claws but he dodged it and reevaluated his options. How could he hit it? Its whole body was made of shadows.

Except the eyes.

Locking in on his new target, he dashed toward the creature and stabbed the tip of his sword through one of the glowing yellow dots.

A sharp pain split his forehead as the beach and everything around him suddenly vanished. The soft crashing of the ocean waves was replaced by the roar of a large crowd.

He was back in the cage, standing over the small and shriveled body of the shadowmongrel. Instead of indefinite shadow, the corpse was now hard and wrinkled, like an old piece of fruit. His own wounds appeared to have healed, but he felt more exhausted than he had ever felt before. He had actually killed it, and Eira had been there. Was she nearby or had he imagined her?

He walked to the side of the cage that wasn't covered by the tarp and looked out. Ulagan stared back at him with wide eyes and mouth slightly agape. The crowd that had roared with violent passion moments before fell completely silent. No one moved. Like him, they were all stunned.

"Have no fear!" Ukhel's voice echoed around the coliseum. "What you just witnessed was all part of the demonstration. The shadowmongrel used to be the most fearsome presence in Amidral, but now there is a new power: Gurvel. It's time for the real celebration. Guards, bring him to me."

Ronan searched the crowd for Eira, but all he saw were hundreds of Gurvel faces staring down at him in fear and awe. As the guards neared, something felt different. He didn't just feel their physical presence in his mind, he felt the edges of their thoughts too. Eira had explained mind reading to him, but he had never been able to move beyond simple emotions. Now he could sense each guard's thoughts with ease as if reading from the pages of a book. Still in shock, he swept his foot back into a defensive position and waited.

CHAPTER 45

The Eternal Flame

*But not even the piercing yellow eyes of death could smother
Ravenel's persistent passion. As soon as one beast
hit the ground, Ravenel moved on to the next one.*

Khartsaga

KHARTSAGA STRAINED AGAINST THE GUARDS that held him back. The satisfaction he felt when Ukhel had stared dumbstruck at the cage was short-lived. Ronan was miraculously alive, but he still didn't have any way to escape. The cage was completely surrounded.

"You were right about one thing, Son," Ukhel said, eyeing him from the side. "Humans are clever creatures. I don't know what trick he used to kill a shadowmongrel, but it won't happen again."

He ignored his father and stared intently at the arena floor. One of the guards unlocked the cage and stepped inside to grab Ronan.

"This could actually work in our favor, Son. My pet will serve as a perfect practice tool to help with your re-education. We'll start by cutting out his tongue and then burn out his rebelliousness with cleansing fire. That sounds fun, doesn't it?"

Not if he could help it. Khartsaga squinted his eyes and peered into the cage. The guard hadn't come out yet and some of the other guards surrounding the cage looked concerned. Ukhel leaned forward as well. Something was wrong.

Ronan leapt out of the cage unscathed. A murmur swept across the stands. One of the more seasoned soldiers moved first, but Ronan tripped him with his foot to avoid the attack. Ukhel frowned and gripped the balcony railing tighter.

Two more guards ran at Ronan this time, but he dodged both of them and maneuvered himself closer to the pyre. The murmuring in the crowd increased in volume as the other guards scrambled to try and apprehend him, but as if following a set choreography, Ronan evaded every attempt at capture.

"It's like he knows their every move," a nearby guard said in awe.

"That's impossible," Ukhel growled.

Khartsaga smiled as he watched the scene play out below. They couldn't lay a hand on him. Somehow, Ronan was reading their minds and acting on the knowledge quicker than the guards could catch him. Before too long, he made it to the pyre and began to untie Alvina and Esen. He didn't have much time. The guards were starting to catch on to his tactics. It was time to intervene.

Using the guard's shock as a diversion, Khartsaga went limp and dropped to the ground as a deadweight. The two guards released their grip, giving him just enough time to leap over the balcony and roll onto the arena sand.

Eira

EIRA FOUGHT THROUGH THE POUNDING pain in her head to look for Ronan. Utter chaos was unfolding in the arena, but he was alive! He did it. He killed a shadowmongrel. Now he dodged guards left and right with an accuracy that indicated mind reading. Just like the first time he had been sentenced to death, his powers had grown stronger, as if sparked by danger. Despite the circumstances, she smiled as she watched her pupil defy every odd stacked against him.

"You've taught him well," Einar said. "When this is all done, maybe we can start that school after all."

She chuckled. "If we somehow survive this, I'll consider it." Maybe teaching wouldn't be so bad. First they would need to kill Ukhel, but once that was over, she could see herself teaching others like Ronan.

Guards swarmed the pyre while Ronan tried to untie Alvina and Esen. There were too many of them. Mind reading only worked as long as you could comprehend the information fast enough to act. Too many minds made it difficult to concentrate.

"He needs help," Eira said.

A Gurvel jumped out of the viewing box and rolled on the ground. Unlike the other guards, his uniform looked ruffled and incomplete.

"That's Khartsaga!" Einar said. "He's going for Ronan. We need to get down there, now."

"No, we need to kill Ukhel," Eira said. "That's how we can help."

The cult leader was trying to regain control of the crowd but they were too excited by the turn of events to pay attention. The murmur had grown to a roar again and continued to build in intensity. If they killed him now, the crowd would be too distracted to notice. It was the opposite of their original plan, but at the moment Ukhel's guards were all occupied.

"It's too risky," Einar said. "Ukhel probably already ingested the Verdant Stimulant."

Eira looked over at Wren who was staring down at the arena floor with his tail weaving back and forth nervously. If the boy used his camouflage ability, he might be able to get close enough to a guard to grab some vials.

"I have an idea," she said, "but we're going to need an Inhibitor or two."

Ronan

FIRE BRUSHED PAST RONAN'S head as he fumbled with the knots around Alvina's wrists. It was becoming more difficult to predict the guards' moves. There were too many minds to keep track of. Sweat poured down his face as he tried to steady his hands. Every part of him was sore, as if the fight with the shadowmongrel had been physical instead of mental.

Alvina and Esen stared at him with wide eyes as if not fully believing what they were seeing. He grunted as a fire bolt hit his leg and singed his calf. The guards seemed more intent on burning him than catching him.

"You're alive," Alvina whispered. "How are you alive?"

Esen shook his head in amazement as he watched Ronan work. "Good to see you again! Any plans for getting out of this death pit?"

"Not yet," he said, cursing as his fingers slipped. It was too difficult to grip the knots when he had to keep dodging the guard's fireballs.

A thought flashed through his mind from one of the guards behind him. Moving slightly to the left, he pulled the Gurvel's arm forward and used his momentum to push him off the pyre.

"I see you've been learning to use your powers," Esen said.

He had hoped that Esen might be able to fight with him, but his eyes were slightly glazed over from an Inhibitor. How were they going to get out of here?

"Sorry I didn't take you up on your offer sooner," Ronan replied, turning back to the ropes. His hands were too sweaty to untie them. He needed something sharp. Firebolts continued to fly by as he scanned the pyre for stray bits of wood.

Now that the initial shock of his survival had worn off, the crowd had started to yell and jeer again. Gurvel leaned forward in their seats and pounded the railing as they waited for the guards to catch him. It wouldn't take long. More of the fireballs were colliding with him now that his body had reached its limit. He couldn't dodge fast enough.

There had to be something he could use to cut the rope! In a near panic he got down on his hands and knees and tried pulling up loose bits of wood from the platform. There had to be a way. He couldn't let them die. Not like this. Not again.

"Ronan!"

A fireball struck his arm. He grunted and looked for whoever had called his name. Khartsaga waved at him with one of the swords that had been discarded during The Games. The guards weren't watching for attackers from behind, so Khartsaga pushed past them toward the base of the pyre.

Good, now there was a way to cut the ropes. But once he freed Esen and Alvina, where would they run? Could they make it to the prisoners' door before the guards? Unlikely, but it might work. It was the only thing he could think of, anyway. Then they just had to fight past more guards and get out of the city before the soldiers on the wall could kill them. After surviving a shadowmongrel attack, it didn't sound all that impossible.

A cloud of sand rose into the air as someone jumped from the viewing platform. Ukhel emerged from the dust, drinking the remnants of a thick black liquid. He tossed the vial to the side and looked directly at Ronan with a wide grin.

Khartsaga made it to the base of the pyre and raised his arm to grab the edge. Before he could climb up, Ukhel tilted his head to the side and moved the sand beneath him. Like a wave in the ocean, the sand propelled Khartsaga into the side of the coliseum where he crumpled to the ground and lay still.

Ronan's mouth went dry. No Stimulant was strong enough to allow a Manipulator to control grains of sand like that. Ukhel flashed a toothy grin as he reached out his scarlet hand and clenched it into a fist. A piece of the Sklera coliseum broke away and flew through the air toward Ronan as if it were just a rock. He stared at it as it hurled toward him. That was impossible. Sklera couldn't be Manipulated. At the last second he twisted away and watched it crash into one of the guards.

"This has gone on long enough," Ukhel shouted. The guards immediately stopped attacking and stood aside to make room for him, some of them bowing in reverence.

"Don't just stand there, light the pyre," Ukhel ordered.

Ronan stumbled to his feet as the kindling came alive with fire. He struggled with the rope again, cursing as his fingers scraped against the knots. If this was anything like the Fire Purifications he had witnessed before, the guards would continue to control the flames, increasing the heat slowly to prolong the victim's deaths.

"Don't worry about us," Alvina said. "Now's your chance to escape."

He ignored her and tried digging his nails into the rope. Blood trickled down his fingers as he scratched at the fibers.

"You want to pretend you're a real Seyr?" Ukhel asked, raising the sand beneath him to push himself onto the pyre. "Fine. Let The Games begin."

CHAPTER 46

Mind Game

He stood his ground before each eternal shadow,
refusing to cower before death's rattling chill.

Ronan

UKHEL LANDED IN FRONT of Ronan as flames climbed up the sides of the platform, surrounding them in a wall of heat and smoke. Gritting his teeth, Ronan positioned himself in front of Alvina and Esen.

"Ronan! Run!" A voice cried, barely carrying across the roar of the crowd.

"Eira?" He looked up toward the viewing platform and found her. But before he could make sense of what she had said, a searing hot pain cut across his skull, forcing him to his knees. He was under attack. Tears blurred his vision as he watched Ukhel take a few steps toward him. The pain intensified as images and memories flooded his mind.

Clawing at the wooden platform, he tried to protect his thoughts with a barrier, but the pain was too intense. He couldn't hold onto the image of the glowing ocean. Ukhel's presence pressed against him, threatening to take control. Despite the heat of the flames, cold sweat dripped down his face as he fought for his mind. The pain pierced his head like a serrated blade, cutting deeper into his thoughts and memories until suddenly his defenses buckled.

Like his fight with the shadowmongrel, his surroundings and the sound of the crowd disappeared. The heat of the flame also vanished, replaced by the chill of cold metal around his neck. His mouth went dry. He was back in Ukhel's bedroom, surrounded by Sklera. With shaking fingers he reached up and touched his hair. It was long again.

"I'm almost offended that you look upon this memory with such hatred," Ukhel's voice echoed throughout the room, even though the Gurvel was nowhere to be seen.

This was no memory. Everything, from the feeling of the cracked paint on his face to the color of the drapes over the windows was more vivid and more detailed than any memory he had ever had—more detailed even than reality itself. Even his emotions seemed magnified under the scrutiny of Ukhel's attack, piercing more deeply than the pain he had felt in his skull moments before.

"Well, if this memory doesn't suit you, perhaps you'd prefer another?" Ukhel said, his voice reverberating as the room dissolved and reformed into another familiar scene.

Lying on a bed covered in rich crimson blood lay the dead queen. Her newborn son was pinned to her with the hilt of Ronan's sword. In Ukhel's version of the memory, there were no guards to pull him away from the sight before him, and so he stood, paralyzed by the vivid imagery and unable to tear his gaze away from the haunting reality of what he had done. A part of him still wanted to fight Ukhel, but the fervency and ability to do so were quickly draining away as the weight of his own guilt and anguish closed in on him, choking out his very will to live.

◇◇◇

Eira

"WE NEED TO GET DOWN there!" Eira shouted, swinging her leg over the railing to jump into the arena. The fire was starting to obscure Ronan's crumpled form. He didn't stand a chance against the Stimulant that Ukhel had taken. They had to kill that monster now, while he was distracted.

Before she could push herself over the edge, Einar grabbed her by the shirt and yanked her back onto the viewing platform.

"We talked about this, Sister," he said with an urgent edge to his voice. "We can't fight Ukhel, especially when he's taken the black Stimulant. Not to mention all of those guards."

"This could be our only chance!" she said, meeting his violet eyes. "We need to kill him before it's too late."

"What happened to saving Ronan?"

Beside them, Wren climbed onto the railing, tail flicking back and forth. Their original plan had been to fight Ukhel while Wren stabbed him with an Inhibitor. They hadn't expected him to go after Ronan.

"If we kill Ukhel, we'll do more than save him," Eira said, taking a step closer to her brother. "We'll weaken Firekin and create an opportunity for the Scarletts to launch a counterattack."

"That's not why you want to jump down there. You're still stuck on revenge. Just help Ronan fight Ukhel the same way you did with the shadowmongrel!"

"That won't be enough," she said, heat rising to her cheeks. Didn't he get it? This was about more than saving one man's life. They had a chance to end Firekin's tyranny and avenge their people.

Wren suddenly threw himself over the edge of the railing and fell to the ground, landing lightly on his feet like a cat.

"What's he doing?!" Einar cried, gripping the railing as he looked over the edge.

The boy pointed at the pyre and then scampered off without waiting for them. In silent agreement, she and Einar both lifted their legs over the railing and jumped into the sandy arena. None of the guards noticed as Wren ran past them; their attention was fixated on Ukhel.

"Focus on getting Ronan away from Ukhel. I'll help the others," Einar shouted over the roar of the crowd.

Now wasn't the time to argue, so she nodded and ran beside him until they made it to the base of the pyre. Covering her face, she passed through the wall of flames, hissing as the heat burned her skin. On the inside, the air was hot and difficult to breathe, but the platform was large enough that they still had time to act before the flames reached the center.

"You're supposed to be in the safe house," Esen yelled, coughing fiercely as he inhaled smoke.

"So are you," Einar said.

Eira quickly surveyed their surroundings. With bloody nails, Ronan scratched at the wooden boards of the pyre. His face was pallid and covered in sweat. She needed to act quickly. There was no time to encourage his mental state on the slim chance that he could somehow defeat Ukhel.

While she would rather use a dagger, she instead curled her knuckles into an assassin's unarmed jab. With the right hits, she could paralyze Ukhel long enough to get a choke hold around his neck. Not wasting another moment, she shifted her weight back and lunged toward Ukhel with her knuckles extending toward his neck.

"Sister, wait!" Einar shouted, appearing before her and shoving her off balance so that she stumbled to the side and missed.

With a growl, she snapped her head up to yell at him, but the anger that had flared in her veins suddenly vanished when she saw his eyes frozen in wide-eyed shock. Drops of crimson dripped to the platform as he swayed and then fell forward toward her.

In a daze she caught him as he fell, blood pooling around the dagger sticking out of his back. Not taking his eyes off of Ronan, Ukhel smiled and lowered his hand. Somehow this monster was still aware of his surroundings even while engaged in a mental battle.

Shaking, she looked down at Einar's violet eyes.

"Don't forget to smile, Sis. For me." Her brother's warm voice filled her thoughts as he started to choke up blood.

She watched with blurry tears as the life faded from her brother's eyes. The fire continued to crackle around her but it was muffled now. Somewhere inside she knew she needed to get away from the flames that crept toward them, but all she wanted was to sit there and hear Nar's comforting voice in her head one last time. To walk the streets of their home one last time. To watch a smile brighten his violet eyes one last time. Eira gently set her brother's body down and closed his eyelids with her finger tips. There were scuffling sounds around her but she didn't take her eyes off of Nar's bloodstained and sleeping face.

CHAPTER 47
Of One Mind

*Emboldened by Ravenel's courage, the army fought with renewed passion,
striking down the shadow beasts until there were none left.*

Khartsaga

SOUND EXPLODED IN KHARTSAGA'S ears as he regained consciousness. Every part of him ached and his head pounded. How had his father been able to move the sand? The Verdant Stimulant only allowed someone to use Manipulation and Seyring together, but never had it given the user enough power to move something so fluid.

With great effort, he sat up. His breath caught in his throat. The platform was ablaze and completely surrounded by guards. Through the flames and smoke he could make out the tall stature of his father looming over someone. It looked like there were others moving around on the pyre as well. Maybe Ronan had managed to free Esen and Alvina without the sword, but none of them would survive for long in those flames.

The guards glanced at one another while gripping Stimulants in tight fists. A few of them shuffled their feet as if trying to decide whether they should jump in and save their leader or not.

Gritting his teeth, Khartsaga stood up and limped toward the pyre. He might be under the effects of the Inhibitor but his relationship to the Eternal Flame still carried weight.

"Put out that fire!" He shouted, holding his shoulders back. "Now!"

Without hesitation the guards drank Fire Stimulants and lowered the flames until they became nothing more than smoldering embers. Hopefully this would buy Ronan some time.

Ronan

IN DESPERATION, RONAN CLOSED his eyes, trying to block out the horrible scenes forced in front of him. Ukhel was rifling through his memories like the pages of a recipe book. Each one was more vividly detailed than how he remembered them, especially the way they felt. Ukhel magnified his guilt and fear until his emotions were as tangible as the scenes themselves.

Even with his eyes closed, the memories were still there. The dead queen. The Shadowmongrel. The collar around his neck. The squad that had been executed when he had first joined the militia. His parents and sister.

Ukhel lingered here.

No.

His knees buckled and he sank to the sandy ground with his eyes squeezed shut, but that didn't prevent him from recognizing the acrid smell of burnt skin and hair mixed with smoke. Knowing exactly what he would see, he cracked his eyes open slowly and looked upon the memory that he had replayed in his mind almost daily for twenty years. His mother and father cried out to him while Aprika merely smiled gently in his direction.

His mouth went dry like ashbark. Ukhel's chuckle echoed in his mind, sending shivers down his spine. His stomach plummeted as the Gurvel guards stretched out their hands and lit the fire.

This was his fault. Tears welled in his eyes as the flames caught onto Aprika's shirt. The sound of crackling wood was drowned out by the screams of the others who were being purified that day. If he had remembered to pack his jacket the night before like his mother had told him to, he never would have seen the neighbor sneak into the wrong house. He never would have alerted the school about their secret meeting. Aprika and his parents would never have suffered a fate like this.

The screams mixed with the putrid stench in the air was too much. He puked up the little food he had eaten for lunch, choking on it as tears continued to stream down his face. There was nothing he could do.

A small hand tapped him on the shoulder. Looking up, Ronan expected to see one of his old classmates, but instead he saw Wren standing beside him, eyes wide in concern.

"Wren?" he asked in disbelief.

The boy hugged him and for a moment, the smell of smoke almost seemed to evaporate as he felt the warmth from his small body. Ronan wiped the tears away and shook his head to clear it. This was just a memory. He didn't know how or why Wren was here, but this scene was just a memory that Ukhel had pulled from his mind.

"That's not possible," Ukhel growled, his form materializing in front of them as the memory lost some of its vivid intensity.

Eira

IN ONE MOMENT, SHE lost everything. Nar's thoughts were quiet. The thunderous cry of the crowd now sounded muffled, as if the world lost some of its vibrancy without her brother in it. Even the heat of the flames lessened as she sat before his sleeping body. People were speaking around her, but she didn't care. Their voices were indistinguishable from the distant roar of the crowd.

Someone touched her shoulder. She expected them to drag her away, but they spoke to her instead.

"I'm so sorry, but we need you," Alvina said. Her calm voice cut through the sea of noise and broke the wall of silence. "Esen is still drugged and can't break into either of their minds. We need you, Eira. Ronan needs you. He's dying."

Alvina was right. Ronan was still kneeling on all fours and his pallid skin had turned a sickly shade of gray. The prolonged attack was slowly draining him of life. However, he wasn't shaking anymore. Wren crouched beside him, clinging to his arm with his eyes closed in fierce concentration. It was almost as if...

She leaned forward, astonished. "They've made an assassin's connection."

Fresh waves of sorrow cut through her heart as she remembered the way it felt to connect to someone in such an intimate way. For it to work, both parties had to be of one mind and willing to open up their deepest desires and pains. She and Einar had been a perfect fit for the technique because of the bond they had shared from birth, but non-siblings could form a connection as well. There was usually a grueling process required to form such a bond. It was a secret that the Speki had guarded for millennia, but here before her very eyes, the bond had been formed out of desperation.

Einar had seen the potential in Wren and Ronan and had longed to watch them learn and grow. These two were her brother's legacy and they needed help. Forming the bond was a miracle in and of itself, but they wouldn't know how to utilize it.

With Alvina's help, she got to her feet and moved closer to them. Shaken out of her shock, she finally noticed that the loss of heat she felt was real. For whatever reason the guards had drawn back the fire.

She knelt down in front of her two pupils and forced her mind open so she could touch their thoughts. It would be difficult, but she only needed to get one message through to them.

Ronan

NOT SURE IF WREN was a figment of his imagination or actually present, Ronan wiped the vomit off of his face and forced himself to stand. He couldn't even fathom the thought of what Ukhel might do to the boy, so he stepped in front of him and faced Ukhel.

Wren ran in front of him and shook his head. *"I can help you. Like Eira and Einar."*

"How?"

The scenery around them suddenly intensified as Ukhel walked toward them. The fire from the pyre grew brighter as the tumultuous sound of the crowd in the stands around them crescendoed to a roar again. Gritting his teeth against the raw emotions that flooded his mind, Ronan forced his quivering legs to stay standing.

"Enough games, pet," Ukhel said. His lips didn't move as he spoke. Instead the sound echoed in Ronan's mind. Wren's eyes widened and a shiver passed through him. He could hear him too.

The fire outlined Ukhel's towering frame, casting his features in harsh and shadowed angles. "Humans are so ungrateful. We let you live in our cities. We shared our food with you. We allowed you to walk the same streets as us."

Ronan tried to form a sword with his mind like he had during his fight with the shadowmongrel, but nothing happened. The only option he had left was to fight Ukhel hand to hand. He would lose, but at least it would give Wren a chance to escape.

"Wren, get ready to run."

"I'm not leaving," Wren signed.

"Please, Wren, I can't..." He was cut short when a new voice echoed in his mind. This one was more quiet. Almost like a whisper.

"Work as one. Make him lose concentration. Find the opening."

Wren's ears perked up. He had heard Eira's voice too. But what did she mean?

"We let you benefit off of our glory, and how do you repay us?" Ukhel asked, plastering a wide smile across his face.

Make him lose concentration. If this were a sword fight, Ronan would try to anger his opponent. Maybe the same strategy would apply here.

"Repay you?" Ronan said. "You've done nothing but treat us like animals. You condemn innocent lives to bloody deaths for sport and entertainment."

"So my pet still has a voice after all. I was beginning to think you'd become mute," Ukhel said, his smile widening into a sickening grin. "You should be grateful. I brought meaning to your otherwise worthless existence. Even dead, your body will help me produce enough Stimulant to last centuries."

A wave of painful memories pierced Ronan's thoughts. Suddenly a wall of guilt and shame washed over him. Ukhel was right. Ronan was nothing. His life meant nothing. He should kneel before this Gurvel and grovel in heartfelt gratitude.

Wren stepped beside him and gripped his hand. The weight of the emotions lessened and he was able to think freely again.

"And yet, despite all your effort, you haven't been able to kill me," Ronan said, his voice straining as he fought against the strong desire to kneel before Ukhel.

The heat and light from the burning pyre faded as Ukhel frowned. Emboldened, Ronan took a step forward with Wren. Something like electricity crackled along his skin. New strength flooded through him.

"Despite all of your Stimulants and power, you let this small Forestdweller escape from your hand."

In the Sklera seating above them, the crowd started to vanish. One by one, the jeers grew silent. Ukhel's eyes darted over the levels of seating.

"Despite your pathetic attempts to manipulate your own son, he still broke free from your control," Ronan said. The pyre slowly started to fade away, but heat rose to his face regardless. Beside him Wren's tail swished back and forth, like a cat ready to pounce on its prey.

Ukhel twitched, frozen in place as his face turned a darker shade of crimson. Just moments before he had boasted about using Ronan's corpse to make Stimulants, but now his smirk was nowhere to be found. While Ronan might not understand what Ukhel had meant by that comment, one thing was now evident.

"Despite how weak you say I am," Ronan said as he took the final step that brought him right in front of Ukhel, "you need me."

The coliseum shattered into small pieces of crystal, shimmering in a sea of nothingness. The veins on Ukhel's neck bulged for a moment before his form evaporated into the shards. Gripping Wren's hand, Ronan looked around at the sea of glittering glass. Without the sandy pit of the coliseum they floated among the crystalline fragments, watching them pass by like leaves drifting in a calm current.

Wren pulled on Ronan's hand and pointed below them. Amidst the crystals, a young Gurvel, covered in scars and fresh wounds, kneeled in a pool of blood. Despite the marred features and young physique, Ronan would recognize that face anywhere. It was Ukhel.

Body tensed, Ronan grabbed one of the crystal fragments like a dagger and moved to lunge at the figure, but Wren's grip tightened on his hand and held him back. The power that had flown through Ronan moments before wavered. It appeared that the strength he now possessed would only work with Wren's help.

"You don't want to kill him, do you?" he asked, lowering the crystal.

Wren pursed his lips and shook his head.

Of course not. Wren was just a child. But Ukhel still needed to be stopped.

"Can we inhibit him?" Wren asked with his free hand.

"Maybe. Let's try."

With their hearts in agreement, they floated through the crystals toward the young Ukhel. As they approached, Ronan searched for signs of aggression, but he found none. Instead, Ukhel wept in the pool of blood beside the corpse of a Gurvel woman.

Without looking at them, Ukhel spoke with a raspy voice. "You. It's your fault. It was your kind that killed her."

Ronan was speechless. This was Ukhel's mind? What had happened to him?

"GET OUT!" Ukhel thundered. The sound came not from the young Gurvel kneeling before them, but from all around them. A high pitched hum erupted from the crystal fragments as they began to vibrate.

Wren reached out and touched young Ukhel on the shoulder, closing his eyes in concentration. Getting a similar sense, Ronan did the same thing and placed his hand over Wren's. Like a gentle rain on a warm summer's day, he could feel Wren's mind mix with his own. Together, with one heart, they reached further into Ukhel's mind and blocked his access to the very power he clung to with such desperation.

The vibrations in the crystals became violent, escalating into a cacophony of tones that made Ronan's bones feel like they were going to burst. Then it all vanished, replaced by the ear-splitting roar of the crowd in the coliseum. He was hunched over on all fours, nails bloodied from where he had scratched at the wood of the platform. Pain erupted across his entire body as if he had been flayed and beaten at the same time.

Gasping for breath, he collapsed. Somewhere nearby, Ukhel's scream cut through the cry of the crowd as he entered into a reality in which he had no power.

CHAPTER 48

Prosperity

*After the battle, Ravenel was nowhere to be found.
Some say he rejoined the Forestdwellers, others say
he still fights crime in the shadows of night.*

Khartsaga

THE CROWD FELL SILENT. One by one, Gurvel peered over the Sklera railing, trying to figure out what had happened. Bare-chested cultists stood around the pyre shifting nervously from foot to foot as Ukhel fell to his knees screaming in agony. Even their Eternal Flame had been unable to subdue the human—an outcome they had been told was impossible. Their entire worldview had just shattered before their very eyes. Now, uncertainty radiated from them as they stood before the Gurvel they had once worshiped. Khartsaga felt sympathy for them as he watched them. Could they be blamed for the lies that had been hammered into their head day after day?

On the pyre, Esen and Alvina crouched beside Ronan. He looked winded and had a few burns on his skin, but otherwise the color had come back to his face. Eira had gone back to her brother's body to wipe up some of the blood with her skirt.

He tore his eyes away from her and turned toward the crowd. Einar's death was his fault. All of this was his fault. He could never take back what he had done, but maybe he could try to repair some of the damage.

Taking a deep breath he looked up at the crowd and lifted his arms to get their attention like his father had done. Esen watched him curiously from the pyre. He probably didn't trust him, and why should he?

Hundreds of Gurvel looked at him with wide eyes, craving answers and direction. Even the guards turned to him, staring at him with stunned expressions.

"Today you have witnessed an impossibility!" Khartsaga said, raising his voice and holding his head high like he had seen his father do. "You have been taught that humans are worthless because of their short lifespan and inability to become Seyrs or Manipulators, but today you have witnessed otherwise!" He looked over at Ronan who gave a small nod in response. "This man has done what no Gurvel has ever been able to do. He defeated a shadowmongrel without the aid of Stimulants or Inhibitors.

"And with the help of this Forestdweller, he defeated the Eternal Flame in a mental battle without Stimulants or Inhibitors. This should have been impossible, and yet you witnessed it for yourselves. You have been lied to about the reality of worth. It's never been about power or lifespan. True worth is found in life itself and in the drive to defend it."

The crowd murmured quietly but continued to listen. The cultists looked toward Ronan and Wren in utter bewilderment. It would take time for them to truly believe this for themselves.

"We were wrong about the New Age. It hasn't come yet. We were taught that all creatures would prosper when Gurvel prospered, but what you have seen in the past few weeks has not been prosperity." Khartsaga paused and looked around at the audience to gauge their reactions. Some looked terrified and gripped the railing with white knuckles. Others glared at him with piercing eyes filled with hatred. "These other races are not creatures. They are like Gurvel and deserve to rule alongside us. Only then will we prosper."

At this, the crowd began to grow restless.

"Traitor! You're no better than a gutter pet!" An old Gurvel with disheveled hair yelled from the lower stands. Similar insults filled the air from around the coliseum as the audience grew emboldened.

Khartsaga continued, speaking clearly so his voice would carry. "Before his death, King Chono named me his heir. Now that my father is unfit to rule, I take back that command."

A few in the crowd nodded their heads in agreement, but otherwise the crowd grumbled in dissatisfaction. There was nothing they could do about it though. The law was the law. From the corner of his eye he saw Esen ease himself off of the pyre and walk toward him. Esen didn't need to worry though. His reign would be short-lived. All he had to do was pass off the authority to someone who deserved it.

"But I am unfit to lead you, as I have failed to understand the true meaning of the New Age until now. So as your king, I decree..."

Esen put a hand on his shoulder, causing him to pause. "Now's not the time. I know you mean well, but these people need a leader right now, and you're the rightful heir to the throne—regardless of how you got here. We can work out details later."

"But you'd make a better king," Khartsaga said, turning toward him. "You've been fighting for humans this whole time."

"Then let me advise you," Esen said. "These people need stability. Now is not the time to renounce your throne."

"I don't deserve to be king," Khartsaga replied, looking down at a red splotch of sand where a splatter of blood had dried. He had been the cause of so much pain and suffering. Innocent lives had died here because he had been too weak to stand up to his father.

"That's not what this is about," Esen said. "If you care about these people, you'll give them what they need—stability. Besides, right now, you're the only one these Firekin members are going to listen to. We don't have the power to stage a coup at the moment, so think carefully before you act."

Khartsaga looked from the crowded stands, brimming with expectant Gurvel waiting for his next command, to the cultists standing around the pyre, looking at him in shock and fear. "I decree," he spoke to the crowd again, "that Esen should be made advisor to the king. Secondly, I order that Ukhel be arrested and brought to the castle prisons for his crimes against citizens of Galynkhot."

None of the cultist guards moved. A stab of fear pierced his gut. Esen was right. They didn't have any actual power if the guards refused to obey him.

Movement in the lower stands caught his eye. A handful of Gurvel soldiers wearing King Chono's emblem jumped into the sandy arena and made their way toward Ukhel. Two of them grabbed him by the arms and dragged him toward the prisoners' entrance while the others walked over to Khartsaga and stood beside him.

Satisfied, he nodded his gratitude. Hopefully there were more soldiers like these who were still loyal to the throne. He looked up at the crimson faces awaiting further direction in the stands. This was only the beginning. Not everyone would accept this change in leadership so readily, but it was a step in the right direction.

Eira

LOOKING DOWN AT NAR'S peaceful face, Eira could almost believe that he was just sleeping. Any minute now, he would open his violet eyes and crack a wise joke about how messy her hair had gotten. She could almost believe it.

Once Ukhel had been removed, the crowd calmed down. They seemed content to do what they were told. She didn't pay any attention to them. Instead she sat beside her brother, preparing herself for what she had to do.

When a Speki died, the Seyr that was closest to them was responsible to gather their memories before they faded from the mind. Normally it was an intimate moment done in private, but Eira didn't dare wait any longer. She wanted Nar's memories to stay crisp in her head.

Wren crawled up beside her. After a few moments of silence, he tapped Einar's chest with the tip of his tail and then placed it over his own heart. Then he closed his eyes and hummed softly to himself.

So solemn and heartfelt was the gesture that a fresh wave of anguish gripped Eira's heart. Tears freely flowing down her cheeks, she bent down and touched Einar's forehead with her own, willing her mind to find the remnants of his memories. She had never performed this ritual before, but she had watched her father receive the memories of her grandmother.

Vaguely aware of the others who had gathered around her, Eira closed her eyes and blocked out everything else until she found her brother. His memories welcomed her like warm sunlight on a chilly day. Knowing innately what to do, she opened her mind and allowed the memories to combine with her own—similar, yet distinct.

As the warmth slowly faded from her thoughts, she sat up and opened her eyes, still wet with tears. Across from her, Alvina, Ronan, Esen, and even Khartsaga, sat around Einar's body, solemnly guarding her last moments with him. She looked at each of them in turn and felt not only her own emotions, but echoes of how Einar had felt about each of them.

Wiping her eyes on her shirt, she stood to her feet and looked down at her brother's body. "It is done. I will carry his memories and knowledge as long as I live." These were the same words her father said on the day her grandmother died. "And I will carry out his dream," she added with a whisper. She didn't know how, but she would find students. She would teach them all she knew about Seyring and Manipulation, just like Einar had wanted.

Ronan looked at her. His face was covered in soot, but he was alive. Einar had seen more potential in him and Wren than she had realized. Perhaps she would continue what he had started and worry about finding more students later. For now, that was enough.

Ronan

IT WAS OVER.

Everything was over.

During Eira's ritual, a throbbing ache had settled deep in Ronan's bones. Even his ears pulsed from the pain. He had felt this level of exhaustion only once before when he had crawled his way into the Scarlet Forest. It wouldn't be long until he passed out from the Seyring fatigue. Although, after everything he had been through, slipping into a coma sounded like bliss. Battling the shadowmongrel had been terrifying on its own, but then Ukhel had invaded his mind. If it hadn't been for Wren, Ronan would have died. Yet against all odds, they had won. Waves of relief washed over him, churning inside until they settled into a mire of fatigue and sorrow. Their victory had come at a great cost.

Einar, the final victim of The Games, was gone. Anguish radiated from Eira like the blazing pyre that had threatened to consume them moments before. Ronan was powerless to ignore his mentor's tormented thoughts. The raw emotion cut through his battered mind, ripping away his last shred of strength. Tears fell freely down his face, spattering the blood-stained wood of the pyre.

Pain.

Horrible, unending pain.

Someone leaned up against him. The weight of the pain lessened. In a daze, Ronan realized that Wren had curled up beside him. Warmth filled his heart. The world was still tainted, but not all its vibrancy had been lost. He wanted to comfort Wren, but his limbs were too heavy to lift. He would have expected himself to feel panic at the thought of losing consciousness again, but he didn't. At least for now, he was safe. The last thing he saw before falling asleep was Eira's face, filled with concern as she kneeled beside him.

Epilogue

But this we do know: Ravenel was more than a man. He was hope itself.

One Week Later

Esen

FROM THE VIEWING PLATFORM, Esen looked out across the coliseum at all the people gathering to hear King Khartsaga's announcement. It wasn't mandatory, but a good portion of the city had decided to come. They were skeptical about the change in leadership. Most of them were Gurvel, but there was a section of humans gathered together in the lower seats. All of the other humans had left to start new lives in the surrounding villages. The streets felt empty without them, but he couldn't blame them for leaving.

Beside him, Khartsaga fiddled with a button on his new navy uniform. Esen didn't need to push very hard to hear that the new king's thoughts were filled with uncertainty. Esen stepped up beside him, wearing a similar uniform, and placed his hand on Khartsaga's shoulder. "You're doing great, my King. The changes you've made in just one week are remarkable."

"I shouldn't be king," Khartsaga said, frowning as he looked out across the stands. "I should be in prison."

"Perhaps," Esen agreed. Khartsaga looked taken aback. They had discussed this same topic every day since he had become king. In every case, Esen had tried to assuage his fears, but Khartsaga continued to wallow in guilt. It was time for a new tactic. "But you don't have that luxury."

"Luxury?"

"This city needs a king, and by law, that's what you are. If it makes you feel better, you can go lock yourself in a Sklera cell after you make this announcement, but it won't change the fact that the majority of this city's population trusts you. If you isolate yourself in a cell, maybe it would be a proper punishment for what you've done, but it won't make anything better."

"Even if I worked every day for the rest of my life," Khartsaga said, not meeting Esen's eyes, "I could never make up for the crimes I've committed."

"No. You can't. But I'm not asking you to make it perfect. I'm asking you to help me improve what we have."

The gong sounded from the coliseum pit, signaling the king's speech. Immediately, the crowd fell silent. After a week, everyone craved further explanation and direction. Riots had erupted in various parts of the city following Ukhel's arrest. Since then, Khartsaga and the guards loyal to the throne had fought to regain control. At the moment, they had the upper hand, but tensions were high.

With a deep breath, Khartsaga stepped forward, lifted his head high, and addressed the crowd. "Thank you all for your cooperation as we've worked to repair the damages done by Firekin. In the coming weeks, I will be dedicating most of my time in service to the city by reeducating the former members of Firekin who have agreed to reintegrate into society. There is still a lot of work we need to do to repair the city, so today I'm appointing a second advisor to aid me alongside Esen."

Khartsaga turned around and held out his arm to invite Alvina up to the front of the viewing platform. She stepped forward with her head held high and took her place beside Esen. Even though they had practiced this the day before, Esen couldn't help but notice again how her eyes seemed to shine while wearing her navy uniform.

"Alvina of the Scarletts has agreed to advise me in matters of the kingdom," Khartsaga announced, looking around the coliseum. "Together we will work to bring Galynkhot one step closer to the true New Age. A New Age that will be beneficial for all races: Gurvel, human, Forestdweller, and Speki."

Most of the audience clapped and cheered, but there were many who stood with arms crossed while they glared at Alvina. Never in recorded history had a human held so much power in the Gurvel government. While Esen was excited by the idea of working more closely with Alvina, he had actually advised against it. Khartsaga, on the other hand, had insisted. He wanted to show the humans that he was adamant about improving the city. Either way, it would take centuries to change the minds and hearts of the general population.

The gong rang again, this time signaling the entertainment to start. As the metal reverberated around the coliseum, a set of fire performers appeared from what used to be the prisoners' entrance. They wore royal blue sleeveless uniforms and had belts filled with vials of Fire Stimulants. Each one in unison drank a vial and began moving around the coliseum in choreographed movements, shooting fire before them as they passed by each other.

Never again would this place be used to shed human blood. Khartsaga had replaced The Games with a weekly performance. Hopefully it would become a way for Gurvel and humans to enjoy something together, but it would take years before the shared experiences outweighed the horrible memories. Esen's skin crawled as he remembered how helpless he had felt tied to that stake just one week prior.

The performers danced around each other and coordinated their fire blasts to form delicate designs in the air. When used like this, fire Manipulation had a special beauty to it. Each burst flickered in the air like a bird in flight before being redirected by the Manipulators.

In between sets, Esen let his eyes scan the crowd. He needed to find Ronan and Eira once the performance was over. Now that Ronan had recovered from the Seyring fatigue, it was time to tell him about the discovery in the dungeon.

"You owe me an ale," Alvina said softly.

He turned and looked at her in mock surprise. "Do I?"

"I distinctly remember you promising to buy me a drink if we somehow managed to survive the Fire Purification."

He smiled. "You can't hold me to that! We were on the brink of death. Regardless, I keep my promises. How about tonight?"

A soft smile played at the edge of her lips. "Seaside Tavern?"

"I was thinking somewhere a little less rowdy. How about Sarnai's tea shop?"

"A tea shop? You promised there'd be ale."

"Forgive me for changing the terms. If you'd like, I can bring some ale. Sarnai won't mind."

She smiled in response as they continued to watch the show. After a series of elaborate cartwheels rimmed with flames, the performers eventually ran out of Fire Stimulants. They took a final bow and waved at the applauding audience before packing up their things.

Again, Esen noted the handful of Gurvel who stood pointedly with their arms crossed. There would always be those who craved violence. For them, a show without bloodshed was probably boring and pointless. He couldn't force anyone to change their true nature, but together with Khartsaga and Alvina, consequences would be created for anyone who chose to act on it.

"I should get going," Khartsaga said as the crowd started to disperse.

Esen eyed him carefully. "You're not going to throw yourself in a Sklera cell, are you?"

The corner of Khartsaga's mouth lifted with the slightest hint of a smile. "No. I need to talk to Ronan. I think I saw him on one of the lower levels."

Esen smiled in affirmation. "I have to talk to him too, but I'll catch you in a bit."

The king nodded and walked down the stairs, one body guard following closely behind him. In order to control the rebellions around the city, they had to spread their guards thin. Hopefully everything would settle down over time, but so far they had had to arrest multiple people each day. With Esen's standing as an outlaw, he was able to scrounge up a few volunteers who had been receptive to him during Ukhel's reign, but soldiers couldn't be made overnight.

"I should be going too, actually," Alvina said, looking toward the stairs.

"So soon?"

"I need to meet with Holt to talk about the future of the Scarletts. My hope is that we can move them here, to the city."

"Just don't forget about tea tonight."

She smiled and walked toward the stairwell, turning to look at him before leaving. "Don't forget the ale."

"I wouldn't dream of it," he said in a mock serious tone.

He watched as her blue uniform disappeared down the stairs and then he turned back toward the coliseum to look for Ronan. With fewer people in the stands, it didn't take him long to find him sitting next to Eira whose hair stood out in stark contrast to the black seating. He memorized their location and headed down the stairwell.

A bright green color flashed through his mind as he rounded a corner. He smiled and found the chroma snail slowly slithering along its journey, oblivious to the world around it. At least something in the city had been left untouched by Firekin.

He stepped into the city square and admired all of the people, Gurvel and humans, milling about in the streets after the performance. This was how the city should feel. Alive with all kinds of people. Of course, he hoped there would be more humans someday. If the Scarletts decided to relocate here that would help, but it would still be years before Galynkhot felt as full as it once was.

He waved to a merchant who handed out free samples of cinnamon sweets. A familiar set of ears was visible among the pack of children waiting their turn. Ronan and Eira could wait for another minute or two. He smiled and made his way toward Wren, who had yet to see him.

274

A gruff-looking man with graying hair stepped in front of him. Another person that he had been planning to run into sometime this week.

"You must be Holt?" Esen said. "Wren told me a lot about you. Your son is probably the bravest person I've ever met."

Holt's eyes lit up despite the rest of his emotionless expression, and Esen could hear pride swell to the front of his thoughts. At the sound of their voices, Wren's ears perked up. He turned around and ran toward Esen with a large grin spread across his face. With a chuckle, Esen bent down and welcomed him into a hug. Over the boy's shoulder, Holt gave Esen an intentional look and mouthed 'Thank you'. Esen held his gaze and nodded in understanding. Then he pulled Wren away and pointed toward the cinnamon treats. *"Better grab one before they're gone,"* he signed.

Wren smiled and grabbed Holt's hand to pull him toward the treats. They owed that boy a lot. Without him, they would probably all be dead. The Assassin's Bond he had formed with Ronan was what had finally saved them all.

Esen gave Holt a final nod before continuing toward the lower coliseum entrance to find Ronan and Eira. A pair of soldiers stood on either side of the archway and saluted him with a fist to their foreheads. He returned the salute and stepped through the arch.

Once inside he looked around the seats and found Ronan talking with Khartsaga. They sat on a Sklera bench and looked out at the empty coliseum. Beside them, Eira stared at the wall with a blank expression, either listening or lost in thought.

"There you are!" Esen called out. "I've been looking for all of you. Seton wants to treat us at the Seaside Tavern. He told me to come find you after the performance."

Ronan waved at him and then gingerly stood up. His thoughts were guarded, but Esen could tell from the way he moved that his body was incredibly sore from the exertion he had used to fight both the shadowmongrel and Ukhel. As if in a daze, Eira also rose to her feet and followed Ronan, but Khartsaga stayed where he was, looking out at the coliseum.

"You too, Khart. Come on," Esen said. "Let's not dally too long, or all the spiced ale will be gone."

Eyeridges raised in surprise, Khartsaga quickly followed them outside where children ran beside the Sklera buildings and families chatted in the afternoon sun. With the help of the militia, they had made a lot of progress in a week. A few human merchants had set up new stalls, this time next to the

Gurvel merchants, per Khartsaga's command. It was an odd sight, but it felt natural all the same. With any luck, these small changes would slowly soften some of the more calloused hearts.

The castle loomed before them as they turned left onto the next street. Khartsaga had opened the gates to anyone who wanted an audience with him, but so far none of the humans had decided to venture inside the walls. With any luck, the garden party they were hosting next week would help alleviate some of their fears.

"Gutter pet." A haggard-looking Gurvel with heavy bags under his eyes stepped in front of Ronan and shoved his finger against his chest. "You should have burned with the others, you ungrateful pile of Sklera dust."

Both Esen and Khartsaga took a step forward to intervene, but Ronan was already ahead of them. Without making a sound, he stepped around the Gurvel and continued walking down the street while his adversary raved and ranted to an illusion that wasn't real. Still wanting to do something, Esen caught up to him, but the man just shook his head.

"He's drunk," Ronan said. "Let him rant."

Esen didn't want to draw any more attention to the altercation, so he let it go. Ronan was right. They couldn't arrest every drunken fool stumbling around the streets. Their soldiers were spread thin as it was. Besides, not all Gurvel were so ornery. In fact, quite the opposite was true. After Ronan's display in the arena, many revered him as almost mythical. Merchants and playful children frequently stopped to stare at him, but Ronan ignored their goggling eyes with stiff determination. For better or worse, he could no longer escape attention.

They passed by Batu's Books which, like many of the stores on this street, was closed. Losing the entire population of humans had wrecked some of the smaller businesses that relied on both races for income. Ronan glanced at the bookstore with a deep sense of longing. Just like when they had first met, Esen saw an image of *The Legend of Ravenel* flash across Ronan's forethoughts. After everything that man had been through, he deserved a copy of that book.

When they reached the Seaside Tavern, Esen opened the door to an almost empty establishment. It was still early in the afternoon, but even so, the tavern used to be a popular location for lunch. That had all changed. There were a handful of patrons making casual conversation, but the Gurvel and humans were still sitting apart from one another.

Seton saw them enter and waved them over to the bar where he was busy filling glasses with spiced ale. Their party of four grabbed stools and sat across from the lively bartender. He sported scrapes and bruises from his time in the mines, but otherwise, his optimistic spirit seemed to have survived unscathed.

"One Scarlet whiskey," Seton said, sliding a glass toward Ronan. "One spiced ale." He slid a large mug toward Esen. "And dragonbreath tea for you?" He asked Khartsaga.

"That's my favorite. How did you know?"

"Read your mind." Seton winked and poured him a cup from the tea kettle on his stove. He handed the cup to Khartsaga who accepted it with a skeptical look.

"Anything for you?" Seton asked Eira.

"Just water."

"Water it is. Best in the land." Seton slid her some water and then left to deliver the glasses of ale to another table.

They each took a swig of their drinks. Esen sighed with content as spiced warmth hit the back of his throat. He had missed this. But they had come for more than drinks, so he reached into his pocket and pulled out the vial of black liquid that Ukhel had been working on.

"I wanted to show this to you," he said, setting it down on the bar. "We found this in the prisons."

"It looks like blood," Ronan said, leaning forward.

"That's because blood is one of the main ingredients. Your blood."

Ronan stiffened and pulled away from it.

With a frown, Khartsaga picked up the vial and held it up to his eye. "I've never seen this before."

"I doubt you would have," Esen said. "From the sound of it, Ukhel was working on this in secret. We questioned him yesterday, but the only thing he told us is that he calls it the God Stimulant. Eira helped me work out the other ingredients. Apparently, Ukhel learned the recipe from *The Legend of Ravenel*. That's why it's been so hard to find a copy. He bought them all to keep anyone from figuring out what he was doing."

They were still looking for Ukhel's assistant, Tarkhan, but hadn't been able to find him. According to Ukhel, he was the only other person who knew about this secret weapon.

"What does it do?" Khartsaga asked, handing the Stimulant back to Esen.

"It's like the Verdant Stimulant but stronger," Eira said, staring at her glass of water. "It gives you the power of both Seyring and Manipulation, and allows you to penetrate an Inhibitor mind cloud."

"That's what Ukhel took before he fought you in the coliseum, Ronan," Esen added.

"That's how he was always one step ahead of us too," Eira said, finally looking up at all of them. "He was developing this new Stimulant, but it wasn't until he found Ronan that he was able to finish it."

Esen put the vial back in his pocket. "It lasts for hours instead of minutes, which would make it a phenomenal asset if the ingredients weren't so costly. We're going to destroy what's left and keep it a secret, like Ravenel intended. Good news for you, Ronan. Since the secret ingredient is blood from a human Seyr, all you'd have to do is drink the other ingredients and you'd get the same effects."

"Good to know," Ronan said, taking a sip of his whiskey.

That had been Esen's main reason for bringing them here, but there was one more thing he wanted to do. He walked around to the other side of the bar and grabbed the package that he had asked Seton to keep safe for him. "Before you all leave, there's something I wanted to give to Ronan. I think the rest of you will be interested as well."

Ronan tentatively took the package from him and slid open the flap. A hard object fell into his hand. With wide eyes he stared down at the gold embossed title of the book: *The Legend of Ravenel*. A small smile crossed his face as he traced the title with his fingers.

"How did you get this?" he asked.

"I convinced one of the Gurvel families in town to let me have it," Esen answered with a smile. "They had a change of heart after the display we put on last week. I told them you'd been looking for it, and they wanted me to give it to you." In reality, he had paid the Purevs another visit to see if they had decided to join with the rebellion after Ukhel was dethroned. They had been more than accommodating when he had asked to have the book.

With the soft clinking of glasses echoing around the tavern, Ronan cracked open the book and gingerly turned the pages until he found the depiction of Ravenel standing over a dark shadow with his black cape swirling out behind him. They all watched as he pored over the ancient story. Even Eira's eyes seemed to light up slightly as she watched him read.

Now that they knew there was some truth to the legend, Ravenel's tale held new significance for all of them. Like the defeat of the shadowmongrel, the dark cloud of despair that had suffocated the city for centuries had finally dissipated into the dawn of a new age.

Appendix

Glossary

Amidral – the known world

Assassin Bond – strong connection between a Seyr and Manipulator

Base Stimulant – Gurvel Stimulant that enhances Serying and Manipulation

Cinnamon grass – plant that blocks Seyring and Manipulation

Chroma snail – creature that projects colorful illusions with Seyring

Corpse tree – plant that uses toxins and Seyring to paralyze prey

Fire Creed – set of beliefs held by Firekin

Firekin – Gurvel cult

Fire Purification – Firekin ritual in which someone is burned at the stake

Fire Stimulant – used by Manipulators to create and control fire

Forestdweller – reclusive race of people with keen senses

Forethoughts – easiest part of the mind for Seyrs to read

Galynkhot – capital city in southern region of Amidral

The Games – event where humans and Gurvel fight to the death

Gurvel – long-living race of people with crimson skin and ridged foreheads

Inhibitor – substance that blocks Seyring and Manipulation

Manipulation – ability to control nonliving matter

Glossary

Manipulator – someone who has the ability to Manipulate

Moss frog – creature that can Manipulate small objects

New Age – belief held by Firekin; a future in which Gurvel reign over everything

Prime Stimulant – Speki Stimulant that enhances Seyring and Manipulation

Relief leaves – plant that temporarily relieves minor pain

Ropesnare – vine used to restrain Manipulators

Ropesnare milk – substance that cannot be Manipulated

Scarlet Forest – infamous forest where many dangerous plants and animals live

Scarletts – group of humans living in the Scarlet Forest

Sklera – grown over hundreds of years; also known as "living rock"

Sklera sculptor – artisan who shapes and cares for Sklera

Seyr – someone who has the ability to Seyr

Seyring – ability to project illusions and read minds

Shadowmongrel – rare and mysterious beast that feasts on fear

Speki – long-living race of people with white hair and violet eyes

Stimulant – substance that increases Seyring and Manipulation powers

Verdant Stimulant – substance that temporarily gives the ability to use both Serying and Manipulation powers

The Legend of Ravenel

Contains spoilers

Long ago, when the four races still lived in peace with one another, rumors of a new dark threat spread throughout Amidral.

At first, the darkness was just a rumor and nothing more. Reports of terrifying visions and bodies found frozen in fear spread through every town like phoenix fire.

Kings and city officials assuaged the commoners' fears by telling them the reports were nothing more than the ravings of drunken fools.

And so life went on. The rumors continued to spread, but no one believed them—not unless they found themselves alone in the woods at night.

During this time, there was a man named Ravenel who worked as a merchant, traveling from city to city with his wares.

It used to be assumed that humans, like Forestdwellers, couldn't become Manipulators or Seyrs.

But fear has a way of forcing discoveries about the unknown, as Ravenel soon found out.

One day, Ravenel was on his way to the great Speki city, Mikiltoft, when his cart broke down, forcing him to make camp in the woods.

The air had grown unusually chilly for that time of year, so when Ravenel laid down to sleep,
he used an extra blanket for warmth.

He also noted that the moon that night wasn't shining as brightly as it should have been, even though the sky was clear.

Not able to sleep because of the silence, Ravenel got up to look around.

What he encountered that night, alone in the woods, was a beast like death itself.

At first, Ravenel thought he must be dreaming. His surroundings were the same but he found himself running from every fear he had ever imagined.

But worse than his own fears was the beast itself.

Clicks in the shadows. Yellow eyes that bore into the soul. And an inescapable sense of unending dread. Terrible, eternal terror.

Ravenel fought for his life, trapped in his own mind by a beast born from the shadows of fear.

But somehow, Ravenel found a way to survive. He barely escaped with his life that day
and claimed that something inside of him had been awakened.

What was once impossible suddenly became a reality for Ravenel.

Not only could he read thoughts and cast illusions into minds, but he could also perform skills that would normally require a Stimulant.

But there wasn't time to explore these new powers.

As the rumors of attacks in the night increased, Ravenel became more aware of the danger that lurked at the edge of civilization.

If left unchecked, the beasts would destroy every human, Speki, and Gurvel town from the Ashcapped Mountains in the north to the Turbulent Sea in the south.

So Ravenel met with the Speki order of Knowledge Keepers, but they turned him away, refusing to accept his claims.

Next, Ravenel met with the Master Manipulators among the Gurvel, but they each turned him away, laughing at his tale.

Finally, Ravenel appealed to the courts of men to help him find a way to defeat the shadow beasts before it was too late.

But even his own people turned him away, claiming his tale was a fluke of nature and his powers a danger to society.

And so, with nowhere else to turn, Ravenel traveled across the mountains in search of the reclusive Forestdwellers, until one day he found them.

The Forestdwellers taught him about the art of listening. With nature as his guide, Ravenel learned how to use his mind in ways previously unknown to the world.

As Ravenel improved his skills, the Forestdwellers taught him how to make vim tea.

They told him that vim tea was as old as the mountains and gave new knowledge to those who drank its leaves.

A secret kept in mind. Feather. Ash. Crystal. Power combined.

These are the only words Ravenel ever revealed when questioned about the power he learned from the Forestdwellers.

When Ravenel returned home, he returned to destruction. The whole town lay strewn about the streets, frozen in fright.

In anguish, Ravenel began a grand search.

Listening to faint rumors and myths, Ravenel tracked down a handful of humans like him.

With their help, he formed the Veiled Paladins and taught them everything he had learned about Seyring and Manipulation.

His small group practiced their skills by hunting down criminals in the night, all the while preparing for their real enemies: the shadow beasts.

Eventually, rumors of the Veiled Paladins reached the ears of the Speki Knowledge Keepers and Gurvel Master Manipulators.

With the number of attacks on the rise, the Speki and Gurvel were finally inclined to listen to Ravenel.

The Veiled Paladins worked with the Speki and Gurvel to plan the destruction of the shadow beasts, attacking them where they were most vulnerable: the mind.

They created an army made up of not only Speki and Gurvel, but also Ravenel's human team of Seyrs and Manipulators.

In preparation, Ravenel worked late into the night creating a new Stimulant for the army. But he worked in secret, revealing to no one what the Stimulant contained.

Finally, with Ravenel's Stimulant, the army marched into the Scarlet Forest where the shadow beasts made their home.

A battle of the mind ensued, but as they fought, it was clear to all that they were greatly outmatched.

But not even the piercing yellow eyes of death could smother Ravenel's persistent passion. As soon as one beast hit the ground, Ravenel moved on to the next one.

He stood his ground before each eternal shadow, refusing to cower before death's rattling chill.

Emboldened by Ravenel's courage, the army fought with renewed passion, striking down the shadow beasts until there were none left.

After the battle, Ravenel was nowhere to be found. Some say he rejoined the Forestdwellers, others say he still fights crime in the shadows of night.

But this we do know: Ravenel was more than a man. He was hope itself.

Acknowledgments

Growing up, I was a *voracious* reader. Despite how many books I consumed it was never enough to satiate my hunger for new worlds to explore. That's why I will forever be indebted to the teachers and librarians who read to me, recommended new books, and taught me how to analyze stories.

Writing a book is a messy business. Without willing Beta readers, I never would have made it past the third draft. Jess, Michelle, and Pat put up with my terrible grammar and left me excellent suggestions to improve the characters and plot. Likewise, I'm grateful to my editor, Grace Rankin for cleaning up my final manuscript which was riddled with the aforementioned grammatical errors.

Finally, I wouldn't be where I am today without my Alpha team. These are the people who saw *Shadow of the Pyre* when it was still in its infancy. My parents supported me the whole way and kept my spirits high so that I had the tenacity to finish. Jason, Kendrick, and Sarah gave me incredibly valuable ideas throughout this project. Whenever I was stuck on a name or plot point, these are the people I turned to.

Words fail to describe just how amazing my husband is. Beyond watching the baby so I could focus, Ethan listened to me rant and rave about my stories since the moment I first decided to write. Not to mention how many times he woke me up at 3 AM to share a genius new idea for my book (he's a night owl—I am not). I will forever cherish the way he loved me during this exciting time.

Lastly, this acknowledgement page would be lacking if I did not thank the first Author for including me in His story. Without Him, story itself would not exist.

About the Author

R.T. grew up in Delaware, Ohio where cherished moments of reading with her parents were complimented by school book fairs and author visits. In the summer of 2020, she decided to pursue her life-long dream of writing a book. Four years later, her debut novel, Shadow of the Pyre, was completed. R.T. enjoys spending time with her husband and son in northern Indiana. When she's not writing, she can be found playing Pokémon TCG, Skyrim, D&D, or a host of other nerdy activities.

rtsilveus.com

www.ingramcontent.com/pod-product-compliance
Lightning Source LLC
Chambersburg PA
CBHW031249160726
47993CB00001B/76